BAY OF

THIEVES

Megan Davis was born in Australia and grew up in mining towns across the world. She has worked in the film industry and her credits include *Atonement, In Bruges, Pride and Prejudice* and the Bourne films. Megan is also a lawyer and is currently an associate at Spotlight on Corruption. She has an MA in Creative Writing from the University of East Anglia. Her debut, *The Messenger*, won the Bridport Prize for a First Novel, judged by Kamila Shamsie, as well as the Lucy Cavendish Prize, judged by Sophie Hannah. *The Messenger* was also shortlisted for the CrimeFest Specsavers 2023 Debut Crime Novel Award. She has lived in many places, including France for a number of years, but now lives in London.

Also by Megan Davis

The Messenger

BAY OF THIEVES

MEGAN DAVIS

ZAFFRE

First published in the UK in 2024 by
ZAFFRE
An imprint of Zaffre Publishing Group
A Bonnier Books UK company
4th Floor, Victoria House, Bloomsbury Square, London, WC1B 4DA
Owned by Bonnier Books
Sveavägen 56, Stockholm, Sweden

A CIP catalogue record for this book is
available from the British Library.

Hardback ISBN: 978-1-83877-862-0
Trade paperback ISBN: 978-1-83877-866-8

Also available as an ebook and an audiobook

1 3 5 7 9 10 8 6 4 2

Typeset by IDSUK (Data Connection) Ltd
Printed and bound in Great Britain by Clays Ltd, Elcograf S.p.A.

MIX
Paper | Supporting
responsible forestry
FSC
www.fsc.org   FSC® C018072

Zaffre is an imprint of Zaffre Publishing Group
A Bonnier Books UK company
www.bonnierbooks.co.uk

Prologue

Roquebrune-Cap-Martin

THE SECURITY GUARD GRASPED THE dog's lead and prepared for another sweep of the property.

It was 5 a.m., the sky a wash of pale blue although the sun had not yet risen above the hills. In another hour his shift would be finished and Milos would head home to his apartment in Ventimiglia, a town just over the Italian border and part of the coastal sprawl that stretched from Marseille to Messina. He took a drag of his cigarette and the smoke stung his throat, a bracing hit against the pure morning air. He whistled softly to the dog, then began his circuit, clockwise this time around the perimeter.

It had been another warm night and there had been some activity on the beach at the eastern end of the property just before 2 a.m. Two drunk tourists had clambered into the sea from the rocks below the old architect's place. They must have scaled the hurricane fence that ran along the railway line. Milos had heard the soft pop of a cork then laughter as he surveyed them from the balustrade, their voices amplified by the water. They spoke in French but Milos's was limited and he had strained to make anything out as he watched the woman strip off. The moonlight glowed on her skin and made a silhouette of her naked body as she lowered herself in off the rocks and then

1

walked along the pebbles with the man. Milos waited until they were in the water again before letting the dog off the lead.

'Make sure no one swims on the beach in front of the house,' Amir had told Milos on his first day at the villa two months ago.

Amir had pointed to the restaurant at the far end of the shingle, beneath the steps that led to the road. Among his other instructions, Amir told Milos that was the place for public bathing.

'People think they have all kinds of rights over this beach just because they're locals. But this is my property and I say who swims here.'

Milos knew Amir was wrong and that although it didn't seem like it, there was no such thing in France as a truly private beach. Milos nodded in agreement though because Amir had the money and he was the boss. Money wrote the rules on the Côte d'Azur and the real locals were those who understood this.

That was back in May and Amir was no longer there. Milos had only worked at the villa for a week before the security company sent him to another estate in Antibes after its owner, a Russian businessman, was sanctioned. Milos had stayed in Antibes guarding the empty estate and this was his first time back to Roquebrune since then. Milos had heard that Amir had been sanctioned too and that the villa had changed hands. He noticed a lot of other things had changed since May, but that was nothing strange. When new owners took over these large properties they usually brought in teams of builders and workmen to fix them up – altering the gardens and the bathrooms, changing the location of the driveways and the helipad. Each owner needed to put his own stamp on a place even though it had never been anything less than perfect.

Milos had worked along this coast for several years and he knew how it went. After the new owners had finished renovating, there would be a flurry of activity and parties. Limousines backed up night after night, helicopters coming in with glamorous guests. This would continue until one day, without warning, the owners would disappear and the place would be shut down again. Milos used to imagine this happened because the owners had become bored, that they'd found better places to go – their yachts, the Caribbean, the Balearics or Bali.

This year had been more difficult than usual and instead of holding one job the whole season, Milos had to follow the work. Many of the luxury villas on the Côte d'Azur were empty now because travel bans meant their owners couldn't visit France anymore. A lot of properties had been sold in anticipation of this and for fear of the market collapse that might follow. Locals were concerned that the absence of Russians meant the absence of cash, but they needn't have worried: there was always money in the world for the Côte d'Azur. If it wasn't the Russians it would be someone else and in the meantime, Milos's job was to guard the empty villas. To him they were like ghost ships that had washed up on shore, their vacant rooms still glowing with chandeliers and bustling with uniformed staff. In the kitchens the champagne remained chilled. Food was still purchased and chefs retained in case of an owner's surprise return.

Amir's villa, Casa di Stelle, was one of the biggest houses on the Cap-Martin peninsula. There was a new resident now – a woman Milos had not yet seen. She must be somebody important though as there were two other guards that looked after the place besides himself, plus a staff of eight – a cleaner, two maids, a butler, a chef, two bodyguards and a driver. Inside the villa there was artwork, antiques and jewellery and it all needed to be protected and polished.

Milos descended the narrow staircase at the edge of the garden and opened the gate to the beach. He gazed along the pebbles to where he had watched the couple lay last night. A gentle tide was coming in, soft waves lapping the shoreline, clinking the stones against each other.

Milos picked up a half-empty bottle of champagne. The sun had not yet touched it and it was still cool. Milos chuckled to himself as he remembered the couple's panicked swim to the other end of the beach. The dog was trained to bark from the water's edge, to keep the beach in front of the villa empty, but not to follow people into the sea nor chase them along the beach. Perhaps the couple had walked naked up the steps to the road and flagged a taxi, or sought refuge in the restaurant. He didn't think they would have dared walk all the way back past the villa again to retrieve their clothes from the rocks.

Milos was still smiling when he returned to the property. The sun shimmered now above the hills, flooding the valley with luminous colour, making pink scars of the limestone cliffs in the forest above Roquebrune. He continued his circuit, threading his way towards the villa past the pool. Beneath his boots fine blades of emerald grass had been mown to bowling-green perfection. Up ahead there was a vast gazebo and to the right classical statues and potted palms surrounded a large rectangular *bassin*, which sat drained and awaiting destruction. The new owner wanted a more modern aesthetic and had started work on an infinity pool perched on an outcrop overlooking the beach. A digger had arrived three days ago and had already excavated two wide trenches along the front boundary wall.

The dog was alert now, pulling at the leash, its nostrils twitching with the morning smells. Milos wound the chain tight around his fist, pulling the animal in close but something had caught its attention beyond the frogs, the cats and the freshly turned earth.

Milos was about to discipline the dog when he saw something near the gazebo that changed the tone of a sprinkler as it rotated past. As he drew closer he faltered. It was the body of a woman, slumped on the grass, ragged and wet. Her chest was unmoving but there were deep wounds that ran from her shoulders across her breasts. Her head was at an unnatural angle, a black rope ostentatiously coiled around her throat. Her face had been slashed too, all red and bloated from the rope and half covered by her wet and matted hair, the gashes peeling open.

Milos ordered the dog back and walked over to where she was, the water from the sprinkler hissing around him, running down his hair and face, drenching him. His first thought was that this was the woman from the beach, but she wasn't naked. The lower part of her body was covered in a fine silk fabric, stained with blood spread thin by the water. A pale arm stretched out on the grass above the woman's head, as if she had been waving for help from something in the sky.

He bent down to check her pulse, averting his eyes from her face. Then he shook his head, stepped back from the arcs of water and crossed himself. Milos stared at the sun and said a prayer for the woman, cursing the thing that had brought her to this place and allowed this to happen.

He lit a cigarette and then spoke quietly into his phone.

SIX WEEKS EARLIER

Chapter One
Monaco

VANESSA'S PHONE RANG JUST AS she was logging out for the evening. It was her boss, Rob, calling from London.

'There's a big tranche coming in tonight,' Rob said. 'I need you to make sure it's dealt with.'

Vanessa checked the time. She had been at her desk since six that morning and was already late for drinks with a new colleague, Kate.

'It's Friday evening, Rob. I was just about to leave. Why are you only calling me now?' Vanessa said, turning back to the computer.

Kate, the new colleague, had just moved from London to work with Vanessa and Rob at the Meritus Monaco office. Kate was no stranger to working late and she would understand, but still.

'Napier's been here all day, following me around like a bloody shadow,' Rob said. 'I've barely had a moment free.'

Coldness gripped the back of Vanessa's neck. Napier was the firm's managing partner.

'What was that about?' she asked.

'Billings.'

'Are you sure?'

'Of course I'm sure.'

Vanessa edged her chair back and looked out of the window to the main port of Monaco. She worked closely with Rob on what he termed the 'more sensitive' matters for their wealthiest clients, but she knew he never told her the complete truth about anything.

'How much money's coming in?' she asked.

'Seven million. But there's been a mix-up and the client has it in a Cyprus account.'

'Why Cyprus?'

'Some of it was cash. Came through the casinos.'

'OK,' Vanessa said, tapping her keyboard.

'And the thing is – the funds need to be here in London for completion on Monday,' Rob said.

'So soon? Why do they want to complete on Monday?'

Rob's voice dipped and he spoke through gritted teeth. 'It's a property deal, Vanessa. They complete when they bloody well like.'

Vanessa didn't usually respond when Rob swore at her. It was her one act of defiance.

Rob waited and then breathed deeply down the line. 'The deal's only available if we complete on Monday.'

'Why is that?'

There was a long pause. 'Sanctions,' Rob said.

'We can't deal with anyone who's been sanctioned. You know that.'

'It's a bonanza here right now. Another round's coming in and everyone's moving property before it's frozen.'

'That's just as bad. If we know what's coming—'

'—and so that's why the deal needs to go through on Monday. This is a townhouse worth at least twice the amount Amir's paying. He wants that property, Vanessa.'

Vanessa shifted in her chair. Amir was their biggest client, a politician's nephew from Belarus.

'It won't be long before Amir and his uncle are sanctioned too, you know.'

'It'll be held offshore. No one will ever trace the property to him. It's a Russian seller though and that money needs to be here on Monday, Vanessa, otherwise there's no deal.'

Vanessa turned to her private laptop and opened the spreadsheet for Amir. 'Which company is he using to buy the property?'

'Peregrine BVI.'

'Right. Well, he can't send that amount to you from Cyprus. And it really shouldn't go via London at all. Have him send it to one of the British Virgin Island accounts.'

'Can't do that. The money needs to be in London.'

'It'll raise too many red flags. He'll have to do it in several tranches at least.'

'Can't do that either. It won't be here in time. You'll have to run it through the firm's account this weekend. Amir's already cleared it with his bank. It's on its way.'

Vanessa stared at her phone as if it were malfunctioning. 'The trust account? You know I can't do that.'

'It'll be in the Monaco account tonight and you can pre-clear it for sending on to me here in London on Monday morning.'

'Not with Napier breathing down your neck. No, Rob, it's too much.'

'We did it last month.'

'We were desperate. We had no choice.'

'We're desperate now.'

'It's way above the reporting amount.'

'You can override it.'

'We shouldn't even be having this call. You know the protocol.'

Vanessa glanced around the room, her eyes coming to rest on a half-empty bottle of gin. She'd only had one drink so far – at 6 p.m., or at least that's what she told herself. Normally a few drinks wouldn't make any difference. They'd slip down easily, hardly touching the sides, and would make her sharper if anything. But tonight there was something off. The light in the room seemed hazy somehow, and the shadows cast by the evening sun seemed to tilt unnaturally towards her.

Rob sighed. 'It's the only way. I'll be in Monaco next week. We can chat then if we need to. In the meantime, get the transfer cleared for Monday.'

Despite her unease, Vanessa was thinking fast. It was only her voice that gave her away. It was a little shaky, as if it were having trouble keeping up with her thoughts. 'Stephen's on tonight. He'll check everything before he finishes. You know what he's like.'

'It won't go through till late. You can pre-authorise it now.'

'Come on, Rob, I can't—'

'And another thing. You need to change the beneficiaries of the French villa to Elanka and her mother.'

'Elanka and her *mother*?'

Elanka was Amir's girlfriend and Casa di Stelle was his French villa.

'For fuck's sake, Vanessa!' Rob barked down the line. 'Do I have to hand-hold you every step of the way? I'm fighting fires here. Just get it done!'

Rob didn't wait for a response before ringing off.

The gin fizzed in her head as Vanessa texted Kate to say she would be late. Then she reached for the bottle and poured herself another. Vanessa drank to calm her nerves and to drown the guilt she felt about the deals she did for Rob. Sometimes she couldn't tell these feelings apart, but tonight it was mainly her nerves that needed soothing.

Vanessa brought the glass to her lips. There was no ice and the gin was warm, but the aromatics pricked her nostrils like a blast of smelling salts. She swigged the gin as she typed the authorisation codes then glanced out to the shimmering bay. Yachts flanked the port, three or four storeys high, their carefully oiled decks packed so tight in the harbour that there seemed barely enough room for the water. Each vessel was equipped with the kind of luxury that was now required for life at sea – Jacuzzis, wraparound bars and tiers of lounging furniture, all jutting out over the marina in a sun-drenched, open-air display of inaccessible wealth. Vanessa usually liked the sight of all that floating real estate but tonight it unnerved her. She moved her laptop closer, logged into Amir's account and waited for access.

Rob was such a bastard. He had always shown the potential to be one, even back at law school where Vanessa had met him. She remembered their first day – how he strode into the lecture hall in a cloud of expensive aftershave and sat right next to her. She thought he was being ironic with his chalk-striped suits and button down collars, like the parody of an old-school lawyer, and so she gave him the benefit of the doubt, but she really shouldn't have.

He said he wanted to be a partner before he was thirty as though that was the pinnacle of human achievement. He managed it by twenty-nine with the kind of ruthlessness that made it look easy. It was hard not to admire his drive – he was in the office every weekend, burning the midnight oil while his peers were out drinking it and having fun. Like most successful lawyers, he perfected his skills through monotonous repetition and now, fifteen years later, he was the highest billing partner at Meritus.

For her own part, Vanessa had been much more cautious. Her prudence had paid off however, and she now ran the firm's compliance department. Her job was to vet clients, to monitor the money coming into the firm, and to be on the lookout for suspicious transactions. It was the perfect place to work if, in fact, you were going to get involved in some suspicious transactions yourself.

Vanessa helped Rob's clients launder money, illegally of course and without the rest of the firm knowing. Most of Rob's clients had accumulated vast fortunes through embezzlement, organised crime, or by being part of the ruling clique in a corrupt state. Money laundering restrictions meant they couldn't use the traditional banking system to move their money around easily, and without assistance from people like Rob and Vanessa, these funds were grounded in their country of origin and practically useless.

Rob had devised ways of liberating this cash by funnelling it through an ingenious matrix of shell companies and offshore banks that cleaned the cash by disguising its source. Once the funds had passed though Rob's laundromat to a bank in the West his clients could use it to buy mansions, yachts, sports clubs, businesses, jets and jewellery, and to generally fund a luxury lifestyle without raising suspicion.

Vanessa scanned the figures on the screen once access to Amir's Cyprus account had been authorised. She saw the seven million had come in from various sources. The bulk of it was from an Austrian bank account in the name of a company based in the British Virgin Islands, and there were several large cash deposits that had been made directly in Cyprus – no doubt the gambling money Rob had mentioned. Finally, there was a tranche that had come in from Dubai. Vanessa saw that instructions had been given to send it all to the firm's Monaco trust account. She moved back to her workstation and filled in the necessary forms authorising receipt of the money and assigning the codes that would make sure it passed under her colleague Stephen's overworked radar.

This part of the transaction was simple and one she had done countless times before, but tonight the reality of it all made her feel nauseous. She put down the empty glass. Once the money arrived in Monaco it had to go through a second authorisation to be transferred to London on Monday. She couldn't log into the account remotely so she would need to come into the office tomorrow morning and do it then before anyone picked it up. She set her alarm for 6 a.m. now to make sure she didn't forget.

Vanessa wiped her hands and poured another gin as she looked across the port to the Rock of Monaco – the vast limestone cliff the locals called Le Rocher. Her gaze drifted up towards the sun which burned a golden disc over the Prince's Palace. It was a warm evening and people would be out in force in the bars along the marina and later, filling the terrace restaurants of the Old Town. However shaky she felt now, she knew she would feel fine when she was outside, among others who, like her, serviced the rich and hid their money. There was comfort in numbers, in knowing those around her shared a common goal. She would feel better on Monday when the transfer to London was done, and her adrenaline could release. Better still Monday evening when the property deal completed.

She knew the deals she did for Rob were wrong, and there was even a time she used to say each one would be the last. These days, though, she didn't tell herself that or even think she should and she smiled at the irony: deception had taught her to stop lying to herself. That was something at least, she thought as she changed her clothes and fixed her make-up. It was best not to think about it too much. It was easier to just get it done, Vanessa thought as she gathered up her things, and then went outside into the sunshine.

Chapter Two

ALTHOUGH IT WAS AFTER 7 p.m. when Vanessa left the office, the warmth of the afternoon still hung over the marina and in it Vanessa sensed the remnants of another day missed, like the lingering waft of a delicious meal smelled through an open window.

As she navigated the steps that led to the quayside car park, Vanessa thought of Rob – how offensive his manner had become, the increasing number of risks he had asked her to take recently, and above all, how awful it was that she still worked for him.

Vanessa reached the bottom of the steps and walked along the waterfront. The Grand Prix had taken place just the week before and while some of the barriers had been taken down, thick black tyre marks looped the city's asphalt like an extravagant stain.

Vanessa knew of course that money was the reason she still worked for Rob. She had never fooled herself it was otherwise but there were still days she resented it. She also knew that however offensive Rob was, clients loved him and he always poured on the charm when needed. His smooth words slid into the ears of regulators and officials who enabled the deals no one else could pull off, and of course he talked his way into his clients' pockets too with his sky-high bills and crazy, money-making schemes.

He had even persuaded Vanessa to sleep with him once – twenty years ago when they were junior lawyers in the London office. It should never have happened – she was his supervisor, and he was not her type. The incident only occurred because they shared an office fourteen hours a day for six months solid so frankly, neither of them had much choice. Stockholm syndrome, they called it later when they could laugh about it, and although it was true then, it didn't explain why she was still trapped with him years later, and even worse, why Rob was now her boss.

Vanessa scanned the bars as she passed. Long wooden tables stretched along the quay, conversation and laughter carrying across the tarmac to the yachts packed in the harbour to her left. In a couple of hours these bars would be raucous, but right now they were calm, full of people entering the first stage of intoxication and still high on the simple pleasure that comes from having finished work for the week.

Vanessa found her Porsche in the car park and from there it was a twenty-minute drive east over the French border to The Maybourne Riviera hotel where she was meeting Kate. Two hours ago, this road would have been backed up all the way to Menton, but now the traffic was light as Vanessa wound up into the hills.

She could see the Maybourne from every bend in the road. The hotel was a white modernist cube perched high on a rocky crag overlooking the sea and it jutted out over the cliff's edge in defiance of gravity and the rules of tasteful construction.

The whole edifice gave the impression it was about to come tumbling down at any moment, bringing half the hillside with it. Although the Maybourne was a massive eyesore from sea level, the most stunning views of the coastline could be had from its terraced balconies. It was Kate's first week in Monaco and Vanessa had booked a table on the rooftop from where they could watch the sun set.

At thirty-five, Kate was almost ten years younger than Vanessa and had already made a name for herself in London as a top-notch litigator. She was a high-flyer, headed for full part-nership, and the Monaco office was lucky to have her, Rob had told Vanessa in a tone that made it clear the same did not apply to her. Although Vanessa was a junior partner, she had been passed over for full partnership twice and she knew she wouldn't get another chance. Rob always made Vanessa feel she was on borrowed time at Meritus and even though she was pretty sure he needed her as much as she needed him, she could never really count on it.

As Vanessa pulled up to the hotel's sweeping driveway, she cursed Rob under her breath. It wasn't her style to play tour guide on a Friday evening but she liked Kate and didn't want to let Rob succeed in his agenda of setting them up as rivals, so she had offered to show Kate around. Rob had done it before – driven a wedge between Vanessa and the other lawyers who worked for him so as to ensure no solidarity developed that would be a threat to his control and she didn't want it to happen with Kate.

Vanessa handed over her keys to the valet and steeled herself for the evening. Ten years ago, Vanessa would have been well into her weekend by now with any number of fun-loving friends but these days, those friends were all married and busy with children, even on a Friday. Ten years ago, Vanessa would have been chatted up before she even crossed the lobby of a hotel, but now it took a little longer.

Vanessa checked her reflection as she strode past the Maybourne's mirrored reception and then took the lift to the rooftop. She wore a midnight blue silk halter dress and heels with silver straps that wound around her ankles. The dress set off her tan and her dark hair, and was an outfit she hoped would ensure their access to the nightclub she had planned for later that evening.

When Vanessa arrived, Kate was already on the terrace with a glass of white wine and to Vanessa's dismay she was wearing a floral print dress and flat shoes. Vanessa couldn't help but stare – Kate was very pretty with a fair, English rose complexion and Vanessa wondered why she always hid beneath clothes that made her look like a chorister.

Kate took in Vanessa's outfit and then looked at her own, 'Oh no, have I got it wrong again?'

Vanessa beckoned the waiter over and ordered a Martini.

'I'm always misjudging it,' Kate said as they air kissed. 'I'm overdressed for work and underdressed at night.'

'It's my fault, I'm sorry,' said Vanessa, taking the seat opposite. 'I should have said.' She wondered how she was going to pass this off to the doorman at Jimmy'z later on.

Kate shook out her dress. 'You did mention a nightclub, but I'd wear this anywhere in London.'

Vanessa raised her eyebrows. 'Really? Even with those shoes?'

Kate looked down at her feet.

Vanessa laughed. 'I'm teasing. But as I keep saying, this isn't London.'

'I feel so *awkward* here,' said Kate, looking around at the rooftop splendour. 'So *English*.'

'Well, you are English and so am I, but here it's best if we don't look it. It singles you out as a tourist or worse, a *newcomer*.'

When her Martini arrived, Vanessa raised her glass. 'To appearances.'

'To *appearances* then,' said Kate.

They gazed at the view. The sun was low over the hills to the west and the sea was shot with gold, the sky pink on the horizon and deep blue above. Several yachts moved slowly through the bay, their wakes shining on its glassy calm.

'This place is just so beautiful,' said Kate, sipping her wine. 'I've never experienced anything like it. You can see all the way along the coast to Italy.'

'Not only Italy, Corsica too,' said Vanessa pointing out over the sea to a land haze on the horizon where a blood red moon was rising.

'It's incredible. But the cocktails are forty euros each and there isn't a bottle of wine on the list for less than a hundred, even the rosé. Who on earth comes here?'

'Everyone. Tourists. People who like to show off. Us.'

'But it's madness.'

'It's Monaco.'

'No it's not, it's France.'

'It's on the border. It's close enough.'

Vanessa settled back in her seat. 'So you've been here a week. Where have you been so far?'

'Nowhere! I've worked late every single night. But I've heard there are some small bars in Cannes that are nice.' Kate smiled hopefully. 'A few in the Old Town apparently—'

'Oh, no,' Vanessa groaned. 'I know those bars and they're not nice. You won't like them. They're full of conmen and chancers. I'll show you some much better places.'

A small crowd had gathered at the far edge of the balcony. The sun was setting and people posed for photos. Vanessa took Kate over to join them and asked a waiter to take a few snaps.

'So tell me the real reason you came to Monaco?' Vanessa said when they returned to their table. 'Are you escaping someone, or were you lured by the cash?'

Kate laughed and smoothed back her hair, ruffled by the soft breeze. 'Both actually. Well, I didn't *escape* anyone. I broke up with my boyfriend not long ago and needed a change of scene, and yes that's also true – I really need the money.'

'There's no shame in that. We all need money.'

'Oh, I'm not ashamed. My mother has dementia and her care home in the Midlands costs a fortune. There's no way I could afford it on my old salary and still live in London. Here I'm paid double, it's all tax-free and the apartment is paid for. But you know all that.'

Despite the bad luck about her mother, Vanessa felt a stab of envy. The mention of Kate's salary reminded Vanessa she hadn't had a raise in over a year. She also knew Rob had assigned Kate an apartment which although it was smaller than hers, was much nicer, and in a better part of the city.

Vanessa swallowed her annoyance, knowing it was unreasonable. 'And you can't rely on the rest of your family for your mother's care?'

'It's just my sister and everything she has goes online.'

'Online?'

'Gambling,' said Kate, gazing out over the sea. 'She can go for months when it's fine and then suddenly she's back on it and loses everything. I can't even give her money for Mum's prescriptions.'

'That's rough.'

Kate nodded and drained her glass. 'You know I was off on a month's stress leave.'

'I had heard that,' Vanessa said. 'There aren't many secrets at Meritus.'

'Particularly as Rob won't stop going on about it. Anyone would think I'd been in the Bahamas for a year.'

Vanessa lit a cigarette and offered one to Kate who declined. 'Don't worry about Rob, he's an arse,' she said under her breath.

'How have you managed to work with him all these years? He's so offensive.'

Vanessa took a drag of her cigarette, her chest heavy as she remembered the money transfer she had just authorised for him. She had an urge to give Kate a hint of the things Rob might ask of her, but she checked herself. If Vanessa said too much about Rob she would implicate herself and it probably wasn't wise to trust Kate like that at this early stage of their friendship. She noted, not for the first time, that Rob had done a good job of isolating her with his secrets.

Vanessa blew smoke towards the horizon. 'He gets things done.'

'So I've heard,' said Kate. 'Apparently he gets all sorts of things done.'

'Yes,' Vanessa said, not meeting Kate's eyes.

The sun had set and Vanessa beckoned the waiter over for the bill. 'I know a great restaurant back in town.' She glanced down at Kate's dress and smiled. 'We can still go to Jimmy'z afterwards if you feel like it.'

The restaurant Vanessa had in mind was a short drive away on the eastern end of Monaco. When they arrived, a table outside on the terrace had just become free and Vanessa caught the attention of a passing waiter, his arms laden with plates. The man looked them over and told them to stand at the side of the terrace until the table was ready, and they walked a little further away from the diners so Vanessa could smoke. As they were waiting, a swoop of headlights rounded the corner and a Rolls-Royce mounted the pavement, forcing them to step back against the wall to let it pass. When the Rolls came to a stop, the driver leaped out to open the rear door and a pair of stilet-toed feet emerged. The woman turned and shot Kate and Vanessa a look of apology and then said something to the driver before strutting on ahead. Two thick-necked men joined her from the car. When the woman stopped to let one of them take her arm, Vanessa realised she was Elanka, the woman to whom Rob had just asked her to transfer ownership of one of Amir's properties.

Vanessa and Kate squeezed past the Rolls to the restaurant and saw Elanka and the men seated at the table the waiter had indicated was for them. Elanka looked stunning, displaying her tanned legs to the other diners on the terrace, most of whom were gawping at her.

The waiter appeared beside them. 'Sorry *Mesdames*, I made a mistake,' he said. 'That table is reserved. Please come inside with me.'

Vanessa stood her ground. 'But how can it be reserved?' she said. 'You don't take reservations.'

The waiter frowned. '*Madame*, that table is taken. If you'd like to dine here I can show you to a table inside, but if not, I'm afraid we have nothing else.'

'Let's leave,' said Vanessa to Kate. 'I need to sit outside.'

'No. It looks fun. I've heard about this place. Please, let's stay,' Kate said, taking Vanessa's elbow and coaxing her in behind the waiter who led them through the main restaurant to a table not far from the toilets.

Vanessa looked around sourly as the waiter swooped in with two glasses and several plates of antipasti.

'At least he's given us champagne,' said Kate brightly, taking one of the glasses.

'He didn't give it to us – it'll be on the bill. This is just one of their scams,' Vanessa said. She took a sip and made a face. 'Ugh. It's not champagne either, it's Prosecco. Now I'm really insulted.'

Vanessa called the waiter back and told him to take away the glasses and return with a bottle. 'Of champagne.'

Kate leaned in towards Vanessa. 'Those people outside. They obviously arrived in a Rolls and the waiter knew who they were, but what about everyone else? How do they decide who gets the best tables?'

'Monaco is a small place. The waiters know everyone and give the best tables to the biggest tippers. I always tip well, but don't come here often enough. Other than that it's the way they're dressed.'

'Back to appearances then?'

'Exactly,' said Vanessa grimly.

The champagne arrived, and the waiter made a fuss of opening it, setting it ostentatiously in the middle of the table in a crimson ice bucket.

'So talk me through the appearances of the people at the next table,' Kate said.

Vanessa glanced over at the two men. 'First look at bearded one's suit. It's an unusual shade of blue. Not off the shelf. The way it fits him perfectly around the ass and thighs.'

'How can you tell? He's sitting down.'

'They came in when we were outside,' said Vanessa, laughing.

'So you check everyone out too?'

Vanessa took a sip of champagne. 'Of course.'

Kate sighed. 'Clothes. How do people know what to wear? It's one of my total blind spots,' she said. 'I have no idea.'

'It's easy if you want to play that game. First, give people an obvious reference point. For women – it's labels, jewellery and if you really lack imagination, a big-name handbag. You saw that beautiful woman outside in the diamonds and the Gucci mini dress. Her name's Elanka and her boyfriend is a client of Rob's, incidentally.' Vanessa took a sip from her glass and then coughed slightly, pointing at Kate. 'Amir Fedorovich. He bought Falkon Racing, the Formula One team last year.'

'No way,' Kate said, looking towards the terrace. 'Is that Amir with her now?'

'I assume so. I met Elanka once a couple of years ago but I've never met Amir. Rob likes to keep his clients to himself.'

'I didn't notice the men. I was looking at her.'

'Exactly. No one's going to put Elanka out here in the back room. Or Amir, for that matter. He's the only client Rob fears. He's utterly ruthless.'

'God, really?' said Kate, alarmed.

'So as I was saying – for men, it's high status arm candy, an expensive suit, a big name watch.' One of the men at the next table rose. 'See, he's wearing a Richard Mille.'

Kate nodded to the man as he headed into the toilet. 'So why are they in here with us if they're so rich, I mean, *stylish*.'

'Because they're not as rich as those outside. Here there's always someone richer, just like there's always someone younger and more beautiful. They're the ones who get to sit outside on the terrace. But it all comes and goes, fortunes rising and falling like oil and water. When someone's wealth takes a nosedive, there'll always be someone else to take their place at the parties, buy their villa and their yacht.'

Vanessa raised her glass and slugged back the champagne. 'And our role is to help them navigate all that. We help them on the way up, and we help them on the way down. And we skim the fat on the way through in the form of our fees.'

When they finished the champagne, Vanessa ordered wine and several more dishes to share and they spoke about apartments and their plans for the weekend. Vanessa offered to take Kate on a shopping trip to Nice to buy some things she needed.

When they had almost finished their food, the conversation turned back to work.

'So what is it Rob does here exactly?' Kate said. 'Does he even live here?'

'He lives between London and Monaco but he doesn't have an apartment here because he prefers to stay in hotels. The Hôtel de Paris, the Hermitage or the Chèvre d'Or up at Èze. He likes to spread himself around and his clients prefer hotel bars to offices.'

Kate swirled the wine in her glass. 'In London no one seems to know what he actually does. He swans in from Monaco every week or so, has a few lunches, and then he's gone again.'

Vanessa stared at Kate for a couple of seconds. Could it really be that Rob hadn't told her anything about the kind of work he did?

'Isn't that what all those partners do?' said Vanessa airily.

Kate laughed. 'So who are his main clients?'

Vanessa poked at the remains of the salad. 'He acts for high net worth individuals. People from the ex-Soviet bloc mainly – Kazakhstan, Belarus, Azerbaijan.' If Rob hadn't told Kate who he worked for then it really wasn't Vanessa's place to say much more. 'What has he told you you'll be doing here?'

'I know I'll be continuing with some litigation I did in London for Falkon Racing, and that there'll be other Formula One work, but beyond that I don't really know. He was fairly vague when I asked what other work I'd be doing.'

Vanessa wound an anchovy around her fork and brought it to her mouth. 'Here in Monaco we provide the usual things rich people want. Tax sheltering, company structuring, immigration advice, property, trusts, divorce, litigation. A diverse practice, as they say.'

'And what's your role?'

Vanessa shifted in her seat, thinking again about the transaction she had just authorised for Rob. It was annoying of Kate to hound her like this, and Kate was now staring intently at Vanessa like this was some kind of inquisition. Paranoia got the better of her and Vanessa had a sudden frightening idea Kate might even be an undercover cop. She then quickly dismissed the idea: cops were never that clever.

'I do some tax work for Rob and I also coordinate the money flows and vet the clients. Technically I'm the Compliance Officer here, so I make sure all the financial aspects of the transactions comply with the law and that we don't act for anyone dodgy.'

Vanessa knew she'd had too much to drink to continue. She might say something incriminating, and so she indicated to the waiter they had finished their meal. The waiter cleared the table and brought over two glasses of limoncello, but Vanessa waved them away. The men at the next table had gone and the room was almost empty.

Vanessa reached for her bag. 'There's usually more action in here on a Friday night. Speaking of which, let's go to Jimmy'z.'

They paid the bill and walked to the nightclub, which was just a couple of streets away. The sea air was refreshing and Vanessa relaxed a little.

The entrance to the nightclub faced the water, in front of a bank of high-rise hotels. The exterior of the club was decorated with Balinese style totem carvings and fat white candles in a garden of palm trees.

'Is this really a helipad?' Kate said, pointing to a tarmacked area a few feet from the entrance.

'It's a bit early in the year now, but during the season that's how most people arrive. They come in off the yachts.'

There was a red carpet leading from the helipad down some steps to the club. A small queue had formed outside the main doors – the women in silky dresses and heels, the men in tight, dark clothes with tattoos and footballer haircuts – part gangster, part sportsman.

Kate stared at the group. 'There's no way—'

'Come on, let's try.'

As they approached the door, the bouncer asked for their membership card.

'Members' night only,' he said.

Vanessa turned to Kate, mouthing the word, bullshit.

'It's because of what I'm wearing, isn't it?'

Vanessa took her by the arm. 'Don't worry. I don't want to go in anyway. Let's just go to one of the hotels for a nightcap.'

Kate checked her watch. 'I'm sure it will be the same there. Anyway, I have a session with my personal trainer in the morning.'

Vanessa rolled her eyes. 'On a *Saturday*?'

'What about dinner one night?'

Vanessa smiled. 'I'm going to London later in the week but when I get back, sure let's do that,' she said.

They said goodbye and Vanessa walked to her car. Once inside, she wound down the windows and let out a sigh of relief. A breeze was coming in off the marina, turning the night cool, and Vanessa was now wide-awake.

Vanessa drove to the casino. All the effort of putting a positive spin on Meritus, Rob and his corrupt clients on top of her stressful day had unnerved her and she wanted to be around others who, like her, took risks for a living. She would restrict herself to a few hundred euros on the roulette but it would be worth it. She would get a thrill and then that sweet release, regardless of whether she won or lost. And who knows, she might even get lucky.

Chapter Three

Nice

VANESSA WOKE STARING AT HER reflection. She was lying on her side in an unfamiliar bed, her head sunk into a leopard print pillow, and in the pale blue half-light she could see the shape of a body behind her. He was face down beneath a white sheet, his shaved head resting on the pillow beside hers, and his back rose and fell gently in time with his breathing.

She rolled onto her back and took stock of the room – a studio apartment not much bigger than her bedroom in Fontvieille. There was a small kitchen to the left, a length of mirrored wardrobe beside her, and a door to a bathroom on the right, she recalled, assisted now by the sound of a dripping tap. Straight ahead, behind a blue gauze curtain, a set of glass doors led to a terrace where they had sat last night. They had drunk a bottle of champagne, smoked a lot, and then he had kissed and caressed her throat, she remembered as she rose from the bed and walked softly across the bare wood floor to the bathroom.

There were still puddles on the tiles and the showerhead was leaking water onto the tray in a steady trickle. The towel rail had dislodged from the wall and one side was hanging down, the screws exposed. She remembered gripping hold of it during the shower they'd had before bed. After it broke, he made her go down on her knees, the water pouring on her head, soap stinging her eyes as he pulled her towards him.

She stared at her reflection in the mirror – bloodshot, raccoon eyes, and her hair was wild. Vanessa dabbed her face gently with the wet corner of a towel, wiping off the smudged make-up, then used his toothbrush. She went through the bathroom cabinet, swallowed two paracetamol and then tip-toed back to the main room. She found her phone on the floor under a blanket. It was just before 7 a.m. and she'd slept through an alarm.

'Shit!' she said aloud, remembering she needed to get back to work for Rob. She looked at the man in the bed, her eyes straining against the shadowy light for his face but it was completely buried in the pillow. She couldn't remember what he looked like and she certainly didn't know his name.

She walked to the small round table next to the television where they had flung their clothes. The contents of her bag had spilled across the table together with his wallet, splayed open and surrounded by her keys and a handful of coins, trusting gestures on both their parts, but also somewhat hollow given they had both lost all their cash.

She winced at the sight of her keys, recalling that he had driven her car from the casino to his home in the hills above Nice. She had been in the cocktail bar after her loss at roulette and he had taken the seat opposite. He told her he had just lost everything too – at poker – and they commiserated over vodka Martinis. After that, she was certainly too drunk to drive, she remembered him saying.

'I'm sure you are too,' she replied, laughing as she handed her keys to the valet. She let him drive her car, however, justifying the recklessness of that decision on the basis that they'd both had their share of bad luck that night and it couldn't possibly get any worse.

As she reached across the table to extract her keys from beneath his wallet, several of his cards fell out, including a French ID. She peered at the photo, recalling that broad jaw and those dark, intense eyes now staring back at her from the mugshot beneath the official watermark. Her hand hovered a moment over the card before picking it up and turning it towards the light for a better view.

Normally she wouldn't go looking for a man's date of birth, but good god, he was twenty-eight years old! She stared in awe at the numbers on the certificate and then over to the sleeping form on the bed. This man was sixteen years younger than her. She was old enough to be his mother, she thought, with a strange mixture of euphoria and disgust that was quickly replaced by a sudden, crushing sense of responsibility for his well-being that seemed to arise out of nowhere. What had possessed her, she thought, as she recalled snippets of their conversation on the terrace last night. He'd had a hard life – you could tell from the way his mouth turned down at the edges, and the dark shadows under his eyes, but she didn't remember thinking he was *that* young.

She must have been awfully drunk.

He certainly had the stamina of a younger man, she thought with a flicker of satisfaction, unable to recall the number of times they'd had sex during the night. She remembered the way he had turned from her after they had finished, announcing with a slight note of apology that he always slept on his front. It was a protective measure, she assumed at the time, not really wanting him to hold her anyway, but it now took on a childish quality. She remembered David used to sleep like that when he was a baby and she felt suddenly panicked at the comparison between this young man in the bed, and her son.

She scooped her belongings from the table, stuffed them into her handbag and then gathered her clothes. As she arched her back to pull the zip on her dress, she saw their cigarettes on the terrace outside, next to the glasses and the empty bottle. She could see that her packet of Marlboro Lights, with the picture of the diseased cornea, was still half-full so she slid the glass doors open to squeeze through. Outside, the air was cool, and she leaned over the balcony taking in the sweeping view of Nice spread out below now tinged a delicate pink in the early summer sunrise. Beyond the apartment blocks of the suburbs, she could see Castle Hill wedged between the densely packed terracotta roofs of Port Lympia and the Old Town. To the west was the wide curving stretch of the Baie des Anges, its flat glassy calm melting into the horizon and the endless blue sky.

When she came back inside he was propped on the pillows.

'What were you looking for?' he said in French. There were crease marks on his face like a series of carvings etched deep in the skin.

'My cigarettes.'

He pointed to the table. 'No, over there.'

She glanced at her bag. 'I was just gathering my things.'

'No you weren't,' he said aggressively.

He flung back the sheets and came to stand beside her, his body shocking in its sudden, unfamiliar nakedness. 'You were snooping through my wallet.'

She stepped back. 'I – I saw your ID.'

He drew her close, grabbing her wrist so tightly that his nails dug into her tendons. She felt the heat of his body as he pulled her to him, flicking through his wallet with his free hand, checking his cards.

'What have you taken?' he said, tossing his wallet on the table and fishing in his jacket now, which was draped, together with his jeans, over a chair.

'Nothing,' she said as he felt through his pockets.

'What the hell were you doing then, going through my wallet?' he said shaking her wrist angrily.

'Just checking.'

He dropped her arm, his anger dissipated, as if satisfied his belongings were still there. 'Checking what?'

She stepped back. 'You don't look twenty-eight,' she said, her voice wavering. 'And I would have remembered if you'd said your name was Pascal. My ex's name is Pascal.'

'I'm not twenty-eight,' he said, reaching over to his jeans pocket and throwing a passport on the table. He grinned and the creases on his face gained prominence. 'I'm thirty-nine and my name's Jeremie.' He pulled a driving licence from his wallet. 'Or Craig Saunders, forty-two.'

'Why do you have all these cards?'

'Why do you think?' he said, walking over to the coffee machine.

His body was very lean from behind, his back tanned and deeply arched, with prominent clefts at the side of his buttocks. The muscles on his arms flexed under his tattoos as he yanked out the coffee filter.

'I don't know. I don't know anyone who does,' Vanessa said, her voice trailing off as she stared at his body. 'Anybody who has separate ID cards, I mean.'

He filled the machine and reached up to the cupboard for a fresh packet of cigarettes, taking one in his mouth as he turned to her. 'It helps at the casino. They can't keep track of me that way.'

'In case they what? Ban you?'

He nodded as he lit his cigarette. 'They keep tabs on the big winners. You need ID to get in, so I have a few different names.'

He pointed to the ID that had fallen from his wallet. 'Pascal doesn't normally lose. That was unusual for him. He's usually quite lucky, which is why he found you, but you took all his luck last night.'

He came forward for a kiss but Vanessa stepped back.

'Why are they all different ages? Excuse me for saying this, but you don't look thirty-nine either.'

'Sometimes I do. I have different disguises.'

'*Disguises?*' Vanessa said, as she sat on the edge of the bed and eased on her shoes. This was great, she thought, she had just spent the night with some kind of criminal.

He came over and took her leg in his hands.

She pushed him away gently with her foot and then stood up.

'I can't, sorry,' she said, smoothing her dress. 'I have work.'

'On a Saturday?' he said, standing in her way as she moved towards the door. 'You didn't tell me what you do.'

'No,' she said, her heart beating quicker as she pecked him on the cheek and stepped around him. She was suddenly aware of his physical strength. He could very easily force her to stay, force her to do anything.

'Do you have a number?'

She shook her head.

'Well if I can't call you then you'll have to call me,' he sai.
reaching over to his jeans and handing her a yellow and black
laminated card.

'Joe?' she said. It wasn't a very French name.

'Yes.'

'OK, *Joe*. I'll call you sometime.'

Joe had parked her car behind his apartment block and its glossy
red body stood out in the suburban street like a beacon. Vanessa's
Porsche was an extravagance she had allowed herself after her
divorce and since then, it had always felt like a bit of a sanctuary.
No matter how bad she felt about the mess she seemed to have
made of her life, she always felt better when she was inside,
enveloped in its soft, calf-leather upholstery. The car was a refuge
now more than ever, and as she pressed the key fob, the vehicle
replied with a wink of lights and a soft beep. Vanessa opened
the door and slid into the driver's seat. She locked the doors
and sighed heavily, bracing for a moment at the wheel, overcome
with relief at being alone. Then she started shaking. She had
spent the night with a stranger before – in fact it was becoming
increasingly common, but this was a new thing. She had let
herself go home with a thug, some kind of low-life from the
casino, and a wave of nausea washed over her leaving a sense of
panic in its wake. She had extracted herself without too much
hassle, but she had been reckless and her wrist was red and
smarting where he had hurt her. The incident with the ID card
could have gone either way, especially if he was a serious criminal and she felt overwhelmed with gratitude to be out of his
apartment, aware that she'd probably just had a very lucky escape.

This kind of luck eventually ran out, Vanessa told herself sternly, as she started the car and drove through the suburbs of Nice. Risky behaviour was becoming the norm, and it often occurred after she had authorised an illegal money transfer for Rob. At first she thought such behaviour was an outlet – an expression of relief at getting the deal done or a way to get her mind off things, but now it felt like a form of self-harm.

Vanessa dug into her handbag for some Valium. She hit 'home' on the satnav and saw there were already long queues on the roads around Nice – day trippers no doubt, enticed by the promise of a beautiful day on the beach. Vanessa sniffed gingerly under her armpit and recoiled in disgust – the adrenaline from her tussle with Joe had released a strong animal smell. There would be no time to go home for a shower. She would have to change in to the gym kit she kept in the boot and head straight to the office.

As Vanessa drove along the motorway, she went back over the previous night. She was pleased she had risen above Rob's attempts to drive a wedge between her and Kate, and she was happy to take Kate under her wing at least for a few weeks until she settled in. Vanessa's mind spooled back to their conversation at the restaurant. Kate had been digging for information about Rob, and Vanessa shuddered as she recalled her urge to disclose more about Rob than was wise. While Vanessa had thankfully kept her mouth shut, it was clear from Kate's line of questioning that rumours were circulating in London. Vanessa couldn't remember whether Kate had mentioned anything in particular, but Rob's dealings were obviously raising suspicions.

It had been a long time since Vanessa had worked in London and she didn't know what the other lawyers at Meritus thought of Rob these days. Some of them were no strangers to dodgy dealings themselves, of course – the City of London was renowned for it, but London lawyers were good at hiding their tracks, and turning a blind eye. There had been a change of management at the firm however, and she had heard the new managing partner was much more inclined to toe the line.

Vanessa reached the first of the tunnels, then ground to a halt in the early morning traffic. Her head had cleared a little and she felt a bit calmer after the Valium, but her mouth was dry. As she leaned over for a bottle of water, she saw Joe's card peeping out of her handbag:

Joe Lebeau
Antiquaire

There was an address in the Old Town of Nice and pictures of some kind of antiques shop. She wouldn't throw his card away just yet despite his intimidating nature. Her losses at the casino had been bad, but they could have been a lot worse had she not met Joe. Often after a series of stinging defeats, she retired for drinks in the bar but then went back to the roulette once her courage had returned, sharpened by alcohol and the prospect of further recklessness. Vanessa played the Martingale, which with its system of doubling up on losing bets frequently resulted in rapid losses. She chose the technique because betting on defeat somehow eased its blow. She also reasoned that it made her less inclined to return to the wheel after her initial wager had been lost. It rarely worked out like that however, and often in her half-cut state she would carry on gambling until she lost even more.

He had saved her from herself, she thought as she pulled onto the hard shoulder and sped towards a slip road leaving a cacophony of angry horns in her wake. Joe might be useful, too. He knew about gambling and if he had gone to all that trouble disguising his identity, then he must be good. She had never visited the casino with a professional gambler before, and the idea appealed to her. Now that she had left his apartment she could think about him more objectively. Men like Joe needed careful handling that was for sure, but he might be worth it. He might be able to teach her how to win. Although Vanessa had no desire to see him again immediately, she tucked his card into the inside pocket of her handbag.

In the meantime, his card could be her lucky charm, she thought, smiling to herself for the first time that morning. It could be her *mascotte*.

Chapter Four

Monaco

V ANESSA PARKED NEAR THE QUAY and changed into her gym gear. Then she hurried towards the office, retracing her steps from last night. The cool morning air stung her face, erasing some of her tiredness and on the pavements too, the staler remnants of the evening were being swept away. Vanessa hadn't yet had a coffee and she was desperate for one now as she caught a whiff of the strong Italian roast coming from the cafés, but she was already late.

Arriving at the office, Vanessa went directly to her terminal. What she had to do now was straightforward and it wouldn't take long to authorise the transfer of money through to Rob, provided it had arrived in the trust account overnight.

As she tapped in the codes, Vanessa noticed one of her hands was shaking. She was hungover and had barely slept, but this had never happened before. She hadn't drunk *that* much, surely? Perhaps it was the pill she had taken on the motorway, Vanessa thought, as she rummaged through her bag to check precisely what she had taken. She usually carried all her prescriptions with her but she couldn't find the little blister packet the pill had come from. It must have fallen out in the car.

She didn't like coming in to the office on a Saturday – it made what she did feel that much more illicit, so perhaps what she was experiencing now was the edge of a panic attack. Vanessa had occasionally authorised a transfer to London directly through the firm's Monaco trust account as she was doing now, but never in such a large amount, and flouting the rules in such a flagrant manner unsettled her.

Vanessa was aware of the risks she took when she broke the law, but she knew that laws were blunt instruments and useless in sculpting the complicated financial arrangements that Meritus clients demanded.

And anyway, Vanessa had no real respect for the law. The law had not protected her when she had nothing, nor had it helped her in her bitter divorce from Pascal. As far as Vanessa was concerned, laws were there to unfairly maintain the status quo.

Vanessa knew the whole system was corrupt, but at least she didn't waste time thinking it could be otherwise. At Meritus Vanessa saw how much money the clients had, how it insulated them against life's blows and how it grew to staggering amounts with clever investment. It was impossible not to want to participate in that bonanza, and if Vanessa helped her clients launder money, then she could. Everyone at Meritus was richly rewarded if they did a good job and Vanessa didn't know any lawyer who was able to resist the lure of cash. People spoke about lawyers being guardians of the law and officers of the court but that was expecting too much of human nature. Lawyers were not monks or priests. They were not men and women of the cloth who had taken vows of poverty. They were ordinary folk, often from humble backgrounds themselves, so why should they be held to such high standards? It was naïve.

Vanessa had considered all of this when she first started working at Meritus. She knew that when she authorised these transfers and did other illegal tasks for Rob, she passed through into another morality which had no bearing at all on real life. The world of rich people who circulated vast sums of money through exotic places was so different from the ordinary world that it was impossible to compare the two realms. You just couldn't apply the same rules.

The super-rich, the gangsters and the oligarchs Vanessa worked for were beyond the law, but not because they were better than others. Far from it. They were beyond the law because the law did not stretch to them. The rules were too blunt, too coarse, too unsophisticated, or simply too easy to circumvent. When it came to the rules that applied to their clients, Vanessa and Rob had to make up their own.

These days, Vanessa did not often question what she did and rarely did it affect her emotions, but today was different. She was strung out and tired, and the thin veneer that separated her conscience from reality had fractured a little. The risks involved in what she was doing were at the forefront of her mind causing her hand and her thoughts to wobble from the task ahead.

One thing however, that remained steadfast was her reason for doing all this. Vanessa took these risks, suffered the batterings to her conscience and put up with Rob's bullying in order to provide for her son, David.

Before they divorced, Pascal threatened to withdraw all financial support. By then, Pascal was already one step ahead and had put what was left of his money and assets beyond the reach of his creditors and also, as it turned out, of Vanessa, and so her attempts to force Pascal to support David came to nothing. In the end, all Pascal left her with were debts. While she continued to rent the apartment in Fontvieille and allowed herself the extravagance of the Porsche, she had very little other money and had to support David alone. If Vanessa wanted David to be properly educated and given a decent shot at life then it was up to her to provide it.

Vanessa had access now to the Meritus trust account. She saw the seven million was in the Monaco account and so she gave authorisation for the transfer to London on Monday with a few taps of her keyboard.

Once Vanessa completed the authorisation she felt better. The money would soon be in Rob's hands and he would make sure the property transaction completed. She sent him a text about the football – the latest Arsenal score, which was the code they used whenever she had successfully completed something for him. Then she put in a quick call to David at his boarding school in the UK. Vanessa told David she was coming over next week and would take him out for his thirteenth birthday at the weekend. His real birthday was at the end of term, but that didn't matter. It would be a special pre-birthday treat.

As she was on the phone to David, a text arrived from Rob.

Did you tell Elanka about the football scores? 😠😠😠 😊😊😊

'Oh, shit!' Vanessa said out loud, realising she had forgotten to initiate the transfer of Amir's French villa to his girlfriend, Elanka.

'What Mum?'

'Nothing, darling. Just an email I received.'

'Are you at work?'

'I'm just leaving darling. I'll see you next week.'

She opened Outlook and started typing a message in code to the agent at the firm in Jersey who ran all the trusts.

Vanessa instructed the agent to draft documentation transferring beneficial ownership in the company that owned the villa to Elanka and her mother. She told him to send it to Rob to sign as he held power of attorney for Amir. Amir must be transferring ownership of his French villa to Elanka in anticipation of being sanctioned himself, Vanessa thought. She wondered why Amir would need to do that, as Rob was always so confident Amir's ownership of his assets was hidden. He was probably just being extra cautious with such a valuable property, Vanessa concluded upon further reflection.

As a precaution, Rob often advised his clients to hold property in the name of trusted friends and relatives through companies and trusts set up in the British Virgin Islands and Jersey because that way the true ownership of assets could be hidden and the clients' privacy safeguarded. This was particularly helpful if a client was worried about the imposition of sanctions, freezing or seizing orders, for example, or if they simply wanted to hide the source of their funds. Offshore companies and trusts operated like a cone of silence and protection, wrapping around property better than brick walls, barbed wire and guard dogs. These kinds of corporate structures made it easy to avoid unpleasant scrutiny, keeping out nosy intruders like journalists, regulatory authorities and the taxman. Ironically, it was also how Pascal had hidden what remained of his money and assets from Vanessa.

In the bathroom half an hour later, Vanessa stared at herself in the mirror. Her face looked gaunt in the cold fluorescent lights, which emphasised every wrinkle and blemish. She took one of the soft hand towels, dabbed water under her eyes, and applied a fresh layer of make-up over the residue from last night. Then she left the office.

Outside, it had turned into a beautiful morning – one of those gifts of early June that held the full promise of summer, and a reminder the cold weather was gone. It had been a warm spring, a season whose vitality along the coast was contagious and although each cycle meant another year passing, the season always made Vanessa feel young again.

There were other reminders of her youth on the streets that morning and wherever Vanessa looked she saw glimpses of the woman she had once been – young, happy and full of hope.

The women around her now were dressed immaculately in the latest designer clothes and unlike Vanessa, these women were not dashing from work in their gym gear, unwashed and tired after a sordid evening with a stranger. Instead, these young women were heading out to brunch on a lovely sunlit morning, wonderfully unencumbered by the prams and toddlers that earned them the right to such leisure. Vanessa had taught herself not to yearn for the lives these women lived because she'd had it once herself. She knew what it was like to be a trophy wife – someone whose existence was securely mapped out because that was the life she'd had with Pascal.

Pascal was the reason Vanessa had come to the Côte d'Azur in the first place. He was an entrepreneur and for many years, they flitted between homes in London and Monaco. Their life was wonderful to begin with – a dream in which she had everything she wanted – an interesting job, a child and the love of her husband, but then gradually the fantasy fell away. It was the usual story. A few years after David was born, Pascal was staying in the office a little later each week, then drinks after work that spilled into the early hours. There were work trips that gobbled entire weekends, and even when he was in Monaco, he was hardly at home. He invented lame excuses at first, but there came a point when he didn't even bother. For her part, Vanessa pretended not to care – she busied herself with David and her own projects, and so Pascal stayed away even more. His affairs were bad, but she learned how to deal with them and eventually she had her own lovers too. It was what married people did, she told herself.

When he turned forty, Pascal's drinking escalated and he started gambling again. He was losing money on his investments and once things began spiralling downwards, they didn't stop.

When Pascal told Vanessa he was filing for bankruptcy and that he had no money left, Vanessa was shocked, but not surprised. She formulated an escape plan during one of his long absences. She took David and moved from Monaco to a small town near the Italian border.

Vanessa didn't want to return to London as a failure in marriage and a failure at life, so she contacted Rob who gave her a job back at Meritus in the compliance department. It was perfect timing, Rob said. He had just set up the Monaco office and was looking for someone to oversee the firm's transactions and help him navigate money through the firm's accounts.

It was a lack of imagination on her part and Vanessa often dreamed of what she might have done had she not been so desperate.

Vanessa was prepared for the onslaught of young and glamorous women on the streets of Monaco that morning as usual, but nevertheless it still shocked her when reminders of her past potential leaped out at her in this manner. Vanessa bypassed the fashionable cafés where the young women congregated and stopped instead at Marcello, a quiet restaurant in a side street. It was an Italian place with flirtatious waiters, which at this time of the day was inhabited almost entirely by women her age or older. If the younger women in the cafés were reminders of who she once was, then the women on the terrace around her now were projections of the woman she might have become.

Often, when she dashed from the office at lunchtime to grab a sandwich, Vanessa had to turn away from these older women with a force of will that was almost as strong as if she had reached up and wrenched her head around. If she didn't look away, the waves of regret would become so vast they would feel part of the blue sea and sky all around her. Yes, Vanessa thought as today she let herself look at them all. These were the women she envied now with their reassured and hard-won freedom.

These women had been trophy wives and their husbands were most likely philanderers too, of course. But their husbands hadn't risked and lost everything like Pascal, and some of the more considerate ones had died, leaving rich widows behind them. The comfortable lives these women possessed represented the future Pascal had snatched from her. Vanessa would never know how it felt to be a woman like this – older for sure, but beyond the turbulence of motherhood and free on a calm vessel that she alone steered, away from the hazardous whirlpools of one-night stands with dangerous men, and the constant anxiety that came from working for someone else.

Vanessa thought about how violently she had been thrown from the course she had once mapped out for herself, and the rough seas that now lay ahead. She had never imagined she would work this hard, and that even in her mid-forties she would be working on a Saturday.

This particular morning it felt like there were more women than usual on the terrace and Vanessa gazed at their contented faces, bathed in the warm sunshine as they chatted and laughed. The light shone upon them all so perfectly that Vanessa felt as if she was looking at a scene from a painting. She smiled ironically to herself, thinking that if an artist were to capture the scene around her now, she would not be one of the striking women occupying the centre of the frame. She would be the haggard, stressed-out woman at the side; someone the artist might think to include in order to highlight the glamour and indolence of the main characters. Vanessa sighed as she realised she had become a sideshow to the life she once had, a supporting actor in the future she had once imagined for herself.

As Vanessa's eyes drifted over the terrace, she saw another woman sitting alone, but instead of a coffee, the woman held a glass of champagne, lightly smudged with the bright red lipstick she wore. Vanessa couldn't see the woman's face but she noticed she was dressed expensively in something subtle – Valentino or Hermès, and it reminded Vanessa of the way she used to dress and how confident she had once been. It was as if this woman was poised at the exact place where Vanessa's life had diverged violently off-course many years ago.

Just then the woman looked up to the waiter to pay her bill and Vanessa realised she was Amir's girlfriend, Elanka, the woman who would soon possess his beautiful coastal property.

Elanka saw her too and smiled as she collected her things from the table and then nodded a goodbye.

Vanessa was tempted to hurry after Elanka to renew their acquaintance and to properly say hello, but the waiter arrived with her food. And what would Vanessa say to Elanka anyway? Meritus clients didn't pay to be accosted on the street and so Vanessa turned her attention to her Caesar salad.

She used to be like Elanka and she could be like that once more. Vanessa smiled up at the waiter. 'A glass of champagne, please.' There was still time to reinvent herself again.

Chapter Five

I**T WAS MILD ENOUGH IN** the mornings for Kate to drink her coffee on the balcony before work. She sat among plants the previous tenant had left behind – ferns, cactuses, a thriving red and yellow orchid and a rose bush that had just started to bloom. This would never happen in London where she had to coax plants along with careful tending, bringing them in for the winter, and even then they all withered and died. Warmed by the balmy air, the roses released such a powerful scent that Kate peered over to the neighbours' balconies, wondering if the smell was coming from there.

The metal grilles that had been pulled across the neighbours' glass doors were covered with a layer of dust, confirming what the relocation agent had told Kate when she showed her around. Although the apartments on either side were technically occupied, no one actually lived there.

Kate's apartment was in Saint Roman, a prestigious area on the eastern tip of Monaco. The floor plan was roughly the same as her basement flat in Camden – just one bedroom next to an open-plan kitchen, dining and living area, but the full-length glass doors across the entire front of the apartment gave it a much more splendid feel than her damp London flat. Sitting up in bed, Kate had a view right across the city to the stunning cliffs above La Turbie. Although she had no view of the sea, her balcony got the best of the afternoon sun and was still sunlit well into the evening.

Kate had only been in Monaco a week but already she had fallen in love with the place – the sunshine, the sub-tropical plants, the citrus trees with their pungent blossoms, the bright purple bougainvillea that tumbled down the hillsides. With the sea on one side and the mountainous hinterland on the other, there would be plenty to explore on weekends, long evenings on warm terraces to look forward to, and cocktails in the sun. The transfer to Monaco had been competitive, with many other Meritus lawyers vying for the post. Kate had assumed she was out of the running, thinking her recent stress leave would count against her in the last round, but it was Rob who'd had the final say. Kate had successfully concluded some litigation for Falkon Racing in the months prior to the decision and Rob said he wanted her to continue working on other aspects of it in Monaco. The litigation had been unpleasant, but Kate was grateful for it now as she sat on her balcony sipping coffee with the delicious smell of roses on the warm air around her.

When she arrived at the office half an hour later, Kate took out the Falkon Racing files and fired up her computer. She worried loose a thread on the sleeve of her jacket as she checked the progress of the Monaco litigation, the public relations strategy, and then went through Falkon's on-screen financials. The red line on the profit and loss statement pointed steadily downwards and then flattened out. Kate squinted at the screen and sighed. Falkon's performance had fallen off a cliff last month, and even now, there was still no sign of recovery. She zoomed out to the longer-term view. It resembled the mountains above Monaco – up, down, up, and then down again steadily, before tapering into the sea. The past weeks were more like a cardiac flatline. There had been sporadic blips, intermittent signs of life, but overall, the prognosis was bleak. Kate pulled the thread from her jacket, balled it between her fingers and flicked it at the screen.

Falkon Racing was a Formula One team owned by Amir Fedorovich, and it was mired in litigation. It was Amir's pet project, and since Amir was Meritus's biggest client in Monaco, Falkon Racing was now Kate's problem. The cause of its financial woes was a class action that had been brought by a group of mechanics and garage workers against the team for hearing loss. Initially, Falkon thought the men would go quietly, so Falkon had held out against paying any big settlements. One of the employees, however, turned out to be the father of a top driver for Red Bull and so the litigation hit the spotlight. Slurs were made in the press against Falkon and its treatment of workers, and this was whipped up on social media by the other teams and their drivers. The more exposure the cases received, the more ex-employees came out of the woodwork with similar claims, and the harder it became for Falkon to attract the best drivers and mechanics. Kate had worked relentlessly to settle the claims cheaply and quietly while she had been in London, but the work had been difficult and draining.

Amir wasn't particularly interested in Formula One, and he had bought the team three years ago with one purpose in mind, which was to establish a beachhead of soft power in the south of France and in Monaco, where motor racing reigned supreme. Although the casino and the other luxury businesses run by *Société des Bains de Mer* propped up the finances of the principality, motor racing supplied the glamour. The Grand Prix was the pinnacle of the social calendar and the fulcrum around which everything else revolved. Overnight, Amir went from being just another rich man with a murky past to a glamorous tycoon and a sportsman of the world. He was suddenly at all the best parties and events, part of Monaco's inner circle as though he had been there forever.

Thanks to his uncle, a corrupt politician from Belarus, Amir was accustomed to a life of privilege, and glamorous parties were nothing special. Thanks to Rob and other clever lawyers and accountants in London, Amir had both a British passport and many ingenious ways to hide his money from the taxman and his countrymen too, and so Monaco citizenship or residency wasn't the endgame either. The real reason Amir had bought Falkon was to establish a benign smoke screen to obscure his other, more sordid activities along the coast.

Although no one had ever proven anything against Amir, he had a reputation for involvement in all forms of trafficking – drugs, arms, money and human. Most of this occurred in Belarus and the neighbouring oblasts of Ukraine, but since the war, several of these activities had relocated to the West where Amir had other interests. At the same time, things had tightened up against oligarchs and the like, and Amir needed a safe haven for his money and a soft power front from which to control his hard power base.

No one at Meritus except Rob knew the extent of Amir's business interests and provided Amir paid Rob's over-inflated bills, no one at the firm ever asked. Buying the Formula One team had been Rob's idea and initially, it was genius. Following the acquisition, Amir's status rocketed. Since he was now a high-profile businessman and significant contributor to the economy of the Côte d'Azur, Amir pulled in favours and perks from the Monégasque and French governments alike. He received planning permission for alterations to his villa at Roquebrune, together with private beach rights, which had never before been granted. He also got permission to run a small gambling circle at the villa, and everyone turned a deaf ear to the rumours that circulated about the many indiscretions there and on his yacht. His Formula One team ownership smoothed the way for everything, just as Rob had promised. It covered up and excused all kinds of bad behaviour.

What neither Rob nor Amir had fully appreciated, however, was the capriciousness of Monaco society. In a shallow world, a person is only as deep as their social media profile, and as soon as one's reputation is even slightly tarnished, it rusts fast. If that happens, everyone runs scared for fear of contagion. The Falkon litigation had thrust Amir into an unflattering spotlight and it was now an uncontrollable PR disaster. During the Grand Prix, Amir saw just how far he had sunk. Everyone had given Falkon a wide berth at race week, and no A-listers came to any of the parties that took place in the Falkon hospitality tent. Amir was enraged and had been on the phone to Rob every day since. Falkon was so integral to Amir's business strategy and his reputation on the Côte d'Azur that the litigation had to be stopped at all costs.

Kate had worked all morning on the most recent claims and at 1 p.m., the sun was high and streaming in through her office window. As Kate stood to adjust the blind, her gaze panned over the yachts glistening in the harbour, then above to Le Rocher. She was just about to head downstairs for lunch when her desk phone buzzed. It was Julia, another partner in the Monaco office who also worked closely with Rob.

'Can you pop into my office? I'm with Rob. It's about Falkon,' Julia said, ringing off before Kate could reply.

'We'll cut straight to the chase,' Rob said, as he ushered Kate in and closed the door. He pointed to a seat facing a large mahogany desk where Julia stood in a bright fuchsia trouser suit.

'We're worried about these new claims,' Rob said. 'We need to do something before they get out of hand.'

Kate glanced at her watch, wondering why this couldn't wait until after lunch, then stared back at Rob. In London, she always thought he looked out of place with his thuggish physique and cold blue eyes, but here in Monaco he seemed to fit right in.

'I was just going through the files, actually. We got a great settlement on some of the claims last year—'

'—which is why you got the promotion to Monaco,' said Rob tersely. 'But we need to act soon, to stop any further claims coming out of the woodwork. Amir is very worried about how it looks.'

'How it looks? I've been working closely with the team on Falkon's image while trying to combat any negative fallout from the litigation. We've contacted a number of celebrities, offering member tickets to next year's Grand Prix and key influencers have been approached to do some soft messaging. I've got it covered.'

Kate cursed herself. That last statement was just what Rob had been waiting for.

'I'm not sure you have got it *covered*,' Rob said, looking at Julia as they passed the conversation between them.

'It seems some of the older claims weren't properly dealt with while you were . . .' Julia said, her voice trailing off.

'While you were *away*,' Rob added.

Kate was used to her stress leave being referred to as if it were some kind of vacation and she braced herself.

'Not dealt with at all, in fact,' continued Rob and rolled his eyes absurdly, placing his upturned palms in the air. This unnerved Kate – why the jocular manner? At Meritus humour was often used as a way to soften up your victim for the kill.

Julia saw Kate's eyes harden and she smiled benevolently. 'Now you're here we need you to fix it.'

'It's not something we can give to any of the others,' Rob said.

'Resolving these claims swiftly will really improve market confidence,' said Julia, letting the words drift around the room like a promise.

'*Resolving* them?' Kate said. 'I am resolving them and so far the client has agreed to pay out the claims I've negotiated. Now I'm here in Monaco I'm sure it will happen much quicker.'

Kate looked first at Julia, then at Rob as Rob and Julia looked at each other. They didn't seem quite sure whose turn it was to speak so Julia grasped the opportunity, her voice smooth and even. 'The ones that concern us are the much older claims. Some of them are a complete waste of time.'

Rob scratched his ear. 'We can't afford to go to court, Kate. It would send out the wrong message about Amir and about Meritus.'

'What is it you want me to do?' Kate said slowly, shifting in her chair, as the heat rose beneath her jacket.

'We need you to find a document,' Rob said casually.

'Find?' said Kate.

'Yes. *Find*. We need a certain key document *found*,' said Julia, mouthing the words slowly while moving a pile of papers to the outer reaches of her desk. 'Something that will unlock all this.'

The pause drifted on a little too long and in its depths Kate sensed what they wanted her to do.

'We need you to go through the files and find something you might have missed,' said Rob.

'What kind of thing?' Kate said, the hair follicles behind her ears tingling.

'A disclaimer, a get-out clause, something like that,' said Julia, wafting her hand casually in the air. 'Something the claimants themselves have overlooked.'

Rob looked to the ceiling, arms crossed over his chest as if deep in thought. 'You know, these claims are really very old. All the employment contracts are in hard copy, there's nothing digital. I'm sure you'll be able to find something in those older files,' he said. His thin lips had levelled into a straight line. 'You're a lawyer. You know how this works.'

A strange coldness seized Kate's stomach. Men like Rob didn't usually intimidate her. She had worked with enough of them to know that beneath the hard-man exterior, they were all just cowards, but now he seemed positively evil. The glare from the fluorescent lights made the wrinkles radiate from his darkened eyes like brooding sunbursts.

Kate stared at Rob, trying not to break eye contact. 'Right. I see. You want me to make this up? You want me to manufacture evidence?' she said flatly.

Rob walked towards the window and shrugged, his back to her. His spiky black hair glistened in the sun and Kate realised the moisture on his scalp was sweat rather than any hair product. Rob was scared about all this, scared of the client.

Kate felt a sudden stiffening in her spine. 'There are criminal sanctions, Rob. I could be struck off . . .'

Rob spun around. 'It's only a crime if you're caught.'

'If *I'm* caught?'

'Yes,' he said, glaring at her. 'So make sure you're not caught.'

Rob's face altered and he grinned at her, and then at Julia, snapping his fingers in the air, his voice conversational now. 'What's that saying? If a tree falls in a forest and no one hears it, does it make a sound?'

Julia seized the philosophical baton. 'If a tree doesn't make a sound, does it even fall?'

Rob threw his arms in the air, hallelujah style. 'If nothing falls, there's nothing to catch.' His grin was the ugliest Kate had ever seen. 'So don't drop anything. And make sure you're not *caught*.'

Julia smiled coldly and finally sat down at her desk. 'Look, Kate. Everyone wants it fixed – Amir, the claimants, the bank, the other investors, the insurers and most of all – us. Even the other teams want it gone. The whole thing is bad PR for the sport – everyone accepts that.' Julia glanced at Rob. 'This will be worth it for you, for all of us. Our interests are completely aligned.'

Kate shook her head. 'Amir knew about the problem when he bought Falkon Racing. That's why he got such a great deal. He can afford to be generous.'

'*Generous*,' Rob growled. 'People like Amir don't come to us because they want to be generous.'

'*Fair*, then! Falkon can afford to be fair. The insurers have agreed to settle. It's all on file. The press release goes into all that. Think of the amazing PR if we settled these cases fairly for everyone.'

Rob glared at Kate. 'You haven't met Amir, but I can tell you now he's the furthest thing from *fair* you can possibly imagine. This is all a huge embarrassment for him.'

Rob sighed and swivelled his trousers around his waist as he walked over to her.

'The timing isn't good, Kate,' he said, softly now. 'More claims will come in if word gets out and we can't afford to have any further payouts. This could destroy Falkon Racing and god knows what damage it will do to *our* brand. Meritus could go under. This is your issue too.'

'We'll make this work for you, Kate,' said Julia.

'*Work?*' said Kate.

'It will be worth it. We'll make it worth your while,' Julia added, sitting back and smiling generously.

Later that afternoon, Kate went over the conversation as she looked out at Le Rocher. It was a warm day and crowds of tourists swarmed up the ramparts to the palace and the streets of the Old Town. Kate toyed with a takeaway salad then pushed it away, her hunger curbed by the hard ball of worry pressing against her navel.

Kate had met the claimants Rob and Julia wanted her to manufacture evidence against. They were respectable men with modest expectations, each with beige hearing aids tucked behind their ears. Like the men, the claims were old and Rob's strategy was to dispute every one, dragging out the cases in the hope of exhausting the men or sending them to the grave in which case there would be no payout at all. When Kate was in London she had negotiated settlements that had satisfied the men as well as Falkon, and while she considered herself resilient, the process had been gruelling. There was one old man who had particularly affected her. He was as deaf as a haddock but had insisted on coming to settlement conferences even though he couldn't hear a thing. In meetings he had watched Kate with a deference she found completely unnerving. His death, just after settlement had been reached, prompted her stress leave and afterwards she applied for a transfer to Monaco thinking a change of scene would do her good. She couldn't explain why the old man had affected her so much, but in her darker moments she questioned her job, knowing she was ripping these men off, negotiating them out of more generous deals.

Kate tapped her pen on the file as she thought about the conversation in more detail. What Rob and Julia wanted her to do was to falsify a document between Falkon Racing and the union. The purpose of the document would be to absolve Falkon Racing from any responsibility for the health and safety of its workers, specifically related to hearing loss above a certain amount. Such clauses had been included in contracts for other Formula One teams but so far none had been found for Falkon, hence the current series of claims. Rob and Julia said they only had a couple of weeks before they needed to act definitively. Kate stared at her screen, willing the flatline into an uptick.

What they were asking her to do was illegal and very risky, but what were her options? Falkon was in trouble. If Amir was forced to sell as a result of this litigation, his reputation would be in tatters and Meritus would suffer too. If Meritus's standing fell, then Kate's reputation would follow: she would lose her job, and it would be difficult to move anywhere else in the pall Falkon's losses would cast. No one would employ a litigator who had been responsible for such a high profile loss.

The idea of just resigning and not working for a while scudded across her mind, followed quickly by a lonely vision of herself in the white laminate kitchen of her apartment as she waited for calls from recruitment agents. There was also her mother to consider. How would she cope without Kate's salary? Another surge of anxiety uncoiled within her at the thought of her sister who was just beginning to recover from a series of self-harming episodes linked to her gambling debts. Kate saw the consequences of her decision not to do Rob and Julia's bidding reverberate through her life like a series of toxic dominoes, each one setting off multiple disasters. She would never be able to replicate the kind of package she received at Meritus. Kate took a swig from the glass of water at her desk and wiped her palms on her jacket. No, she had to work this out somehow. She had to stay at Meritus.

For the remainder of the day, Kate's stomach lurched as she thought about what she had been asked to do. As the afternoon wore on, the fear that initially overwhelmed her was slowly replaced with the beginnings of a strange kind of curiosity as she considered how quick and easy it could be. A disclaimer drawn up and backdated, signed by the union on behalf of the men. The old union was defunct and the new one had no way of knowing it hadn't happened. She could draft it on her laptop at home so there was no trace of it on the office system. She could print the document out, forge the signatures and then *voilà! – find* it in an old file. She would just need to circulate it to everyone and the claims would be struck out of the court lists. Like most acts of dishonesty, it was small and mean, quick and easy. Foolproof even, and while she knew it was wrong, she was annoyed that her conscience was such a burden when others around her seemed to have no qualms.

Kate glanced out over the yachts in the marina and thought back to her evening with Vanessa. Vanessa had worked with Rob for years. She would know how to handle this.

Chapter Six

WHEN VANESSA THOUGHT OF TAKING Kate under her wing she hadn't imagined it quite so literally. Vanessa didn't mind the occasional outing with Kate, and she had enjoyed their evening chewing the fat about all things Monaco and Meritus, but that was barely three days ago. Vanessa had a date planned for tonight, and on Thursday she was going to London so her week was already cut short. Kate had sounded so anxious on the phone, however, that Vanessa cancelled her date and arranged to meet her at the Brasserie de Monaco on the waterfront at 8 p.m.

'So how's the second week going?' Vanessa said, placing an order with the waiter and then bringing her attention back to Kate. 'Not too good from the sound of things.'

'No. Something's come up.'

'Tell me.'

'You have to keep it quiet. Confidential.'

'Of course,' Vanessa said. 'Absolutely.'

'So as you know I've been brought here to work on the Falkon litigation.'

Vanessa nodded. 'You must know it all backwards by now. What's the problem?'

'I thought I'd settled the biggest claims, but some others have come in. Rob and Julia are worried Amir will have to make a big payout.'

Vanessa moved aside as the waiter delivered their drinks. 'So what? He knew about the claims when he bought the team, didn't he? They would have factored it into the price. Amir can afford it.'

'At the time he bought the team, there was only one claim. The man was on death's door and so Rob knew he could settle it quickly. But then other claims appeared and now they don't want to settle.'

'So they litigate.'

'They don't want to do that either. It would be a PR disaster.'

'So what are you saying?'

Kate glanced over her shoulder and lowered her voice. 'I've been asked to manufacture evidence.'

'What kind of evidence?'

'A false document, a waiver, a limitation of liability.'

'On what?'

'On the older claims.'

Vanessa shook an ice cube into her mouth and looked over to the bar. Rob had barely given Kate a week to settle in. He must be desperate pulling this stunt so soon.

'How complicated is it?'

Kate paused for a second. 'Not very.'

'Is it traceable?' Vanessa said carefully, crunching the ice.

'Everything's traceable.'

Kate was staring at Vanessa, anguish pouring from her face and it was hard for Vanessa not to feel sorry for her as she considered how to respond. Vanessa could pretend she knew nothing about this kind of thing, make out as if Kate had just got the wrong end of the stick. Alternatively, she could bring Kate in on how things worked with Rob and save her a lot of time. It was brutal of Rob to throw her in at the deep end like this, but Vanessa had seen him do it with other new recruits. It was a way to disorient and manipulate them quickly before they'd had a chance to find their feet in the already overwhelming world of Monaco.

Vanessa could let Kate stumble on and find out how it worked for herself, or she could guide her towards the truth. Vanessa decided not to beat around the bush. It was the kindest thing to do and would give Kate some thinking time.

'What I mean is could you hide it easily?'

Kate paused as confusion clouded her face. 'Probably.'

Vanessa shrugged and looked at her watch, then scanned the bar. 'I always had this place down as livelier than this,' she said.

'What?'

'This bar. There used to be a lot more action in here. Even on a Monday.'

'Vanessa, I just asked you something.'

'No, I asked *you*.'

Kate looked at her blankly.

'And you answered. You said you could probably hide it,' Vanessa said, finishing her drink and shaking the last of the ice into her mouth.

Kate raised her eyebrows and settled back in the chair, crossing her arms over her chest. 'You seem pretty casual about it.'

Vanessa waved her hand in the air. 'You said you wanted advice. But I see now what you really want is an ethical debate.'

'Have you ever done this kind of thing?' said Kate weakly.

'What kind of thing?'

'I mean you've been here a long time.'

Vanessa gestured to the waiter for two more drinks. 'Thanks for reminding me.'

'Have you ever been asked to do anything illegal?'

Vanessa shrugged her shoulders gently.

'Have you?'

Vanessa looked away. She didn't want to admit such a thing of course, but she had started off down this path and she couldn't now deny it outright.

'I'll take that as a yes, then.'

Vanessa's face softened. '*Illegal*,' she said, meeting Kate's eyes and smiling, as if it was a newly invented word. 'Come on, Kate. Don't give me this babe-in-the-woods routine.'

Kate was taken aback. Vanessa was kind-hearted and was going out of her way to help her settle in, but this was a shock. Kate knew Vanessa didn't pull any punches when it came to saying it how it was, but she now sounded a lot like Rob.

'*Babe-in-the-woods?* It's not every day I'm asked to do something so brazenly illegal, so apologies if I come across as a little confused.'

'I know. I'm sorry,' said Vanessa quietly.

'No, really, I want to know.'

Vanessa paused as fresh drinks were delivered. 'Well occasionally, you know, I do a few things to ease the transactions through. The odd thing here and there, small things.'

Kate's eyes grew wider. 'Small things?'

Vanessa put her drink down impatiently. She didn't want to have to go into detail. She was still exhausted from her evening with Joe and wasn't up for much more of this wise-woman mentor routine. It was making her feel old.

'What kind of small things?' said Kate.

'Look, everyone does it at some point. You hide evidence, find evidence. Cook the books, ice the books. So what?'

Vanessa wouldn't normally admit she had done anything of the sort, nor would she so openly advise a colleague to commit fraud, but she had the urge to shake Kate up a bit. She would find out what Rob did sooner or later.

'You told me on Friday you doubled your salary coming to Monaco. I know you were one of the best lawyers in the London office but really, Kate, what do you think they pay you for here – skilful drafting?'

A waiter delivered a plate of nachos smothered in cheese. Kate wasn't hungry and pushed the plate towards Vanessa who dug in.

'Don't look at me like that. You know how these things work. It saves everyone money in the end. I imagine in this situation it will get the cases cleared through court quicker and that's got to be a good thing for everyone, right?'

Kate was appalled. 'What if I'm caught?'

'No one's ever *caught*. Not here anyway,' Vanessa said, but a sliver of fear pierced her heart as she thought of the transaction she had authorised for Rob at the weekend. Money laundering through the trust account for Amir who was buying property in London from a soon-to-be-sanctioned Russian. What was she thinking?

Kate fiddled with her bracelet. 'Do you ever worry about it, though? It's such a terrible risk.'

'Don't look so stressed. The regulators here are still pretending to audit files from ten years ago and don't get me started on the UK authorities. The truth is, those organisations are filled with people who were never smart enough for private practice, and are on a tenth of our salaries. We run rings around them,' Vanessa said, stuffing a handful of cheese-fused nachos into her mouth.

'But there are criminal sanctions. Jail terms, not just fines,' Kate said, her voice high pitched and whiny.

'Tell me one person you know who's been caught,' Vanessa said through the nachos. 'One person.'

Kate shrugged.

Vanessa was on a roll now and words were just coming out. Speaking like this was an outlet for the tension she carried over from the weekend and the look of horror on Kate's face was almost cathartic.

'No one thanks you for being honest, being straight. That's not what people want in a lawyer. They can do all that themselves. They want someone dynamic who can cut through the crap.'

Vanessa opened her phone and delivered a quote from the firm's website. "*Meritus provides a full range of legal services to meet the needs of our clients and gives creative, effective, cutting-edge advice for special situations.*" She rolled her eyes towards the bar. 'In other words, we align ourselves to meet our client's demands. God, do I even need to tell you this?'

Kate knew Vanessa had been involved in enough deals in Monaco to know what she was talking about.

'Tell me honestly, Kate. Why did you come here?'

Kate shifted back. Of course the main purpose in coming to Monaco was to earn money. It was why she worked at Meritus in the first place.

'Like I said the other night, I was getting burned-out in London. I needed a change of scene. Meet new people, save money. I thought it was a good idea.'

'And it *is* a good idea. So focus on that. Make the most of it here. Have fun. Take it less seriously. Meet people. Join a dating app.'

'And this thing Julia and Rob want me to do?'

Vanessa looked at Kate vacantly.

'I can't believe your advice is to just get it done.'

Vanessa slouched back in her chair and loosened the button at the waistband of her skirt. She felt quite tipsy but it was good to be dishing out advice for a change rather than taking it from Rob. It felt like she was purging herself.

'Look, you know what my real advice to you would be? Think seriously about what you want. If you really want to be an honest lawyer then you need to get out now. Join those bleeding hearts with their losing cases down at Legal Aid, or try working at some community centre. Heaven forbid, you could even go into *human rights!*'

Vanessa waved her hand around – taking in the bar, the marina outside. 'Open your eyes, Kate, and look around. These kinds of concerns have no place here. Surely that's obvious to you by now.'

She leaned forward and tapped her nails on the table.

'Your real concern should be what's in it for you. This is an opportunity. If I were you I'd be cutting my deal with Rob and Julia now. You need to make sure you do this in a way that works for you. You're helping them out here, big time. Do your deal in advance.'

'So, that's your advice? Just get on with it? Cut a deal?'

Vanessa shrugged. 'Why not? Everyone's at it in London as well as here. Coming to Monaco as an honest lawyer is like being a vegan in an abattoir. Why be the odd person out?'

Chapter Seven
London

TWO MEN SHOULDERED THEIR WAY off the Tube and onto the platform at Bank station. They fell into step and pushed through the crowd. One of them checked his phone for signal then returned it to his inside jacket pocket. Rob was still a little hungover, his round face flushed with the afterglow of a stag party he had attended at the weekend. His associate, Lensley, was tall and slim with a waxy complexion. There were shadows under his eyes and he had small, discoloured teeth. Rob drew half a step ahead of Lensley, keeping a straight course up the stairs, ignoring the instruction to keep right. Rob's bulk commanded respect and ensured the pair carved their way quickly through the crowd, onto the escalators, through the ticket barrier, and up the steps into Lombard Street.

Rob reached for his phone and started scrolling. 'Footsie's down,' he uttered, more to himself than to Lensley. The screen's light shone in his dull blue eyes, heavy lidded and tinged with red.

Lensley retrieved his own phone. He kept one hand in his pocket, rattling loose change and keys while he worked his phone with the other. *Down*, he thought. That was about the measure of things. His jaw tightened as he considered his career at UBank, which, by anyone's reckoning, had taken a nose-dive recently. Lensley had missed out on a promotion and he had just learned his bonus would be non-existent this year. By contrast, Rob was at the top of his game. In addition to being the highest billing partner at Meritus, Rob ran what he called an 'investment fund' on the side, and Rob and Lensley had offices in the same building.

Although they had known each other since school, theirs was an uneasy friendship. It was more symbiotic than anything else, similar really to that of a parasite living in the gut of a shark. Lensley made money by attaching himself to deals Rob set up through his fund. Rob let Lensley in because he needed someone to do the dirty work – to be the frontman in case anything went wrong. Although he couldn't seem to make a success of his day job, Lensley did well through Rob's deals. He had a way of getting into the middle of things, hooking in at the right time and then cutting loose when things got hot. He knew when to get out quick, like a man whose turn it was to shout a round of drinks. Teflon Len, Rob called him, and nothing stuck except the name.

The pair forged along Threadneedle Street, the steel tips on their shoes marking time as they walked. They kept their eyes on their screens, a signal to oncoming pedestrians that they had more serious business to attend to than pavement gallantry. The crowd dispersed as they passed the Wellington Monument and they walked alongside the Bank of England. London's Old Lady sat impassive and stony-faced, forever clad in a matronly iron grey, and outside the building, a holy roller strode back and forth proclaiming the end of the world.

Ye cannot serve God and Mammon, said the man's tattered sandwich board as damp air from the Thames gusted up Queen Victoria Street, blowing rubbish and leaves around his ankles.

'Where did you say you met her?' Lensley asked, wiping a fine band of perspiration from his brow as they waited for their coffee in Taylors.

'Knightsbridge a few weeks back. A party – one of the Monaco clients.'

'She's a Meritus client?' asked Lensley, impressed.

Rob dumped two tubes of sugar into his espresso. 'No, the guy who had the party is a Meritus client. The one who tipped us off about that telecoms deal.'

'What about the girl?'

'June, or Dawn – name like that,' said Rob, downing his coffee. 'Sweet.'

'She was sweet all right. I picked her up in the Maserati – we had dinner, went to a nightclub, the whole bit. But then she turned me down.' Rob slapped a note on the bar and led the way out of the café into a side street.

Lensley lit a cigarette. 'Talk about taking the wind out of your sails.'

'Mate, she left me gasping for air. And she waited until *after* I'd paid for everything to deliver the bad news.'

Lensley shook his head but the corner of his mouth twisted into a smile and his eyes darted over the street like dark brown beads.

Rob's other phone rang. Lensley jangled the change in his pocket as he scrolled through his texts. It was irritating to stop and wait while Rob took his call, and he'd have gladly walked on, but he wanted to hear the end of the story. Rob told him at the weekend that he had another deal brewing and from the way Rob was strutting around it was probably worth waiting for. It was usually worth listening to Rob. His father ran one of the big investment banks in the City and although Rob had all of his father's contacts and polish, his great-grandfather had been a grifter. Rob mentioned this to anyone who would listen, and he often spoke about his heritage as if he were the product of an unbelievable miracle of evolution. Everyone laughed, of course, and shook their heads in disbelief, but Lensley knew there was something to the story. He knew Rob's bloodline throbbed with the pulse of a swindler's good fortune – an umbilical mooring chain that led straight back to his great-grandfather.

Rob wound up his call and began texting as they headed down Finch Lane.

'And then?' Lensley asked, trying to conceal his impatience.

'So then I thought if sex was out of the question, I'd see what *intelligence* I could get out of her. I thought she was in tech but it turns out she's in *crypto*, and she comes over all enthusiastic about her latest venture. Starts explaining the sector to me. I'm listening to her yabber on, thinking sooner or later she'll come to her senses and decide to sleep with me.'

The bells of the Royal Exchange sounded out nine o'clock as they came to the bottom of Change Alley where they paused in front of the UBank building.

'Come on, wind it up. Did she put out then, after all this patient listening?' Lensley said.

'She did not.'

'Bad luck, mate.'

'Nah, it gets better,' said Rob, winking at Lensley. 'I start tuning in and I realise she's talking about a new crypto asset they're launching. She gave me an idea.'

The men entered the building, and handed their bags to security.

'What's the deal?' said Lensley.

They cleared the turnstiles, Rob sucking in his belly and turning side-on to crab through. He waited for Lensley, then the pair carried on.

'Everyone thinks crypto is over, but it's not. It's got too much of a foothold in certain, shall we say, *innovative* sectors.'

'You mean money-laundering and the Dark Web,' Lensley said under his breath.

'If I didn't jump into this one now, everyone would think I was an idiot,' said Rob.

'No one thinks that.'

'I'm the smartest guy here.' Rob gestured broadly with both hands, taking in the building, possibly the entire City as they walked across the marble lobby towards the lifts. 'It's like the dotcom boom.'

'Oh yeah. How's that?' said Lensley.

'Or even further back. The South Sea Bubble. Tulips.'

'*Tulips?*'

'Speculation. People don't realise it's a wave, but not like you think. You wait till it passes and then hunt out the secondary ripples. Those far-off shores, the little places where the water's still lapping.'

Rob pressed the up button, smiling at a young woman standing next to him.

'You think this is the same thing?'

'What?' said Rob as he dragged his eyes back to Lensley.

'As tulips. You think crypto is the same as tulips?'

'Not the same. Better.'

The lift arrived and when it emptied at the third floor, Lensley turned to Rob, nodding for him to carry on.

'The unbanked poor. Micropayments. Microcrypto.'

Lensley raised his eyebrows. 'Microcrypto?'

'In Africa. Someone needs to buy something but they don't have any cash,' said Rob as the lift doors opened on the sixth floor. 'So they use micro.'

Lensley stepped out but kept his hand on the doors.

'Look into it. I'll send you some stuff,' Rob said, grinning as the lift closed.

At lunchtime, Lensley walked down to the river. The tide was out and he leaned on the railing watching the gulls squawk and bicker over things they had found in the sludge. He sat on a bench, breathing in the dank iodine smell of the water and thought of Rob's new scheme. He said it was a way to bring the unbanked – those without enough cash to qualify for a regular bank account – into the financial system, but really it was just a way to get their money. It was a way to fleece the poor of their pennies by dangling a line of hope. There was something desperate in the way Rob had spoken about it over the phone later that morning. He seemed more keen than usual that Lensley play a part. Lensley wondered whether it was for real. The damp air tugged at his stomach and he couldn't tell whether he was nauseous, or just hungry.

On the way back to the office he went into Pret and bought a salad of hand-caught baby crayfish. Standing in the queue to pay for his food he texted Rob.

You got a name?

The response was immediate.

LuckyCoin. I'll need your help.

While he was looking at his phone, Lensley saw he had missed a call from his wife, Allegra. This was unusual. As far as Lensley was aware from the bank statements and the little she told him, his wife's mornings were busy with Pilates, shopping and beauty appointments. Allegra hardly ever called him until later in the afternoon when she needed help with what she called 'admin' which was really just more spending – paying the boys' boarding school fees, arranging family holidays or booking the cars in for a service. He decided to respect the timetable she had established and not call her back until later.

Then a text came in from her:

AMEX declined in Harvey Nix. Call me ASAP

Lensley turned his phone to silent. When he got back to the office he switched his desk phone to automatic answering and started up his computer.

When Lensley met her, Allegra was a reality TV producer. But it turned out she didn't really like reality after all, and she quit her job soon after they married. She said at the time that working didn't suit the *flow* she wanted in her life. Well, thought Lensley grimly as he prised open the salad box, placed it in front of his keyboard and jabbed at his food with a plastic fork. She was about to get a shock: a dose of grubby reality was about to come flowing her way. She wouldn't like hearing that his bonus from UBank would be non-existent this year. He wouldn't like delivering the news either, but he would need to tell her this afternoon, before she ran up any more bills. The crayfish was cold and woolly but he ate it all as he flipped through his research on micropayments. After an hour or so he pushed back his chair and sighed.

He walked over to the window and looked down at the sluggish grey slick of river winding through the City. Further along the Thames, the office buildings and skyscrapers of Canary Wharf jostled together in staggered geometry against the hazy outline of the horizon. He felt lethargic as he surveyed the panorama, immense in its tarnished, silvery-grey brutality. The office lights flicked off behind him and in the gloom of the late afternoon his reflection was superimposed on the view. He took in this image of himself looming over the City and he wondered why he had to swim faster and faster just to stay still. He had the sense of everything rushing past him, and that he was slipping down into something dark and uncomfortable. He closed his eyes and realised he was sweating and that his fists were clenched.

That evening after work, Lensley and Rob went for a quick drink at Chitas, their regular watering hole.

'I've done some research into the micropayment deal. This is a controversial scheme you're talking about,' said Lensley as Rob eased himself into the booth.

'You've done your homework. Good boy.'

'This is taking money from people who have *nothing*.'

'Not money, micropayments.'

'It's still money.'

Rob flashed a grin. 'It's only money when we get hold of it, when we turn the pennies into pounds.'

Lensley didn't want to push it, but this deal, even on Rob's non-existent principles, was depraved. It involved swindling the poor by enticing them into a crypto Ponzi scheme. It was designed to pass under the radar because the amounts involved from each investor were so small.

'And there's nothing behind this coin. Getting in on that—' he shook his head. 'It's immoral, not to mention illegal.'

'Man, you're killing me with your bleeding-heart *morality*.'

The waitress delivered two pints of beer and a bowl of nuts. Lensley wasn't hungry. He pushed the bowl towards Rob who scooped up a fistful.

'Doesn't this one stink just a little bit, even by your standards?' said Lensley.

'If you're worried about the smell, mate, then you should wear a stronger aftershave.'

Rob let out a roar of laughter then toasted Lensley and took a swig of beer.

'It's just—' Lensley cleared his throat.

'Look, I don't care whether you're in or out. I already have one big investor lined up and others will jump in on the set up side if you don't.'

Rob tilted his head back, peering at Lensley down his nose.

'No ... no, I just—'

'Just what?'

Lensley looked towards the door.

'You just want the stink kept away from you?' Rob pointed a cashew at Lensley as he spoke. 'Is that it?'

Lensley pulled himself together. 'No, not really. I'm just not sure about this one. It's not like the others. They were all risky, yes, but this one is high profile, this is ...' Lensley searched for the word, 'emotional. This one goes against the flow.'

Rob looked towards the bar and loosened his collar. After a moment his eyes swivelled back to Lensley. 'I don't know if you've been paying attention, Mr Morality, but all my deals go against the flow.' Rob drained his glass and gestured to the waitress for two more. He made a squiggling downwards motion with his hand splaying it out flat on the table. 'Only dead fish go with the flow.'

Lensley shrugged his shoulders and sat back as Rob went into further detail about the deal. When he spoke about money, Rob became unusually eloquent. He let the words whistle slightly as he outlined the offshore arrangements he wanted Lensley to put in place, and the faint hissing sound Rob's breath made against his teeth was like a pile of cash being shuffle-counted. Rob spoke softly, letting the soothing sound of limitless wealth settle in to the depths of Lensley's mind.

'I know it *looks* bad, but when you get closer you'll see it's a win-win scenario. These people are left out of the mainstream. They have no credit rating so banks won't deal with them. How do you expect them to ever get ahead and pay for stuff? Micro is the solution,' Rob said.

'But there's nothing to it.'

Rob put his hand on his heart. 'Aww, Mr Morality. There's nothing to a lot of things. There's barely anything to you!' Rob said with another roar of laughter as he jabbed Lensley in the ribs. 'Haven't you figured that out yet?'

Lensley had hardly touched his second beer, torn between the unscrupulous ingenuity of the scheme and his own conscience. He knew Rob had, at his fingertips, an archipelago of tax havens at the shores of which his clients' fortunes lapped and swelled continuously, and he knew Rob's arrangements were always well thought through and watertight. The mechanics of the deal seemed straightforward, but the whole thing stank. Lensley pursed his lips and shook his head. 'No, I'm not sure I want in on this one. It's a bit depraved.'

Rob eyed him critically. 'I'll let you think about it tomorrow but then we'll need to get moving. There's a rumour MicroFund are planning something similar. Vanessa's coming to London tomorrow. She's going to love it! Come and join us for dinner. We can discuss further details then.'

Chapter Eight

WHEN VANESSA LANDED AT MIDDAY on Thursday, London was blanketed in a thick grey fog. Stepping off the plane, Vanessa felt as if she had plunged head first into a wet and filthy sponge. Even though she had been born in England, coming home was always a shock and the damp weather overwhelmed her mood, making her feel heavy and slow.

The people were like large sponges too, she thought as she stood in the taxi queue. Everyone was bundled into oversized clothes – fleeces, puffer jackets and ugly technical gear – names like Karrimor, The North Face. They all looked drab and sullen, as if they were about to dissolve into the bleak landscape around them.

Rob had summoned her to London on the LuckyCoin deal, saying he wanted to discuss it in person. They could have gone through it over the phone of course, but Rob demanded face-to-face meetings when there was something new in the pipeline. Even during the pandemic, Vanessa got special clearance so she could fly to London once a month. Rob had been very excited about the potential of Covid-19. Huge opportunities emerged when people were consumed by the same panic, he said when lockdown struck, and a chance like this only came around once in a lifetime. Rob was in there at the forefront, setting up deals for PPE procurement and arranging government-backed loans for his clients. It was important they were at the cutting edge of what was happening. They couldn't afford to be left behind.

Vanessa didn't mind the frequent trips to London because it meant she could visit her son, David, at his boarding school near Windsor. She glanced at her watch. She had dinner with Rob and Lensley tonight, and then on Saturday she would spend the day with David.

She soon found a taxi and on the way in from the airport, the water in the atmosphere finally gave way, coming down in huge sheets, causing the traffic on the motorway to come to a complete standstill. She needed to do some work before she met Rob and Lensley at 8 p.m., so she perched her laptop on her knees and did the bulk of it before she arrived at her hotel near St Paul's an hour later. She now had the afternoon free – enough time to find a present for David.

He was going to be thirteen in July. Vanessa wasn't sure she would be back in the UK before his birthday so she needed to buy a present now. She wondered what on earth teenage boys liked as she walked around Moorgate, past endless shops selling cheap, disposable fashion and dull city wear. There was enough polyester to clothe the entire female population, but what about thirteen-year-old boys? Probably something techy, she thought, entering an electronics store where she bought a new game and the latest noise-cancelling headphones. Feeling guilty after such expenditure on tech, she went into a bookshop but then realised she didn't know what kind of books David liked. Did he even read anymore? She wasn't sure, but anyway, they had a huge library at school. He would be able to get any book he wanted there.

Rob's favourite restaurant in the City was not far from Vanessa's hotel. It was an Italian bistro that served international food on checked tablecloths, but where the cheapest bottle of wine on the menu was over a hundred pounds. It was the kind of restaurant you had to call on a secret number and even then you still had to make it past the doorman who guarded the entrance like a Rottweiler. Bar Barolo's cachet, like all exclusive places in London, lay in the fact that it was a club for insiders. Since the sanctions had come in, ostentatious displays of wealth had become unfashionable. Gone were the days when you could buy your way around town and declare your status with bottles of expensive champagne on the table. These days, you had to find a lower-key way of signalling superiority and Bar Barolo had quickly transformed to meet this new trend. It looked cheap and welcoming, but it was just as expensive and exclusive as it had been when it was a caviar emporium.

Rob ordered champagne, two-dozen oysters, followed by medium-rare steaks and Pinot Noir. He liked to take control of the menu and thought it was more convivial if everyone ate the same thing. Oysters were non-negotiable, even though he knew Lensley hated them. In Rob's view, oysters were made for celebration because their wrinkled shells and icy crispness always made him think of money.

Once the champagne was opened and the oysters had arrived on huge zinc platters, Rob started outlining the deal. The individuals LuckyCoin targeted were being excluded from the system,

Rob said. They were economically disenfranchised and it was time someone brought them in and introduced them to the benefits of retail finance.

'So how does it work?' said Vanessa.

Rob took an oyster, ladled in a teaspoon of vinegar, sprinkled it with red onion and then poured the concoction into his mouth, letting the juice drip down his chin.

'Take Michael,' Rob said through the oyster. 'He operates a small-time bicycle repair business on the outskirts of Lagos. The banks won't deal with him because his turnover is too small, he has debts and a bad credit rating. Michael is therefore excluded from the financial system. He has no bank account, and no way to buy anything online. So he opens a LuckyCoin account with us and the next person who pays for their bicycle repair pays him in LuckyCoin.'

'How do *they* get hold of LuckyCoin?' said Vanessa.

'They open an account with us too. They buy LuckyTokens which generate LuckyCoins which go into their account.'

'And where do they buy these tokens?'

'At a shop. It's just like a phone card. Once they buy a card, a LuckyToken, they use the code on the card to top up their LuckyCoin wallet. In fact we're going to team up with telecoms providers and give bundled deals on data and LuckyTokens.'

'But there are already schemes like this,' said Lensley. 'NorthWold launched a microcoin in India a few years ago, and Argonaut has just announced one in Venezuela.'

'This one's different,' said Rob, pointing his oyster fork at Lensley. 'This is Africa and there's an incentive.'

The incentive was that when people used LuckyCoin, they earned credits on a virtual gaming platform for phones called

LuckyPlay. The concept was simple. The more LuckyTokens people bought and the more LuckyCoins they used to buy things, the more credits they earned on LuckyPlay which was linked to a TikTok-style video sharing app. Rob outlined the scheme proudly and then sat back for the *coup de grâce* which went above and beyond anything NorthWold, Argonaut or any of their other competitors had come up with so far: the credits the users accumulated on LuckyPlay allowed them to bet on the outcome of a completely fictional and virtual football event involving African players.

'Crypto, gambling and football! My three favourite things,' said Rob, beaming.

'Hey, you,' he said, snapping his fingers at a passing waiter and then tapping the champagne bottle. 'More of this.'

'Crypto is banned in a lot of African countries and gambling has issues too. We looked into this before with Yandex,' said Vanessa.

Rob's piggy eyes gleamed above his flushed cheeks. 'We don't call it crypto or gambling. We call it a *gaming platform* and we put the servers and the companies in the Dutch Antilles so it's well outside the jurisdiction. If we structure it as a game of skill, then we get around the rules. Capital Leisure did that with their gambling hotels.'

Rob paused to look from one to the other to make sure he had their full attention. He reached for another oyster, squeezing lemon juice over it this time and then slurping it up. He wiped his chin and carried on.

'There are millions of people like Michael in Africa. When the concept takes off over the country – as indeed it will, the value of LuckyCoin increases. This will cause more investors to pile in. Once Michael holds a certain amount of LuckyCoin he can extract it from his account and get naira or pounds or euros. He can use it to invest or buy things online.'

'And presumably we have to pay someone off,' said Lensley, who was struggling with an oyster, prodding it gingerly with a fork.

'Swallow it in one!' barked Rob demonstrating by gulping an oyster and then swigging champagne.

'Naturally, we would share the profits with certain officials,' said Rob.

Vanessa sat forward. 'And what's our role apart from arranging that?'

'Your role,' said Rob, swivelling back to Vanessa, 'is to sell it. Lensley will deal with the investor side. Amir has already said he'll come in with ten per cent, by the way, and I'm meeting Elanka to seal the deal this week. I need you, Vanessa, to sell it on the ground.'

'What do you mean, on the *ground*?'

Rob sucked down the last oyster, followed by more champagne. 'Sell it locally. That's where the money is. I need you to do a deep dive into our contacts in Africa. Make contact with people at the source to do the intermediate selling.'

'Middlemen,' said Lensley.

'Exactly. We need trusted middlemen,' Rob said to Lensley and then turned back to Vanessa, 'and women of course, to sell this. We need people who are plugged into the local community – teachers, nurses, religious folk.'

'*Religious folk?*' said Vanessa.

'Yes. People with a network, trusted local people who can encourage their communities to get on board with LuckyCoin.

We're going to set up a pool of ambassadors and offer them a commission on all transactions made with the coin.'

'*Ambassadors?*' Vanessa stared at Rob as the waiter cleared away the oysters and laid down the steaks.

'Is it me, or is there a fucking parrot in here?' Rob said, cupping his hand to his ear and looking around.

Rob cut into his steak, and Vanessa and Lensley watched him scoop it into his mouth in huge quivering forkfuls.

'We need to stay ahead of the pack,' Rob said through the steaming meat. 'The Russian ride is over with all these sanctions. That work has dried up – *poof* – all that money's gone to Dubai.'

Vanessa leaned forward. 'Rob, these people are unbanked for a reason: they have no money.'

'They have very little money, it's true,' said Rob, licking sauce off his knife. 'So we need to scale up and that's what's great about Africa: there are *millions* of people! The population of Lagos alone is over sixteen million, and they all have phones. Think about it. One million, two million people giving even just a buck a week. Once we get a foothold in Africa we can roll it out in India and bring in other virtual sports like boxing, for example, to include alongside the football. Now there's an opportunity if ever I heard one. This is the best idea I've had for years.'

'And you think they'll just give it away.'

Rob stabbed a pile of buttery mangetout and brought them to his mouth. 'Not give it away. You're both missing the point so let me explain how the idea came to me. It was in the airport in Dubai at Eid. I'd been in the first class lounge watching the World Cup and when I came out I saw all these construction workers waiting to board the plane for Abuja. They were watching the football in rags, some of them still filthy from the

Emirates building sites they'd all come from. They didn't look like they had two pence to rub together, but I looked over one's shoulder and sure enough, there they all were, making bets on their phones!'

'Jesus, Rob.'

'Everyone wants a little bit of magic in their lives. Everyone needs some stardust, some distraction and hope. And do you know who needs it the most?'

'I have a feeling you're going to tell us it's your construction workers.'

'It's people who have nothing. They're the ones who need the magic. Crypto, gambling and football! It's a magic combo, I'm telling you.'

Vanessa pushed her plate away then crossed her arms over her chest. 'It's just so ...' She paused as she searched for the word, 'So *depraved*.'

'*Depraved!* Ha! That's exactly the word Mr Morality here used yesterday,' said Rob wagging his knife between them. 'Have you two been talking out of school?'

Vanessa looked at Lensley. 'What makes you think Lensley and I are the best to do this? I have no experience in Africa and neither does he.'

Rob laughed again. 'You're not the *best*. Oh no, neither of you are the best.'

'Excuse me?'

'You're just the most desperate,' Rob said. He pointed at Lensley. 'Lensley has a wife he can't afford and two kids at the country's most expensive boarding school. He needs the money. You have a kid at the same school, no loser husband to support anymore, lucky for you, but you still want to keep your job.'

'What makes you so sure?'

Rob grinned. 'Because you haven't left.'

'Because I haven't *left*?'

'You're the oldest lawyer at Meritus. You know it yourself, you're not blind!'

'You're older than me, Rob.'

'The oldest non-full partner, I mean. Look, it's one thing not to be a full partner at thirty, or even forty, but after that you start looking like a busted flush. Everyone does! Not just you. There's the reek of failure about it all.'

Vanessa reddened. 'I do my job and I do it well.'

'It's not good for our image, Vanessa.'

'I even work evenings and weekends! Look at me now. I'm spending my evening with you two and I'll be at your place on Saturday night.'

'I know you've been looking for other jobs. My friends at Carnage & Screets told me. You interviewed there in September but you didn't get a call back. There will have been other interviews too, that I don't know about.'

'It was London-based. I'd be closer to David.'

'This isn't just about loyalty, Vanessa. It's about your *relevance*.'

'I do have options, Rob.'

'Don't give me that bullshit. We both know your ship has sailed.' Rob stretched out his arm, making a wave motion with his hand. 'It's sailed right off into the sunset without you on it. Your only real option is to stay at Meritus, so cut the *depraved* crap, OK?'

'What about Lensley?' Vanessa said. 'He's not a partner at his bank but you never attack him like this.'

'He's got a consistent track record.'

'A *consistent track record*. You mean he's a man?'

'I think he's a man, but his wife has his balls, so I'm not sure anymore,' Rob said, laughing cruelly. 'You could have been a full partner, Vanessa, but you left and followed Pascal.'

'I didn't *follow* Pascal. I married him and had a child.'

'That's right. And then you became the lowest billing lawyer in the least profitable sector. It was me who let you back in years later and gave you a job in the compliance department.'

Rob placed his hands on the table and stood up. 'You needed me then and you need me even more now. You're coming up to a performance review with Napier soon. There are a lot of other people in London who want that cushy job down in Monaco, down there in the sunshine now all the Russian work has dried up here. So far I've protected you, but loyalty swings both ways, you know. Lensley understands that. Don't you, mate?' Rob slapped Lensley on the back.

Lensley grunted.

'Are you threatening me?' asked Vanessa.

'I'm giving you a chance, Vanessa. You don't make luck, you take it. And if you don't take this chance, someone else will.'

Vanessa watched Rob as he threaded his way across the crowded restaurant to the toilet.

'Honestly, Lens. Where does he get off?'

Lensley just shrugged. He had hardly touched his food.

'You didn't say much over dinner.'

'I've learned not to say much around Rob when he's in deal mode.'

'How long has he been like this? In deal mode.'

'A week or so. I could tell something was up when he came back from Dubai. He met someone. A woman who works in crypto. June, or Dawn he said.'

Vanessa shook her head. 'I don't like this deal. It's real bottom feeder stuff. Lowest of the low.'

'And we feed off him so what does that make us?'

'I try not to think of it like that.'

'As he said, things are getting tougher. This is where the money is now.'

'I know. But where there's this kind of money, there's a lot of risk. I've got no idea how to sell this scheme. I'm not a sales agent!'

Lensley leaned back. Some colour had returned to his face. 'Yes, but you're a good talker, a good scammer. That's why he likes you.'

'He likes you more. But really, what do you think?'

'I don't like it all. For the same reasons as you,' Lensley said. 'I don't think this one has legs.'

'Well fortunately you won't be doing the legwork. Sounds like that falls to me.'

Lensley reached over and filled her glass. The red wine swirled around the bowl. 'You know it's always like this with Rob's deals. They sound crazy to begin with, but they usually work out. He's got a good nose and he has an awful lot of luck.'

Vanessa smiled reluctantly. 'Luck has a habit of running out.'

'That's what you always say. But look at you – still here.'

'That's not luck,' said Vanessa. 'It's desperation. Rob's right.' Vanessa didn't really believe in luck. She believed in a malign force that dogged her when it came to certain things – men, marriage, money.

They looked across the restaurant. Rob had seen someone he knew, a client perhaps, and they were backslapping and laughing together. The man Rob was talking to was huge and he couldn't get in close to the table because of his girth. A napkin was stretched across his gut to deal with the inevitable slippage of food that occurred between plate and mouth. The man gripped his wine glass by the bowl as though his life depended on it.

'Have you two finished complaining about me yet?' said Rob when he returned to the table.

'It's crazy. Neither Lensley nor I have ever even been to Africa,' said Vanessa.

'Well you should go since you have such empathy for the people.' Rob pointed at her plate. 'Those beans. I bet they're from Africa and you haven't even touched them. Think of the poor bastard who had to trim them for you.'

Vanessa glanced at her plate. 'They're mangetout, Rob, not beans. No one fucking trims them. Mangetout means you eat all of it.'

Rob's eyes gleamed. 'Oh, don't swan in from Monaco and try to bamboozle me with your fancy French words,' he said, leaning over to pierce her mangetout with his fork. He raised his glass and grinned like a shark. 'And don't you worry. I intend to eat all of it.'

Chapter Nine

THE TAXI DROPPED LENSLEY OFF at the corner of his street. Lensley's terrace house, or villa as Allegra liked to describe it, was tall and imposing, clad in white stucco and it sat in the middle of a row of identical villas. A pair of plaster sphinxes the size of large dogs straddled the steps at the entrance to each villa and their staring eyes gave the street an expectant, eerie look. Lensley glimpsed into his neighbours' basements as he passed. In the low buttery light he saw Persian carpets, modern art, and brightly coloured children's toys strewn over exposed wooden boards.

The entrance to his own house was dark and gloomy. He walked up the steps to his front door and stood between the sphinxes whose eyes glowed wetly under the streetlights. He entered the house and went downstairs. At the front of the basement was a media room where he usually spent the evening if he was at home. To the rear, the basement extended out in a tesseract of steel-framed glass which, when the sun shone, cast diamond patterns on the antique French dining table and produced a concentrated subterranean light of such airlessness that Lensley sometimes found it difficult to breathe. Now, the dark rain sent splinters of light all around the muted greys and greens of the bespoke kitchen, giving the marble island worktop the cold hue of a mortuary table.

There was an open bottle of wine on the side. Lensley poured a glass, sat at the island and thought about the deal Rob had outlined at dinner. He didn't like it, but what Lensley liked was irrelevant because Rob was right – he needed the money and he needed it now, more than ever. As always, when he thought about how cornered he was financially, Lensley's mind went straight to Allegra and to his two boys, Felix and Teddy, who were now fast asleep in their boarding school dormitory twenty miles away. Lensley paid a fortune to rarely see his boys and he felt bad they didn't live at home. Lensley had grown up without a father so he knew what it was like. He'd had to shape himself early around the void his father left and so he had the edges and outline of a personality long before his friends did. Felix and Teddy weren't like that though. They were a little bit soft, it was true. Lensley had always meant to spend more time with them to make up for sending them away but he had never quite managed it. There was always work and in any case, Allegra had claimed the boys' domain.

There were no decent schools in London, Allegra had said when they sent off the applications five years ago, or none whose entrance exams didn't need months of expensive tutoring. Felix had been just eight when they sent him away. He was now twelve and Teddy was sixteen and doing his A levels. It occurred to Lensley that he didn't even know what subjects Teddy was taking. Was it chemistry, English and maths, or maths, French and history? Whatever it was, he was sure maths was in there somewhere. Lensley had tried to persuade himself it wasn't so bad the boys were at boarding school but he realised now how much he missed them. A wild thought entered his head: why not leave everything behind? Just say no to it all – his dead end job at UBank and Rob's crazy deals. He certainly wouldn't miss London if they left, which they would have to do, he thought, with a spike of pleasure. They might just be able to afford a small cottage in the countryside if they sold the London house and paid off their debts. They wouldn't have the boarding school fees anymore and the boys could live at home.

These were pleasant thoughts and Lensley's heart grew lighter as he walked slowly upstairs to bed. It was half past twelve and he could see from the gap at the bottom of the door that the bedroom lights were out. Lensley stood on the landing, listening. The air seemed recently ruffled, as though Allegra had only just passed through and gone to bed.

Lensley went to the bathroom and examined himself in the mirror as he brushed his teeth. He saw sagging jowls beneath day old growth, and the shadows that were permanently etched under his eyes seemed darker now than usual. A chill crept up from the marble floor to his calves, settling into a cramp in his lower back.

He rinsed his toothbrush, placing it in the container next to Allegra's. He smiled grimly as the movement in the jar caused her toothbrush to swivel away from his own. He took a mouthful of water from the tap and gargled softly. You could dedicate your life to something, he thought, you could work with purpose and sacrifice and even then you still might not make it. He spat in the basin, grimacing in the mirror as he inspected his teeth. He ran the tap, rinsed the basin and stared into the mirror as he wiped his face with a towel. You had to dream big, isn't that what they said? Well, what the fuck did that mean, if not this, he thought, looking around at the marble-clad bathroom with the double sink, intricately plumbed antique bath and expensive gold fittings.

Lensley took off his shirt and stepped back from the mirror. He looked small and ugly against the luxurious backdrop, his skin all grey and flaccid, and he realised then just how hard he had worked to buy a lifestyle that didn't even suit him. He thought about how much harder he would have to work to keep it, and remembered the surge of pleasure he had felt just now on the stairs at the thought of chucking it all in.

There was a tap at the door that led to the bedroom. Allegra was standing there wearing a shimmering, pale blue dressing gown.

'I'm sorry. Did I wake you?' Lensley asked.

Allegra dimmed the lights, walked past him to the bathroom cabinet and took out a vial of pills. 'Not really. Can't sleep,' she said, her eyes downcast.

He undid his belt and took off his trousers, folding them neatly across a chair. She shook out a couple of pills, moving past him to the basin. He watched her fill a cup with water but still she didn't meet his eyes. She was circling around him – hesitant and emotionless, like she had been this afternoon when he had finally returned her calls and broken the news of their precarious financial position. He explained on the phone that she would have to rein in her spending, at least until he could correct the situation. He even raised the prospect of moving out of London. While he spoke, Allegra had deployed a battery of pauses and sighs and he felt beneath her helpless noises and silences the deep, black-rimmed heat of her disappointment in him. He looked at her pale, graceful neck as she twisted her hair behind her head and swallowed the pills. Her cool blue eyes appraised him in the mirror, then narrowed. The depths of loathing in her gaze made his blood run cold.

He walked to the bedroom and took his pyjamas from under his pillow. She followed him, switching out the bathroom lights. Her dressing gown made a rustling sound as she passed, as though the silk was whispering insults to him.

She lay in bed with her back turned and he felt his isolation as a deep pain in his heart. He reached over to her. She let his hand rest on her hip for a second and then slithered from his touch. It was unbearable. In her eyes he had seen reflected his own disgust in himself. He rolled over to face the wall. He was overcome with self-pity, but it was not a passive, helpless kind of pity. It was the kind of shame that made his stomach roil and churn with rage. He saw himself for what he was – a small, pathetic figure standing at the foot of a Goliath whose stony gaze was fixed beyond him towards the golden horizon of an ever-expanding future. He was little more than a tantruming child to the giant looming above him. *Mr Morality,* he recalled, and Rob's sarcastic laugh. He was powerless against this monster of money, finance and expectation that overshadowed everything and hissed all around him. Recognition of his own insignificance engulfed him as he stared helplessly ahead seeking clarity in the vacant blackness.

Sometime later that night it hit Lensley head-on. He didn't need to kick so hard against it all like this. Why was he making everything so difficult for himself? Rob's deal was terrible, it was true, but it would go ahead regardless of whether Lensley was involved. Rob wasn't doing anything others wouldn't do given half a chance, and if Lensley didn't help him, the next guy would. And why shouldn't it be Lensley? He had put in the time with Rob. He deserved the pay-off. The alternative was to stagnate or worse, be washed downstream. What Lensley had seen in Allegra's eyes was the truth. Without her, the house, the money, the job at UBank, he was nobody.

He could be better than that. He had worked all his life for money because it had the power to make him a better person. And it still could. It occurred to Lensley now as he lay in bed that all this time he had been playing the part of a man he didn't believe in. He had been playing the part of poor old Lensley the failed banker, the guy who only got things half right. While he had been playing that role, it had become his reality and he had turned into a loser, nipping along at the heels of his more successful friends. Well that needed to change. It was time to fully become himself, to earn big money and to join the big league. Why on earth not? Who the hell was going to stop him?

The next morning Lensley felt better. The confusion of the night dissipated in the cold purity of the day. Beyond his office windows, the buildings opposite winked at him in the sunshine.

He rang Rob that afternoon.

'How will it *look*?'

'What do you mean?'

'Will it be traceable?' There was a tremor in Lensley's voice.

Rob laughed, then said softly, 'Listen mate, I told you. I've got it all worked out. The money, the trading company, the investor vehicles, they're all offshore. I got a guy down in St Helier setting it all up. The investment itself will come from a shell company incorporated in Vevey and that company will be held by a network of offshore trusts. No one will be able to trace it to us.'

'You sure?' Lensley's monitor went on standby and he saw his silhouette traced in its dark screen.

'Of course I'm sure. I've got some of the money in already. Amir loves the idea – Elanka too. And there's a pastor in Lagos who's going to be our first ambassador.'

Lensley exhaled deeply, wiping clear a faint sweat from his upper lip. It sounded like Rob had a firm grip on things.

'OK, then I'm in.'

'Good.' There was a pause before they hung up and Rob said, 'Hey, I know it stinks now, but if you hold your nose and grip your balls you get to the right place. Then when you let go you'll find the smell of all that cash is sweeter than anything you can ever imagine.'

Lensley put the phone down and went to work on Rob's deal. After he had made some calls and completed the preliminary steps on the investment structure he paused, staring out of the window in a dead reverie. He looked down at the river – a curving artery of bile coursing through the City, its source somewhere to the west in the shifting murkiness of the horizon. He shook the tension from his shoulders and told himself he was doing the right thing.

He felt nervous as he closed down his terminal that evening. He turned it back on twice to check he had wiped all traces of the work he had just done. Of course he shouldn't be working for Rob using the UBank resources. He shouldn't be working for Rob full stop, Lensley thought as he took the drafts to the shredder and stood by the machine until it was done.

He took a deep breath as he left the building, then realised he had forgotten his jacket.

'Working too hard, mate,' the guy at security joked as he went back to retrieve it. Lensley laughed hollowly. In the lift one of the night traders asked if he was feeling OK. He hardly recognised himself in the mirrored glass. The anxiety had sharpened his features and had given him a ravaged look.

Lensley knew he couldn't go home feeling so agitated. He walked aimlessly down one street and turned into another, which led to a dead end. He stood there wringing his hands and a surge of adrenaline went straight to his bowels, so he entered a pub to relieve himself. As he left the men's room a strange sense of calm came over him. He didn't need to go home just yet. He would have a few drinks at the bar.

He was drunk and disoriented when he left a nightclub near Smithfield several hours later. He had met some younger colleagues in the pub and they had done shots together, followed by lines of coke in the toilet. When the pub closed he went with them to the nightclub. The place was heaving, and Lensley saw Rob dancing with a woman and then afterwards, he saw them in a booth at the back of one of the rooms. Rob saw him too and waved him off, although Lensley wasn't thinking of approaching anyway.

Sometime later, Lensley went to the rooftop for a cigarette. He felt incredibly drunk and he hoped it might sober him up. The night was cold and he was the only person there, he assumed, until he saw a couple in the dim light of a fire escape. He could only see the back of the man but he was sure it was Rob. The woman was struggling against the man who had his hand around her throat. Lensley could only see the lower half of the woman's face but she was slack-jawed, her mouth open. In the instant Lensley saw her she pulled free and let out a scream.

Lensley tried to step forward intending to help her, but he stumbled and fell. He knew he ought to go over once he had dragged himself to standing, but his body wouldn't move from inebriation and fear. The woman screamed again but all Lensley could do was take a step back and stagger down the stairs, the woman's cry ringing in his ears.

Lensley's head was spinning and the heat of the nightclub made him feel nauseous. He fled the building, walked down the alley that ran alongside the club and threw up. There was a row of bins stacked up against a wall and they gave off a sick, sour reek. Something lurched out of the dark at him – a cat or a fox, its sudden movement dislodging a stack of bottles that cascaded around his feet. He looked to the side where the animal had come from. Under the streetlight he saw bloodied fur, flayed skin and the pulsing guts of something in its death throes. He retched again and backed out of the alley.

Lensley woke the next morning with a painful stiffness in his arms and shoulders, the sheets damp with sweat. There was an oily taste in his mouth and the same confused, sick feeling from the night returned. He lifted his head from the pillow and the bed pitched and rolled. He lay back, frightened. The bile rose in his throat as isolated scenes came back to him. Was it real? He had been wandering the streets, unsure of where he was going. He thought he had seen Rob at a nightclub molesting a woman, but he couldn't be sure. He searched the dark recesses of his memory and recalled an argument with Allegra when he got home, an endless rising tide of rage, a struggle and then blackness.

His hands trembled as he reached across the bed. Allegra felt ice cold beneath her layers of silk. He turned and in the grey dawn he made out her face. She looked just like the woman on the roof: slack-jawed, her mouth open. Lensley felt a stabbing pain in his gut as he shook her lightly and her shimmering silk dressing gown moved around her like streams, gullies, rivers of water. He sat up, coughing and gasping for air, his heart pounding and terrified of what he might have done to her in his drunken, drugged state. He shook her again, more urgently now.

Her gown fell off her shoulder and finally, she stirred.

'Get your hands off me,' she hissed and then rolled away.

Sweating and weak with relief that she was alive, Lensley put on his dressing gown and went upstairs to the spare room.

Chapter Ten

IT WAS MEANT TO BE just the two of them spending the day together but when Vanessa arrived at David's school on Saturday morning to collect him, he was waiting in the porter's lodge with another boy. The traffic had been slow on the M4 because of the rain and Vanessa was half an hour late. She was flustered and full of loathing for England and its appalling weather, and it now seemed she wouldn't even get David to herself.

'Hello Lai,' she said, forcing a smile when David introduced his friend.

Lai had a regal air, despite his slight build and he offered his hand graciously.

'Shall we go then?' Vanessa said to David who had stepped back after their initial hug and now stood stiffly by the porter's desk.

'You need to sign me out,' Lai said, pointing to a book on the desk. 'My bodyguard needs to come too.'

Just then, Vanessa noticed a man on a leather sofa at the far end of the wood-panelled room. She hadn't seen him when she arrived and she wondered now how she could have missed him. He was heavy-set and wore an earpiece and shades, despite the overcast day.

The man walked towards them, speaking on his phone.

When he reached them he removed the earpiece. 'I'm Jonathan,' he said, extending his hand.

Vanessa signed the boys out and the group walked from the lodge in single file with Jonathan at the head talking again on his phone, then down some steps and onto a huge sweep of gravel driveway, flooded now with rain.

'I thought it might be easier if I drive,' Jonathan said, pointing his key fob to a Mercedes 4WD with tinted windows parked next to Vanessa's rental car.

'I booked a pizza restaurant in the village,' said Vanessa. The simple day she had envisaged didn't include rocking into town like gangsters and she was about to say so, but stopped herself. David had had trouble fitting into this school and Lai was the first friend she had met since he had started there a year ago. She didn't dare object to Lai, Jonathan, or his car, at least at this stage.

'That suits us fine,' said Jonathan, who was already in the driver's seat.

Vanessa hesitated at the side of the car, not sure which area of the vehicle was Lai's domain. She waited until the boys slid into the back before getting into the passenger seat.

She glanced around at the boys. The two princes were already helping themselves to sweets and soft drinks from a mini-fridge sunk into the upholstery between them. She could tell David had been in the car before and this annoyed her more than the sugar before lunch. Lai had to be signed out so why had no one at the school sought her permission for any excursions? Why had David not told her? She made a mental note to raise this with David's housemaster when they returned.

'Lai's father is Minister for Aviation in Nigeria, and a cousin of the President,' said David through a mouthful of sweets.

'Why aren't we flying then?' said Vanessa.

She meant it as a joke, but her tone was too sharp and David's mouth froze mid-chew. Vanessa was about to apologise but to her astonishment, the other two laughed.

Vanessa bit her tongue for the rest of the journey, hoping David would volunteer further information, such as why Lai needed a bodyguard, but she guessed she had blown it now. She wondered whether Jonathan lived full-time at the school, or whether he had an apartment nearby and just appeared for outings like this. Perhaps the school even had a special wing for security staff. The school's buildings were incorporated into the village, Oxbridge style, so perhaps Jonathan escorted David to lessons. She had quite a few other questions but she kept them to herself and directed the conversation to the boys, asking them about football, which David loved, and their after-school clubs.

Things went smoothly over lunch. Vanessa recalled that she had already met Lai's father at a school picnic and she learned now that Lai's mother was his father's third wife and that she lived mostly in Dubai, which was where Lai spent his holidays. Lai wore a Rolex and had the latest iPhone, both of which he consulted quite a lot. When the pizzas arrived Lai called his mother. The food was inspected and the phone passed around so Vanessa met her too.

It occurred to Vanessa that Lai's parents and their network might be useful contacts for LuckyCoin. She was reluctant to leverage her son's friendships for her work, but she knew most other parents had no such qualms and so she filed the thought away for future use.

After lunch, David asked whether they could visit a gaming centre in the next town.

On the way there, Vanessa checked her phone. There was a barrage of furious messages from Rob. He said he was having trouble raising Lensley and that he needed someone back at the office urgently that afternoon.

'I've been calling for an hour. Where the fuck are you? Both of you have let me down!' he roared down the phone when she called him.

Vanessa hung up.

'It's Saturday, Rob. I'm with my son,' she said when he called back.

'Well you're going to have to cut it short. This is urgent. I've been working all morning myself. We have a huge opportunity this evening.'

'I can't. I just got here. I'll see you tonight.'

'I need you to cast your eye over some investment documents this afternoon. Get here as soon as you can,' Rob said and then hung up.

Vanessa cursed Rob and took a deep breath before turning to David.

'I'm really sorry, darling, that was my boss. He needs me back at work.'

David looked out of the window for a while, and then turned to Lai. 'Let's play Beat Saber together. It's more fun than Pistol Whip.'

Jonathan said he would stay with the boys for the rest of the afternoon and Vanessa caught a taxi back to the school to retrieve the hire car.

Vanessa arrived in London at about 4 p.m. Rob had called her en route to let her know he had finally managed to raise Lensley and she should go straight to his house.

Lensley answered the door in a terrible state. His pale complexion was even more sickly than usual and his hands shook as he made coffee in the basement.

'Big night then?' Vanessa said.

'Honestly, I can't remember.'

Vanessa walked past him to the windows and stared out to the back garden. 'Come on, you can tell me.'

'No, seriously I can't remember. I went for a drink after work.'

'And then?'

'And that's it. Shots at the bar with some guys from UBank then a nightclub.' Lensley rubbed his forehead as fragments of the evening came back to him. 'After that it's a bit of a blur.'

'Jesus, Lensley. You're regressing,' Vanessa said. She saw the work papers spread over the kitchen table. 'Speaking of which, this is like being a trainee again.'

'That's pretty much what we are. Hope it didn't spoil your plans?'

'I was with my son. Rob said he couldn't raise you, and that he needed someone here this afternoon. This *huge opportunity* he mentioned had better be good.'

'God, Vanessa, I'm sorry. I spoke to him earlier and then I had a nap, but—' Lensley picked up his phone and started scrolling. 'There haven't been any other calls from him. No messages, nothing.'

Vanessa walked past Lensley and sat at the head of the table. 'So what does he want? Let's get it over with.'

'An investment outline. I did most of it yesterday but he wants you to have a look at it too.'

'And this couldn't wait until Monday, or even tomorrow?'

'He wants me to bring it along tonight. The big crypto investors are in London. They'll be there this evening.'

Just then Vanessa's phone beeped. It was a message from Rob.

Don't be late tonight 8 p.m.

'Honestly, sometimes I think he's listening in,' Vanessa said, showing Lensley her phone.

'I wouldn't put it past him.'

Lensley gave Vanessa the outline and watched her go through it as he gulped his coffee. He debated whether to tell her what he had seen on the rooftop of the nightclub but he couldn't be sure what it was. He knew he had been very drunk and now his recollections slipped and weaved like hallucinations. Lensley tried to recall the scene and whether he had been involved. He didn't want to be implicated in what Rob had done but whatever it was, he couldn't shake the feeling he was somehow a participant.

He imagined being cross-examined in a packed courtroom.

Was the woman blonde or brunette?

What time was it?

Did you intervene or try to help?

Lensley didn't know the answer to any of these questions but he was pretty sure he hadn't tried to help anyone. It had been late and very dark up there. He hadn't seen either of their faces properly, they were quite a distance away and they could have been kissing. But there was a scream, which caused Lensley to turn and run. A fox in the alley had left a terrible mess of fur and guts, so perhaps that was the sound he'd heard?

Rob had been strange on the phone earlier, and why had he told Vanessa he couldn't *raise* him? He hadn't said anything about the nightclub and it wasn't like Rob not to say what was on his mind, even something as nasty as that.

Perhaps Lensley had dreamed it all. Perhaps the cocaine or whatever it was had been spiked with a hallucinogenic. There were a lot of weird drug mixes going around these days – GHB, ketamine, fentanyl and the like. Lensley tried to remember who had been handing out the powder at the pub. He had lost the guys in the crowd soon after they had arrived at the nightclub.

Lensley trembled as he remembered thinking he had hurt Allegra. That moment in bed this morning had felt so real and he had been convinced she was dead. They had definitely had an argument last night and Allegra had left after breakfast without speaking to him at all.

Lensley glanced over to Vanessa who was making notes on the investment outline. How would he broach it with her? *Oh, by the way, I think I saw Rob molesting a woman on the rooftop of a nightclub last night, but I'm not quite sure because I was so pissed. I also think I might have been involved too, but I can't remember.* He couldn't tell Vanessa he had failed to prevent a woman being attacked, that not only had he not helped her, he had run off. It was a cowardly thing to have done. If it wasn't real, he would make it real by saying something and the last thing Lensley wanted was to make any of it real.

'What's this here?' Vanessa said, pushing the investment document over. 'My god, Lensley, you're sweating.'

She touched his forehead. 'You're boiling up. Perhaps you should have a lie-down. Where's Allegra?'

Lensley told Vanessa they'd had an argument last night.

'That must be why you look so awful. Go and rest. Open it up on your laptop. I'll make all the changes and then let myself out.'

'I can't leave you to do it.'

'Why not? It's not as though you're any use now, in this state. Go on. Have a sleep. You'll feel much better.'

Vanessa worked for a couple of hours and then returned to her hotel to get changed. In the shower she thought of the empty look on David's face when she told him she was needed back at work, and how cold his cheek felt when she kissed him goodbye. They had hardly spent any time together and no time alone. She had meant to ask him about his other sports and how his subjects were going.

When she came out of the shower she went to her laptop, wet patches forming on the carpet at her feet as she checked the airlines for a later flight – perhaps she could see him tomorrow. She remembered with another pang that in her haste to leave the boys that afternoon, she had forgotten to give David his birthday presents. He had mentioned the school sports day was scheduled to take place on his birthday this year, so if she couldn't make it to Meetham tomorrow, she would try her best to come back for that.

She put on a navy blue dress and lawyerly pearl earrings and cursed Pascal. She was all David had. There weren't any details she could give him about his father's whereabouts because she didn't know herself. After the divorce came through he had simply disappeared. There was so much children didn't understand and so much you couldn't properly explain. It reminded her of one of her father's sayings: *If you can't explain it to a child then there's something wrong with it.* God, how true that was. There was something wrong with Pascal all right.

Lensley answered the door of Rob's mansion in Highgate. He said he had slept for a couple of hours and that he felt much better. He took Vanessa's coat and handed her a glass of champagne.

Vanessa saw the gathering in the drawing room and groaned inwardly. There were about thirty people there. She recognised several financial advisers and their wives: tight faces above black dinner suits, sombre dresses and the glitter of diamonds. Low voices and no laughter. Amir's girlfriend, Elanka, was also there. Vanessa slugged back the first glass of champagne and took a second.

She entered the room and began talking to one of the financial advisers, Stuart, about LuckyCoin. Rob had roped Stuart in to sell the scheme to investors in London and to also help sell it 'on the ground'. Stuart told Vanessa he had made contact with some intermediaries in Lagos, a local pastor and a nurse, who had large followings on social media and were keen to be ambassadors for LuckyCoin.

'We need people who have the trust of the community,' he said.

'Influencers,' she said.

'Exactly.'

'And what commission are you giving them?' Vanessa asked. She knew from the documents that advisers like Stuart got a healthy cut of the money they brought in. There had been no mention of any payments to the ambassadors.

'It varies,' he said. 'On how much they sell.'

It was all off the books in other words, and subject to Stuart's discretion. In fact, the ambassadors were probably getting paid in LuckyCoin themselves.

Stuart was thick but he was cunning and he could sell ice to Inuits. Vanessa had seen him sell non-existent C-grade films to investors at Cannes. She had seen him sell the same films with different names the next year to the same investors when none of the films were made, nor ever intended to be made.

Stuart sold dreams and bullshit and there was never any shortage of buyers.

Vanessa needed the bathroom and the ground floor was occupied so she went upstairs. She had visited Rob's place only once before but she had never been upstairs and she marvelled at the art on the landings. She could only imagine what was in the bedrooms.

It wasn't obvious where the bathroom was so she followed the corridor, quietly opening doors as she went along. The bathrooms must all be en suites, she thought as she entered one of the bedrooms. The room was a mess with sheets and pillows strewn across the floor.

She heard a flushing sound and Rob emerged.

'I was just looking for the bathroom,' she said.

'Not this one,' he said, putting his hand on the door to block entry.

A sound rang behind him. Metal hitting a stone floor.

Vanessa craned past him, intrigued. Most of the women at the party were with their partners so who was Rob carrying on with up here? A housekeeper?

Rob took Vanessa by the shoulders and steered her from the bedroom into the corridor.

They went downstairs and despite her increasing desperation for the loo, Vanessa spoke to another financial adviser so she could keep an eye on the stairs. Finally Allegra appeared on the landing.

She was flushed and as she glided down the stairs, Vanessa glanced over at Rob. He was holding forth with a group of investors, his conscience untroubled by the fact he had just been having it off with one of his associate's wives. This aspect of Rob amazed her: brazenly carrying on with Allegra when her husband was milling about downstairs. He was so full of conceit that he didn't care whether Lensley knew, or anyone else for that matter.

Amazingly, Allegra still looked bored after all that activity upstairs. What did it take to get her excited, Vanessa wondered, as Allegra's blank gaze panned around the room. Lensley went over and pecked her on the cheek.

Just then, Elanka appeared on the landing where Allegra had been and Vanessa suppressed a gasp. Surely not? Rob knew better than anyone what Amir was capable of so what was he playing at? Surely he wasn't stupid enough to be dipping into such treacherous waters. And more to the point, what on earth would Elanka see in Rob?

Later, Vanessa caught up with Lensley alone.

'How are you holding up?' she asked.

'I'm fine,' he said grimly, holding up his drink. 'Third glass of champagne.'

'Allegra seems very at home here.'

'Yes, she gave Rob some tips on the design of his new kitchen.'

Vanessa raised her eyebrows. 'And the bedrooms too, from the looks of things.'

Lensley seemed puzzled.

'Oh, come on, Lens, don't tell me you didn't see that.'

He shook his head. 'What are you talking about?'

'What does Allegra know about kitchens?'

Lensley turned away. 'Quite a bit, as it turns out.'

'Don't be naïve.'

Lensley flushed and looked at her sourly. 'Who are you to be calling me naïve anyway? What is it – two, or three divorces?'

'Just the one, actually. And it's just an observation. One day you'll thank me for it.'

There was an uncomfortable pause before Vanessa changed the subject. 'And what's Elanka doing here without Amir?'

'Elanka?'

'Elanka Aleksandras. Amir's girlfriend.'

'Which one is she?'

'You can't miss her, she's over there, talking to Allegra,' Vanessa said, nodding towards them. 'She's invited us all to their villa in France to launch LuckyCoin. That must be what they're talking about – Allegra seems delighted for a change.'

The colour suddenly drained from Lensley's face. He hadn't met Elanka and as he stared at her now, he realised she was the woman he had seen with Rob last night on the rooftop.

Chapter Eleven
Monaco

I T WAS LUNCHTIME, EXACTLY A week since her discussion with Rob and Julia, and Kate was in the bathroom at work studying her reflection in the mirror. She knew she had an overly expressive face, one that often revealed too much of what she was feeling and right now, it was pale and her jaw muscles were taut from overuse.

She had looked like this before her stress leave when her skin had turned all grey and waxy. Afterwards, when it didn't recover, Kate thought London was the problem and that moving somewhere sunnier would fix it, but the tension in her face was worse now, if anything. Kate had spent the past week scouring the Falkon files, trying to find an alternative solution to falsifying evidence, but all to no avail. The men had solid cases and the only way forward that made any sense was for Falkon to pay them out.

After a stressful week, Kate had had a solitary weekend with too much time to think. She had visited a museum in Nice, and then on Sunday she had walked along the coastal path to a beach in Cap-d'Ail and although it had been pleasant, she had barely spoken to anyone and had eaten every meal alone.

Kate pinched her cheeks and forced herself to smile. If she was going to be expressive then she may as well express something friendly, she said to herself in her mother's voice as she swiped on the red lipstick. She needed to meet more people and she wouldn't do it with a face like this.

Kate had taken Vanessa's advice and joined a dating app. It was a distraction from work and when she got back to her office, she checked her phone. She had drawn a lot of interest but the prospect of sifting through all the profiles seemed like yet another job, so she deleted most of them, although there were a few people she liked back.

As she was busy on the app her phone rang.

'Do you fancy lunch?' a man said.

'Who's this?'

The speaker laughed. 'Don't sound so worried. You just liked my profile.'

Kate almost dropped the phone. It was as shocking as if the caller had leaped through the screen and was now sitting on her lap.

Kate stumbled over the words. 'Where did you get my number?'

'You're on the dating site.'

Kate hung up, her palms sweating as she went frantically through her profile page. She was sure she hadn't given the app her phone number and she couldn't see it displayed, so how did he find it?

The caller rang back.

'What the hell do you want?' Kate said.

'I smiled at you in the lift the other morning, but you looked straight through me.'

Kate's phone slipped in her hand as she swivelled her chair to face the door. Was he following her now?

She spoke slowly, not wanting to know the answer. 'How do you know where I am?'

'Because I work at Meritus too. I did your tech set-up when you arrived a couple of weeks ago. You don't remember?'

'You *what?*'

'My name's Marc. From the IT department. I recognised you from your photo and realised you'd just started at the firm.'

'Are you kidding?'

'Monaco's a very small place. If you want any privacy you'll need to delete a few things.'

'Like what?' asked Kate, staring at her phone.

'Your location details for a start. I can see you're in the office now. You can't see it, but those details are accessible if you know where to look. Meet me for lunch and I'll show you.'

'And my phone number. How did you get that?'

'From the office directory.'

Marc suggested they have lunch at a pizzeria nearby. He said he was on his way there and sent her the address.

'And don't worry,' he said. 'I don't date co-workers.'

While she debated whether to join Marc at the restaurant, Kate went through his profile. Looking closely at his photos now, she thought she recognised him from the office, but most men on the site looked vaguely familiar. They all had the same smiles, wore the same clothes and worked their abdominal muscles to the same extent. They all had the same hobbies too – mountain climbing, kite surfing and trail biking.

She scanned through Marc's pictures and saw him flashing his Rolex behind a large platter of seafood at the Hôtel de Paris in Monaco. And there he was in Balenciaga trainers in front of a skyscraper in Dubai.

She could tell he wasn't her type. He was younger for a start and good-looking. He was also an extrovert if the phone stunt was anything to go by. Attractive, overly confident men made her wary. When she met them, she felt a strange sense of vertigo, as if she had entered a place she didn't belong, or a trap had opened somewhere up ahead.

She found him on the office system and tapped her pen on a file. She was always having technical issues in London. The set-up here seemed better and it was a smaller office but still, she needed friends and a friend in the IT department could be useful.

She arrived at the restaurant ten minutes later. He was on the terrace looking exactly like his photos, only smaller.

'Don't look so suspicious,' he said.

'They said security was paramount on that site,' Kate said, taking a seat opposite.

'Nothing online is secure,' he said. 'Surely you know that. Give me your phone.'

Kate handed it over and watched as he gained access to her profile on the app without even asking her password.

'That's why you should install thumbprint or facial recognition,' he said, flicking through several pages. 'You also need to disguise your location.'

'How easy is it to access all this?'

'Very easy if you know how. Don't mention you're a lawyer at a boutique firm in Monaco,' he said, continuing to scan her profile. 'There aren't many firms like Meritus here.'

He showed her the adjustments he had made to the settings on her phone and then gave it back. 'And you really shouldn't hand your phone over to anyone either.'

They ordered pizzas and while they ate they spoke about work. Marc told her he was from Brittany, and had been at Meritus for three years.

'Though I'm leaving soon,' he said, his face hardening. 'They're outsourcing the IT department, apparently.'

'Really? I haven't heard that.'

'They're not making any kind of announcement. They're just going to sack us all in a few weeks' time without notice.'

'How do you know?'

'I monitor pretty much everything that goes on here. I know what everyone's up to.'

Kate stared at him, horrified. 'So where did you learn this?'

'On one of Rob's calls last week.'

'On one of his calls?'

Kate wondered how far his surveillance extended and whether he had overheard the conversation she'd had with Rob and Julia last week.

When the bill came she offered to pay half but he insisted. 'I'm running it through the expense account. I know they won't pay us out properly, so I'm taking advantage of it before I leave.'

Kate tucked her purse away. 'You shouldn't be telling me all this.'

'I don't care, I'm leaving.'

On the way back to work, Kate steered the conversation towards safer topics and Marc gave her tips on nearby beaches and other places to visit. He had a spare bike and offered to take her on his favourite cycle route up in the hills.

When Kate got back to the office there were some clothes hanging on a cupboard door with a note from Vanessa.

None of these fit me anymore. I think they'd suit you.
(PS They're WORK clothes!)

The clothes were all designer, vintage items, worth a fortune from the looks of them, and hardly worn. Packed carefully in plastic garment covers was a dark blue Lanvin dress, a cream Ferragamo trouser suit, two skirts still with their tags on, a couple of day dresses and some silk shirts.

Back at work that afternoon, Rob and Julia were overly friendly, bringing her coffee and asking about her weekend. Neither of them had a soft side, let alone one each and their behaviour unnerved her. She almost preferred them when they were unpleasant – at least she knew where she was. She had seen how quickly their moods could turn and she felt the sourness in the air, just waiting to curdle.

Later that afternoon, Rob came into her office. 'I know I don't need to tell you this, but that conversation we had last week, don't mention it to anyone.'

'Of course not.'

'And nothing in writing between us about it all, of course.'

Kate nodded as Rob stepped forward and handed her a blank white card with a UK number printed on it. 'I'm away for the rest of the week but if you need to discuss anything, call me on this number. It's a private line.'

Rob paused as he left the office, his hand on the door frame. 'I knew from the very first day you started here that I'd made the right decision.'

Kate felt her skin crawl, but she smiled weakly. Then he winked, giving a little tap at the door as he left.

As she removed her make-up that evening, Kate examined her overly expressive face and wondered how it might change if she did what Rob and Julia had asked. Would her furrowed brow and sunken cheeks disappear along with her worries, or would her anxiety just retreat for a while only to fester and get worse? She thought of Rob and whether it was true what they said: that people get the faces they deserve. At some level she knew it was right and that you didn't get a face like Rob's unless you'd done some pretty awful things.

Kate wasn't used to going beyond her limits and this move to Monaco was probably the most daring thing she had ever done. Kate knew her reluctance to do Rob's dirty work now wasn't due to any overdeveloped moral code so much as an excess of caution and it made her feel more cowardly than proud. Risks, although they might seem manageable were unpre-dictable, and Kate had always tried to avoid anything too impulsive. She had seen how quickly things unravelled for her sister once she started gambling, and how one bad move always led to another.

Kate splashed her cheeks with water then stood back from the basin to see her face scrubbed clean. She wondered what might happen if she went ahead and made this one dangerous move. Would the boldness of the act eclipse any remorse, or would it throw her off balance, setting her down in an unfamiliar place? Even if she felt no immediate qualms, guilt was the kind of thing that lay in wait. She imagined it biding its time, germinating and planting roots, and then gradually working its way out onto her face like some kind of lesion until in time she no longer recognised herself.

Chapter Twelve

KATE SLEPT RESTLESSLY THAT NIGHT, heart thudding through her dreams. She was running down the corridor of a skyscraper, chasing someone – or was someone chasing her? At 3 a.m. she woke with her chest tight, hair damp across her forehead. She found the anti-anxiety pills her London doctor had prescribed and swallowed one, leaning on the basin as she pressed her forehead against the cool bathroom tiles.

The packet was now empty, each ragged blister a souvenir of a night like this. Kate went online, made an appointment with a local doctor for the next day, and then returned to bed. A few hours later she rose again, her anxiety subdued by the sluggish haze the medication had left behind. She showered, dressed and then went to work.

At midday, Kate emailed Julia saying she would be working from home that afternoon and then walked to the doctor's surgery a few streets from her apartment.

In the waiting room, Kate took a number and sat in a lozenge of sunlight that slanted in through the high windows. It was a

warm day, the room silent and still, and the woman opposite
Kate shivered and coughed. When the woman stood to remove
her jacket their knees touched for a moment triggering the
anxiety Kate was struggling to contain. Kate waited a moment
and then moved to the other side of the room.

A little while later, Kate realised she didn't have her ticket so
she returned to her old seat. There was a man in it now and he
smiled as he moved his jacket from the space beside him.

'No I don't want the seat. It's just I've lost my—'

'This?' he said, holding out the crumpled ticket.

She took it with a quiet thanks.

'It's a good number,' he said.

'What?'

'Thirty-six. It's a lucky number. I was tempted to keep it.'

Kate laughed and offered it back. 'Go on, keep it then.'

'No, it's yours.'

Just then the machine above them beeped.

'I told you,' he said, as the screen flashed her number.

When Kate finished with the doctor, she checked the waiting
room but of course he wasn't there. She lingered by the water
cooler until the next person appeared from the doctors' rooms
but it wasn't him. Next door in the pharmacy she realised she
still had the ticket screwed up in her palm. She was about to
throw it away but instead she smoothed it out and tucked the
scrap of paper into her purse.

Once the prescription was in her bag she could relax, and
outside in the street she noticed how vividly blue the sky was
against the terracotta rooftops on the hills. She couldn't face
going home to her computer just yet so she decided to have
lunch in one of the restaurants on the waterfront.

Walking down a narrow street towards the harbour she saw him sitting outside a café. She thought he had seen her too – a quick glance in her direction, but his head was down now, studying something on the table in front of him. She followed the line of sun, pretending to browse the shops along the street until she reached the café.

He didn't look up when she stopped at his table, so absorbed was he in the task before him.

'More lucky numbers?' she said, pointing to his notebook.

He removed his sunglasses and squinted up at her, smiling already.

The sun was behind her, beating down on him and on the back of her neck. She moved aside, shielding the light from his face. There were scores of numbers in the notebook crossed out and rewritten in spidery writing like a complicated mathematical formula.

'What's all that?' Kate asked.

'I'm working out the odds,' he said, as he moved his bag from the chair beside him. 'Of whether you're going to sit down this time.'

'Whether I'd like to, or whether I will?'

He laughed. 'Aren't they the same thing?'

'No,' she said, tempted to prove her point by walking away, but at the same time not moving. If she left now she might never see him again. Twice in one day, what were those odds?

She sat down, then regretted her decision when she saw the pencil he was using. Silver letters glistened along its spine: *Casino de Monte-Carlo*.

'You're a gambler,' she said.

He shrugged, closed the notebook and placed the pencil on top. 'Sometimes.'

She ordered a coffee and he a beer. She thought about telling him she knew a bit about gambling, but where would she start?

'Numbers relax me,' he said after a while.

'They do the opposite for me.'

It sounded abrupt and so she corrected herself. 'If I were a gambler I'm sure I'd lose everything on the first game, like those stories you hear.'

'Or you might have beginner's luck,' he said. 'Not everyone loses straight away. It's usually only once you get hooked.'

'That's even worse.'

He scooped up the notebook and the pencil and shoved them into his bag. 'I like the way numbers work. Probability and odds. I like the simplicity of it.'

Kate thought of her sister – how in her case it wasn't simple at all, but she held the thought back.

They chatted for a while and she told him she worked in Monaco. He was interested in her job, half teasing her with questions and jokes about being a lawyer, pretending to be impressed. He said he lived further up the coast, at Menton near the Italian border and that he was an artist but supplemented his income with gambling, since he was good with numbers. It seemed unlikely but she went along with it.

After they had finished their drinks he took off his sweater. The skin on his neck was tanned and it set off his eyes, which were very blue. He looked up at the sky. 'It's going to be warm again today. Why don't we go swimming?'

The possibility of it leaped up at her, sharpened by his cologne and the sweet rush of caffeine. Kate smiled, savouring the moment before it retreated beneath more sensible concerns. She wasn't dressed for the beach. Her buttoned-up navy suit with its tight waistband encased her like a protective shell.

'My car's around the corner. We could go for a drive along the coast.'

He said this casually, as if it were just an idea, but he was already on his feet, rattling the keys in his pocket.

It seemed like the most normal suggestion in the world – he had a car and the sea was just there. What could be lovelier than a drive up the coast and then a swim, especially after the stress of the past week? She glanced back towards the doctor's surgery, aware of the sequence that had led her here. It wasn't completely random. She had willed herself to meet him again, had probably even made it happen with the lucky ticket in her purse. Although none of it was planned, it had a certain momentum to it and while her readiness to give in to his sugges-tion seemed natural, it also scared her a little.

'But they're always so crowded,' she said, twisting the watch on her wrist. Her instincts felt out of kilter, as if the dilemma she faced at work had disturbed her judgement somehow. That same restlessness had made her seek out a stranger, and now it was telling her to spend the afternoon with him.

'Not during the week,' he said. 'I know some quiet places.'

She cast around for further excuses.

'I don't even know your name,' she said.

Looking down at her, his eyes stood out against the sky even brighter than before. He wore an aqua T-shirt and his irises were like shards of sky that had somehow found their way onto his face, which was now totally surrounded by blue. She could hardly look at him.

'Anton,' he said, offering his hand.

Kate had an image of herself running into the water, her navy suit strewn wildly across the sand. Her underwear was really not fit to swim in and the prospect of swimming naked with him almost made her pass out.

'I'm really not dressed for the beach.'

He dropped her hand to fish in his pocket for some coins and immediately she wanted it back. Her anxiety surfaced and spoke to her: *This is a stranger! Don't take unnecessary risks! Think of your underwear!* Her legs felt weak, like she was treading water.

The café was filling up now, the faces on the terrace warmed by the sun and flushed with wine. A woman smiled at them and asked if she could have their table. Laughter floated out from inside the restaurant, and the waiter shouted something back as he moved past them with plates of food.

He took her hand again as she stood. 'We'll get some things at the market for a picnic,' he said. 'Come on.'

They walked from the café to the marina where seagulls bickered between the ice cream vendors and the boats, their hulls and sails glinting in the light.

At the market Anton bought a couple of cheeses, a baguette, grapes and a bottle of wine. He bought these things without asking whether Kate liked them, and instead of finding this presumptuous, she found it reassuring.

His car was parked in a street just back from the marina – a sleek black Ferrari. Kate had never seen such a beautiful car and she made him take a picture of her in the driver's seat. As they loaded the food into the boot she saw he had towels and a cool box monogrammed with the same yellow rearing horse insignia of the car.

The traffic was slow leaving Monaco, but once they had cleared the city, Anton hit the accelerator and the car surged ahead following a road that wound into the hills. As they gained height, the corners got sharper, tyres skidding beneath the engine's throaty roar. Beneath them, the land fell away revealing a vast expanse of glistening sea all the way to the horizon where water and sky merged in a soft blue haze.

They sped along the Corniche and then came off the main road, descending abruptly onto a thinly tarmacked track, the sudden change in height hollowing Kate's stomach. She felt the power of the car as Anton applied the brakes, changing gears and pulling hard around the bends, sending up clouds of dust. Looking out at the endless bay, Kate held tight to her seat, feeling the energy and power of the car, unsure if it was the motion causing such a rush of vertigo or her current situation. The risks in meeting people on a dating app were obvious, but the hazards involved in jumping into a car with a stranger from a café were as close to insanity as it got.

Tyres padded off the tarmac onto a rougher track. The dirt ended in a clearing before some rocks and the car came to rest in the shade of a tall pine tree. Its engine groaned like a sated beast after all the exertion on the road and the wild flowers and pine needles around them released a sharp herbal tang.

All was silent apart from the cicadas and the creaking car and slowly, a sickening sense of doom threatened to close in around her. The twists and turns in the road had made Kate nauseous and her palms were prickling.

She leaped out of the car to get her feet on solid ground, trying to quell the anxiety that rose in her throat. Kate took several deep breaths as she pushed away fear and told herself she had chosen this course and she had to now see it through.

Anton went to the boot and came back with the cool box, putting the food and wine into a gym bag. He passed her a pair of flip-flops. They were too big for her but better than her work shoes and she felt the smooth indents of his feet on the rubber soles as she followed him down a steep path, grasping branches as she stepped through the rocks and trees. It was well into the afternoon now, the heat rising from the bare stone on either side of the path as they wound towards the beach.

'This is the old customs path,' he said, as they dropped onto a track near the sea. 'The Sentier des Douaniers.'

A small dirt track wound ahead between the pine trees and to the right was an uninterrupted view of the ocean and the rocky coastline. 'Where does it go?'

'From Monaco all the way to the Italian border,' he said. 'I've only travelled this stretch because the landowners around here always try to keep people out, but there are some beautiful inlets for a swim.'

Finally they were at the water and they walked along a small pebbly beach until they found a shady area beside an overhanging rock where Anton set down the bag, arranging the food on a towel beside it. The spot he had chosen was stunning – a small sandy beach, clear aqua water between limestone rocks, pine trees beside them, framing the view. He tore an end off the bread, pressing a piece of cheese into the crust before handing it to her. She took it gratefully, realising she hadn't eaten anything since breakfast. He opened the wine and poured some into a cup. It was delicious – cool and sharp, and she sipped it slowly as he told her about the kind of art he made and that he was having a show soon at a gallery near her office.

When she finished her wine, he poured another cup and she relaxed against the rock feeling the weight of the past week lift a little.

'It's crazy,' she said.

'What is?'

'We only just met. One minute, you're a total stranger in a doctor's surgery and the next minute we're here together on this beach.'

'C'est la vie.'

Kate stared at him. This might be his kind of life but it certainly wasn't what she was used to. This was something she would never do in England. She would never get into a car with a stranger and then walk along a deserted path with him. Never in a million years.

But why not? The wine had gone to her head and she laughed at herself. The whole situation was exhilarating. Maybe she had been wrong all this time. She had taken a risk and it had worked out. It made her wonder why on earth she hadn't done this kind of thing before.

She leaned forward and tore another chunk of bread, filled it with cheese. 'Tell me about risk.'

'Risk?' he said.

'Yes, with your gambling. How do you know when to take a risk and when to back off?'

His face grew serious. 'I don't take risks. I calculate the odds, assess my opponent. Every risk is actually a choice.'

'And how do you do that? Assess your opponent I mean.'

'It's about paying attention, working out how they think. Once you get in the habit, it becomes an instinct. A kind of confidence.'

'If it's just confidence, then how do you know whether to trust it when the stakes are high. How do you know it isn't just wishful thinking?'

He laughed. 'Ah, that's the million dollar question. I usually trust it. It's a bit like self-belief. What else do you have? You have to trust yourself.'

That was all very well provided you were on familiar ground, Kate thought. Kate wasn't sure she trusted herself now.

She took a grape. 'Back at the café you said you liked the simplicity of numbers. But it's more complicated than that, isn't it?'

'Not always.'

Kate persisted, thinking it was something important for her to understand, something that was relevant to her sister's constant battles and to the dilemma she faced at work.

'Taking risks is more than instinct and choice though. Don't you think people crave the thrill of risk? Even if it means losing. Even if they *know* they'll lose.'

His eyes suddenly intensified. 'Partly that, but it's also deeper. What they're looking for is hope. People take risks because of the hope it gives them.'

'How is that?' she said.

'Take roulette. The croupier spins the wheel in one direction,' he said, drawing a circle in the sand between them.

He took her hand and used her index finger to draw another, outer circle. 'Then he spins a ball along an outside track in the opposite direction. Eventually the ball loses momentum and falls onto one of the pockets on the wheel.'

'Why is that hopeful?'

'Even if the odds of red or black are less than fifty-fifty, which they are because of the zeros, people always think it's more. It's not addiction, it's hope. Hope is the wild card, the invisible hand on the wheel.'

Kate looked at him, puzzled.

'The hope is in the movement, in the forward momentum of the ball while the wheel spins the other way. In those seconds waiting for the ball to land, you're a winner against gravity, against all probability and chance. All your dreams are fixed upon the ball while the world turns. Your whole future is concentrated in that tiny white ball.'

'You make it sound like the moment of death when your life flashes before your eyes.'

'Yes, but instead of dying and looking back over the past, you're glimpsing ahead into the future.'

'A future full of hope.'

Kate leaned forward to kiss him, and in that movement she felt the blood in her cheeks, the sun on her back and the weight of the past week fall away.

Chapter Thirteen

KATE TOOK A LITTLE MORE time in the mornings before heading into work. The afternoon with Anton had shifted something, and the past two days she had woken with her mind clear. Meeting Anton had deepened her infatuation with Monaco and she now saw its full potential, provided she dealt with her problems at Meritus.

As Kate made coffee, she thought back to Vanessa's words: *Your real concern should be what's in it for you.* She wondered if Vanessa was right – that the solution to the dilemma was to somehow make it work for her. Kate knew that Julia and Rob would want results soon and so she needed to be smart, to devise a better plan than simply saying no.

Kate slid the doors to the balcony. The jacket she had worn to the beach was still hanging on the back of a chair so she lifted it off and tossed it inside. She sat down and flicked through her photos – smiling behind the wheel of Anton's Ferrari, shots she had taken during their walk to the beach and finally, the selfie of the two of them just after they had kissed.

She hadn't heard from Anton since Tuesday evening when she had texted to thank him for the trip. She had spent a while composing the message, veering away from the too eager first draft which listed the things she had enjoyed about the afternoon. The message she sent in the end was short, just

Thanks, hope to see you soon

She signed off with one restrained, lowercase *x*. She decided that was too cold, so she added another. He replied straight away his tone similarly reserved, saying he'd had a lovely time too. She opened WhatsApp and analysed the exchange. She should have gone with the first draft as he hadn't contacted her since. There was nothing to suggest he had any interest in seeing her again and the word 'hope' in her restrained little message now came across as vulnerable and needy. She wanted to send him one of the photos, but according to the rules of texting, it was up to him to initiate the next exchange.

She refilled her coffee and flicked to Google Maps, trying to work out what beach they had visited. It was a place near Menton, a cove not far from the Italian border, she recalled, as she scanned the names of the beaches and the bays until she recognised it. She zoomed in on the village and then the coastline. She saw the path they had walked along, the series of small inlets and the little sandy beach among the rocks where they had sat.

Menton was only a short train ride from Monaco along a railway track that hugged the coast. Kate glanced at the blue sky above La Turbie. It was another beautiful day – she could have a quick swim at lunchtime, or at least a walk near the sea. She had a call with some US clients that evening and it would be a waste to spend the whole day indoors. Kate finished her coffee and went inside. She grabbed her swimming costume, stuffed it into a bag with a towel then left for work.

The same logic that told her she couldn't text Anton before he texted her also said she couldn't go back to the same beach they had visited. When she arrived at her desk, she checked the map again, scanning the coastline and she found a town even closer to Monaco with a train station next to the beach. She could swim there or else walk along another section of the customs path Anton had told her about.

The café terraces were heaving as she walked from the office just after midday. Locals in suits and heels jostled for the best tables – far away from the tourists who lounged in the sun with their holiday faces and beer. Kate entered the station and in less than ten minutes the buzz and commotion of Monaco was gone and she was standing on the railway platform at Roquebrune-Cap-Martin.

Kate walked through the station car park, past a food truck with tables and umbrellas around it. A sign for the customs path was hidden at the edge of the car park behind some cactus bushes, the metal rusted through in part. Kate followed the path behind a line of bungalows until it dropped down some steps onto a small beach after a set of black metal gates. The gates bore the emblem of a ship's wheel and the words 'Casa di Stelle' in bronze letters beneath a row of gilded spikes. Through a narrow opening to the side, Kate glimpsed a sweeping driveway flanked by two guardhouses that led to a three-storey white villa. There was something ominous in the precision of the vast gardens surrounding the villa, their meticulous perfection like a military encampment.

The property occupied an entire waterfront plot and Kate trekked along the pebbly beach in the shade of a high stone wall surrounding the gardens. A few small fishing boats had been hauled onto the beach and next to them, on a rocky promontory, a man stood with his dog, gazing out to sea. A little further on, a woman was preparing for a swim.

When Kate reached the end of the beach, she looked back towards the station to the cluster of pretty, pastel-coloured houses that clung to the steep hillside and made up the township of Roquebrune. Balconies shot out at all angles taking advantage of the panoramas that came with the height, each one cantilevering over the next in an effort to steal the best view. It was warm and still, and the light was so clear she could see the ruined castle perched high on the limestone cliffs above the village, the scene as perfectly luminous as a postcard.

The path ahead with its canopy of trees was far more enticing than the hot beach so Kate left her towel and swimsuit rolled up behind a rock and followed the dirt track towards the cape.

Kate had heard about the glamorous people who lived for a short time each year in the massive villas that occupied this stretch of coast and she had always wanted to come this way to see them for herself. To her left, behind hurricane fencing, vast gardens full of palm trees, shrubs and bushes seemed to grow out of the rock itself. Towering over this ground cover, pines and cypresses provided a frame for the imposing villas and mansions set much higher back.

To her right, the land dropped away into small coves, the water rippling where the wind caught it and shimmering across the bay to Monaco – now a concrete mirage against the beauty of the landscape around it.

As Kate walked towards the cape, the gardens on her left grew wilder, each villa more breathtaking than the last. Gaining height, the plot size increased and the green canvas expanded. The sea did the same, the endless blue growing darker near the horizon where it melted into a cloudless sky.

Finally, Kate reached the tip of the cape where the landscape collapsed into a mass of brown rocks that tumbled into the sea. It was a desolate view, strikingly at odds with the beauty of the terrain she had just passed. Kate paused and looked over to Monaco. Skyscrapers gathered at the water's edge, their reflections giving the city roots in the water, as if the whole place had erupted out of the sea like a futuristic Atlantis.

The sun was at its peak now and she was hungry. The sight of Monaco brought back thoughts of work and she glanced towards the shore, to the beach she had just walked along. She saw there was a café at the far end, tables and umbrellas in the sun, and Kate decided she would head there. She wanted to spend time among people whose carefree lives meant they could eat lunch in a beachside café instead of an office. Perhaps she wouldn't go back to work at all.

As Kate drew closer to the beach, she had a bird's eye view of the mansion she had walked beside earlier. She peered down at the white stucco facade with its tiered balconies, columns and balustrades. The mansion was surrounded by acres of manicured lawns, palm trees and pines, an Olympic-sized swimming pool and a gazebo that looked capable of accommodating an entire orchestra. Finally, at the eastern end of the property there was a helipad.

Kate descended to the beach, collected her belongings and headed towards the café. The man and the woman had gone and in their place was a group of boisterous young women lounging on towels in their swimming costumes, laughing and throwing pebbles at each other. As Kate approached, two men and a large dog joined the group from a door that led to the beachfront property. As Kate got closer she saw that the women were all quite young, girls really, and that there was a kind of untamed energy to them, as if they were on a school trip. As Kate passed, the girls fell silent and stared at her. One of them smiled and Kate was about to say something but then one of the men stepped forward, the dog straining at the leash. The aggression in the man's bearing stopped Kate in her tracks.

'This is a private beach,' he said in heavily accented French. He wore thick clothing and boots despite the warm day.

'I'm sorry,' said Kate automatically. She looked around for a sign saying the beach was private but saw none.

Just then at the edge of the group there was a scuffle. One of the girls was trying to snatch something back from the other man who appeared to have taken it from her. Kate couldn't see what it was but it looked to be a phone as she saw metal glinting in the sun.

The girl was on her feet now lunging at the man. She managed to get whatever it was from him, but he snatched it back from her so roughly that her bikini top snapped. The girl continued to fight for the metal object, half-naked now but seeming not

140

to care. Finally the girl gave up and stormed back to the house, leaving the others watching in stunned silence.

'Is she all right?' Kate said to the man with the dog.

The man didn't reply, just released the dog on the lead a little so it moved closer to Kate. The animal was panting, its glistening pink tongue lolling over its strong jaws. The man pulled the dog back, winding the chain around his fist.

'I said is that girl all right?'

'Over there,' the man said to Kate, nodding towards the café. 'The public beach is over there.'

By now the rest of the girls had gathered up their things and were walking back towards the property with the other man. The scene, combining the man's hostility and the girl's half-nakedness was unsettling, but by the time the girls reached the property they were all laughing again.

'Over there is the public beach,' the man repeated.

'Then that's where I'm going,' Kate said, but she continued to watch the girls until they disappeared through the door.

Kate walked slowly towards the café. There were some other people on the beach now, sprawled on towels, sunning themselves and reading, but no one seemed to have noticed the altercation.

She went over to a woman sunbathing alone.

'Excuse me, but did you see that group of girls?'

The woman looked up, her heavily tanned face squinting at Kate as she removed her headphones.

Kate pointed over to where the girls had been. 'Those girls. Did you see them?'

'Spoilt oligarchs' kids,' said the woman, adjusting her bikini. She shrugged and then waved towards the villa. 'Russians. You see them on the beach a lot. They make a lot of noise. A real nuisance.'

The woman planted her head back into her towel and Kate moved away. She considered asking further questions, but the woman had replaced her headphones.

As Kate drew closer to the café, a waiter came out to clear a table. He was side-on and although she couldn't make out his face, she registered his stance, the dark hair falling across his face, and the same blue T-shirt he had been wearing the day they met.

Anton seemed to sense her too and he put down his tray. Then he glanced in the opposite direction, out to sea. Kate was the only person moving across the beach to the café and she knew that if she waited a second longer he would look back and notice her. She was disorientated after the disturbing scene with the girls, and the surprise at seeing him at the café made her turn abruptly and walk towards the steps that led to the road. She had come here half looking for him, of course, but now seeing him was the last thing she wanted.

By the time she was halfway up the steps she began to doubt what she had seen. Was it really Anton at the café, and had he seen her? If he had, then why didn't he call out or come over. Maybe he had been equally shocked to see her too. She was wearing a hat and her hair was tied back, so perhaps he hadn't even recognised her. Kate removed her sunglasses and squinted towards the café. The glare almost blinded her, and she couldn't make out any figures at all in the heat haze coming off the beach.

She reached the top of the stairs and walked slowly along the path to the station. She thought back over what Anton said he did for a living. What reason did he have to lie?

As she neared the entrance to the villa, a limousine appeared up ahead and Kate stood back to let it pass. As she did so, the gates to the villa swung open and a pair of security guards waved the car in. They wore army fatigues and carried machine guns, surreal against the palm trees and the quiet, luxurious backdrop. The sight of the guns made Kate double take, fixing her to the spot and despite being acutely conscious her presence was unwelcome, she stayed watching the house until the gates closed.

When Kate arrived back at work, Julia was in her office rifling through some papers on her desk.

'Sorry I'm a bit late—'

'Not at all,' said Julia, smiling broadly. 'I'm just looking for a file.' She glanced over. 'You look a little flushed. Is everything all right?'

The effort of being pleasant manifested on Julia's face as if she were in pain, making her smile into a grimace, and so Kate grimaced back.

'I'm fine, it's just a little warm out,' Kate said, hanging her jacket behind the door.

'*Voilà*,' Julia said, holding up a file. 'Here it is.'

Kate saw it wasn't one of the Falkon files. 'What do you want with that?' she said.

'I'm giving it to Lucie since you're so busy with Falkon.'

Kate glanced at the file. It was a high profile case she had brought with her from London and it had almost completed. There was no need to give it to Lucie, or more importantly, let Lucie take the credit for its resolution.

Kate took the file back. 'I can do both.'

'OK,' said Julia. 'I just thought it would be helpful.'

'Really? No one discussed this with me.'

As she was leaving, Julia turned back as if something had just occurred to her. 'I was a bit disappointed by your attitude the other day.'

'What attitude?'

'I didn't get the feeling you were on board with the solution on Falkon, despite our generous offer.'

Julia matched Kate's stare with a blank one of her own. 'We need to know we can rely on you to get that document done.'

Julia pointed to a piece of paper. 'If you change your mind you can help with that instead.'

Kate scanned the desk.

'With the interviews,' Julia said as she stepped from the room.

Kate picked up the sheet of paper Julia had left on her desk. It was her own job description in four neatly typed lines.

Litigation Associate
Candidate should have at least 10 years' experience in all aspects of litigation, including class actions.
Ability to thrive under pressure essential.

As she was staring at the sheet, there was a knock on the door and Marc came in.

'God, she looks even worse than usual,' Marc said. 'I don't know what Julia is on, but she just gets meaner. Speaking of which,' he said, 'I've just seen written confirmation.'

Kate wasn't in the mood to chit-chat and barely looked up. 'Of what?'

'I was reading some emails between Julia and the managing partner today. They're restructuring. In a couple of weeks there will no longer be an IT department. They're just going to sack us all and outsource it.'

'Right,' Kate said, not sure what he expected her to say. 'Do the others know?'

'Not yet. I've only just seen it myself and came straight here because I saw something about you as well.'

'About me?' Kate said, paying attention now.

Marc sat down heavily. 'Well, actually, I saw it the other day. It was one of the reasons I contacted you when I saw you on the dating app.'

'What are you saying?'

'Your head's on the block too.'

'*What?*'

'A list Julia put forward to Napier on Monday set out all the lawyers in the Monaco office. You weren't on it.'

'What do you mean not on it?'

'At first I thought it was a mistake, some kind of oversight since you've only just arrived, but then I went back over the emails. Napier queried why you weren't there.'

Kate rose to close the door. 'And what did she say?'

'She said you were having – and I quote "teething problems". She said she thought you were having trouble settling in and that she may need to send you back to London before the end of your probationary period. Alternatively, she said they could give you a paralegal role.'

'A *paralegal* role? But I'm a qualified lawyer.' An image of Kate's mother in the nursing home flashed across Kate's mind. The paralegal pay would be barely half of what she was getting now. 'What are they playing at?'

Marc swivelled in his chair. 'I don't know, but I'm sick of the way they treat us here. I'm going to do something before I leave,' he said.

'Like what?'

'Something to make them think. A virus. I'm still deciding,' he said, tracing a line on Kate's desk.

'I said you shouldn't be telling me this.'

'I don't care who knows. In two weeks I'll be out on my arse. None of us in IT are on contracts. We're all consultants and Julia told Napier there won't be any payouts. They shouldn't be able to get away with this so if that happens, I plan to cause as much disruption as possible.'

'Disruption? Like what?'

'There's a lot I've learned during my time here. I know what Rob's up to, for example. Some of Julia's more colourful deals. I'm no lawyer but I know they're not supposed to be working for sanctioned clients. I know some of the other things their clients are up to as well.'

'So what are you planning to do?'

'I'm not sure yet. I've started collating stuff though. Just so I have some leverage in case things get nasty.'

'Blackmail never works. Be careful.'

'Don't worry,' Marc said, standing up to leave. 'I'll probably just mess with their documents and emails or something. Let's see what happens.'

'Their documents and emails?' Kate said, her mind racing. 'You have access to everything on their computers?'

Marc was at the door now but he turned back. 'Of course.'

'How easy is it to access all that?'

'Child's play.'

'And for me?' Kate said, pointing to her computer. 'Could I do it from here, for example?'

Marc grinned. 'Absolutely.'

Chapter Fourteen

B Y THE TIME VANESSA ARRIVED home, the sun was well over the hills, casting bronzed light back upon the bay. She had finished work early and had returned to her apartment to prepare herself for an unpleasant meeting back in town. After that she would have to go into Nice.

Vanessa made a coffee, which she drank on the sofa in her bright sitting room. Her apartment faced the marina of Fontvieille, which was separated from the rest of the town by the Rock of Monaco and from her sofa Vanessa had a view of the Prince's yellow palace high upon the cliff on the other side of the water. Fontvieille had been built on land reclaimed from the sea in the 1980s and while it looked surreal from a distance – a mass of high-rise apartments topped with palm trees jutting into the Mediterranean like a mini Dubai – up close it had a certain charm. Unlike Port Hercule whose every cubic foot was packed with yachts, the marina at Fontvieille was laidback and calm, home to smaller motorboats and sailing dinghies, pleasure craft their owners actually used at the weekends. Vanessa finished her coffee and slid open the balcony doors. The smell of grilled meat drifted up to her apartment from Le Beefbar four doors down, and she could hear voices and laughter from the bars and terraces lining the marina.

Vanessa showered, dressed and then travelled through the maze of escalators, tunnels and stairs that lead from Fontvieille through Le Rocher to the Place des Armes. From there it was a short walk to a bar near the station where she was meeting the cash mule.

As head of compliance, Vanessa assisted in Rob's money laundering schemes by circumventing the procedures she should have been enforcing, and by relying on the services of trusted contacts. Most of the people at the firms and banks Vanessa dealt with were willing to overlook their legal obligations for a healthy cut, or because dealing in such huge volumes of cash inflated their bonuses. Even if her contacts weren't corrupt, they were often satisfied that because their instructions came from a well-respected law firm with offices in London and Monaco, the money was legitimate.

In terms of the services Vanessa helped Rob carry out for his clients, Vanessa had convinced herself long ago that although what she did was illegal, simply moving money through bank accounts didn't actually harm anyone. This fantasy was assisted by the fact that while her day-to-day work was dubious, it felt anonymous. Although the various steps involved dealing with real people, they were just email addresses and phone numbers. Vanessa could do it all from her desk and rarely did she have to meet anyone.

That was not the case however when it came to physical cash.

Processing funds through the offshore banking system for Rob's Eastern European clients was one thing, but it was becoming increasingly difficult for Rob's local clients to deal with the large volumes of physical cash they generated through their illicit operations along the coast. Since the pandemic, most people had drastically reduced their legitimate use of notes, and so attempting to make large cash deposits at a bank aroused much more suspicion than before. As always, Rob had seen the opportunity in adversity and he had come up with new and innovative ways of dealing with the cash his clients generated.

Like the bank transfers, Vanessa didn't ever ask where this cash came from. If pressed, she would say that she assumed the bulk of it was from illegal gambling, which Vanessa knew was rife along the coast. She also knew there were other illicit things that were traded in cash and that frankly, gambling was the least of the vices on the Côte d'Azur. Vanessa had long since trained herself not to think this way, however, and the people with the cash didn't say.

Vanessa didn't like dealing with the cash mules – it was a new low – but Rob's scheme relied on her as a middlewoman, at least for the time being, because the people in the stash house in Nice didn't want to deal with the cash mules either. Rob said it was important for security that none of his clients knew about the stash house, so they couldn't deposit their cash directly, and he didn't trust any third parties to act as a go-between. Vanessa had initially refused to do it but as always, Rob wore her down with enticements and threats until finally she agreed. The drop-offs were to happen once a month and Vanessa was free to make whatever arrangements she liked to get the money to Nice.

The mules were usually young men who carried out other roles for their bosses. Sometimes they were students, unrelated to organised crime, who took the courier job as a risky trade-off for a free holiday, and other times it was a professional who did this for a living, but rarely was it the same person. If the mules arrived at the airport, Vanessa would collect them with a driver. She would pretend to be a friend and would be waiting straight off their flight. She would bundle them into the car, take the suitcase of cash, give them their payment and drop them at the nearest bus stop. If they came by train she had to make more complicated arrangements.

The cash mules were rarely women, but this time she was.

This evening, the young woman sitting opposite Vanessa at the bar near the station went by the name of Nikki Jazz. Vanessa was always sent a copy of the mule's ID for security purposes and she always looked them up online before meeting them. It was work for desperate people so Vanessa needed to make sure she wasn't dealing with anyone who might hurt her. This was why she always met them in a public place, not a car park or a hotel room, or even her car, which was how Rob had originally suggested the local drop-offs should occur. The woman she had looked up on Instagram that morning however, bore no resemblance to the one now toying nervously with the umbrella in her drink. Online, Nikki Jazz was a DJ in Cyprus with long blonde dreadlocks and glowing skin, whereas the woman Vanessa saw before her now had a sallow complexion, sunken cheeks and a buzzcut. If she hadn't been the only person on the terrace, Vanessa wouldn't have recognised her.

The only other things Vanessa knew about Nikki were that she had travelled from Italy via Casa di Stelle, Amir's mansion at Roquebrune and beside her in a suitcase was a hundred thousand euros. The suitcase was locked but Vanessa had been sent the combination earlier that afternoon and she would open

151

it later when the cash was counted. The plan was to meet at the bar and then Nikki would go, leaving the suitcase with Vanessa who would take it straight to Nice.

There was no requirement to speak, but just after Vanessa sat down, Nikki wiped her eyes with the knuckle of her finger.

It was a very childlike gesture.

Vanessa wanted to ask if she was in trouble, but of course she was in trouble. Why else would the girl be here?

'Are you OK?' said Vanessa.

Nikki was about to speak, but then she glanced towards the station and her expression hardened as a man sat down at a table next to them. The man had a shifty, wasted appearance with bags under his eyes although he couldn't have been more than thirty years old. He wore a black waistcoat like Nikki and a string of beads around his neck.

Nikki glanced at him and then quickly pulled herself together, but Vanessa could tell she was new to all this. 'I'm fine,' she said with a sniff, sliding her jacket over her shoulders. She took the small paper bag Vanessa had placed on the table, which contained her payment, and Vanessa saw that the girl's hand was shaking. Then she got up and left without saying anything to Vanessa or the man.

The man leaned forward and asked Vanessa for a cigarette. His breath reeked of alcohol and he stared at Vanessa rudely while he used her lighter and took a drag of the cigarette. Then he left and caught up with Nikki.

The interaction had barely taken two minutes and Vanessa felt a sense of dread as she watched the pair disappear into the station. She wanted to call after the girl to see if she needed help. The man was clearly some kind of pimp, or at best a controlling boyfriend and she should have intervened, but what could Vanessa do now? Chase after them with the suitcase? It would just make a scene, and could even be some kind of scam meant to take Vanessa's eye off the cash. She moved the suitcase closer and cursed Rob. This was exactly why she didn't like dealing with the mules. You never knew what kind of lives you were getting involved in. She couldn't believe she was doing this, it was too much. Rob needed to find someone else for this.

Vanessa stubbed out her cigarette, took the suitcase and hailed a taxi.

Half an hour later the taxi dropped Vanessa at a building two streets back from the Old Port in Nice behind the Eglise Notre Dame.

From the outside, wedged between a jewellery store and a milliners, the unremarkable nineteenth-century building looked just like its neighbours. A sign hung from the second floor: 'Hotel Lympia'. Masquerading as a three-star budget hotel, it was perfect cover for a stash house. In Monaco, a hotel like this would be out of place but here in Nice, where everyone was a tourist, it didn't draw attention when people trailed suitcases in and out of the building at all times of the day and night.

The only thing setting the Hotel Lympia apart from other buildings in the street was that it had two small CCTV cameras guarding the entrance, whereas the other buildings had none.

Vanessa entered a code on the keypad beside the door. She heard the lock disengage and pushed hard. The facade was deceptive and the six-foot high polished oak doors were rein-forced with steel, making them very heavy. She looked behind to make sure she hadn't been followed and then entered the building with the suitcase.

The lobby was furnished like a regular hotel with a short corridor leading to an unmanned reception desk. To the right there was a characterless breakfast room with a bar at the far end, a coffee machine and several shelves filled with glasses and bottles. The windows were sealed with metal plates and the room was lit by a series of lamps above the bar.

Vanessa placed her right index finger on a sensor on the reception desk. A screen on the wall behind lit up and her passport image appeared.

Vanessa stood still as a beam of green light from the screen scanned her face. The image on the screen pixelated, enlarging her eyes, and then disappeared.

The screen behind the desk went black and a heavy steel door next to the screen slid open to reveal the interior of a lift servicing floors one to six.

Vanessa wheeled the suitcase into the lift and pressed the button for the third floor. Instead of going up, the lift took Vanessa two floors down to a basement crypt at the very bottom of the building.

Vanessa went through another security procedure to exit the lift and passed through into a small antechamber. She was familiar with the process having done it many times before, and she stared at a small screen attached to the wall while putting her finger on a sensor mounted beside it. The needle was so fine that she didn't feel anything as it extracted a microscopic drop of blood.

Vanessa heard the door to the left unlock and she stepped forward into a low-ceilinged concrete bunker.

'Hello, Franz,' Vanessa said to the man who greeted her at the door. Franz showed Vanessa to the vault he kept for Rob, which was piled high with bricks of cash shrink-wrapped in plastic. The money was from illicit operations carried out by Rob's clients and the arrangement was for Franz and his team to move it steadily into traditional banks. They did this in small batches to avoid detection using contacts they paid off within the banks themselves. It was risky work and Franz's commission was usually a generous fifteen to twenty per cent. Vanessa didn't know exactly how much was in Rob's vault at any one time, but by her calculation there was probably about five million euros in front of her now.

Vanessa unlocked the suitcase and waited while Franz's two assistants put the cash through several industrial-sized money counters.

Once they confirmed all the cash was there, Franz gave Vanessa details of the possible countries he could send the money to, depending on how soon Rob's client needed it to join the regular banking system. It depended on his contacts at the banks and at the moment, it was the Austrian banks Franz could rely on to take large sums of physical cash.

Rob had said that Amir needed the money as soon as possible in Switzerland and so Vanessa asked Franz to move the money into an Austrian account and then on to an account in Switzerland when that was available. After Franz had transferred the money to Switzerland he would give Vanessa control of the company that held the account and she would move the money to wherever Amir needed it next – usually offshore in the British Virgin Islands or Jersey. From there Amir could use the cash however he wanted. It had been properly laundered.

They said goodbye and Vanessa went upstairs, leaving the building by a back exit that led to an alley.

Vanessa caught a taxi back home to Fontvieille. She wound down the window and let the cool night air rush over her face. Even with the window open it was hard to breathe and Vanessa was unable to shake off the sense of dread that crept alongside her after meeting Nikki at the bar. Vanessa didn't want to acknowledge what she knew the girl was mixed up in, but something about Nikki's frightened, newly trapped manner reminded Vanessa of the way she had felt the first time she had done something illegal for Rob. He had presented her with a problem – a small mistake he had made on a document. He had looked so helpless and he gave her his smooth talk, asking for advice and complimenting her, saying he was sure she would know what to do. He hadn't bullied her that first time; he had appealed to her ego.

She was flattered he had come to her before anyone else, and that he thought she could fix it. They both knew there was an easy way around the problem, and it took just half an hour for Vanessa to alter the document, backdate it and forge the signature. Rob had been so grateful.

That first time it had been easy and no one had ever found out. But in the end that wasn't what mattered. What mattered was that Rob now had something on her. Vanessa remembered the feeling afterwards when she realised she was hooked in. Everything had closed in around her and it was like being suffocated.

Chapter Fifteen

WHEN KATE WOKE ON FRIDAY morning there was a message from Anton on her phone, just a simple *Ça va?* and an invitation to meet up that evening. She had no plans and so she agreed to meet him in a bar near the marina. As soon as she arrived, he suggested they drive out of town again. They headed east on the coastal road towards Menton – the same direction as last time. Just after the turn-off to the beach where she had seen him the day before, Anton turned left and took the winding road uphill towards the ruined chateau at Roquebrune.

'I'm taking you to the best restaurant in the area,' he said, pressing his foot down on the accelerator. The tarmac was heavily potholed and the road fell away steeply on one side.

Kate clutched her armrest. 'Great,' she said, her stomach lurching as the car skidded into the gravelly edges. 'I hope we make it.'

He took the turns quickly, the car screeching through the bends and Kate stayed silent so as not to distract him from driving. The road was in a terrible state with a vertical drop a mere foot from the car, and the sun's glare made it difficult to see. The near-death experience didn't seem to faze Anton who stared ahead with utter focus, his hands flying from one side of the wheel to the other, a slight sweat breaking out on his forehead. As long as Kate kept her eyes on the dashboard, concentrating on the power of the car and thinking about how well the expensive tyres must be gripping the road, she managed to supress the urge to scream.

'No one comes up this way,' Anton said finally, bringing the car to rest in a gravelled area just below the village. Kate waited a moment until her pulse subsided and then emerged gingerly from the car to join him at a viewing platform on the edge of the car park. There was a sheer descent straight down to the sea, houses clinging to the hillside, the blue sky all above and around them. The sudden drop caused a hollowness in the back of Kate's legs and she leaned on Anton's shoulder trying to regain solidity as he pointed out the landmarks – the beaches just below them, the Maybourne hotel perched on its promontory, Monaco, and then further west where the sun was setting, Saint-Jean Cap-Ferrat, Nice and Cannes.

'All the tourists come as far as Monaco and then something happens – they kind of give up and turn back, or else they roar straight on to Italy. No one bothers with Roquebrune. They leave it to the locals and the retirees.'

'So there are still some locals here then?'

'A lot of people live here and work in Monaco,' said Anton. Then he added, with an edge of bitterness, 'Well, actually they live here in order to *service* the people of Monaco.'

As they walked up to the village the air grew cooler, clouds gathering above the chateau. The steep hills protecting the town from the cold northern winds made the climate here unique, almost sub-tropical judging by the plants sprouting between the rocks and clinging impossibly to the cliffs. Palm trees and acanthus, aloe vera and wild herbs, their fragrance bringing Kate's senses alive. Hardy cactuses grew among orchids, roses and sprays of purple bougainvillea. There was even an avocado tree in the citrus grove of one of the gardens they passed.

At the restaurant, they ate in a courtyard filled with flowers and vines.

'Everyone here speaks Italian,' Kate said, tuning in to the voices around them, the alluring sound of Italian being spoken in France.

'This stretch of coast used to be part of Italy. Now the Italians just run the restaurants and the bars.'

Kate noticed how Anton sipped his wine, only ever holding the glass by the stem. She tried to copy him, moving her fingers halfway down, but the glass felt unbalanced and she moved her hand back, cupping the bowl again.

'If you hold it like that it warms the wine,' he said, reaching over to take her glass. He took her fingers and placed them around the stem. 'Hold it like this.'

'Everyone's so sophisticated here,' she said. 'So well dressed, so' – Kate glanced around the courtyard, searching for what she meant – 'confident and at ease with themselves. I feel so awkward here, especially in Monaco.'

'Well, you are English. You're at a disadvantage.'

She laughed. 'It's uncanny though. If I dress casually, everyone else is dressed to the nines that day. If I make an effort, everyone's dressed down. I can never get the right register. The other day I felt so uncomfortable just walking down the street in Monaco that I had to check I was in fact dressed.'

'You look great,' he said.

'I do not,' she said automatically. Kate was wearing Vanessa's blue Lanvin dress and despite what she had just said, for once she felt as though she had got it right. 'And anyway, these are work clothes,' she said parroting Vanessa, relieved she hadn't gone home before meeting him as she would probably have made a mess of it.

'Monaco's a strange place, but you'll soon get the hang of it. In a couple of months you'll be totally at ease.'

Kate took a sip of wine. 'I don't know if I'll be here that long.'

'Why's that?'

She frowned. 'Problems at work.'

'It didn't seem as if you liked it much when you spoke about it the other day.'

'At the moment I really hate it,' she said, draining her glass. 'In fact, I think I'm about to get fired.'

Anton raised his eyebrows. 'You've only just arrived, haven't you?'

She nodded, feeling the need to explain further, to clarify that it wasn't because she was incompetent. 'I don't agree with some of the things they want me to do. I could get into a lot of trouble.'

'OK,' he said slowly.

Kate lowered her voice. 'And if I don't go along with what they want me to do, they'll probably sack me.'

He paused, as if considering what to say, and then shrugged before refilling her glass. 'I guess there are worse things that could happen,' he said.

Kate reeled back, wondering why people here were so blasé. 'For me, right now, that would be the very worst thing that could happen.'

'I mean for someone as smart as you it would be easy to find something else, surely.'

'Well, no, it's not that easy. The whole thing is stressing me out. It was why I was at the doctor's earlier this week.'

Kate took her glass, moving her hands down the stem and swirling the golden liquid. 'I probably shouldn't discuss it. Not here anyway.'

'You can talk about anything here. But not work because it's officially the weekend,' Anton said, toasting her glass. 'Try and put it out of your mind.'

The waiter brought over plates of antipasto and fat green olives followed by linguini with sweet, garlicky clams, and then another bottle of wine.

It turned out Anton knew the owner of the restaurant, Silvano, who came out to meet Kate and then later he and Anton spoke in rapid-fire Italian, none of which Kate understood. When it came time to pay the bill she reached for her purse.

'You paid last time,' she said when he objected.

He laughed and put his hand over hers. 'We don't pay here,' he said. 'Silvano is an old friend. And anyway, you're about to be fired.'

'That's not funny.'

'Then you can buy me a drink later. Come on, let's walk up to the chateau.'

They said goodbye to Silvano and stepped out into the cobbled streets of the ancient town. The sun had set but there was still plenty of light and they followed the signs to the ruined chateau. The route was lined with artists' studios and small ateliers, and from hidden terraces came the murmur of conversations and the clink of cutlery. As they climbed the steps to the ramparts of the chateau, they gazed down at the indigo sea set out beneath them like glass. Above them the sky was the same deep inky blue and it felt as if they were suspended on a parapet between sea and sky, the air perfectly still all around them.

'Why are we here, Anton?' Kate said softly after a while, emboldened by the wine and the exhilarating view.

He glanced at her, and then back to the sea. 'What do you mean?'

'Why *here*? Why did you bring me to this village, take me to your friend's restaurant. Why this spot? Why tonight?'

Her question sounded ungrateful and the air thickened around them, souring a little like the look on his face – his mouth downturned, staring out and saying nothing as if challenging her to continue.

'Why not this spot? Why not tonight?' he asked. 'I wanted to show it to you,' he added, after a while.

'You wanted to show me for a reason. You wanted me to work it out myself, didn't you?'

He turned to face her. 'I wanted you to work what out?'

'The thing you don't want to tell me,' Kate said, placing her arm on his shoulder. 'What you do for a living.' She felt his muscles tense beneath his shirt.

He lit a cigarette and turned fully away from her now, pretending to be absorbed in the view. There were several yachts in the bay, pinpricks of light on the water. As they watched several more came alight, flickering like stars.

Kate removed her hand from his shoulder. 'If you were an artist, like you said, you would have pointed out the studios on the way up here, or said something about the small gallery we passed. But you didn't even look at them.'

There was a long pause as he smoked. Above them the chateau was perfectly lit from storm lights around its base, and its crumbling walls stood out against the inky dark like a mirage from a dream.

'You saw me, too, didn't you?' she said. 'Yesterday.'

He took another drag. 'I saw you first. I was serving in the food truck in the station car park and I watched you head off along the coastal path.'

'Why didn't you call over? Why not say something?'

'At first, I wanted to hide so you didn't see me. But I knew you'd find out sooner or later so I went down to the restaurant and watched the beach until you returned. I wanted you to see me there.'

'So this evening was some kind of test?'

He shrugged.

'A test to see if I'd still have dinner with you even though I knew you were a waiter.'

'Something like that,' he said quietly.

She drew a step closer to him. 'And how am I doing so far in this test? Have I passed?'

He didn't answer but there was a hint of a smile on his lips.

Kate laughed. 'I don't believe for a second you're a waiter, or an artist either for that matter.'

He turned and leaned his elbow against the ramparts, looking at her fully now.

'You don't believe I'm just a waiter?'

'That's not what I said.' She reached for his cigarette, took a drag. 'What's a waiter doing driving a Ferrari for a start? I know Monaco is strange and a lot of weird things happen around here, but that's a bit upside down, even for Monaco.'

163

His face wore a look of defiance. 'Maybe if I told you what I was then it would make more sense.'

Kate felt a cold tightening of her heart. 'What you were?'

'Yes,' he said. 'What I was once, a long time ago.'

'OK,' she said cautiously. 'Tell me what you were.'

'I was a professional footballer.'

Kate laughed out loud at the absurdity of it, managing to disguise the outburst in a smoke-induced cough as she passed the cigarette back to him. This was even less credible than the story he was an artist, a gambler, or a Ferrari-driving waiter.

'I came to Monaco when I was nineteen,' he said, taking her hand and putting it on his leg, tracing the muscles around his knee. 'You don't get that from being a waiter, even on these hills.'

'I did wonder where you got that physique,' Kate managed to say, her chest tight as he kept her hand pressed to his leg. 'I thought it must be genetic.'

Kate wasn't sure if he was joking or whether this was just a ruse to get her hand on his knee. She held her breath, trying not to react to her hand now being slowly guided up his thigh.

'But why Monaco? There are no tax breaks here if you're French.'

'I'm not French, I'm Italian.'

'Italian,' she said. 'OK.'

'And Monaco isn't just about the tax.'

She laughed and pulled her hand away but he caught it and held onto it. 'They've always wanted to attract sports people here. Tennis players, footballers, racing-car drivers. It boosts the image of the place, and we get preferential treatment.'

'Like what?'

'Free entry to all the bars and clubs, free drinks, tickets to all the events. You name it.'

'So the whole team moved here?'

'Most of them stayed in Madrid – I was with a Spanish team. Only the top players came. But it was too much. I was already struggling.'

'Struggling with what?'

'The partying lifestyle. All the cocaine, the sex, the benders. I'd spend a week here off my head, then two weeks back in Spain training hard to get my fitness back. It was before the football clubs had alcohol or smoking bans, or any kind of curfew.'

She didn't say anything for a while, wondering whether he was for real. 'And how long did that last?'

'A few years. And you're right, it was all tax-free so I was earning a fortune. More money than I'd ever seen in my life. More money than anyone in my family had ever made.'

'You were a good player?'

'I was very good. The best. I was their star player, their main striker.' Anton's face was still, and he held his breath as if he couldn't maintain the conversation for much longer. Then she felt him sigh. It was slight but seemed to wrack his whole body. 'I could have been great, but I wasn't serious.'

Kate knew almost nothing about football as a game, but she knew how serious it was as a business, how much money was at stake and how crazy the fans could get. 'How serious did you need to be?'

His laugh was bitter. 'You have to take the training seriously. By the end I wasn't even turning up to that. I missed flights, spent weeks here when I should have been training. I could barely stand up some days, let alone kick a ball.'

'So what happened?'

'I was shunting back and forth from Monaco to Madrid and to games within Europe, barely holding it together, but the team was still winning. There was so much money, too much to handle. I took everything I could – more and more and more – no one ever refused me. One night I woke up in a hotel bedroom full of strangers. I didn't know how I got there or who any of them were.'

He laughed again, another bitter laugh. 'I still have no idea who they all were or where I was. After that I had a kind of breakdown. Then my mother died and I totally lost it. I knew she'd been ill but I'd neglected her for months. Then during a game I had an accident. A big problem with my hip.'

Anton's hand moved to his hip in a reflexive way, a movement she had seen him make before, rubbing it as if it still hurt.

Kate put her hand on his shoulder. 'Oh god, Anton, how dreadful.'

'I tore all the ligaments and had months of operations, but it was never the same again. At twenty-three my life was over.'

'You didn't recover?'

'I did and I still played, but I was no good. Still on the cocaine. *Finito.*' He wood-chopped the side of his palm against his other hand.

'But you stayed here?'

'I continued to live the life. I was sure things would get back on track but when you're on coke you lose yourself in a tunnel of madness. I was so far into the game, into the lifestyle, I never thought I'd come out. It was unimaginable that football would no longer be my life. What did I know about failure?'

'And your family? Did they help you?'

'My family have nothing, there was nothing they could do. Initially, the club supported me. Their insurance saw me through for a while and I did an IT course, got some work that way, but I had become addicted to painkillers and they led to heavier drugs. I kept it together though with a few computer jobs here and there, and with gambling because it turned out I had a talent for that. I thought I would start playing football again, get back to where I was, but eventually I gave up on that fantasy too.'

She moved in closer but he turned away, facing out to sea. 'You don't need to feel sorry for me. It was the life I chose.'

She wanted to tell him it wasn't his fault, that he was barely an adult then. How could he be expected to make a serious choice when no one his age knew what that meant? But the sentiment felt thin, it missed the point and she felt his loss as if it were her own. The bitter way he pulled on his cigarette showed that he had moved way beyond justifying himself and any words she could come up with now would just be wasted.

To have had such a gift so young and to have lost it before it ever fully crystallised. And then to live forever in the shadow of that loss – it was tragic.

Chapter Sixteen

THEY DIDN'T TALK MUCH ON the return trip to Monaco and Kate thought back to their first meeting. Anton had lied to her because he didn't want to admit he was a waiter, but why would she care? Why did it matter to him what she thought on that first meeting? It was clear he was ashamed about the course his life had taken, but what he had told her this evening only served to intrigue her further. She wanted to ask about the intervening twenty years – had he spent it all in Monaco? Had he married or had children? He still hadn't explained why he was driving a Ferrari either, but she didn't want to ask him about any of that, wary now of his responses. That was the thing about exposing a lie. It always leads to more questions and afterwards, whatever is presented as the truth feels like further deception.

Anton pulled up outside her apartment block in Saint Roman and despite wanting to invite him upstairs, she felt things were moving too fast in a direction she hadn't anticipated. Although he interested her, she wasn't ready to fall for whatever he might spin next and she certainly wasn't sure if she wanted to embark upon any kind of relationship with him. His stories seemed larger than life and with all that related baggage, he suddenly felt like too much to handle.

The next morning he texted her. When she didn't reply he sent another message, Checking, he said, that she hadn't gone in to work on a Saturday. He said he hoped she wasn't working too hard and she felt a stab of regret, realising she had probably told him more last night than she should have. The beautiful surroundings, the delicious wine and the relief of finding someone to talk to had relaxed her too much and she remembered making vague references to the situation she was in at work. It felt good at the time to get it off her chest, but she cringed now at how indiscreet she had been. She never discussed work socially, let alone with people she barely knew. She remembered he hadn't pressed her for details, thank god. He hadn't been surprised at what she had told him either, just nodded sympathetically as if he understood, and at least he wasn't advocating fraud, like Vanessa.

Kate responded to his text about work, but she didn't want to be drawn in further. She was sure he wasn't an artist and for all she knew this story about being a footballer could be made up too. She didn't know who the hell he was.

She remembered the tone of his voice when he told her what he had wasted. *You don't need to feel sorry for me. It was the life I chose.* The words felt genuine, more so because he had said them so lightly – as if the loss of his football career was just one of those things, like bad luck or fate, and not a real choice at all rather than the worst series of decisions he had ever made.

Kate leaned back in her chair. So much for not being drawn in further. She picked up her phone and scrolled through his messages to a picture he had sent her that morning. It was Anton when he was nineteen years old in the Real Madrid colours. She tapped on the screen and expanded the image. The blue eyes were the same but the hair was darker, the smile youthful, face unlined. At the bottom was the name *Massaro*. She typed it into the browser on her laptop and her screen lit up with images of him. There were articles too, some of which had been archived but they weren't difficult to access and she flicked through the headlines now:

In 2004, Real Madrid forked out €24 million for Massaro at the age of 19 making him the world's most expensive teenager.

Davide Massaro overtakes Cristo Berger as Real's highest paid player ever.

Massaro shoots a hat trick!!!

He had got off to a phenomenal start after joining Real Madrid, winning the Young Footballer of the Year twice, but his lust for partying soon emerged. A spate of reports splashed his indiscretions all over the front pages.

Italian maverick Davide Massaro lives one of the most hedonistic lifestyles ever known to football. As Italy prepares to face France, we delve into his wild exploits on and off the field.

Pictures of him on yachts, in sports cars, and stumbling out of nightclubs with beautiful women went on for page after page, each story more extreme than the last. He had a temper too and bitter fallouts with management were the norm when he moved to Roma in 2007. The switch was heralded as a triumphant return to his homeland but Roma paid just five million euros for him. It was at this point his exploits spiralled out of control.

Massaro disciplined after flashing spectators at World Cup qualifier.
Massaro falls out with Roma management.
Massaro strikes manager and lands him in hospital.

His whole life from the age of nineteen to twenty-three was minutely documented in print. Each night-time deed, each girl-friend, every youthful excess analysed in great detail with commentary advanced as to how it affected his game. The tabloids stalked him in a frenzy of gossip and front-page exposés. Not content to simply publish details of his personal life, they posted visuals of his accidents and falls on the pitch, linking his misfires and injuries to his drunken carousing. As the pundits grew more critical, fans began to shun him. They no longer saw his behaviour as entertainment or laddish excess: it was evidence of his contempt and disrespect for the game.

The last article was about his departure.

Massaro retired after shocking hip injury.

Once his demise was complete, there was nothing more to be said about his game and the press, for the most part, retreated triumphant, their premonitions proved correct. The spectacle had played out the way they had predicted and the tabloids and their readers basked in *Schadenfreude*. You couldn't win at everything;

you couldn't have it all. Talent plus a hedonistic lifestyle led to the scrapheap. You had to choose between them, and the name Massaro became synonymous with foolish choices as in: *he did a Massaro*, or, *his Massaro-scale partying*.

But still the papers couldn't totally let him go and each year there would be an exposé of a new, upcoming player whose habits veered towards the same decadence. The moral spotlight would spin around to examine this young player's lifestyle, visiting the same disdain on him. The name Massaro featured in such articles as a warning, and Anton became the poster boy for too much talent, too much excess, too much of everything.

Kate saw pieces as recent as last year and so it seemed even now the press continued to bait him, asking him what he thought of so-and-so a manager, or such-and-such a new player, never letting his wounds heal. Anton's response to being asked for his opinion on other players was often short and non-committal, stating things like 'he's not as good as he thinks he is,' which the press took as evidence of his enduring bitterness.

Kate had been reading about Anton, enthralled, for over an hour and was deep in an article where he was trash-talking another player when a message appeared on her screen. Seeing his profile picture flash up above a news article about him was surreal.

Ciao bella

She waited half an hour and then replied. They texted for a while until curiosity got the better of her and she agreed to meet him at a café nearby.

He wore a shirt that same shade of blue.

'Bonjour, Davide,' she said. 'Or is it Antonio?'

He shook his head. 'It's Anton. And I'm not hiding anything. I knew you'd find out sooner or later. I've told you most of it anyway.'

The images she had seen of his exploits off the field had stayed with her and they now swam through her mind, more vivid than on screen. She felt little more than curiosity at the time, but seeing him here in the flesh she felt strangely jealous of all those women twenty years ago. Although she registered the feeling as a warning against further entanglement, the stories of his wild carousing excited her.

He told her he had just come off his shift at the restaurant, but was due back that evening.

They didn't stay long in the café and in the lift of her building they kissed. When they entered her apartment however, Kate had second thoughts. She left him in the sitting room and went to the kitchen, started rattling around with cups and glasses. It was too early for wine but too late for coffee and in any case he was going back to work. She stood there frozen in front of the cupboard. Water, she said under her breath, taking two glasses from the shelf and filling a jug from the tap. Then she reconsidered, taking a bottle of wine from the fridge and two more glasses, setting it all on a tray.

When she returned to the sitting room he was looking at the photos on her bookshelf.

'Is this your boyfriend?' he said, holding a picture of Kate on a beach with some friends from London. In the picture, Kate's hand was on the shoulder of her ex, Simon.

The photo had been on a corner shelf that caught the afternoon sun and it was now faded and curled at the edges. It had been taken just last year but it now seemed ancient. It was odd to see this photo of washed-out Simon in the hands of this tanned, mysterious man and she was struck by the stark difference between them.

'No,' she said loudly. 'I mean, yes, he *was*. He was technically my boyfriend, but it's over now. We broke up just before I came here.'

He smiled and looked back to the photo. 'You don't need to explain anything, or hide it from me.'

'I'm not hiding anything from you,' she said, thinking that was a bit rich coming from him.

He replaced Simon's picture on the shelf, leaving it a little more prominent than before which she felt was deliberate.

'But speaking of hiding – all those news stories about you. My god, they don't leave you alone, do they? Even now.'

'That's why I changed my name,' he said, refusing the water and taking the wine. 'Even though I was no longer playing, the papers kept hounding me, scouring my social media, interviewing my so-called friends, desperate to see how much further I'd fallen.'

'And you obliged them for a while.'

'Everyone loves a rags to riches story, but they couldn't get enough of the riches to rags.'

'Or riches to rages in your case.'

'The ending was ugly,' he said, draining his glass and pouring another. He went onto the balcony for a cigarette and she watched him from the sofa. She wanted to know more about his past. He had lost so much and should be wallowing in remorse and self-pity, but he seemed untroubled and free, or at least a lot freer than she was with her stressful job, her anxiety and family pressures.

When he came back inside he took the tray of drinks to the bedroom without any discussion and she followed him, almost retreating when she saw the state of her room. She hadn't tidied up all week and the floor was strewn with clothes. The problems at work had unsettled her and she had felt the need to wear more protective clothing to the office. She had rejected the kind of flimsy dresses everyone wore to work in Monaco, and had dug into the back of her wardrobe for the dark business suits she used to wear in London. But it was too hot for the suits, which she had left draped over the furniture together with shirts and several abandoned pairs of tights.

'Sorry about the mess,' she said, bundling the clothes onto the seat of an armchair as he poured more wine. 'It's not usually this bad.'

He took his wine, pushed the clothes off the chair and sat down. 'Show me what it's usually like in here then?'

She took a sip of wine, startled by his change in tone. 'What?'

'Take off your shirt.'

Kate baulked at this demand, but was intrigued by his face, now very focused. She glanced at the clothes on the floor – all those awful bits of cloth that caused her daily anguish and she began unbuttoning her shirt, letting it fall to the floor as well. She kicked it over to join the tangled mess of clothing at his feet.

'Take off your bra,' he said and instead of being repulsed she was ceding to his demands, Kate felt an overwhelming sense of relief that things were taking place beyond her control.

'Now go and stand by the window and take off the rest.'

She stood in front of him for a moment, maintaining eye contact as she finished her wine. Then she walked to the window.

'Leave it,' he said, as she reached to pull the blind. 'I want to see you in the light.'

She hesitated, glancing across the street to see whether anyone was watching. Most windows were dark beyond the panes, some shuttered and so it was impossible to know. She stood there, suspended between fear and excitement as she undid her belt and let her trousers drop to the floor. Slowly she removed her underwear until finally she was naked, watching him as he sat there among her discarded clothes, a master of disorder. She felt exposed to the open window, the apartments and the street behind her.

Kate went over to the bed. 'You do the same,' she said.

He stood at the side of the bed, started taking off his shirt.

'No, over there. At the window, like I did.'

He stood above her for a moment, as if considering whether to comply. With his blue shirt and the sky outside he looked the way he had when they met. He went to the window, turned away from her and removed his shirt. Then he undid his trousers and slid them down his legs.

He paused for a moment presenting himself to the window, his left hand on his hip so his back was perfectly arched, triceps flexed, shoulder blades jutting out. From where she lay, she could only see the back of him, but if she didn't believe he had been a sportsman before, she did now. A network of muscles crossed his back, his spine curving in an arc from his neck, dipping between his shoulders to his waist, before disappearing into the cleft of his buttocks. She couldn't see his pelvis, but his thighs were long and lean, still well defined, and the assembly of muscles around his knees were like knotted ropes.

He was beautiful, still with the physique he would have had twenty years ago and she felt a surge of lust tinged with loss for

176

what he had been. It was a body that had endured, built in his youth when he was full of purpose, his muscles still developing, and it would be like that, more or less, his entire life no matter what he did, or didn't do. She wasn't sure whether that was a good or bad thing. It was like carrying around a relic of the past that had ceased to have any relevance, and yet it was a monument to something important no gym routine could ever replicate.

He came over and lay beside her and it was almost too much. The afternoon wine was making her head spin and her mind spooled back to the rush of images she had seen of him online, these thoughts of his past, then him here now, his smell, his touch.

She could hardly bear to look at those blue eyes either, so she buried her face in his chest, kissing his torso. She touched the scar on his hip – an ugly red gash that had been hacked and crossed again in the course of the multiple operations he had told her about. The brutality of the mutilation made the rest of his body more striking, and she stroked the skin on his scar taut and hairless like silk.

Afterwards, he apologised. 'I'm sorry,' he said. 'I need to go.'

She drew away from him as he checked his watch then glanced around as if suddenly aware of where he was, almost shocked as he sprang from the bed. He looked at the sheets strewn across the floor, then at her. 'I'm late already.'

'Late for what?'

'For work,' he said, looking worried as he ran his hands through his hair. 'For the restaurant. I need to leave.'

He dressed quickly, leaving his shirt unbuttoned as he tucked it into his jeans. 'Let me take you out this week. I'll get the evening off and we'll go up into the hills to a place I know.

A beautiful hotel, Michelin-starred restaurant. We can eat there and stay the night. It's less than an hour away.'

His words were breathless, panicked even.

'All right,' she said, so affronted by his sudden desperation to leave that she almost let him make his own way out.

'This is for you,' he said, giving her a package he had carried with him from the café, then pecking her cheek before racing down the stairs.

She opened the parcel distractedly, still at the door as if she expected him to return but she could hear his footsteps receding, taking the steps two at a time.

The package contained a tiny painted portrait of her about five inches square. In the background was the lit up castle at Roquebrune, the starry night and the sea swirling around her in a haze of blue. It was beautiful, he could paint. Kate was flattered, but at the same time shocked by the abruptness of his departure.

He hadn't even finished his wine.

Chapter Seventeen
Roquebrune-Cap-Martin

ELANKA WANDERED THROUGH THE GUEST rooms of Casa di Stelle, her cream Louboutins clipping softly on the newly laid parquet floors. She opened the door of the furthest bedroom and wrinkled her nose. The decorators had only left last week and the smell of paint lingered in the room, giving the whole floor a just-finished feel. This was a little disappointing. Elanka didn't want their guests to think fresh paint was the ambiance she had been striving for or worse still, that anything had been patched up or done in a hurry. She thought of the suite she had just left at the Hôtel de Paris in Monaco, how it had smelled of musk and spice like the Tuscan hills. She would ask the maids to fill the rooms with bowls of potpourri and in the meantime, Elanka opened the French doors that led from each of the rooms to the balcony. She would leave the rooms to air for the rest of the day, she decided, as she stepped outside. From the wide, colonnaded terrace that wrapped around the villa there was a direct view over the bay – a perfect horseshoe of glittering blue with craggy rocks at either end. Tourists were walking along the path towards the cape, and others were sunbathing on the shore in front of the house. When Elanka was alone, she liked to watch people on the beach from the balcony of the private salon on the floor above. It was the highest room in the house and the acoustics of the bay meant she could often hear people's voices and their laughter too. Amir hated the laughter most of all. If he heard people on his beach he would order one of the security guards down there with the dogs to scare them off.

Elanka and Amir had arrived at the property earlier that morning for their summer vacation. Elanka had phoned ahead and asked the chef to prepare dinner for twenty guests that evening, and then told the maids to make sure all the beds were ready for those who would be staying overnight. Elanka was doing a circuit of the bedrooms now to check that everything was in order, and apart from the smell, everything was perfect. The redecorating work over the winter had been painstaking but Elanka saw now that it had been worth it. She wondered whether her guests would notice that the mouldings on the ceiling had been painted with real gold leaf using the tiniest of brushes. A friend of hers in London, a fellow Lithuanian, had put her in touch with two artists from Vilnius who specialised in historic restoration work. They had even done work for the British royal family. The men had worked for months on the guest rooms alone, their ladders propped outside on the balcony causing the locals to wonder why the owner was renovating the property again when it had only just been refurbished last year.

Elanka had been Amir's girlfriend for four years now and she knew what was coming. Next year she would be twenty-six: closer to thirty than to twenty. Amir was already forty but with advancing age came a taste for younger women. Elanka made sure she dressed youthfully whenever she was with him, but she knew he lived like a playboy, as so many of them did. Of course she knew she wasn't his only girlfriend, but she was content to be the *official* one, meaning she was the woman he woke up with most often. She had asked him already about the future, about marriage and babies, but he had laughed in her face.

He had a point, she was only twenty-five, but she knew what would happen once he tired of her. The Birkin bags, the diamonds and the couture dresses would be gone and she would be sent on her way with little more than the clothes on her back, like a member of staff who had been abruptly dismissed. She had seen it happen to the mistresses and girlfriends of other men, with security watching over them as they packed their bags to make sure they didn't take the jewellery. The only woman who continued to have any standing in Amir's life after they had split up was the mother of his five-year-old son, Roman. Amir had married Roman's mother, Selena, just before she gave birth so as not to render his son a bastard. He had discarded her soon after Roman was born, but they were still married and Selena was well looked-after with a townhouse in London close to Amir's mansion in Highgate and the school Amir wanted Roman to attend. Elanka didn't know the entire story between Amir and Selena, or whether they still slept together when he was in London, but Selena had played her hand well. She had been clever.

Elanka needed to be clever too.

She had come to the south of France as a model seven years ago. She had been due to go back to Lithuania to start an economics degree after the first year, but her father lost his job and since Elanka was earning decent money in France, she stayed on for the sake of her family. With her fair, Nordic complexion Elanka hadn't been one of the most sought-after girls on the coast – the agencies always wanted more bronzed skin for the swimwear jobs, but the work had been steady, particularly in Monaco where she had also worked as a hostess on the yachts. It was easy work and the girls were just required to stand around on deck and make the boats look enticing during the yacht shows. Of course there were girls who did other kinds of work on the yachts when they were out at sea, but Elanka had avoided that. During her third summer, Elanka moved into an apartment with some Ukrainian girls in Ventimiglia, just over the Italian border. A couple of them worked as hostesses at Casa di Stelle and that was where Elanka met Amir.

Elanka overheard a lot when she was with Amir. She usually stayed quiet, pretending to be occupied on her phone but she was always listening in to his calls and meetings and she came to understand Amir's business dealings. Although Elanka hadn't taken up her university studies, finance and economics still interested her and she combed the business pages each day, building her knowledge and reading whatever she could get her hands on about Amir's deals.

She knew Amir was not one of those men who were threatened by intelligent women, but she had never met a man who really liked it, so she was careful not to show off any particular expertise. Mostly she kept quiet when he spoke about work. Sometimes he asked for her advice about a problem if there was no one else around and he always seemed pleased with the responses she gave.

Last year, Elanka had advised Amir to pull out of a sports betting company in the UK after she read it was facing bribery charges in Turkey. She knew from listening in to his calls to Rob that he was over-exposed in this company. At first, Amir was reluctant to sell his shares, but it turned out to be excellent advice when a month later the company went under. Amir had taken his money out just in time and after that narrow escape, he gave Elanka control of several companies in Cyprus which ran lucrative gambling ventures in the region. Seeing as she had shown such an affinity with the sector, her job was to oversee those ventures and to keep him informed of the money that flowed in and out of the accounts.

Elanka loved Casa di Stelle and she loved the Côte d'Azur, but the past year had been quiet with the departure of a lot of Russian friends and this season looked like being quiet too because of all the sanctions. There were fewer wealthy people around and the parties weren't as frequent or as lavish as they used to be. Each setback however held the seeds of opportunity and the sanctions regime was no different. Elanka had heard that many oligarchs had put their assets into the names of trusted family members as a precautionary measure to avoid the effect of sanctions and although he wasn't sanctioned yet, she knew Amir was thinking of doing the same. The problem for Elanka was that Amir was thinking of putting Casa di Stelle into his wife Selena's name. It would be better for Roman if anything happened to Amir, he said, and while Elanka didn't like the idea – Selena already had the townhouse in London after all – it was difficult to argue with the logic.

The relationship between Amir and Selena had thawed quite a lot recently. Roman was growing up and Amir found him fascinating. So much so that Selena and Roman had joined them on a yacht trip to Sardinia at the beginning of May. Roman was very sweet and Elanka liked having a child on board, but it was humiliating to have to take Selena on shopping trips and lunches with the other wives and mistresses while the men stayed on the yacht discussing business. Selena had criticised Elanka's restaurant choices, and had generally lorded it over her all weekend. Elanka put up with it though because it suited her for Amir to have a good relationship with his son and to visit him regularly in London, but she was worried about what this thaw in relations meant for her own future.

Rob had been on the Sardinian yacht trip too. Elanka knew Rob's father had managed a lot of Amir's uncle's financial affairs and that Amir and Rob were like brothers. Amir and his family trusted Rob so much he had made Rob the enforcer of all his offshore trust arrangements. This meant that Rob could quickly restructure and rearrange ownership of Amir's assets to take advantage of tax breaks or simply to hide Amir's ownership if necessary. Several of Amir's companies in Belarus were being investigated on suspicion of profiting from the Russian war in Ukraine and Amir was worried that it was only a matter of time before he was sanctioned too. Although Rob was on the yacht to discuss the restructuring of Amir's assets in anticipation of these sanctions, he also used it as an opportunity to pitch LuckyCoin.

One morning at breakfast, Elanka saw the chance she had been waiting for.

It was the last day of the trip and everyone else had left. The three of them were seated around the breakfast table and Rob was outlining LuckyCoin to Amir, trying to interest him in coming on board as one of the anchor investors.

Suddenly, Amir turned to Elanka. 'This is partly a gambling deal, Elanka. What do you think of it?' he said.

Elanka had been pretending to only half-listen as usual while she inspected her nails and scrolled through Instagram. She thought the scheme sounded terrible and she was stunned at the new depths to which Rob had sunk. People would have to be desperate to buy into the product, she thought, whilst at the same time marvelling at the logic – desperate people were exactly the market Rob was targeting. There had been a series of articles in the papers that week about another crash in crypto, but Bitcoin and other currencies were still flourishing, so perhaps Rob had a point. He was renowned for pulling off crazy deals no one else would touch with a bargepole.

'I'm sorry, I wasn't listening closely,' Elanka said.

Rob looked surprised that Amir was asking Elanka for her opinion but he was more than happy to outline the scheme again. When Rob had finished, Elanka sat back and smiled. At the same time as she had been listening to Rob another, more interesting opportunity had occurred to her.

She turned to Amir. 'I think it's quite a good idea. Why not make an investment of seed capital.'

A few weeks later, Rob sought out Elanka when she was alone at the villa. The crypto market had slumped again and many of the investors Rob had lined up for LuckyCoin had pulled out. Amir had gone cold on the idea too, and for all his bluster, it was Rob who was now exposed and desperate. He had put a lot of his own money into the scheme and he needed to offset the risk with another significant backer.

'I've seen you pull off worse deals,' said Elanka.

Rob moved in close. 'I'm telling you, crypto still has a long way to go. The Chinese love it and it's the main currency of the black market so it's never going away.'

'Amir has some money in Cyprus he needs to deal with. It's gambling money so it might be a good fit.'

'It would be an excellent fit!' said Rob, beaming.

Desperation was written all over him, in fact he was quivering with it and Elanka knew she had him in her hand, like a helpless little bird.

'There's something I need you to do in return,' said Elanka.

'If you can get me that money, it'll be done yesterday.'

Elanka explained why she didn't think it was a good idea for Amir to put Casa di Stelle into Selena's name. It would be much better if the villa went into Elanka and her mother's names.

'If Amir is sanctioned, he'll go back to the UK, where the rules are much more lenient. He'll be on a travel ban but I want to stay in France. I can't live at Casa di Stelle if Selena owns it, and she doesn't need it. She has her place in London, after all.'

'If you can get me that Cyprus money this weekend, there'll be no need to put the property into Selena's name,' said Rob and they shook on it.

Here's a crafty one, thought Rob in the car on the way back to Monaco, but surely not foolish enough to double cross Amir. He didn't trust Elanka and felt uneasy about their deal, but he needed the money, which he would pay back of course once other investors came on board next month which they were sure to do. Amir didn't need to know. In the meantime, Rob knew Elanka was well-supervised so she wouldn't do anything stupid. Once the Cyprus money was in the London account he could rearrange the beneficiaries to include Selena and then spin Elanka some story about how it was necessary to do that for tax reasons. In the meantime, if Amir found out, he would say Elanka and her mother, with their Lithuanian passports, were much better beneficiaries for the French property than Selena. Selena was Amir's wife and mother of his son so she could be liable to sanctions too.

That had been two weeks ago and so far things had gone according to plan. Elanka had forwarded the seven million from Cyprus to Monaco as Rob had asked, and Casa di Stelle had been transferred into Elanka and her mother's names.

The incident on the roof of the nightclub in London had been unpleasant. Elanka had discovered that sure enough, a week after transferring the property to Elanka and her mother, Rob had made Selena a beneficiary too. Elanka happened to be in London and tracked Rob down, confronting him at the nightclub in Smithfield. She threatened to expose Rob to Amir, saying that if he didn't correct the situation, she would tell Amir that Rob had tricked her into transferring the Cyprus money for LuckyCoin. Rob had been very drunk and he had lunged at her while they were arguing on the rooftop.

Elanka had been frightened. She had hit out at Rob first, slapping him hard on the cheek and he had grabbed her throat. While she was struggling against him someone appeared on the rooftop, thank god. It had been enough to bring Rob to his senses and he had backed off. He knew Elanka meant business though, and the next day he made sure Selena was taken off the list of beneficiaries.

Elanka felt powerful. She had used her wits to manipulate Rob and she was on her way to full control of the villa. Amir would soon be in London, sanctioned and on a travel ban – probably for a very long time. He might even be arrested if anyone could prove his links to the Russian weapons business.

All she needed to do now was bide her time. She had one more trick up her sleeve but that could wait until after he was sanctioned. Casa di Stelle was enough for now. It would keep her busy. She might even move the swimming pool.

Elanka looked down to the beach. It was noisier than usual. The new hostesses had arrived for the party that evening and she watched them near the restaurant with concern. These new ones were very young and not at all sophisticated. According to Amir they had made a nuisance of themselves on the beach a few days ago and there had been complaints.

Elanka finished her circuit of the first floor and then took one last look over the bay and smiled. It was a beautiful part of the world. And soon it would be hers.

Chapter Eighteen

Monaco

VANESSA FELT BETTER AFTER HER morning workout, but a clearer mind brought sharper focus, which today was unwelcome. She had lost over a thousand euros at roulette last night and she cringed at the memory as she sipped her coffee. Croupiers weren't supposed to make eye contact, but theirs had looked at her with concern as she bet stupidly and laid down more than she could afford.

Each September, Vanessa paid David's annual school fees in advance. Then each month, she set aside her rent and the money she needed to live on, as well as cash for anything David might require. This money was always ring-fenced but the remainder was hers to use as she pleased. There had always been enough in this pot to cover her casino indulgences, but lately she was losing more and dipping into her savings too.

Vanessa went onto the balcony. The sailing boats shimmered in the marina, their masts swaying gently on the breeze. Apart from last night at the casino it had been a pleasant weekend, largely because she hadn't heard from Rob. He was in Kenya, scoping out opportunities for LuckyCoin and would return via Nigeria later in the week.

Vanessa never understood why Rob insisted on visiting the countries the money came from. He said it was important to gauge the atmosphere of the place and to feel its potential. His view was that problems occurred when you removed yourself too far from the source of your wealth. Look at all those Silicon Valley start-ups, he would say, rattling off a list of the latest disasters. Those execs had no idea where their funds came from. It was all just silly money, figures on a page.

Vanessa didn't know exactly how much money Rob had personally, but she knew about his investments, some of which had been successful but there were many which hadn't. Rob didn't have as much money as his clients, of course, but he had a lot more than most partners at Meritus and over the years, Rob had bought everything he could possibly need – the mansion in Highgate, a fine art collection, a manor house in Norfolk, a Maserati for the city and a Range Rover for weekends. He had things he had no time to enjoy and he had no family to enjoy them either. Although Vanessa had no desire for these kinds of possessions, she understood the drive to accumulate assets, and she thought Rob's obsession with money was not dissimilar to her gambling urge. He hadn't grown up poor like a lot of people motivated by money – it was the thrill of the chase that fascinated Rob, rather than anything he could actually buy with it. Money was also a symbol of power of course, a way of declaring his status to his clients and to others like him. To Rob, money was an end in itself.

Although he didn't really seem to enjoy the things he bought with his money, Rob had a visceral sense for it that went beyond anything rational. Vanessa had seen him fondle the cash in his wallet, shuffling it, then carefully flipping and folding each note.

Sometimes, after he had run his fingers through his cash like this, he would steeple his hands in front of his face, close his eyes and inhale gently as though he were savouring truffles or fine wine. It was as if he sensed how hard people had toiled to get the money as far as his wallet and he wanted to appreciate the smell of all that sweat and labour.

'But you'll see the potential damage too,' said Vanessa quietly when she was in London. Rob had been boasting about his forthcoming trip to Africa, telling Vanessa and Lensley how he planned to go out to the villages and meet the LuckyCoin ambassadors. It made her uncomfortable the way he spoke so freely about the people they were planning to exploit.

'You're asking people to invest their life savings into this scheme when you know there's no prospect of a return.'

There was barely a pause.

'I don't see it like that,' he said, looking at her straight on. 'It's money. It's an opportunity.'

While Vanessa rarely had any qualms about the deals she did for Rob, she thought it would be different if she actually met the individuals they were ripping off.

Vanessa had spent the week working on LuckyCoin, setting up the companies and the bank accounts that would collect the money coming in from LuckyCoin members via the offshore network Rob had devised and that Lensley had put in place. Some money had already come in and Vanessa had been shocked at the amounts – sometimes only the equivalent of ten pounds because that was all those people could afford.

Vanessa had made contact with several of the ambassadors to discuss how they would go about promoting LuckyCoin in their communities. She had made it clear there would be bonuses for those who recruited the most new members and incentives for early adopters. One of the first ambassadors in Nigeria was a woman called Faith, a nurse who had worked in Guinea during the Ebola outbreaks several years previously. Vanessa and Faith were meant to be discussing LuckyCoin, but somehow they got talking about Ebola and how Faith had risked her life to help the community in Guinea deal with the outbreak. Such an act of selflessness was beyond Vanessa's comprehension and she listened with awe and growing unease as Faith spoke about her work, then expressed her gratitude for the LuckyCoin opportunity. She had resigned from her job as a nurse and would be working on promoting and selling LuckyCoin full time, encouraging people in her community to invest in the scheme. Faith didn't know LuckyCoin was a scam and Vanessa couldn't tell her of course. All Vanessa could do was listen as Faith grew more excited, believing she was going to make so much more money as an ambassador than she would if she continued to work as a nurse. Faith was full of ideas about how she would bring that prosperity to her community. She had already encouraged her sons to invest in LuckyCoin and she hoped when they cashed out they would be able to open the small grocery store they had always dreamed of.

When she hung up from the call with Faith, Vanessa felt ill and breathless. She realised that as a LuckyCoin ambassador, Faith would not only be complicit in Rob's depraved scheme to rip off poor Africans, she would be diverted from other, much more crucial healthcare work within her community.

This was exactly why she didn't like speaking to people at the other end of the deals, Vanessa thought desperately. It was just like the experience with the cash mule. She had warned Rob she would be no good on the marketing and sales side. She preferred to stay firmly with the money and a long way away from any people who might be affected.

Like Rob, Vanessa had always been interested in money, but not for the sake of it or for what it could buy – she was never that interested in the trappings of wealth. What Vanessa most liked was the freedom money represented; its fluidity. She saw the way money found its way around barriers, overcame obstacles and eased the flow of life.

That was happening much less, however, and lately, Vanessa's freedoms had become unenjoyable, constrained as they were by intrusive thoughts of LuckyCoin and the people it would affect. It was why she was gambling so much. Visiting the casino had always been a way to unwind, a means to connect with the raw power of money and to be among its other disciples. Recently, however, she had to spend more to achieve the same result and her increasing losses only amplified her problems. In Monaco, money was everywhere, but her own source was draining fast.

On Sunday afternoon, Vanessa drove Kate to Nice to visit some furniture stores as she had promised. After they had bought a couple of rugs, a lamp and several few small pieces for Kate's apartment, they stopped for a late lunch in the Old Town.

They dwelled for a while on Kate's decoration plans and afterwards, Vanessa asked what Kate had decided to do. She was concerned she had been too glib with her advice last week and she didn't want Kate getting the wrong idea.

'Decided to do about what?'

'Listen to you. About that transaction you mentioned the other night.'

Kate reddened.

'The one you've been thinking about all afternoon. You've been quite distracted.'

'I shouldn't have told you about it.'

'But you did.'

Kate put down her cutlery. 'Julia's been on my back all week.'

'And so what have you said?'

'Nothing. I don't want to do it, but what choice do I have?'

Vanessa toyed with her salad. 'You do have a choice, but if you don't do it, they'll give the job to someone else.'

'Well that would be fine by me,' Kate said, knowing that wasn't true. She wouldn't be able to stand by and watch as the men lost their cases.

'And then they'll freeze you out. Meritus won't keep you on if you don't play the game.'

Kate sat back. 'And what game is that?'

'The game where you work for them and they pay you a salary. The game called employment. You're familiar with that one, right?'

'Hmm.'

'If you don't do it, they'll starve you of work, your billings will go down and they'll use that as an excuse to fire you.'

'I need this job,' Kate said, glancing around the sunlit terrace, realising how quickly she had fallen for the place. 'I want to stay. I want to be part of it all. I'm just trying to think of a way to make it work for me, as you said the other night.'

Vanessa's stomach lurched. In her enthusiasm to tell Kate how it was, had she given too much away? She cringed inwardly as she remembered how she had enjoyed holding forth in the face of Kate's inexperience. Vanessa leaned in closer, her voice dropping in tone. 'I'm not saying you should do it. I don't want you to think that.'

'Right,' said Kate.

'There's a lot here I don't like. A lot of the work is really unpalatable.'

'Yes, I'm beginning to see that.'

Vanessa poked at the remains of her salad. 'I wish I'd gone years ago, but I know that if I didn't do this work, someone else would.'

'That's a terrible justification. One notch up from just following orders.'

'But you know it's true. It's the only reason any of us do it.' Vanessa sat back as the waiter removed their plates. 'All I'm saying is that if you decide to go ahead with it, then be careful and cover your tracks. Put nothing in writing.'

'Nothing traceable,' Kate said, nodding. A possibility was taking shape in her mind.

They had coffee and then paid the bill. As they were walking back to the car, Vanessa received a call from David's school.

'Mrs Giraud, this is Emily from Meetham. Don't be alarmed, David's fine. This concerns his friend, Lai.'

Emily told Vanessa that in accordance with the school's privacy policy she couldn't disclose any details, but Lai had left the school abruptly the previous day. Emily wanted to let Vanessa know that David was very upset.

'It's all rather sudden, I'm afraid.'

'What on earth has happened?' Vanessa said, thinking Lai must have been expelled. She hoped David hadn't been drawn into whatever it was – drugs, drinking, or worse. She had heard stories of what boys got up to at public schools, and David was almost a teenager. Vanessa braced herself and waited for Emily to elaborate.

Emily said it wasn't anything Lai had done, and that the school hadn't been aware Lai had left until that morning. She sounded embarrassed and Vanessa felt a rush of panic, thinking back to how familiar David had been in Jonathan's car. She had forgotten to speak to the headmaster.

'Can I speak to David?' Vanessa asked.

'We've not been able to console him. He won't speak to anyone.'

'I'll try calling him now. Do you have a number for Lai's parents?'

'I'm sorry Mrs Giraud, we can't disclose that.'

It was only later that Vanessa got hold of David. At first he refused to tell her anything about Lai, but finally she coaxed some details from him. Lai's father had been arrested earlier that week at Heathrow airport and the family's assets had been frozen, including their UK homes and bank accounts. Lai's mother had arrived with Jonathan on Saturday morning to take Lai away. He'd only had half an hour to pack his things and David hadn't been there to say goodbye.

'I have to go now, Mum, my battery's running low.'

She could tell he was making it up, but she let it go.

'I'll call you tomorrow.'

'I'm on a school trip, Mum, I won't be able to talk.'

'When are you back?'

'Next Sunday.'

'I'll call then,' said Vanessa, making a note in her diary. 'It's not long until your birthday. Perhaps Lai could come to Monaco in the holidays.'

196

When Vanessa hung up she thought about Lai's family. She remembered speaking briefly to Lai's father at the school picnic and although they had spoken about work, she couldn't remember any details.

Perhaps she should go and visit David sooner than his birthday, she thought, but then quickly dismissed the idea. There was all this work to do for Rob before he returned on Friday.

How did her life get so complicated that she couldn't even be there for her child, Vanessa thought, pouring another glass of wine. She saw the clock. It was 7 p.m. How did it get so late? Time, like everything else, was something she could barely keep track of. She remembered thinking she would work for Rob for two years maximum, and that was almost ten years ago.

She took a sip of wine and went to her room to get dressed. She had a date with an oil trader that evening.

Oil! She nearly choked on her wine. As Aviation Minister, oil was what Lai's father was involved in of course, she remembered now. At the picnic they had discussed people they knew in common and it turned out she had even done a deal for someone he knew years ago when she worked in London.

Vanessa took her glass to the computer and accessed the firm's database, searching for the name of Lai's father which she found online. There was nothing recent, only a list of closed matters Meritus had worked on. The firm had definitely worked for him when he was Aviation Minister, but the details had been erased. Vanessa googled him and saw news reports of his arrest as part of a corruption investigation. *Fraud, bribery, extortion, embezzlement, cronyism and nepotism.* These were all unpleasant words.

Lai's father was from Nigeria, and Nigeria was where Rob was this week with LuckyCoin. It wasn't clear what Meritus had done for Lai's father in the past, and although there was no direct link between Meritus and the current investigation into Lai's father, the information unnerved her.

It was late when she arrived home. The date with the oil trader hadn't gone well, mainly because he had let slip during the main course that he was married. Normally that wouldn't bother her, but he looked a bit like Pascal, so she made her excuses and left. On the way home she went to the casino in an attempt to win back her losses from the previous night.

Standing alone in the mirrored lobby of her apartment she saw her sallow complexion with her cheeks all sunk and drawn. She barely recognised herself and she looked the way she felt – spent and dejected. She had lost badly again – several thousand this time, and she went to bed quietly, taking her make-up off quickly and without care.

That night she dreamed of roulette. She was lying naked, spread-eagled on a green felt table with a roulette wheel sunk into her belly. It was turning and money of all denominations was spewing from her mouth in a stream of notes, coins, betting slips and tokens. As the cash emptied from her she felt weaker and giddier, the wheel churning in her belly. All around the table, witnessing this terrible purging, were the faceless people she had exploited. They were pressing in towards her, getting angrier as they got closer until they were yelling with their fists in the air, demanding their money back as the wheel turned and the cash gushed from her.

And behind them all stood Lai's father, egging them on.

Chapter Nineteen

K ATE DIDN'T HEAR FROM ANTON in the hours following his abrupt departure. She drank the wine they had opened as she tidied up, untangling the clothes on the floor and making the bed, while trying to understand why he had left so suddenly. Would it have been such a problem if he was just a little late for work? It was a casual beachside restaurant, hardly the Hôtel de Paris. And there was the thing about the money too. Why had he suggested an extravagant evening with an overnight stay at a place less than an hour away when he worked as a waiter in a restaurant? Did he expect her to pay? Such thoughts felt mean and judgemental, and she didn't want to dwell on them, but the difference in their circumstances was going to come up sooner or later.

Of course there were differences in their circumstances. Anton was unlike anyone she had ever met and she realised now how infatuated she had become with him. Wasn't this one of the reasons she had come to Monaco in the first place? Hadn't she secretly hoped for mystery and passion, a change from her mundane life in London? Seeing Anton holding the faded picture of her ex-boyfriend, Simon was like watching a modern human contemplate an amphibian ancestor. They were practically separate species.

As she finished the last of the wine, Kate recalled his body at the window, his skin glowing in the light. Anton seemed to operate on a much broader canvas than she did and she felt the constraints of her limited world now that she'd had an insight into his. He had seen so much more of life than she had, and despite what he had been through, he was at ease with himself and free – unlike her, boxed in with anxiety and stress.

Later that evening, Kate sent him a text thanking him for the portrait. She took a photograph and used it as her profile picture on WhatsApp. She checked the app several times during her shopping trip with Vanessa on Sunday to see whether he had read her message, but he remained offline.

Monday at work was taken up with Falkon Racing. The timetable was set now for the litigation and the discovery documents were due to be exchanged with the other side in two weeks' time. Rob called Kate by video and said he wanted to present the *new evidence*, as he called it, to the client early the following week and asked her to make sure the document was in his inbox when he was back in Monaco on Friday morning. He smiled as he said this in acknowledgement perhaps of the generous timetable he had just allocated her. Like most frauds, it was almost absurd in its simplicity: just a short deed the client would need to sign and backdate, and it wouldn't take Kate long to draft but although she tried, she couldn't bring herself to start. Instead, she procrastinated: rearranging the documents in the file and shifting paper around.

Kate was cleaning her desk when Julia darted in.

'My goodness! What are you doing?' Julia said breathlessly, closing the door behind her. 'We have cleaners for that.'

Kate sprayed cleaning product over the desk, filling the air with pungent mist as she explained she had spilled some coffee.

'It smells terrible. I can't concentrate and it seems to be getting worse,' she said, wiping down the sides of the desk.

Julia watched as Kate scrubbed non-existent coffee off her desk, and then leaned in close, putting her hand on Kate's. 'I've just spoken to Rob. You've agreed to go ahead with the plan. That's excellent.'

Julia beamed at her. 'As I said, we'll reward you well for this.'

Her face was so close to Kate's that she could see tiny pricks of sweat in the pores on Julia's nose.

Heat rose up Kate's neck, constricting her throat as she pulled her hand away. She wasn't confident in her ability to speak.

Julia stepped back and scanned the desk. She picked up the Falkon Racing documents, smiling as she browsed through the correspondence. 'And it's not just money we're talking about,' she said cheerfully, as if speaking to a child.

Julia went to Kate's shelves and started flicking through other files, making unhelpful comments on several of those cases, before rounding back to Falkon. She was showing no sign of leaving anytime soon, so Kate sat down. Julia didn't elaborate further on how much Kate's integrity was worth, but there was a gleam in her eye as she raised the topic of Kate's three-month appraisal. It wasn't due yet, but Julia said they wanted to accelerate the decision, bringing an end to Kate's probationary period and formalising her position in Monaco right now with an immediate pay rise and an increase in benefits. Kate was doing such an excellent job, was proving to be such an *asset* that they knew now, even after such a short time in the role, that they wanted her to stay.

'The appraisal's just a formality. It'll be good to get it out of the way. Even this week if you like,' Julia said casually as she left the room.

For the rest of the afternoon, Julia visited regularly to discuss an aspect of the case, airing her optimistic views as to how the litigation would proceed after the *new evidence* had been presented. Once or twice Julia came in and repeated what she had said just an hour earlier, but with a slight variation and in a manner Kate perceived as a concerted effort to unnerve her. Kate felt her stress levels rising and she was tempted to get the document done then and there, just to get Julia off her back.

Things seemed to be moving beyond her control, shifting of their own accord, and the more Julia harassed Kate about the case, the less sure Kate was of her own views and the more isolated she felt. She hadn't decided to do it yet. She needed to think properly through the options before they all disappeared and she was left with just one way ahead. She needed to speak to someone she could trust. Kate tried calling Marc but his voicemail said he was in London for a few days. It would have been easy to pick up the phone to Vanessa, but she would just repeat the advice she had already given.

Kate remembered how non-judgemental Anton had been at dinner when she spoke about work, how she barely needed to explain her situation. Anton had lived along this coast for twenty years, after all, so he must understand the culture of the place.

Everyone had warned her Monaco was its own little micro-cosm, how it wasn't that its residents thought they were subject to a different set of laws, it was more they thought they weren't subject to any laws at all. Kate already knew a different morality applied in the place – she could see it in the faces of those who sunned themselves on the yachts in the marina, in the paunches of the diners in the Michelin-starred restaurants, and in the swagger of those who pulled up in their fancy cars outside the casino. There were also other more subtle signs that a different code applied and she felt it in the exclusive nature of the social life, the way no one ever spoke about their jobs or how they made their money. Although everyone in Monaco displayed their wealth, no one actually talked about it. None of the people she knew in Monaco would give her the right advice. They would just repeat what Vanessa had said.

She needed to speak to Anton. He was someone who knew the place and how it operated, but he wasn't compromised by being a millionaire or a resident.

At the same time, she didn't want to appear desperate. It had only been a couple of days since she had seen him so she resisted the temptation to call, but as the day wore into the evening, his complete radio silence began to bother her. He still hadn't read her message. The situation at work was making her needy and she was annoyed at herself for being unable to stop checking her phone, constantly looking for a message and growing increasingly paranoid he was ignoring her.

She slept badly that night, wondering why he hadn't called or texted. At 3 a.m. she woke and saw he had now read her text. He had seen it so why hadn't he replied? Despite her determination not to become attached, images of him with other women overwhelmed her and she dreamed he was cavorting with them at the restaurant. He was pouring them drinks, sharing their wine. The women were all laughing and there was dancing on the beach in the moonlight.

She typed a short, angry message and then deleted it. Sleep evaded her, so she took a pill.

The next day she felt groggy and confused. All of the frustration and indecision she felt at work was now focused on Anton and whether he was ghosting her.

Finally at 10.35 a.m. he texted.

Ciao bella. Sorry – phone problems.

Relief coursed through her, flooding her brain with a rush of endorphins, which were quickly replaced by irritation at the vagueness of the apology. What phone problems exactly? The only real phone problem was a flat battery and she had seen he carried a charger. If his phone had really run out of juice, then why was he only texting her now and not when he had seen her message seven hours ago? As she stared at the screen, her mind did another backflip and she began justifying his behaviour to herself: Perhaps he had only had a small amount of charge in the night – enough to see her text but not to respond to it. Or maybe he didn't want to disturb her. She tried to supress an explanation that involved him being with someone else but graphic images erupted in her mind – Anton in bed with another woman, then several of the beach women she had dreamed him with last night. Irrational thoughts ricocheted through her brain before she finally settled on the explanation that he was just busy. It had been the first warm week of the year and the beach would have been packed. People would have poured in for lunch at the restaurant then stayed for sundowners and dinner. As her mind wove back and forth through the myriad explanations, another message flashed up on her phone.

Are you free tonight?

Excitement spiked again but left her feeling nervous and worried he was manipulating her. It was too much and so she turned her phone off.

An hour or so later, her mood had dipped and she felt flat, bruised by his delayed reply and the lack of any real explanation. Normally a few days' silence wouldn't bother her at all – they had only slept together once and no promises had been made apart from a vague plan to go up into the hills at some point, which she wasn't sure about anyway, so why was she so upset? It was too soon to be feeling attached to him like this and her instinct told her to back off. There was too much going on that was affecting her judgement. It wasn't like her to obsess over a man like this. She waited another hour and replied in the negative.

Not tonight. Maybe tomorrow evening.

She wanted to remind him of the arrangement to go into the hills, but she didn't want to sound whiny or worse, give the impression she had remembered the plan. She knew she was probably too stressed to be able to deal with any kind of relationship with him, but at the same time she really wanted to see him.

Anton didn't reply for another twenty-four hours, which infuriated her again. When he finally replied, he said he had managed to get the night off.

There was no suggestion they head out of town and she didn't want to be kept hanging until a plan emerged, so she offered to cook dinner that evening at her flat.

He arrived late with a whole crate of wine he said was from the restaurant and they ate on her leafy balcony, side by side, plates on their laps as the sky turned pink and golden before the sun dipped below the hills. It had been another hot afternoon and the scent of orange blossom drifted up in warm gusts from the street below.

Kate asked Anton how his week had been but he brushed her off, saying something about the casino.

'Do you go there often?' she said.

'Too often. This week there was a tournament.'

He shrugged when she asked more about it. 'I've had better weeks.'

After dinner she cleared the plates and brought out some cheese. He had surreptitiously checked his phone a couple of times during dinner and when she came back from the kitchen, he was checking it again. Being glued to his phone like this wasn't consistent with his lack of communication the other night. It had been a relaxing evening and she didn't want to ruin it by raising his phone problems during the week, so she pushed the thought from her mind, putting this persistent anxiety down to her problems at work. But he registered her annoyance and when she sat down, he asked her how things were going at the office.

Although she had only meant to give him a broad outline of her dilemma, the relief of being able to speak was immense and the words flowed from her as she explained how Rob and Julia wanted her to fabricate evidence that would ensure the case she was working on was dismissed. Anton watched as she spoke freely, talking through her options and letting her mind unfold on trains of thought she hadn't allowed herself to pursue until now. Kate listened to herself explain her fears, imagining how it all looked to him and the enormity of her predicament was somehow diminished. She felt herself unwind as she told him everything.

When she said Julia had mentioned a *reward*, he smiled.

'You find this amusing?' she said.

'No, not at all.'

'Really though, what does a *reward* even mean?'

His smile fell away. 'It means whatever you want it to mean. They want you to fantasise, to start thinking about the money.'

'Well I did. As soon as Julia said it, an amount popped into my head. I hadn't decided to do it, but I was already thinking of a number.'

'And what was the number?'

Kate laughed and touched her neck. 'There's a lot at stake with the litigation. And the fact no numbers were mentioned made me think I could name my price.'

He filled up her glass. 'Of course. That's the intention. So what is it? What's your price?'

Kate gripped her glass and laughed nervously. 'A million euros! It sounds so fantastical, so life-changing.'

A cooler breeze had started up, and with it came faint music from the marina. Anton stood and leaned on the railings of the balcony.

'A million euros wouldn't change your life that much,' he said quietly. 'It would barely last six months in a place like this.'

'Well I'm not even sure she means that much,' Kate said.

She saw the lights in the sitting room were attracting insects so she went inside to turn them off. She came back outside with his jacket, and a wrap for herself. 'Julia and Rob are mean though. They're always cutting costs and shaving budgets, always going on about how well they've done against the odds, so perhaps it's much less than that.'

Kate felt renewed indignation at the memory of the restaurant Julia and Rob had taken her to on her first day. She had been expecting something chic, a thoughtful introduction to Monaco – white tablecloths, flowers and a view over the water, but they took her to a dingy café in a busy side street behind the casino where the roads looped in tunnels and overpasses. Rob thought it would be fun to show her part of the Grand Prix circuit. They had pizzas and toasted Kate's arrival with cheap rosé as they yelled at each other above the traffic noise.

'They're both so tight – perhaps she means only several hundred-thousand, low six figures max.'

Anton looked at her dubiously as Kate raised her chin. 'I wouldn't do it for that,' she said, struck with mild horror that she was even thinking about it.

Anton went into the kitchen and Kate heard him open the fridge and rattle around in the drawers for the corkscrew. She scanned the distant skyscrapers hunkered in against the hills, their peaks obscured by the darkening clouds that seemed to hover permanently above Monaco. The clouds were an odd aberration against the ever-blue skies of the place, an atmospheric condition caused by the land's dramatic ascent from the sea. During the day, the clouds provided much-needed respite from the heat, but there was something ominous about them too.

She scanned the apartment blocks below the clouds, their outlines dim now the sun had set. Most of the apartments were unlit, the homes of tax exiles who, once they had secured a safe haven for their money, found somewhere else to go. The empty residences were reminders that exile was continuous and that once you started running, you had to keep going.

Kate brought her attention back to the balcony and the small flat behind her. Even with the fantasy million euros she would barely be able to afford a car parking space in Saint Roman, but she wouldn't want to stay in Monaco anyway. She would use the money to get out. She smiled at the irony – if she wanted to leave so much, then why was she even thinking of doing what Rob and Julia had asked?

Anton returned with another bottle of wine.

'It's not that complicated,' she said. 'It would be so much easier to just do it, get it over and done with.'

It was the path of least resistance, but even as she said it she felt her gut tighten, her palms prickle with sweat.

'You'd be theirs then. They'd always have something on you.'

She watched him pierce the cork and remove it gently from the bottle as the truth of his comment sunk in. She had only been thinking about the short term.

'If they threatened me with exposure they'd be incriminating themselves too,' Kate said.

He pointed the corkscrew at her. 'Would they be, though? I don't know how things work in places like your firm, but why do they need you? If it's as simple as you say, why don't they just do it themselves?'

He handed her the glass and she cupped the bowl, it's coolness a relief against her warm hands.

'I'll tell you why,' he said. 'Because they want you to do it alone.'

Kate was an experienced lawyer, she drafted most things alone without their input, so this angle hadn't properly occurred to her, but he was right. She thought back to Vanessa's warning and then to what Rob had said – about how there was to be nothing in writing between them. If she wanted to communicate with him it had to be verbal. Her mind sped ahead and she knew if it all backfired it would just be her name on the documents.

Anton leaned against the balcony. 'That's how these things work,' he said. 'No ties, no connections. Everyone working alone so if someone's caught, it's only the weak link that goes down.'

She thought aloud. 'And you think I'm the weak link.'

He raised his glass in a toast. '*Santé.*'

'And that's the reward.'

'If you fuck it up, yes, it will be you who goes down,' he said. 'But if you do it well then other deals will follow, along with more money. That's the real reward.'

Kate recalled the casual way Rob had proposed the deal, speaking about *finding a document* as if it were the only sensible option, almost a fait accompli. She thought such nonchalance was odd at the time, but then again he was a strange man – his face expressionless, his eyes burning with greed. Julia wasn't as intense but made up for it with a nastiness that was harder to read. She was creepier too, if that were possible. There was a lot that was odd about them and they moved in a strange world, but for all the time Rob and Julia spent together they didn't seem to like each other much. Kate thought about other deals they had boasted about. They had pulled off some incredible feats, refinanced dying businesses, taken on losing cases and won.

It was obvious those other jobs weren't just luck – they had done illegal things together before. It was nothing new to either of them. Rob and Julia were like a married couple trapped in a union well past its use-by date. They had washed each other's dirty laundry and knew too much to let each other go. They resented each other, but neither could escape.

Anton was right. If the past week was anything to go by it was pretty clear what Kate's role would be in this toxic threesome. She would be rewarded and promoted for sure, but afterwards she would be locked in.

She looked up at the hills, at the lonely apartments, bleak against the deepening skies.

If she did this deal she would be stuck in this place.

In this Alcatraz for the rich.

Chapter Twenty

KATE SHUDDERED AT THE THOUGHT of being stuck forever in Monaco. She shifted her chair back and took a sip of wine.

'This is delicious,' she said, swirling the golden liquid in her glass. It had an oily, viscous quality and glancing over, she saw the label was a dusty yellow, mottled like parchment with the name of the wine house embossed in raised gold lettering. She looked at the other bottle and the label was the same. She was a little drunk now, but she knew enough about wine to know these were expensive bottles. Anton had placed the newly opened wine on the stool beside the first bottle, and it seemed like a show – the matching labels facing out as if he wanted her to notice.

She took another sip and realised her palm was cradling the wine so she moved her fingers down the stem and held the glass in the elegant way he had shown her.

'Tell me what you're really doing at that restaurant,' Kate said.

He was smiling, approving of the change to the way she held her wine, but then his brow creased.

'It's my job.'

'Come on, Anton,' she said, pointing to the bottles, then putting her hand on his wrist, touching the thick platinum links of his Rolex. 'That expensive wine. This watch. They aren't things a waiter usually has.'

He pretended to be hurt then spoke, half mockingly. 'Expensive wine? I always drink good wine. And the watch was a present.'

'Your car then.'

'If you don't have a decent car in this place no one speaks to you. The valets are more judgemental than anyone.'

He was teasing her again and the wine had gone to her head, making her wonder about her own place in this alternative reality where waiters wore Rolexes and drove around in sports cars.

'Anton. It's a *Ferrari*!'

'It's an old one and it's nothing compared to the Lamborghinis and the Maseratis you see everywhere.'

She waved her hand in the air. 'All this money you have. Waiters aren't paid *that* well, even with all the tipping that's expected here.'

The words came out harsher than she intended and the comment deflated the moment, the smile vanishing from his face. An electrified stillness filled the air and everything went quiet around them.

His face was tight. 'I'm glad you're noticing everything. It's good to be appreciated,' he said, looking across to the apartments opposite.

He was wounded, but she couldn't tell whether she had really insulted him, or whether it was something else. She felt it was the latter and that she had hit upon some truth. She had gone too far now to attempt any kind of retreat so she carried on.

'It's a display – as if you want me to know. I've told you all about my situation. Why don't you tell me yours?'

He turned to face her. 'Well, the car belongs to my boss. He lets me drive it when I do stuff for him.'

'Your *boss*?'

Anton sighed with exasperation. 'My boss at the restaurant.'

'And what *stuff* do you do for him?'

'Picking up supplies. Things like that?'

'A Ferrari as a delivery van? Come on. I'm not that gullible.'

There was a pause as they stared at each other.

Kate lowered her voice. 'The gambling? Is that where you get your money?'

Anton threw his hands up. 'Money's always available. It's every-where here, and flows through the place like water. Look at it all!' he said, pointing to the billion dollar high rises. 'This place is built on it. That's what people don't understand and they act grateful for each cent that comes to them, as though it's luck.'

'It is partly luck, or good fortune. Having money is a product of birth and education. Most people would agree with that.'

'No, what I mean is that most people let money enslave them. The way they squirrel it away, careful not to waste it, worried each dollar might be their last. I prefer to spend it.'

Kate was sure he didn't really believe what he was saying, but there was something in his extravagance, in his disregard for the obsessions of others that was intriguing. It made him seem reckless, but also not beholden to the things that preoccupied everyone else. It was the freedom of someone who wasn't worried about tomorrow.

A round of fireworks had started up in the bay. Anton stood as the noise grew louder, craning over the balcony as if trying to catch a glimpse of the show even though he must have known there was no view of the water from Kate's flat.

Kate waited until the noise had died down a little. 'What you said just now about the reward I was offered. You know quite a lot about this world.'

'It's just an outside perspective. You can't see it because you're too close.'

Kate got up to stand next to him. 'You seem quite close to it, too.'

'It's complicated,' he said, still not looking at her.

His expression in profile reminded her of when she asked him up at the village whether he really was an artist. He couldn't look at her then either.

He reached for the wine and refilled their glasses.

'I would tell you, but you'll judge me,' he teased. Kate took her wine and held it to her chest.

'But I can see you're already judging me.'

'No, I'm not. Come on, I just told you my story.'

He thought for a moment. 'Frankly, it's no real secret.'

'What's no real secret?' she said.

'The restaurant – La Terrasse – is part of Casa di Stelle.'

The image of a set of black metal gates bearing the emblem of a ship's wheel sprang into Kate's mind. The words 'Casa di Stelle' beneath a row of gold spikes.

'That mansion near the station,' she said.

'The people who own the restaurant own the mansion and all the land around it too.'

Kate remembered the girls on the beach, the pair of heavily armed guards she saw afterwards when the gates were opened to admit the limousine. She thought at the time it was overkill, but from the look on Anton's face now, possibly not.

'Your boss owns that villa?'

'My boss runs a concierge service for them, and he runs their finances.'

Kate got the sense Anton was now talking in code, that she was supposed to understand him, but her mind was blank.

'A *concierge service*? At the restaurant?'

Anton laughed wearily. 'Not there exactly.'

'Where then? In Monaco?'

'Cannes, Nice, Monaco. All along the coast.'

'A concierge for what?'

'Arranging things.'

'Arranging what things?'

'Everything you can imagine.'

His voice sounded sinister and Kate felt panicked as a flood of images rushed into her mind. 'Tell me.'

There was a long pause and then finally, Anton met her eyes. 'Everything rich people want,' he said, his voice trailing off.

His tone chilled her. She had a fairly good idea of what rich people wanted. She forced a laugh but her voice faltered. 'Like what? Arranging shopping trips?' Her voice sounded hopeful but she felt anything but.

'Shopping trips, yes.'

'Tourist visits? Restaurants?'

He turned away once more. 'Of course, all that.'

'What else?'

He took a long drag of his cigarette, exhaling slowly, the smoke gathering around his face. 'Parties,' he said finally, not meeting her eyes.

She laughed again nervously at the way he said it, his voice flat and emotionless. '*Parties?* Come on, Anton, what's so strange about that?' But even as her laugh rang out, a knot tightened in her stomach.

He didn't answer, just leaned in to the ashtray.

She held out her hand for the cigarette, took a drag. 'Rich people. Parties. So what? What's the craziest thing?'

'Delivering things to yachts by helicopter.'

She laughed properly then. 'Deliveroo by chopper!'

She saw a box of groceries – apples, cucumbers and bread, being traded between liveried staff across a windswept helipad.

'What kind of things, Anton?' she said, taking another drag, her voice catching a little with the smoke. 'A bottle of wine? Maybe they ran out of cigars?'

'Nope.'

'What then?'

'You can guess.'

She handed back the cigarette and pulled the wrap around her shoulders. 'OK then. Drugs?'

He shrugged and said quietly, 'Yeah that's right, drugs.'

The wine and nicotine surged as Kate stood up, her fingers slipping on the glass doors as she went inside. She placed her wine on the table next to the sofa, lowered herself onto the cushions. The cigarette had given her a head rush and the wine had left a sour film in her mouth.

'What do you mean, Anton?' she said once her head stopped spinning.

He didn't answer, just rested wearily on the balcony and lit another cigarette, his body hunched over the railing.

'*How*, Anton? What are you saying?'

He lifted his head and spoke to the night sky. She could barely hear him. 'At first it was just drugs. A bit of hash here and there, then harder drugs when I needed cash to pay for my own. Cocaine mainly. Rich people always want coke with their champagne. *Champagne avec de la cocaïne.* Then it got more serious.'

'How serious?'

'Armed robbery.'

He said the words softly, in French, as if he didn't want her to hear. In fact she was having trouble hearing. There was a ringing in her ears, they were burning. She went to the kitchen for a glass of water and leaned over the sink for a couple of minutes.

'*Armed robbery?* You're kidding me,' Kate said, when she came back to the room.

'I needed money. I fucked up big time at the casino. It was a few years after my accident. I was drinking and taking too much coke. I lost everything and afterwards, I was desperate. I couldn't pay my rent. I had nowhere to sleep. I couldn't even feed myself properly.'

'Gambling?'

He nodded. 'I went in one evening blasted on cocaine. I was feeling lucky, invincible, and I started with roulette. At first I played it safe and thought I had a system. I won the first three bets and so then I was just gambling on the house's money. Then I hit a losing streak and lost it all. All my money. Everything I got from the insurance, all of it.'

Kate winced.

'The loss was bad. But I was sure I'd get it back so I returned the next night, chasing losses. I thought I could win again and then leave straight away, but the winning was worse. That initial success – that's where it got me. Those first blissful moments, but then I lost everything. All my savings and maxed out on credit. Gone.'

'I don't understand. How did that lead to armed robbery? And . . .' Kate waved her hand in the air.

'I borrowed money from the people I was working for. At the time I was doing their IT work. It was the easiest thing to do. I did two big jobs to pay them back but the second one didn't work out and they blamed me.'

'And so you decided to diversify into drugs trafficking?'

'No, it wasn't like that,' he said, his voice low. 'I owed them a lot of money and I had to pay it back.'

'And who are *they*?'

'The group that runs Casa di Stelle.'

'Who are . . . ?'

'I don't know for sure. Some say it's a businessman from Lebanon. Others say they're Eastern Europeans, Kazakhs or the Chinese.'

'How long have you been doing this?' Kate said. She felt overwhelmed by a surge of disbelief so strong she wanted to grab him and shake him, make him tell her it was all a joke, the product of an overexcited, wine-fuelled imagination, but even as she thought it, she knew it made sense – the money he splashed around, the way she knew he wasn't telling the truth. When she thought back to her agonies over his harmless unreturned phone messages, she almost laughed.

'And you stayed working there with them, knowing this is what they do?'

'I paid off the first debt but then I borrowed more. It's not easy to say no to money. You know that.'

'Not easy? We're talking about drug trafficking, about people's lives. About people's *ruined* lives.'

Kate didn't want to know more, but her head was spinning with questions. 'And what does the house have to do with all this? This Casa di Stelle.'

'The house is where the parties take place. People stay for a few nights, sometimes a week. We supply the drugs and entertainment.'

'Ugh,' Kate said, her stomach twisting with disgust. 'The *entertainment*?'

'*Siii, Siii,*' Anton said, the words so soft and rushed with shame they were almost a whisper. 'And the gambling. They come mainly for the gambling.'

'Jesus. Can't they go to a casino? There are enough of them along this coast. You can't move for the casinos here.'

'Those are just for the tourists and the losers, places for small time gamblers. The real gambling happens privately. Casa di Stelle is gambling on another level – there's a whole basement of poker, roulette tables.'

'Illegal gambling?'

He nodded. 'The Casino de Monte-Carlo even gets a take. They send the real high rollers out privately.'

'And the police?'

'As long as it all happens in the villas, on the yachts, and not on the streets of Monaco, then the police turn a blind eye. To everything.'

'How can you work for these people?'

'I could ask you the same question.'

'At least I don't work for drug runners,' Kate said, feeling a confusing rush of something like gratitude for Rob and Julia who, as unpleasant as they were, were not drug runners, at least as far as she knew.

He raised his eyebrows as if tracking her thoughts. 'How do you know who you work for?' he said softly.

'I don't work for scum,' Kate said, this time with a surge of outrage she knew had no foundation in certainty. 'It's not the same! You know what they do.'

'And just because you don't work for scum that makes it OK, what you do?'

'If I knew they were involved in the drugs trade—'

'If you knew, you wouldn't do it. But what if you didn't know? What if you made sure you didn't know? What if you didn't ask questions?'

'We do ask questions. We comply with the law,' Kate said, realising she didn't have a clue most of the time who she worked for, or what any of them really did.

Anton lit another cigarette. 'I know what the law says. It says you can work with criminals as long as they don't tell you they're criminals. So as long as they don't tell you, it's fine. And you sure as hell don't ask.'

'Not quite, but you certainly can't help them with any illegal activity,' Kate said primly, aware that the straws she was grasping for were getting further out of reach. 'You're obliged to carry out checks. I mean, if they're obviously criminals you can't act for them. If they come from exposed countries. If they are a politically exposed person,' she said, racking her brains to remember the law, to remember what she was *supposed* to do, and thinking of ways to justify what she actually did and feeling the gap between the two. The hypocrisy of it all constricted her throat as her voice drained away. She was aware of how pathetic she sounded, weakly trotting out the rules no one ever complied with, aware of how easy they were to circumvent, and how simple it was to hide what people did and who they acted for.

Anton persisted. 'But you can help them with their legal activities.'

'Yes.'

'And help them make their illegal activities legal.'

'In some circumstances you can, yes.'

'And *in some circumstances* perhaps even do the illegal activity for them.'

Kate shook her head but yes of course that was exactly what she was considering. She felt really ill now, as if she had just swallowed something rotten.

'Why are you telling me all this?' she said. 'Why are you telling me what you do and then attacking me like this?'

'Well for a start, you asked me. And also' – there was a pause as he moved towards her and took her arm gently – 'I need your help.'

'Help?' Kate said, chills spidering up her neck. 'You need a loan?'

'I need help dealing with some cash.'

'Some *cash*? I thought you said you owed money.'

'I did owe money. But now I have money.'

'What kind of money?'

'Money I paid myself,' he said.

'Money you took from them?'

'Yes, since you put it like that. It's money I skimmed off my gambling winnings.'

'Is this the work that you do for them now?'

'Among other things.'

'What other things?'

'I look after their computer systems, some courier work, and yes, sometimes I gamble with their money, clean it through the casinos.'

'Clean it through the casinos?'

'I need a bank account. I need you to set up a legitimate account for me and put the cash there. That's all.'

'That's all?'

'You can say I'm a client.'

'You want me to launder cash for you, my *client*?'

Kate looked out through the glass, to the lights of the city, wondering if he was out of his mind. It was too much – him telling her all the terrible things he did and then asking her to help him with it.

'Set up a company and an account for me at the Credit Suisse branch next to your office. I know Meritus banks there and so it will be easy for you. I'll take the cash there. You don't need to touch it.'

'Are you out of your mind? If this is drug money you're laundering, and I'm assuming it is, then what you're asking me to do is a criminal offence. I can't believe you're asking me to do this,' she said, trying to clamber back on her high horse. She spoke more urgently now, carefully articulating every syllable. 'Listen to me. I don't want anything to do with what you're doing.'

'I'm in trouble, Kate. I have no one else to ask.'

He looked pathetic, his face all deflated, eyes pleading.

'Why can't you do it yourself?'

'My credit is shot. No bank will deal with me.'

'How much is it?'

'Just over a million euros.'

She took a step back, overwhelmed by the irony that it was the figure she had just referred to herself.

'It's been through the casino. I have all the slips and documentation. The private banks don't ask questions on casino winnings.'

'It's still money laundering. Originally it was drug money.'

'I can't travel with all that cash. I need to get it safe first and then I can disappear.'

'*Disappear?*

'Once I've banked the money, I'll stage an accident. Something serious – enough to land me in hospital for a few weeks, but nothing permanent. A fall. I'll ham it up, saying I can no longer do what they want and then I'll gradually disappear. But I need you to help me with an account first. It's the only way I can get out.'

'I can't do it, Anton. You can't ask me to do that.'

Kate felt herself disengage from the room. It was as if she had floated up to the ceiling and was looking down at herself and Anton. She saw the cool way he asked her to compromise herself for him, and she wondered if he had planned this all along. Her mind spooled back to when they met at the café, and before then, to the doctor's surgery, the way his eyes lit up when she told him she was a lawyer. Was it a coincidence they met that day? Was she *marked,* or did he just decide to use her once her usefulness became apparent?

He took her hand. 'Forget it now,' he said.

'Are you crazy? I can't just *forget* what you've told me.'

'Let's talk about it later, then.'

'Talk about what later? I just said no.'

'I know,' he said, kissing her softly, and smiling. 'Let's not talk about it anymore.'

She felt her temples throb where he kissed her.

'I need to lie down,' she said and he led her into the bedroom and sat beside her.

He leaned towards her, kissing her and caressing her neck and his face looked distorted in the half-light. His touch inflamed her, and as he got closer, she felt she was being eaten alive. She wanted to resist, but it was exhausting and he was right here with her now, whispering and telling her how it would be when they were together. They could leave Monaco with the cash, go somewhere else. It would be enough for them to start a new life. When she pushed him away he let out a sigh as though she was being unreasonable. She moved away from him but he pulled her back.

She woke later to the soft click of the front door closing quietly behind him. She reached for her phone just as a message arrived:

I'm sorry. I shouldn't have asked for your help. Forget it.

Kate rolled onto her side and stared out across the darkened apartments towards the hills. Her chest ached as she thought of the drugs, the helicopters and the stolen, laundered cash. She couldn't just forget these things. What he had asked her to do was crazy. He was as bad as Rob.

Her first impulse was to run away from it all. Not with Anton, as he had suggested, but by herself. She could book a flight right now and be back in London tomorrow afternoon leaving Anton, Meritus and Monaco behind her. But she knew if she did that

225

Rob and Julia would just find someone else to do the dirty work on Falkon like Vanessa said. Kate couldn't just walk out and let them carry on with their plan to fabricate evidence and shaft the men. She needed to find a way to stop it, to figure out her own path before Rob and Julia dragged her further along theirs.

Kate wasn't going to do what they wanted, but she needed to make it work for her and for the men – *nothing in writing, cover your tracks* – but how?

Chapter Twenty-One

T HE JOURNEY FROM KATE'S APARTMENT to work was easy to navigate when the air was cool and the sun still low over the Menton hills. Kate loved the luminous mornings and her easy commute along the palm-lined streets that hugged the bay, heading inland past the Casino Gardens and then uphill through a maze of side streets to the Meritus office on the Boulevard de Suisse.

While the route was straightforward in daylight it was more fraught now, at midnight on a Thursday evening. Kate was worried for the very reason the streets held no physical threat – there were security cameras everywhere. Surveillance equipment peered down at her from street corners and shops, and she imagined them following her, zooming in and tracking her movements. Monaco residents often boasted there were more security cameras than people, and while it was sometimes reassuring – Kate knew she would never be attacked on these well-watched streets – the degree of surveillance was intimidating. Kate hoped her generic jogging gear would ward off unwelcome attention from cameras, and she walked quickly, like someone who had just come from the office after an evening's work, rather than someone who was just heading there.

She had done it before of course – been in the office at night, but that was years ago when she was much more ambitious. It was one of the reasons she didn't have a serious boyfriend, Kate's mother used to say, expressing exactly what Kate had suspected herself. Kate had watched her friends' relationships develop and she thought there would be time to have that too, once she had sorted out her career. Kate always felt her personal life was much more manageable than her job, which seemed to sway beneath her like a rudderless boat driven by the whims of fickle bosses. She hoped that once her career stabilised, she could fill out the rest of her life, choosing the right partner and packing in kids like last minute stowaways. She didn't realise back then that life needed to be prioritised if it were to happen at all.

It was why she had come to Monaco in the first place, she reminded herself as she passed her favourite café, its windows darkened, shutters drawn. She needed to get out of London, away from the endless cycle of weddings, baby showers and christenings. As soon as her friends hit thirty, they became more interested in marriage and children, and as the stakes grew higher, the choices got fewer. It was why she had settled for Simon. He worked at Meritus too, a property lawyer, and so their relation-ship had been easy. It was so easy, in fact, that it was almost non-existent and they passed whole weeks where they barely saw each other outside work. When Simon dumped her she wasn't surprised but when even the most ineligible bachelor had gone, Kate realised the game was up.

Kate reached the office at half past midnight. She paused at the door to check no one saw her enter the building and then crossed the lobby to the lift.

That morning, Kate had phoned Marc and asked him to meet her for coffee. She explained to him the plan she had hit upon in bed the previous night as she lay there staring out at the empty apartments after Anton had left: she would frame Rob and Julia for the very thing they were trying to pin on her.

Kate told Marc that her scheme would only work if she created the false document Rob wanted her to draft on Rob's own computer.

'I can give you his login details, but you'll need to do it when he's offline,' said Marc.

'Which is when?'

'At night, early hours. Rob usually works until midnight but he's unlikely to be online tonight because he's flying back from Lagos via Dubai. Julia's less of a risk. She rarely works in the evenings.'

'I'll do it tonight then,' Kate said. 'Using Rob's login.'

'It's best if you actually go into the office and draft the document on his terminal there. That way you can change the settings and make it seem like it was done during normal office hours. It will look much better if there's ever any doubt.'

Marc gave her the entry codes to Rob's and Julia's offices and said he would disable the cameras and security systems for her visit.

During the course of their conversation, Marc told her he now had confirmation he would be fired the following week. He said he was pleased to be able to help her out like this and then admitted he had been working on a farewell gift of his own.

'I was planning to leak some of Rob's dealings to the press.'

'God,' said Kate, 'be careful.'

'I know what Rob does and for whom. All the offshore trust arrangements out of Jersey and Luxembourg. Sanctioned clients.'

'So what are you thinking?'

'Rob's in charge of determining whether I get a payout. I thought I would threaten him gently first. See how he responds.'

'I told you blackmail never works.'

'I left a great job to come to Meritus. They said there would be a permanent contract after the probationary period but now they're just going to sack me with nothing.'

'Leaking things to the press is one thing but blackmail is something else.'

They finished their coffee and walked back to the office.

'Let's talk about this properly tomorrow. Promise me you won't do anything without speaking to me. No blackmailing Rob just yet.'

Marc was silent.

'*Promise?*'

'I promise,' he said.

Kate used the code Marc had given her to enter Rob's office and set to work. She logged in to his computer, changed his time and date settings to 9 a.m. the next day and then drafted the Falkon Racing deed, making sure Rob was credited in the Properties as the document's creator. Half an hour later, she emailed it to Julia for approval. Kate was careful to put a few minor errors into the deed, things Julia would be sure to pick up on. Then she went into Julia's office, logged in to her computer, changed her time and date settings, and sent Rob an email approving the deed. There were a few points she made about the intricacies of the drafting – Julia could never help herself in that regard, and of course she identified the typos Kate had made on Rob's behalf. Kate waited a while after sending the first email and then followed it up with an irritable message from Julia to Rob.

I thought Kate was doing this!
Make sure you delete this email and any drafting.

Then a couple of seconds later.

This is what we pay her for!!!!

Kate went back to Rob's terminal for the reply.

She emailed in sick this morning and it needs to go out by this afternoon!

Kate sent the deed from Rob's computer to her own email address with a surly covering note from Rob, telling her to send it to the client as soon as possible and to deal with all other aspects of the matter leaving *no loose ends*.

Kate printed out copies of the emails and documents she had just sent, double deleted them all from Rob's and Julia's computers and bundled them together in a manila folder. She retraced her digital steps – reinstating the current date and time settings on both computers, and then logged out.

It was 2 a.m. when Kate finally left the office and she walked home the long way, past the marina with the yachts creaking in their docks, the sea breeze cooling her face.

When she arrived home, Kate sent an email to Rob saying she was feeling unwell but that she would try to make it into the office that afternoon. She slept soundly that night and for once she wasn't worried about Rob or Julia or any of their sordid schemes. They had tried to intimidate her and they had nearly succeeded. But it was time to do things her way now. It was time to put both of them back in the frame.

Kate woke later to a series of angry messages from Rob telling her she was taking the piss with all this time out of the office, especially today when there was important work to do on Falkon. She checked through the documents she had brought home from the office and then texted him on the private number he had given her several weeks ago. She told him to calm down, that she had the document ready today as he had instructed and all was in order. She said she was sure it was good to go, but asked him to get back to her if he had any comments. Kate went into her emails, found the document she had sent to herself from Rob's computer during the night and without even opening it, she sent it back to him.

I think this looks great.
Let's discuss when I'm back in the office.

This was followed by two calls from Rob on his private number, which she ignored, then a text message.

Jesus Christ! I said nothing on email.

She took a screen shot of the text.

Before Kate dressed, she checked her phone for a message from Anton but there was nothing. She had sent several long-winded texts explaining why she couldn't help him. Reading her words back now, they had a ring of desperation about them, and he had left them unread, poised in the air like plaintive cries.

Kate felt ashamed she wasn't trying harder to help him – not necessarily to do what he wanted, but to find another way to deal with the money he had taken. Perhaps she should encourage him to leave the country or go to the police, but then she realised of course he couldn't do that.

She texted him again and waited, but he didn't reply. In fact it didn't look like he had received her message at all. It looked like he had blocked her.

After dressing, Kate made two copies of the documents in the manila folder and put one set in an envelope addressed to the lawyer for the mechanics' union. Although she had planned how to frame Rob and Julia for the fraud, she didn't want to put the scheme into action without speaking to the lawyer first. She couldn't stand the idea of the old men thinking the document was real and that they might in fact lose the litigation. She hated to think of their devastation once they got wind of the *new evidence*. Some of the men were very old and such news might push them over the edge, so she called the lawyer and told him everything.

At first he didn't want any part of it but Kate convinced him to hear her out. She knew that he had dealt with Rob for years, that he loathed him and wouldn't be able to resist participating in Rob's demise. After Kate explained the detail to the lawyer, he finally agreed, but only if Kate got Rob and Julia on tape discussing the transaction and exactly what they planned to do.

Kate thought it was too risky to use her phone in case it cut out or rang while she was recording Rob and Julia and she decided she would need a special recording device. There was a shop in Nice that sold electronic gadgets, Kate remembered passing it when she was with Vanessa on Sunday. After she had finalised the dossier for the union's lawyer and hidden the other file of documents in her apartment, Kate caught the train to Nice. She went straight to the electronics shop and purchased a small voice-activated recorder. It took a while to get the hang of it and the shopkeeper took her through it a few times.

Kate pinned the tiny microphone behind the collar of her jacket, experimenting with it by making orders in a café and then listening back to the recordings, but mostly the sound was muffled and indistinct. She took apart the casing of the device and the sound was much clearer if she stayed still, facing directly towards the person who was speaking.

On the train back to Monaco, Kate texted Rob, setting up a meeting with him and Julia that afternoon saying she wanted to fully understand the next steps of the litigation. She pretended to have lost the thread of what he had told her over the previous weeks.

'How can you be sure they won't challenge the document?' Kate said, once they were assembled in Julia's office. 'Won't it seem highly suspicious if we've only just found such a crucial document at the eleventh hour.'

'No it won't,' said Rob, his mouth a thin, bloodless streak.

'But how do you know they won't challenge it? The document needs to have been signed by the union on behalf of the workers.

There's an official stamp they use, and it needs to be notarised. The fact they haven't done this will raise a huge red flag.'

Rob looked at her incredulously. 'We've been through all this before, Kate.' Then he looked at his watch. 'I don't have time for this,' he said under his breath. 'I've got another deal blowing up and I need to be on a flight this evening.'

'Tell me again,' said Kate.

Rob rolled his eyes theatrically and explained it all in a patronising voice as if to a child. He really only got animated if he was being cruel or demeaning and Kate had counted on him relishing the opportunity to be nasty even if it meant having to go over it all again.

'Who says they won't have used the stamp and had it notarised?' he said when Kate asked again about the signature.

Kate affected a look of confusion. 'What do you mean?'

Rob whispered conspiratorially, his eyes darting sideways to Julia. 'We have a contact at the union. They'll get it signed on Monday.'

Kate was startled. 'A contact? You've never told me this.'

'A man on the inside. The union rep,' said Julia, unable to avoid bragging, and Rob nodded as if this were the only sensible thing he had heard all afternoon.

Kate had met the union representative – a grey suited, beaky man who did everything by the book. Surely it wasn't him, she thought, her mind racing. She wondered whether the *contact* was even the union's lawyer, the one she had confided in that morning. If so, she was already compromised.

'He's an ex-colleague,' Julia crowed. 'It's how we've obtained all the information so far – how much each of the claims were worth, how much the men would settle for. Only this time we're going to knock them out of the water.'

'You guys have thought of everything,' said Kate.

Julia smiled and came in close, putting her hands on Kate's shoulders.

Kate winced at Julia's proximity to the microphone and swung away, smiling up at Julia through her loathing. 'So who is this ex-colleague?'

'I probably shouldn't say,' said Julia, touching Kate's hair.

'So don't,' Rob growled.

'Why shouldn't we tell Kate?' Julia said. 'She's proven whose side she's on now.'

Kate hated having Julia touch her like this and she was concerned Julia's hands might venture towards her collar again and ruin the recording so she moved her chair further back and shifted so that the microphone under her collar was nearest to Julia.

After they had discussed some other steps in the litigation, Kate repeated it back to them for clarity and had them confirm what they wanted her to do.

'It's still risky,' Kate said finally.

'We'll stand right behind you if anything happens,' Rob said. 'We're very grateful.'

'You can count on us,' echoed Julia.

Kate smiled nervously, her palms sweaty as she left the meeting room.

When Kate returned to her office, she put an out of office on her email and went straight home. She was still shaking when she downloaded the recording onto her laptop and put the recording device with the dossier she had hidden.

After work, Kate took the train to Roquebrune and followed the path to the beach. It was hot and she was melting in her office clothes. When she reached the bottom of the steps she took off her shoes and walked gingerly across the pebbles towards La Terrasse. The beach was crowded and people were milling around an ice cream vendor near the restaurant. Towels and umbrellas studded the beach and everyone was tanned and relaxing in the sun.

Kate drew close to the restaurant then stopped. With so many people on the beach Anton would be busy, probably even annoyed to see her. She wanted to talk properly through his options with the money, but how would she do that among this throng? She stared through the open doors, her eyes straining against the restaurant's dark interior as she moved closer. To her surprise the entire place was empty, just a dark-haired woman at the coffee machine.

'Ciao,' said the woman without looking up. She stabbed the buttons on the machine irritably, as though it were faulty.

'Is Anton here?'

There was no answer.

'Can I leave a message?' Kate said, peering into the main dining room in case Anton was there.

The woman turned from the machine and pushed a pen and an old receipt stub towards Kate. 'He's not working today.'

'When's he due back?' Kate said.

The woman shrugged as Kate wrote her number on the scrap of paper together with a message: *Call me.*

'You'll make sure he gets it?' Kate said.

The woman read the note and leaned towards Kate. 'He'll be at the casino,' she said softly.

Kate opened her mouth to ask further questions but the woman had turned away.

Instead of going back to the station, Kate took the path to the villa.

When she arrived at the property, the gates were ajar and three cars with tinted windows were parked in the driveway. Two security guards milled around the cars moving several large crates.

Kate stood to the side of the entrance watching the activity around the cars. Then, to her astonishment, there was a loud grinding of gears and part of the asphalt driveway with the crates on it sank slowly downwards. An entire square of driveway about the size of two cars dropped down silently on some kind of hydraulic lift.

Kate took a couple of photos of the strange scene while the guards were occupied. She placed herself in the frame and pretended they were selfies.

'It's a lovely house,' said a voice behind her.

She turned to see a bearded man in a dark suit. She couldn't see his eyes beneath his mirrored aviators and his Panama hat, in fact she couldn't see much of his face at all, other than his mouth, which was smiling.

'I saw it from the coastal path,' she said.

The man looked at her shoes. 'You don't look like you've been on the coastal path.'

'Not today,' she said hurriedly. 'I saw it last week when I came up here.'

'So why are you here again now?'

Kate was annoyed. What business was it of his?

'I was just on the beach.'

His smile grew wider. 'You don't look like you've been on the beach either.'

'I was looking for a friend,' she said, flustered now.

'In here?' he said, gesturing to the villa.

'No,' she said. 'On the beach.' She saw her reflection in his sunglasses – two images of herself trapped in his gaze.

The man raised his eyebrows. 'And now?' he said. 'Why are you taking photos here?'

She lowered her phone. 'It's such a lovely house,' Kate said, the heat constricting her throat. 'I thought I'd just take a few pictures.'

'Then let me help you,' he said, reaching for her phone. 'Let me take a portrait with the house behind you.'

'I've got enough now. I should be going. I'm sorry.'

'Don't apologise,' he said, stepping forward until he towered over her.

She released her phone to him and he stepped back. 'Let me get the right focus,' he said, adjusting the phone and then examining the photos he had taken.

'There,' he said, handing it back. 'Those are even more gorgeous.'

Kate thanked him and walked quickly to the station, expecting to hear the man's steps behind her. She glanced back. He wasn't there and the gates to the villa were now shut.

On the train she looked for the photos of the house but he had deleted them all.

Chapter Twenty-Two

VANESSA WOKE WITH A STINGING headache, her throat dry and painful. As she reached for the glass of water on her bedside table, hazy memories surfaced.

She had met a man last night at the Brasserie de Monaco where she went for a drink after work. An American – she recalled now, who was in town for something to do with the yacht show. They had dinner there and more drinks, but then the memory submerged.

Vanessa scanned the room for her handbag and saw it hanging on a hook near the wardrobe. As her head sank back into the pillow, she thought she heard the guest toilet flush. She froze, eyes darting to the bedroom door, which was shut, then to the other side of the bed. There was no indent on the pillow and the sheet was still tucked in, thank god. Vanessa closed her eyes and pressed her fingers to her temples.

The smell of fresh coffee reached her just before the knock at the door.

'I thought I'd surprise you,' a man said, entering the room in her dressing gown. The surprise wasn't the coffee but the fact she couldn't remember having seen him before in her life.

'Thank you,' she managed to say.

He wasn't the American but he smiled as he handed her an espresso. 'Don't look so worried. We didn't have sex. We considered it, but neither of us were up to it.'

He shrugged off the dressing gown and went into the en suite bathroom.

'When you started calling me Patrick I brought you home and tucked you in. I slept on the sofa,' he said over the noise of the shower.

She was grateful for the coffee, and thanked him again, cringing inwardly at the thought of the state she must have been in last night.

When he came back into the bedroom naked she thought for an awful moment he was coming into bed. But he simply pecked her on the cheek as he passed through to the living room. She heard the jangle of keys and coins and then she heard the front door slam, its ringing echo like a slap in the face.

When she woke again a few hours later she had a better recollection of the night, including the encounter with Patrick, the American she had met first at the bar. They had gone to Jimmy'z after dinner but when Patrick left, she must have met the man who had brought her the coffee this morning. She thought back to the night with Joe several weeks ago. Her drinking was getting dangerous and last night was yet another lucky escape.

What did he mean *neither of us were up to it*, she thought, as she made her way to the bathroom, before catching sight of the puffy eyes looking back at her in the mirror.

She would soon be forty-five, only a few years until this kind of damage would be irreversible, she thought as she pressed the skin on her face with a damp cloth in an attempt to reduce the swelling.

She hadn't behaved like this since her break-up with Pascal. At least she hadn't gone to the casino.

She removed last night's make-up, took an ice mask from the freezer and retreated to bed. As Vanessa lay there, her mind drifted back over the past twenty-four hours.

Rob had been unusually agitated on Friday morning when he returned from Africa. He had muttered something about an investor falling out because of a news story that had been threatened. A journalist from the *Financial Times* had caught wind of the LuckyCoin deal and had written a damning report, alleging the whole scheme was a Ponzi. It hadn't been published yet, but the journalist was planning to run the story that weekend. Rob had spent most of Friday on the phone to libel lawyers in London trying to get the story pulled.

'What do I say to the ambassadors in the meantime?' Vanessa asked. She had a call with Faith and another ambassador later that afternoon.

'For Christ's sake, don't mention it. Just tell them everything's on track,' said Rob in a panic. 'Fucking journalists! The lawyers have threatened to sue the bastard personally for defamation if he runs it. They reckon that usually works to get the story pulled, but I've already lost one major investor. The others will run like rats if it goes ahead.'

That afternoon on the call it was Faith who brought up the story. She said a reporter who was investigating LuckyCoin had called her asking who was behind the scheme. Vanessa found herself lying, saying the reports were all false. A competitor was trying to smear their reputation, she explained. They were jealous because LuckyCoin was going to be so successful and they wanted to create uncertainty in the market.

Vanessa came off the phone feeling queasy. Faith had gone very quiet and Vanessa hadn't been her most convincing.

After that, Vanessa needed some air so she had walked along the marina and ended up at the bar. That was where she met the American. It was only after the third drink that her nausea subsided.

Vanessa rose from the bed and made another attempt at the day.

Twenty minutes with the ice mask, another twenty on the cross-trainer and the face in the mirror was one she recognised.

'You need to stop all this,' she said aloud, sweeping moisturiser over her face. She spent a while at the mirror, puttying up the lines and creases, trying to massage the guilt away, trying to locate a human canvas.

'Wow,' said Vanessa when she arrived on the terrace at Marcello's an hour later. She still felt dreadful, but was upbeat for Kate. 'You look amazing.'

'I took your advice and bought some new clothes. Don't tell me you approve.'

Vanessa stood by the table, appraising Kate. 'No. It's not the clothes.'

Kate's face fell. 'You don't like them?'

'It's not that,' she said as she sat down. 'You don't get that look from clothes.'

Vanessa stabbed an olive with a toothpick and brought it to her mouth. 'Is it that guy from IT I've seen you with?'

'Marc? No, no,' Kate said, realising that Marc hadn't returned her call from yesterday when she phoned him to say that everything had gone smoothly in the office.

'Who is it then? I'm starting to get jealous.'

Kate blushed as the waiter gave them the menus.

'Don't be jealous. He's—'

'He's what?'

Kate sighed. 'It's not *serious*.'

Kate told Vanessa about Anton: how they had met two weeks ago, that things had moved quickly, but that the more she knew, the more troubled she had become and that she was now trying to get him out of her mind. Kate wanted to tell Vanessa more but something held her back. A sense of loyalty to Anton perhaps, or embarrassment at how easily she had almost been played.

'Good luck with that,' Vanessa said. 'If the way you look now is anything to go by, forgetting him won't be easy.'

As the waiter delivered their food, Kate was distracted by a group of people who had arrived on the terrace. 'There's that woman we saw outside that restaurant.'

Vanessa looked over. 'Elanka Aleksandras. Yes, I've seen her here before.'

The man she was with was heavyset and sat between Elanka and an older woman.

Vanessa considered her salad then pushed it away as her hangover resurfaced. 'The guy looks like security. Elanka's just acquired a beachfront villa further up the coast so I'm not surprised. God, can you imagine? A place like that.'

'Where is it?'

'Roquebrune-Cap-Martin. Right on the beach. Sometimes they have parties there. It's like a fairy tale,' said Vanessa wistfully.

'Casa di Stelle?'

'You know it?'

'You can't miss the place. And she owns it?'

'Amir owns it. Or at least he did, until he was forced to transfer it to Elanka and her mother.'

'Why was he forced to do that?'

'Rob thinks he's about to be sanctioned. He's in the process of transferring his assets into the names of close friends and family so they're not frozen or seized.'

Kate put down her glass. 'If he's about to be sanctioned we shouldn't be working for him. I shouldn't be working on Falkon.'

'Rob will have made sure the ownership of all his companies is hidden or changed, including Falkon. Don't worry.'

'How do you know?'

'No one except Rob knows which companies Amir actually owns. And Rob will make sure the authorities never find out. They'll never trace his assets or his companies to him.'

'We still shouldn't be acting for him.'

'He's a big client.'

Kate looked over to Elanka. 'So why has Amir transferred this villa to Elanka if Rob has everything hidden?'

'To be doubly sure.'

Kate leaned in, lowering her voice. 'I've been past that place. Armed security guards, hydraulic lift built into the driveway itself. I heard there was illegal gambling there.'

'Yeah, gambling and the rest.'

'What *rest*?'

Vanessa called for the bill. 'Honestly you don't want to know.'

'Tell me.'

'I'd better not.'

'Come on. If Rob works for him I should know about it.'

'Listen,' Vanessa said, 'what I've heard you won't like and honestly, it's best not to know, but . . .' Vanessa's voice trailed off.

'But what?'

The waiter came to collect their plates. Vanessa hadn't touched her food.

'I can't talk about it now. I'm really not in the mood. The main thing is that Meritus acts for Amir and we just do as we're told.'

Walking back to her apartment after lunch, Vanessa saw she had several missed calls from David's school.

'Mrs Giraud. I'm afraid I've got some more bad news,' said Emily from Meetham. 'It concerns David directly this time, I'm afraid.'

'Oh god,' Vanessa said, her legs weak. 'Is he all right?'

'He was mugged.'

Vanessa found a bench near a bus stop and sat down, clutching the phone to her ear. '*Mugged?*'

'He's all right now. He's fine. David is fine. But he's been quite shaken.'

Emily handed over to David and he told Vanessa a little of what had happened. He had been mugged on a school trip to the north of England to visit Hadrian's Wall. He had been shown a knife by some kids on the train coming back into Newcastle where the school group was staying. Thankfully David had given over his iPhone and his Canada Goose coat to the muggers without any argument. David said he was OK, but that he didn't really want to discuss it and he replied monosyllabically to Vanessa's questions.

Vanessa called the school's pastoral support officer when she got back to her apartment.

'This is happening more and more, unfortunately,' the man said. He was from the north of England and said he had worked at schools in and around Newcastle. 'There's a lot of inequality and deprivation everywhere these days. David naturally feels ashamed but he shouldn't. It wasn't his fault. Muggings like this are very common now.'

They talked for a while and the man said that although David had had a terrifying experience, he would recover. The same couldn't be said of the kids who had attacked him, he added, almost as an afterthought. It was very sad. David said they weren't much older than him.

'What can we do? Can we press charges?' Vanessa said.

'It's up to the police, but really, they won't do anything. They see it as part of a much bigger problem. There's really nothing for those kids.'

But what about my kid? Vanessa wanted to scream down the phone.

My kid, she thought bitterly when she came off the call, *the one I'm not even able to comfort properly when he needs me*. Vanessa's face was damp with tears as she thought of her son alone in his cold boarding school dormitory, and she felt a crushing sense of shame for the work that kept her in Monaco, away from him. All of the guilt she had repressed about Meritus, LuckyCoin, Faith and the other ambassadors came surging towards her now bringing an awful clarity to her thoughts. David's mugging wasn't his fault, the pastoral officer was right, but it did somehow feel very much like hers. Inequality was her stock in trade. Deprivation was the bedrock left behind after Rob's deals swept through. Vanessa knew that LuckyCoin was not just a clever scheme to make money. It was outright theft and it would devastate lives.

It would make more of the things that had happened to David happen to other kids and their families too.

Vanessa had long ago abandoned the kind of introspection that might cause her to properly question her life choices but faced with David's mugging, she could no longer ignore it. She knew the justifications for the things she did at Meritus were thin, that what she did for Rob had effects beyond simply moving money around. What Vanessa hadn't been able to tell Kate about Casa di Stelle was at the root of her deepest shame. That beyond the beautiful facade was a place they brought girls. Hostesses they called them. It was an open secret – entertainment to attract the high rollers. Everyone in Monaco knew and no one stopped them, not the police nor the government and least of all anyone at Meritus. The firm acted for Amir, and Vanessa and Rob dealt with the money generated by his activities without asking any questions.

As Vanessa sat on the sofa watching the marina grow dark, she felt the loneliness of her apartment and the venality of the city outside. Was this what her life had come to, she thought, as she watched the darkening cliffs. All her drinking, her gambling and her one-night stands. The things that distracted her from the guilt and the gaping emptiness of her life.

Chapter Twenty-Three

I T HAD BEEN A WHILE since Kate had entered a casino, and she felt a quickening sense of dread as she walked through the Parc des Spélugues, her eyes scanning the dark paths ahead. Despite its location just north of the glittering centre of Monaco, the park had an aura of menace, especially now at dusk when bats darted in among the canopy of fig trees that obscured the sky's faint glow. Spélugues – it was what they called Monaco when the place was just a rocky outcrop of caves and grottos at the edge of the sea. Back then, Spélugues was notorious for the thieves and bandits who inhabited the area and something of that legacy still hung in place, luring people to risk everything on the spin of a wheel, the turn of a card or the scatter of dice.

There were still places like that in Monaco. Places that held the memory of those wilder times before the belle époque swept in with its trainlines and waves of cultured guests. That was the era when, in a sleight of hand as shrewd as any thief, the founders of Monte Carlo transformed it from a peaceful citrus grove on the edge of Italy into a place where fortunes were made and lost. The Café de Paris was a relic of those times, and Kate passed it now as she emerged from the park and saw the casino looming up ahead, its dazzling facade summoning players like the entrance to an amusement park.

Kate made her way diagonally across the square, weaving around the throng of tourists who posed for selfies beside sports cars queuing for the valet. Some of the cars had number plates from Dubai or the UAE, meaning they could only have arrived by jet, and Kate gaped at the extravagance. At the Hôtel de Paris, gloved waiters hovered over well-fed guests, filling glasses, laying down plates. Further along, the windows of designer stores showcased garish creations of leather, snakeskin and fur – outrageous outfits Kate couldn't imagine anyone wearing, let alone buying with their five-figure price tags.

Kate's heels sank gently into the red-carpeted steps of the casino. She smiled at the doorman whose job it was to bar entry to those who did not look like they had fortunes to lose, and when she reached the top of the steps, she turned to face the direction she had come. The square was milling with tourists, alight with flashing cameras and buzzing with people high on the fumes of extreme wealth.

It was as close as they would ever come to such riches, Kate guessed as she surveyed the scene spread out before her. And as far as they would go if they had any sense, she thought, as she looked to the edges of the square, to the sparkling conveyor belt of temptation she had just passed. She knew from her sister how it felt to win – the heady rush, the silvery air. Pockets stuffed with cash, mind spinning with excitement and possibility.

She also knew from her sister how it felt to lose. Those swift and brutal minutes that confirmed she was a loser; that she was going home with nothing.

Kate dwelled on this, the more likely scenario, as she queued to show her passport at the desk and once inside, the opulence of the Salle Garnier took her breath away. It was unlike any casino she had ever seen. Vast crystal chandeliers hung over the gambling tables like dazzling fires and people milled beneath, mesmerised, as the murmur of croupiers stirred thousands of euros to change hands.

It was still early and there was plenty of room for Kate to see the games as she scanned the tables for Anton. Half of the first room was given over to a cocktail bar where a jazz band played softly from a raised stage. Couples sipped martinis on pink velvet sofas and participated in the fantasy that losing money in a place like this was, in fact, an amusement. Soft laughter rose above the background clatter of chips as players ignored the truism that *the house always wins*, despite stark confirmation in the riches surrounding them.

She could have done with a drink – a Vesper Martini, or even a cool beer, but she didn't stop, drawn forward into an ocean of green felt that stretched on as far as she could see. She closed her eyes and let the buzz of the place swirl around her, giving in to something greater than she was, allowing it to lead her across the tapestried carpets to where the real gamblers were.

She was deep in the casino now, the players' cheeks flushed as they cradled their chips, their eyes staring blankly ahead, searching for themselves in the dots, the reds and blacks, the numerals and the suits.

Kate gazed around for Anton in the small corner bar, but he wasn't there. She drew further into the room where the air was stale and heavy, bodies cramped over chips, their faces greedy

251

and restless. Entering the roulette room she saw him immediately. His skin had a sickly tinge, his hair greasy and unkempt.

Anton's bloodshot eyes were fixed upon the wheel, his body straining over the table, and his hands were cupped around his last few chips like sea defences against a rising tide. There was a large bruise on his cheek, darkened under a two-day growth. He was not only drunk now, she realised as she moved closer, he had been drunk for a while, his clothes all crumpled and slept-in. He had lost a lot of money, she could tell from his hollow stare and his restless feet.

There was a similar look to the others around him, a union of common misery, their eyes fixed on the wheel as if the force of their glare could influence where the ball was going to land. To Anton's right was a bald man of about sixty with a large pile of flecked plaques. To his left was a woman, her arm tightly guarding a smaller stack.

Anton saw Kate but he looked straight through her.

'Anton—' she started to say, but he was focused now on the spinning wheel. As the white ball slowed, his spine stiffened and he came suddenly to life, like an addict who had just seen his dealer emerge from the crowd.

'Anton!' Kate said, gripping his arm.

He turned to her once the ball had fallen, his eyes full of fear.

She had seen it in her sister, this same terror, and she pulled gently at his arm.

'*Faites vos jeux,*' said the croupier.

'I'm not leaving until I'm finished,' Anton said, clutching his last few chips.

She saw that he had a hundred and fifty left. Kate didn't want to play but faced with the desperate look on Anton's face she felt compelled to act. 'Let me do it then,' she said, reaching for a fifty.

To her surprise, Anton moved aside to let her in.

Kate laid the fifty on red. The woman and the man on either side both followed her bet.

Black came up.

Anton looked at her with despair and grabbed her hand but Kate took the second fifty and put it on odd numbers. Three came up and she staked the whole hundred on odd again. Twelve came up – she had lost! Then, with a perverse desire to get rid of all of Anton's money and to leave the casino, she put his remaining fifty on odd. She could tell he wanted to stop her, but his will seemed to have left him and he simply shook his head miserably. The two others who had been following her bets withdrew.

When the ball landed, Kate couldn't believe it! Seventeen had come up and so she moved the hundred to red. Red came up and she moved all the chips to the twelve middle numbers. Again she won and half the money went back to red, with the rest aside. Red came up three more times. Anton grasped her shoulder and she felt his grip tightening with each winning play. Her heart was pounding, face flushed with the thrill of winning and the need to keep going at all costs. She had nearly three thousand on the table now and as she removed her jacket and draped it over a stool, she saw Anton's eyes were wild and shining, his pupils completely dilated. She kept half the money aside and placed the rest on black. Red came up and so she placed the remaining money on her four lucky numbers – 4, 11, 18 and 36. She could feel Anton's breath on her cheek and a wall of heat coming off him. She knew he was desperate to intervene, but unwilling to break her run. Thirty-six came up and she won thousands more. She was well ahead now and with the kind of willpower she didn't know she had, she scooped in her chips.

'*Faites vos jeux,*' the croupier said, looking around for last bets.

'Go on!' Anton breathed in her ear.

Kate shook her head at the croupier.

'Keep going!' Anton urged, squeezing her hand. 'You're winning! You must keep going!'

'No,' Kate said, scraping up the last few chips. 'Let's leave. You've had it.'

'No! Just one more bet. You're on a lucky streak, can't you see?'

He was sweating, his eyes feverish. 'How do you know to play like that? I didn't think you gambled.'

'I don't.'

'It's beginner's luck then! Now we really mustn't leave!' Anton said, pulling her back to the table with such force that he almost knocked over her stool. 'You're only a beginner once and we must take advantage of it!'

'Let's go. I need to talk to you. I want to help you.'

'Help me? You have helped me,' he said. 'Stay and help more.'

Although play had resumed on the table everyone was staring at them.

'Come on. Let's get away from this,' she said.

She pulled on his arm and for the first time she felt his grip release from the table. Kate had made up his losses, but it was impossible for a gambler to leave when they were ahead, when they were supposed to. Anton strained against her and Kate knew he was partly right. Fortune was smiling on them now and it was bad luck to leave.

Anton followed her to the cash desk. Kate gave in the ticket and the cashier handed her twelve thousand in cash together with a receipt.

Anton took a wad of screwed-up tickets from his pocket and gave them to the cashier. The man reached behind the desk to a drawer and placed sealed bundles of cash into a series of envelopes.

'What's all that money?' Kate asked, aghast. 'I thought you said you were losing.'

'I was,' Anton said grimly, stuffing the envelopes into a bag he had slung around his hips. 'I lost all *my* money.'

'*Your* money? But there's thousands here.'

They had reached the main bar where they sat on a sofa and ordered a drink.

'Whose money is that?' Kate said, pointing to his bag.

He didn't answer, just stared between his knees to the floor.

She felt a crawling sensation at the back of her neck. Anton did things she never dreamed of, and under his influence, she did them too.

Anton spoke in Italian to the waiter who brought their drinks. He stuffed a hundred euros into the waiter's pocket even though their drinks only cost a quarter of that.

He turned to Kate. 'How did you know I was here?'

Kate told him about her visit to the restaurant, her conversation with the girl at the bar.

'So this money you have now. Is this what you were talking about the other night.'

He nodded.

'How do you do it?'

'I bring it here, a few thousand at a time, exchange it for chips, play with it for a few hours and then cash it out. *Voilà* it's clean.' He showed her the receipt the cashier had given him. 'They show these when they deposit the money at the bank. My boss trusts me because I play well and don't lose it.'

Kate drained her Martini. 'So who is this boss?'

'Silvano. The guy you met at the restaurant near the chateau at Roquebrune. He works for the guy who owns Casa di Stelle.'

'What goes on in that place?'

He looked away. 'I told you. It's a meeting point for the movement of people along the coast.'

'Movement of *people*?'

'And activity along the coast.'

'What, like some kind of refuelling station?'

'Yeah. It's a central networking hub.'

Kate thought of the cars, the unloading of crates. The strange atmosphere in the restaurant, and the fact there were never any diners there.

'La Terrasse. It's not really a restaurant, is it?'

'They put a lot of cash through the restaurant. On the books it has a huge turnover. Other cash I deal with.'

'And you've been stealing from these people?'

'I don't steal, I *win*. I just take a cut of the winnings.'

'What do you mean a cut?'

'Silvano just wants the money back once I've cleaned it through the casino. Any profit, I take,' he said shrugging as he finished his beer.

Then he stood. '*Basta!* Let's go.'

'And you expect me to help you hide this money from him?' Kate said, walking beside Anton through the cocktail bar.

'Not if you don't want to.'

256

'*Not if I don't want to?* You didn't tell me where it came from.'

'It's money I earned.'

'You *earned?* Look at you justifying it. You're as bad as them.'

'Am I any different to you?'

'But you know what they're doing,' she said weakly.

'And you also know what your bosses do.'

'I don't! I have no idea!'

'That's because you don't ask.'

'I don't steal their money.'

'I don't steal their money either. I just take the winnings.'

'But you use their money to make your winnings. Your winnings are polluted.'

Anton stopped abruptly. 'What do you mean *polluted?*'

'Polluted by association. You wouldn't have any winnings if you didn't use their dirty money.'

'If no one used dirty money there wouldn't be any money.'

They had passed out of the casino, down the steps and into the square. The air was heavy with the greasy, metallic reek of petrol from the sports cars and of dirty cash. Kate could taste it on her tongue.

'If no one used dirty money you wouldn't be paid. You wouldn't have a job and none of this would be here. You wouldn't be here and I wouldn't be here,' he said angrily, pointing to the casino. 'That polluted money just bought you a drink. Did it taste any different from any other drink?' Anton grabbed her hand and pulled her towards the Hôtel de Paris. 'Come on. Let's get something *polluted* to eat.'

Kate pulled away. 'Actually, no. I feel sick. Eating is the last thing I feel like doing.'

'Well, I'm starving,' he said. 'I need a steak.'

She stood in the middle of the square and watched him as he transferred the bag full of illicit cash from one side of his body to the other.

Kate turned and walked away fast. She could hear him calling to her as the taxi pulled away but she didn't look back.

Chapter Twenty-Four
Èze

V ANESSA SWITCHED ON HER PHONE on Monday morning to a series of frantic messages from Rob. He needed to discuss something urgently, he said, over breakfast at his hotel in Èze.

He was the last person Vanessa wanted to see. David's mugging had affected her badly and she had spent most of Sunday on the phone to David and to the school again, then a long time alone with her thoughts. She realised she could no longer stomach LuckyCoin, or any of the deals she did for Rob. She had always used David and the exorbitant Meetham school fees as an excuse for staying at Meritus but this incident had exposed the grim reality she had, up until now, been able to ignore: her work at Meritus was harming people, David included. It was affecting her as well, and if she stayed at Meritus any longer things would get worse.

It didn't take long to clear Monaco and Vanessa was soon weaving through the hairpin bends towards Rob's hotel in a medieval castle perched high on a cliff above the sea.

Rob was waiting for her alone on the breakfast terrace clutching a Bloody Mary that had haemorrhaged all over the starched white tablecloth. Above Rob's head was a canopy of jasmine that dropped fragrant blossoms onto the table and all around him were gorgeous plants. Further out, terracotta urns held an assortment of cacti and palms, living sculptures against the deep blue sky, and beyond this, a balustrade of magenta bougainvillea framed the sea below. The view was equally stunning to the west, towards Saint-Jean-Cap-Ferrat, but Rob saw none of it. He was staring into his phone, his face overcast above his double chins.

He barely acknowledged Vanessa as she approached, so intent was he on his screen. He wore a pair of crumpled shorts, faded blue Rivieras and a dirty T-shirt. His eyes were puffy, and grey whiskers swept his heavy jowls.

'Bloody awful business this,' said Rob, his chins wobbling as he glanced up.

For a second Vanessa thought he was referring to David, but then she realised that couldn't be right: she hadn't told anyone about the mugging yet.

'Christ, Rob, you look terrible.'

Rob went back to his screen. 'That deal you did a few weeks ago, it's got hot,' he said.

Vanessa lowered herself onto a chair, placing her handbag firmly on her lap. 'What are you talking about?'

'Amir's deal,' Rob slurred. 'That property transfer.'

'What do you mean "it's got hot"?'

Rob's head whipped up from his phone and he glared at her, his tone vicious. '*Hot*, hot, hot. As in chilli hot, as in fucking boiling. We need to reverse out,' he said, taking a swig from the drink in his fist. He gazed at her with pink, bleary eyes and she could tell this was not his first drink that morning, probably not even his first that hour.

He stared at her wildly. 'Elanka's screwed me over. They'll be after us. We need to reverse out.'

It suddenly hit her what he meant. 'You mean Casa di Stelle? The documents are done, Rob. Everything's been finalised. We can't just *reverse out*.'

Rob asked for the wine list as a waiter in a bow tie and apron changed the tablecloth and laid down another Bloody Mary.

Vanessa moved the drink to her side of the table, beyond Rob's reach.

'No, we don't want the wine list. Just two black coffees, please,' she said to the waiter. Then turning to Rob, 'Start from the beginning. Explain this to me properly.'

Rob sighed, blasting Vanessa with alcohol fumes. 'Remember when you transferred beneficial ownership to Elanka and her mother?'

Vanessa felt her stomach contract. 'Beneficial ownership in the holding company through the Jersey trust?'

Rob nodded. 'It wasn't authorised.'

'What do you mean?'

'Amir didn't really know about it.'

Vanessa's mouth went dry. 'So why did we do it?'

Rob shook his head and went back to scrolling through his phone. 'What a mess.'

Vanessa took Rob's phone and placed it face down on the table. She took a gulp of Rob's Bloody Mary. 'Explain to me properly what's going on.'

'Amir's about to be sanctioned so we had to move his assets around.'

'Yes. I know that.'

'At first, he wanted to put Casa di Stelle into his wife's name but at the last minute, Elanka persuaded me to put it into her name.'

'And her mother's name.'

'That's right.'

Vanessa stared at Rob incredulously. 'And you didn't run that past Amir?'

Rob rattled the ice in his drink. 'Actually, it's more complicated than that.'

'Rob, you're not making any sense.'

Vanessa paused as their coffees arrived then sipped hers, grateful for its clarifying warmth.

'Elanka and I—'

Vanessa buried her face in her hands recalling the evening in London earlier that month. 'You're not sleeping with her,' she said, lifting her head. 'Good god, Rob. She's our biggest client's girlfriend. What on earth are you thinking?'

'I'm not,' said Rob mournfully.

'Or rather, only a very small part of you is thinking,' Vanessa said, gazing at Rob, taking in his bloated features, his slovenly demeanour and wondering, more aptly, what Elanka could be thinking.

'No, no, no,' Rob said scratching his forehead nervously. 'I'm not sleeping with her. It's worse than that.'

'Jesus,' Vanessa said. 'What then?'

'She conned me. She told me she would persuade Amir to make a big investment in LuckyCoin if I got the property transferred into her name instead of the wife's.'

262

A tiny shard of pity pierced the veil of loathing Vanessa felt for Rob, coupled with new respect for Elanka. 'She must be insane. And she's done this without Amir knowing?'

Rob looked up, his eyes wild with terror. 'She's not insane. She's actually extremely bright. We're in terrible trouble, Vanessa.'

'Oh god, Rob. What have you done?'

'That money you sent through for the property deal at the same time.'

'The money you needed in such a hurry.'

Rob nodded. 'Elanka told me about that Cyprus money. She said I should use it and so I made up the whole property deal as cover. There was no townhouse in London. There was no sanctioned Russian. I lied to you and used the money for LuckyCoin,' Rob said, his face collapsing back into his chins.

Vanessa was speechless.

'It was just meant to buy time until I could switch in another investor,' Rob said.

'Do you still have access to this money?' Vanessa asked hollowly.

'Of course I bloody don't.'

'So where is it?'

'I used it for set-up costs. To pay off some officials in Nigeria. That kind of thing.' Rob gulped his drink. 'I also took some money from his client account.'

Vanessa stared at him in horror. 'How much?'

'Another three million.'

'Are you crazy? Stephen or someone else in accounts will have certainly picked up on that by now.'

'No one at the firm apart from you knows anything yet,' Rob said, unconvincingly.

'Does Amir know about any of this?'

'He doesn't know about the money Elanka sent yet, but he's found out about the three million from the client account.'

'So get it out. Now! What are you doing here? Get it all out of LuckyCoin and back into their account.'

'I need your help.'

Vanessa felt a sinking fear and put up her hands. 'No, no. No way.'

Rob's tragic demeanour altered and he stared at her for a moment, his teeth clenched. 'We just need to make it *look* like it's gone back into their account. Buy ourselves some time.'

'What are you saying?'

'We need to take money from the Meritus trust account and put it into Amir's client account.'

Vanessa reeled back as if she had been stung. 'Are you serious?'

Rob widened his eyes. 'It's just optics. We transfer in some funds now so when the auditors see it on Friday it will all look correct.'

Vanessa moved even further back in her chair. '*Auditors?*'

'The firm is being audited. After Friday we can shift the money back.'

'Why is the firm being audited, Rob?'

Rob threw his hands in the air. 'Because we work for sanctioned clients.'

Vanessa checked her phone. It had just gone 8 a.m. 'Why didn't you say this before?'

'I'm saying it now. That's why I'm here for fuck's sake, Vanessa.'

Vanessa rose from her chair, her knees weak. 'You can't come here pissed out of your mind and tell me you've embezzled money from one of our most dangerous clients, that the firm's being audited and then expect me to fix it! No way, Rob. There's no way I'm getting involved in this.'

'You're going to have to. Amir will kill us.'

Rob's tone chilled her, but she kept her eyes on his. 'Don't think you can bully me into this. This is all your mess. I'm having nothing to do with it.'

He grabbed her arm. 'I need you, Vanessa. I don't have access to the accounts here in Monaco. Only you can authorise this.'

She shook him off. 'No way.'

'Come on, Vanessa. Think of all the times I bailed you out.'

'*Bailed* me out? Don't be ridiculous!'

Rob shifted in his chair, his body so soft and lifeless Vanessa thought he was about to slip off his seat. 'You need to help me, Vanessa. You're tied up with this too. You authorised moving the money from Amir's account to London. You gave the instructions to transfer the villa to Elanka and her mother. Your fingerprints are all over this.'

Vanessa felt her extremities go numb and her blood drained as the ramifications of what Rob was saying sunk in. It was true. Her name was all over it.

'Sooner or later this will be picked up at work,' she said, more to herself than to Rob as she looked around helplessly.

Rob's voice was strained and his lips grew thin. 'That's right. You need to sort it out for both our sakes.'

Vanessa's voice was barely a whisper. 'I can't do that without leaving even worse traces. It's like a trail of blood. It can't just be fixed like that.'

'Think of the times I helped *you*. For heaven's sake, Vanessa, I gave you a job when you were *desperate*. When you had *nothing*,' Rob said, his palms together, pleading with her now.

Vanessa gazed at him coldly. 'You gave me a job *because* I was desperate. You wanted someone who had no choice. Someone who would be easy to manipulate into doing your dirty work. Well, guess what? I'm not so desperate anymore,' Vanessa said, more desperate than she had ever been in her life.

'If you don't do this you're on the line too.'

'I'll tell them it was your idea,' Vanessa said, casting around for an escape plan.

'And I'll say it was yours.'

They stared at each other, eyes locked in an impotent Mexican standoff, each knowing that Amir wouldn't care who had done it – he would kill them both.

Vanessa grabbed her bag. 'I'm going to the toilet. Wait here.'

Vanessa's knees faltered as she walked across the terrace. Her face felt numb as she patted it with water from the basin tap and stared at her reflection. The house of cards Rob had built was collapsing. She couldn't stay in it any longer and coming clean right now would make things worse. She needed to do something to protect herself and not Rob for a change.

She delved into her bag for her lipstick. As she covered her bloodless lips in a smear of crimson, she thought of Elanka and the insane risks she had taken. What was she thinking? The girl lived among these people, she knew what they were capable of. There was nowhere on the face of the earth that could shelter her once Amir realised she had double-crossed him. Why was she in Monaco waltzing around as if nothing had happened? Why hadn't she just disappeared?

Suddenly, Vanessa's gaze darted from the garish red lips in the mirror to her handbag as the fever of an idea coursed through her brain.

She rummaged through her bag and retrieved the black and yellow card Joe had given her several weeks ago. Her fingers slipped on her phone as she dialled his number.

He took a while to answer but when he did a delicious sense of relief overwhelmed her.

'Hi Joe, it's Vanessa from the casino a few weeks back.' She waited for the penny to drop. 'I really need your help.'

Chapter Twenty-Five

I T TOOK A WHILE TO coax Rob from the restaurant and he only agreed on the condition he could bring the Bloody Mary with him to his room. In the end, it was the waiter who steered Rob's bulk across the terrace, through the gardens and into his suite in the chateau.

The restaurant was beginning to fill up and several families had appeared on the terrace. A group of five watched as they passed – two blonde children their plates piled high with pastries, a nanny and the parents sipping lattes in matching gym gear. The mother rolled her eyes at Vanessa as Rob stumbled into a pot plant and then swore viciously at the waiter who was guiding him.

When they entered his suite, Rob made a beeline for the minibar.

'I think it's best if you have a sleep first,' said Vanessa, redirecting him towards the four-poster bed.

Vanessa closed the shutters, removed Rob's shoes and arranged the bedding around him.

'I'm too stressed for sleep,' Rob said, kicking off the covers. 'I need another drink.'

Vanessa pushed him gently back onto the pillow, leaving her hand on his forehead as she spoke in soothing tones. 'We need to sort this out together, but you're no good to me drunk. Have a sleep and then we'll get to work.'

'So you'll help me?' Rob said, his eyes blue pits of helplessness.

Vanessa fished in her bag for the Ambien. 'Of course. But only if you have a lie-down first.'

Rob took the pills, his hands trembling.

'Thank you, Vanessa,' he said, gulping down the tablets with half a bottle of water. 'There's some cash here too. Please take it to Franz.'

Vanessa tucked him in. 'Get a few hours sleep and then we'll sort it all out.'

Vanessa waited until Rob was snoring then opened his wardrobe where she crouched in front of the double-width safe. She tapped their usual code and opened the device. It was empty.

She went through his drawers. Rob said he had some cash, so where was it? Finally, she found a suitcase under the bed with a slip indicating there was two hundred and fifty thousand euros there.

Vanessa put the 'Do Not Disturb' sign on his door. She took the suitcase to reception, said Rob was sleeping and that they shouldn't interrupt him under any circumstances.

'Any problems, call me,' Vanessa said, writing down her number.

Vanessa's heart thudded as she turned from the desk, scanning the terrain ahead. She didn't know how much time she had and who was already after Rob, so she needed to move quickly. The family from breakfast were milling around the concierge desk asking about beaches. Seated on low chairs near the entrance, two men in shades and earpieces were pretending to read their phones, while a tour group waited to check out.

Once she was on the motorway, Vanessa called the cash bank in Nice to arrange a visit later that morning, and then went through the things she needed to do before she left. Mercifully, the traffic was clear and she was soon driving through the tunnels to Fontvieille.

When she reached her apartment she transferred the cash less fifty thousand euros into a larger suitcase together with her laptop, driving licence, passport, credit cards and some other items she might need over the coming weeks. She put a change of clothes and the fifty thousand euros into a shopping bag and left it by the door next to the suitcase. Vanessa gave herself fifteen minutes to move through the flat, collecting only those things she would save in a fire. There were very few objects of any real importance in her life, as it turned out, and they were mostly David's.

She gathered all of David's possessions into a box – his toys and books, the photographs of him spread throughout the apartment, his artwork and a few things he had made for her at school. Any papers he might need while she was gone she put on top of the box and carried it down the hallway to his room. Vanessa usually avoided going into David's room when he was at school because it was so empty, a stark contrast to the way he filled their home when he was there. She always kept the door closed too, so the room's emptiness didn't engulf the whole apartment. Sometimes, though, the cleaner left it ajar and Vanessa would open the front door to a view straight down the corridor to his unslept-in bed. The unhappiness his empty room stirred in her was always confronting and she braced herself for it each time she put her key in the lock.

If Amir didn't get to her first, Vanessa knew she would probably be arrested if she stayed in Monaco and so she needed to go to ground until she came up with a plan. She didn't know when she would be back and she had no idea yet what she was going to tell David. She knew she had just one chance to manage the details of her escape and to focus on doing everything in the correct order. If she worried about David it would only confuse her, but now, seeing his things laid out on his bed, his pictures on the wall, his few clothes hanging neatly in the cupboards giving off his faint milky smell, she broke down, overcome with a tremendous sense of guilt.

She imagined David's face as he tried to understand what the school's pastoral officer, or the headmaster, was telling him had happened to his mother. *Disappeared? Missing?* She imagined him shaking his head, his features collapsing in bewilderment and then his face clouding over in panic. *Did they mean Mum was dead?* David was a clever boy, but he would not understand this.

There were signs and things he might cling to, she thought, looking around desperately as she went to the window and pulled down the blind. Hopefully the methodical way she was going about this process would leave everyone in no doubt that she had deliberately disappeared, that she was still alive, and they would make sure he understood that too.

But what if he thought, as the weeks wore on and still he hadn't heard from her, that she had simply abandoned him? After Pascal's disappearance it was the one thing Vanessa vowed she would never do. What if David assumed that, like Pascal, she wanted a new life and that he had no part in it? No, she couldn't bear that. It was a far worse prospect than if she were dead, but there was no way she could reassure David or tell him the truth about what she was doing. It was too dangerous for him to know anything of her whereabouts.

As she fought against the tears, Vanessa realised she hadn't prepared David for this – for the inevitable day when something she did at work caught up with her. She had never spoken to David about her job, never alluded to the risks and dangers she faced from her clients or the authorities for that matter, thinking it was much better for him if she kept it to herself. As far as he was concerned she was just another office worker.

'What job do you do, Mummy?' David asked once when he was about four years old. She had arrived home late as usual, but just in time to see him before bed. His face shone, all pink and innocent, from the bath he'd just had and as he looked up at her, she wished she could tell him she was a doctor or a teacher, or did something useful with her life. Instead she mumbled something about being a lawyer who helped people with their problems.

'What kind of problems, Mummy?' David asked, hope still shining in his face.

'Well, if they have problems they can't solve themselves, they come to me and I help them.'

'You help people?' David said, still smiling.

'Yes.'

'Your mother helps people hide money,' said Pascal from behind his iPad.

David laughed and looked intrigued. 'Hide money? How do you hide money?'

Vanessa didn't miss a beat. 'Oh there are lots of ways of hiding money, darling. Sometimes people don't want others to know they are rich, and so they squirrel it away. And I help them do that.'

David cocked his head. 'Are we rich, Mummy?' he said, his face suddenly serious as he picked up on the bitterness coursing through the room, souring the conversation into one about money.

Then, like now, she couldn't tell him what she did. She had to leave it to others, like his pastoral officer at school, to confuse him even more.

Perhaps she could just go and get him from the boarding house and then disappear somewhere together. They could head north to Scotland, she thought, imagining a new life in a secluded village somewhere in the Highlands. But as soon as the fantasy took shape, it dissolved. It would be dangerous for David to be with her – people like Amir had no limits, and a woman travelling with a child during term time was much more noticeable than a woman travelling alone. The school would be a problem too: they would alert the authorities if David failed to return after an outing with her. No, she couldn't disappear with David; he was safer at school. She would have to call or get a message to him somehow that she was safe and that she hadn't abandoned him. But how? As she considered her increasingly limited options, her phone pinged with a message.

Are you coming in today?

Her colleague Stephen wrote.

There are some strange transactions here I need you to take a look at.

On my way, replied Vanessa.

She would have to work out how to deal with David later.

Vanessa left her apartment for the last time and locked the front door behind her. No one saw her as she took the lift to the ground floor with the suitcase and shopping bag and slid the keys to her apartment through her neighbour's letterbox in the lobby.

Twenty minutes later she was on the train to Nice looking like an ordinary tourist with her face concealed from the CCTV under a large sun hat. Upon arrival in Nice, she placed the suitcase into a storage locker and took the shopping bag with her.

Vanessa walked north from the station until she came to a residential area where there were fewer CCTV cameras and went into a café. In the toilet she changed her clothes and then ordered an omelette and a coffee. After eating, she walked several blocks until she found a recycling bin where she discarded her old clothes. She caught a taxi to the centre of Nice and found a hair salon. She asked the hairdresser – a young woman with long bleached waves, to cut her hair short and to dye it back to its natural mousy brown, adding in some tufts of grey around the sides. Vanessa said she didn't want anything glamorous, explaining she'd had enough of trying to pretend she was younger, and that it was time to start looking her age. The hairdresser nodded in solidarity and gave her a short cut with grey feathery highlights around her face. It was good to be back to her original colouring, and Vanessa was surprised at how much this new style suited her.

Vanessa went to the address Joe had given her over the phone earlier that morning when she was in the bathroom in Èze, which now seemed a lifetime ago. A short skinny man answered the door, his face puffy with sleep, and led her into a dusty back room where he took her photo and the money and told her to come back in two hours. While waiting for her fake passport to be ready, Vanessa bought three burner phones and a new computer. She then visited several boutiques unable at first to find one that didn't sell bright touristy clothes or glamorous beach wear. Finally, she located a second-hand store in a back street of the Old Town. It was difficult to steer away from the designer clothes that were her preference but eventually she found two pairs of ordinary trousers – one beige and one navy, three pale shirts and a grey jumper.

Once she had bought all she needed, Vanessa went to a park, found an empty bench and took out one of her new phones.

'Vanessa? Is that you? This number—' Kate said.

'It's me.'

'Stephen from the finance department is looking for you. What's happened?'

Vanessa looked around the park in panic as if Stephen might be there.

'Napier's also called me. It sounds serious.'

'Napier? Jesus Christ!'

'Vanessa? What's all this about?' Kate said.

'Kate. I need your help. Listen carefully and don't write anything down.'

Vanessa told Kate she had been helping Rob launder client money for years. She explained that Rob had now embezzled Amir's money and that Vanessa was caught up in it too. Vanessa gave Kate enough details for her to understand the danger Vanessa was in from Amir, and that she was now on the run.

'I don't expect you to help me with any of this but I really need help with David.'

'Just tell me what you need me to do,' Kate said.

'I'm going to tell the school I've had to go away and that you'll call him once or twice a week to check he's OK. The school fees are paid but I'm sending through my bank details now in case he needs anything. I'll tell them you're authorised to act as his guardian while I'm gone.'

'Right,' said Kate.

They agreed that if it was safe to do so, Vanessa would call Kate to check up on David but apart from that and a call Vanessa would make to David now, neither Kate nor David would hear from her.

'And if you don't call me?' Kate said.

'If I can't call I'll try to get a message to you some other way.'

'How?' Kate said.

'I don't know. Letter, email, Facebook.'

'*Facebook?* How will you do that?'

Vanessa turned her gaze up to the trees as a few yellow leaves drifted to the ground, flickering like lanterns as they caught the light. 'I'll set up an alias.'

'An *alias?*'

'I don't know, but whatever it is you'll know it's me. I'll use a nickname.'

That had been Joe's idea. He told her on the phone to use her new identity sparingly and to use a nickname if she had to. She chose one associated with her new middle name.

'Annie,' she said. 'My name will be Annie.'

When Vanessa came off the phone she thought carefully about what she would now tell David. Kate agreed he needed to know she was safe, that she hadn't abandoned him, but apart from that, it was best he didn't know anything at all. She couldn't even tell him how long it would be, which was just as well because she didn't know herself.

When David answered the phone they chatted normally at first. He seemed to have recovered a little from the mugging and told her his team had won their football match yesterday thanks to a goal he scored in a penalty shoot-out.

Vanessa basked in the ordinariness of their conversation, thinking how much she had taken these chats for granted and wishing she could just stop there. The early afternoon sun shone through the leaves, scattering light over the grass around her. She imagined walking away from the bench down the path, through the gates and away from this whole plan.

After David had finished speaking she sat still waiting for her heart to stop pounding.

'Are you still there, Mum?'

Vanessa pulled herself together and tried to keep her voice bright. 'The reason I'm calling you now – and I don't want you to worry – but I have to go away for a while.'

'Go away where?' David said.

'I can't say at the moment.'

David's voice grew more cautious. 'Where are you going, Mum?'

'I'm not sure, darling. But the thing is I won't be able to call you very much—'

She let out a sob, which she disguised in a cough.

'—I won't be able to call you at all.'

There was silence down the line.

'But I need you to know that even if you don't hear from me, I'm all right,' Vanessa said, her mouth dry, her voice utterly unconvincing.

David didn't say anything.

'My friend Kate will call you.'

'Why can't you call me?' David said sullenly.

Vanessa looked around desperately at the trees and the flower beds, and then she spoke without thinking. 'I'll find a way of sending you messages.'

When she said it she felt ill. It was exactly what she told Kate she wouldn't do.

Silence again, and then she heard a bell ring.

'That's the bell for the next lesson. I need to go.'

'OK, darling,' Vanessa said helplessly.

After the call, Vanessa sat on the bench for some time, not trusting her legs to hold her if she stood.

She told herself this was the hardest part, but that she had done it now and apart from the promise to send David messages, she was doing the right thing. There was no going back, she just needed to keep going forwards. She checked her watch. Rob would probably be waking up now, she thought. She was doing this for the future, for her future with David.

After she had collected her new passport, Vanessa went back to the train station, retrieved the suitcase containing the rest of the cash and then checked into a hotel near the Old Port under her new name.

From the hotel, Vanessa emailed her landlord, terminating the lease on her apartment in Monaco. She explained she had to leave town abruptly to attend to her sick mother in Canada and transferred the required three months' notice in rent. Vanessa then found a storage depot online, paid the two months' rental upfront and booked a removalist for the following day. She wrote to her neighbour, giving him the same story about her mother and asked if he wouldn't mind giving access to the removalist so he could take the items from David's room to the storage depot. Then she closed off all her utilities and cancelled all her subscriptions.

She wrote to the school, telling them Kate would act as David's guardian while she was in Canada.

Vanessa retrieved all her important contacts, wrote them out in hard copy and then deleted her email accounts.

She set up a new email account in the name of 'Annie' and another one in case she needed it.

While she was deleting her work account, Vanessa saw a flurry of messages from Stephen. Stephen was also calling her now on her phone together with Rob. Vanessa turned off her phone, took out the SIM card and closed down her laptop, satisfied for once in her day's work.

That afternoon, Vanessa took half the remaining cash from the suitcase to the Hotel Lympia, the stash house near the Eglise Notre Dame. She breathed a sigh of relief as she went through the entry procedures. Despite the changes to her hair colour, the facial recognition cameras worked.

Franz greeted her in the basement.

Vanessa opened the suitcase and pointed to the cash.

'I don't have time to wait until it's counted but I'm guessing there's about a hundred thousand euros there.'

Franz nodded.

'I might need you to place it into an account in this name,' Vanessa said, showing him her new passport. 'I'll send bank details in a few weeks.'

Franz took a copy of her new passport. There was a safe in the back of Rob's vault that contained diamonds. Vanessa opened it and placed her old passport, laptop, SIM card and driving licence inside.

Joe had said for an extra fee he could arrange for an account to be opened in the name of her new identity through a bank in Cyprus, but that it would take a few weeks to put in place. Franz could transfer the cash there when it was set up. Joe said it was best to stay in France, the country of her new identity at least to begin with so she wouldn't get caught up with any residency or social security issues.

Vanessa retraced her steps and left the stash house by a back exit. She returned to her hotel, gathered her things and went to the train station. The next train was for Avignon and she boarded it, not quite sure where the town was.

Life never turns out the way you imagine, Vanessa thought as the train pulled out of the station and took her away from the Côte d'Azur, which had once held so much promise. Life is never what you remember either, she cautioned herself unless she had second thoughts or drifted off down a melancholy path of reminiscence. She reached for her phone but then realised there was no signal – she had left the SIM with Franz. She turned to the window feeling a sense of relief as the countryside opened up. The best thing to do was seize whatever parts seemed real, she thought, and she resolved to do that now as she disappeared into a new life where she hoped she would be safe and, for a while at least, free of Rob, Amir and anything to do with Meritus.

Chapter Twenty-Six

Monaco

KATE HAD JUST HUNG UP from Vanessa when Julia rushed into her office. Julia told Kate an abridged version of what Vanessa had just said, embellishing it with the rumour that Rob and Vanessa had absconded together. The *Financial Times* had run the story about LuckyCoin that weekend and the firm's management in London were trying to piece together exactly what Rob had done with Amir's money. Napier, the managing partner, had traced some of the funds and Rob's bank had frozen his accounts, but the bulk of Amir's cash was missing. What Rob and Vanessa had done with Amir's companies and trusts in anticipation of sanctions was even more opaque.

'Do the other partners know what kind of work Rob does for Amir?' Kate asked.

'They know it involves complicated offshore structures, and that Rob's billings are enormous, but they don't know the specifics.'

'They don't ask questions.'

'Right,' said Julia. 'Rob's clients barely understand the arrangements he puts in place to hide their money and assets.

He uses agents and lawyers in most jurisdictions and he keeps that side of things very much to himself. We really don't know what he's done.'

'Does Amir know what's happened?'

'Not all of it,' said Julia, her voice wavering. She closed her eyes, struggling to maintain composure then cleared her throat. 'Kate, I know I haven't been entirely supportive since you started here, but this litigation has been stressful for me too.' An ugly wash of desperation swept Julia's face and Kate raised her hand to stop her going further. Julia then fixed her with a pleading look. 'Napier's trying to sort through things now. It's more important than ever that we win that litigation on Falkon.'

'Of course,' said Kate, turning to the papers on her desk. Julia was trying to force a sense of camaraderie between them and for the time being, Kate would go along with it.

It was two weeks before the case started in Monaco's *Tribunal suprême* and a week before Kate had to present the *new evidence* to the other side. On balance, it was good news Rob was out of the picture. It would just be Julia's head on the block now and she would be much easier to deal with alone. Kate had imagined she would enjoy exacting this kind of revenge, but it just made her feel small and mean, even without witnessing Julia's desperation. She went through the file again then tried to focus on other matters.

Last week, Rob had made a fuss of giving Kate a high profile case as a reward for doing the dirty work on Falkon. It was a piece of litigation for the Automobile Club de Monaco, which if she did well, would earn her a prime seat at next year's Grand Prix. It also came with a ticket to the VIP after-party where

Rob said she would meet all the drivers and their entourages, not to mention royalty.

'This is what you came to Monaco for, Kate,' he said with a wink, as he thrust the ACM file at her. 'Motor Racing. It could be a real speciality for you.'

Kate couldn't have cared less about the Grand Prix drivers and the idea of hanging around with more big egos made her heart sink. She was struggling to get Anton out of her mind after the episode at the casino and although she had vowed not to contact him again, she thought she would be able to focus better on work if she knew he was all right.

She called him and sent several texts, but there was no answer. Finally, he replied the following evening:

I know you're trying to get in touch with me. Don't worry if you don't hear from me for a while. I'll write to you next month.

Next *month?*

Where are you?

He replied in French, which he hardly ever did, the text erratic and full of mistakes, saying he needed to get away, he needed to think. He said he'd had enough of taking advantage of people and wanted some time out. He was going to the bottom but he would be free.

She texted him immediately. What did he mean *going to the bottom?*

He took a while to reply.

Ma chérie, honestly I don't know. I think a little bit in the street but I'm not afraid. Don't worry about me I'd rather be on the street than doing this anymore. You're right.

What on earth was he thinking? And why did he say she was right? Living on the street wasn't her idea. She was frightened for him and fired back a panicked message.

OK, so you replied to me tonight to tell me this alarming news. If you hate what you're doing so much, why aren't you looking for another job and living a normal life like everyone else. Why this drama?????? It feels like you're blaming me . . .

There was no answer.

You don't have to live on the street!

Nothing came back from him overnight or the next morning.

Kate tried to throw herself into work, but she couldn't focus. She knew things at Meritus were unravelling fast and although she was braced for it, she realised now how little she cared about the place. She dragged herself through the day worried about Anton, imagining him alone in a shop alcove or slumped on a dirty street corner.

It was pointless, but she tried calling him again. There was no response from his phone. He had blocked her for good.

Kate despised herself. Would it have been that bad to have helped Anton somehow? God knows what kind of people she was already helping at Meritus and Anton was clearly in trouble. She was aware of her own hypocrisy – how she was beholden to the likes of Rob and Julia for her salary and in return she was at their beck and call, cutting corners, not refusing them or asking questions, just like everyone else. Although she was engaged in this one act of treachery against them, Anton was right – she was no better than him, or them. She may as well be on the street too.

At lunchtime Kate caught the train to Roquebrune. It was midweek, but there were scores of people on the beach and Kate was reminded of the world she had just started to discover with Anton. A couple of weeks ago they had been on the beach too, enjoying each other's company and if things had turned out differently they might have even been here now.

The same dark-haired woman was behind the bar at the restaurant. It was just after 1 p.m. and there was no one in the place despite the crowds on the beach. As Kate drew closer to the bar, she overheard a couple asking for a table. The woman said they weren't serving food that day. She said this rudely without any hint of an apology and the couple walked away, confused.

Just then a man emerged from the kitchen. It was Silvano, the owner of the restaurant near the chateau Kate had visited with Anton, the man he later described as his boss. Silvano nodded to Kate then wiped his hands on a tea towel tucked into the waistband of his jeans.

'Excuse me, I'm looking for Anton,' Kate said.

'He's not here,' said the woman coldly.

Silvano spoke to the woman in Italian and Kate heard him say Anton's name. Finally he turned to Kate with an ugly look on his face. There was no trace of the convivial character she had met at the restaurant.

'He's gone away for a few weeks.'

The woman was now polishing glasses over the sink in a deliberate way as if determined to stay out of the conversation. Kate could see the woman's profile, her jaw clenching as Silvano spoke.

'Gone where?' Kate asked.

He shrugged. 'Back to Milan for his mother's birthday.'

This wasn't right. '*Milan?* I saw him last week. He didn't say anything about Milan.'

Silvano stood there, glaring at her now and openly hostile as if challenging her to carry on.

Kate maintained eye contact but could see in her peripheral vision that the woman was now staring at her. 'Do you know when he'll be back?'

Silvano threw his hands in the air. 'No one has any idea what he's doing. One day he's here. The next day he doesn't show. How would I know when he'll be back?'

Silvano returned to the kitchen.

'Thanks,' said Kate, to no one in particular as the woman was again polishing glasses.

Kate took the stairway to the station, deep in thought. Silvano was clearly lying and she remembered, as she stopped on the stairway, Anton telling her his mother had *died*. Kate was trying to piece it together when she heard quick steps behind her.

It was the woman from the restaurant. She was agitated and pulled Kate to one side so they were concealed from the sight of those below.

'He left his keys with me so I could feed his cat,' she whispered. 'I sometimes look after her when he goes away and he always texts me, but this time he hasn't. He hasn't called since he left on Sunday.' The woman glanced over her shoulder. 'I'm worried about him. Silvano and the others are looking for him because he's stolen money from them.'

'Is there any way to track him down?' asked Kate. 'There must be someone who knows where he is.'

'I have no idea. I've tried calling but his phone's dead.'

'Before he went away I said I would help him, but then we fought. I feel like his disappearance is my fault,' Kate said.

The woman shook her head and a hard expression crossed her face. 'It's not your fault. It's—'

'What?' said Kate.

'I'm sorry. I need to get back.'

'Wait—'

'I've got your number. I'll call you if I hear anything.'

'Wait—' Kate called again, but the woman was already at the bottom of the stairs.

The next evening, Kate and Julia had a dinner with clients on the eastern edge of town. The Monte-Carlo Bay Hotel was another luxury resort on its own man-made peninsula. With arched windows, palm trees and landscaped swimming pools, the place resembled a Caribbean theme park.

Kate got through the dinner but when everyone headed to the hotel's casino, she made her excuses and left.

It was a warm evening and she decided to walk home along the section of customs path that led from the resort to her apartment in Saint Roman. She accessed the path directly from the hotel as it dipped down towards the water. Reaching the rocky shoreline, she stood facing the sea. The moon cast a silver path across the water, illuminating the surf between the rocks with an eerie fluorescent glow.

There were several yachts in the bay, each of them keeping their distance from the others as they fanned out from the port. The vessels shone upon the water and she could hear through the still night air the purr of their on-board generators and she saw the frothy wake of a tender travelling out towards them.

Kate turned back to the path and headed inland. As she walked, Kate imagined nights when smugglers would have tracked along this route, hidden as she was now by the foliage growing densely on either side. The path was a relic of that time – still rough and unkempt with thick roots stretching across, warping the earth underfoot, as if the plants were determined to regain the territory they had lost to the villas and the country clubs all around them.

A train rattled past, her heels scuffing the path and the gentle swish of the sea below. The ground rose steadily past a tennis club then skirted a car park full of luxury cars. Through bushes and hurricane fencing Kate saw the edge of a swimming pool – a dazzling aqua glow in the dark, heard music and laughter from revellers partying into the night. She followed the path until it came to a narrow flight of steps with high walls on either side. Plants crowded in over the walls obscuring the moon and making the steps dark and gloomy. The coolness of the overgrowth sent a chill through her despite the warmth generated from the walk. Kate considered turning on her phone's torch, but the glare would ruin her night vision and she could just about see well enough. A sense of claustrophobia came over her and she picked up her pace.

At the top of the steps, the track took a sharp right past a row of villas before disappearing into a tunnel. As Kate passed through the tunnel, she saw the glow of a cigarette up ahead. She slowed, not sure whether to continue past the smoker in the shadows, or turn back. She stopped and glanced behind her. What a fool she was walking alone at night. Who said this path was safe? Her heart beat wildly and she heard a phone ring – a sharp jolt against the silence. The figure up ahead turned away and spoke into his device. He was probably just a security guard, she thought, trying to calm her breathing as she walked on.

'*Bonsoir,*' Kate whispered softly as she passed the man. He was still turned away, speaking quietly on his phone.

Kate's heart was in her mouth, perspiration pooling under her arms as she entered another dank tunnel. After the tunnel, another flight of stairs led to the road, cars, motorbikes and people.

She could hear the traffic as she raced up the steps, her eyes straining against the dark. The hairs rose on the back of her neck as she took the steps two at a time. There was a landing halfway up and she slowed, her breathing easier with the distance she put between herself and the man behind her.

Kate heard a twig snap up ahead and she stopped, her body stiffening with fear.

There was a rustling and a figure stepped onto the landing.

'*Bonsoir,*' he said.

Chapter Twenty-Seven

KATE SAW A MURKY OUTLINE above her. A grey figure sliding against the dark. Gauzy light from the road obscured his face, but she knew it was the man she had just seen on the path below. Kate took two steps down and he withdrew into the overgrowth, mimicking her retreat. She turned to face the narrow stairwell, wanting to run back to the hotel but she couldn't move, frozen between fight and flight, the depths of the dark stairwell gaping up at her. She put out her hands to stop herself falling into the night and then glanced back to the place she had just seen him. She knew from the speed with which the man had appeared above her that even if she ran now, he would reach the bottom before she did.

There was no option so she edged slowly up the steps, her hand sliding along the rough concrete wall, her footsteps grating against the stone.

When she had almost reached the landing, the man came out of the shadows. There was a gentle click as he lit a cigarette into his cupped hands.

'We've met already,' he said softly, taking a drag and then dropping his hands to reveal his face.

His voice was calm, and she shuddered with relief as she recognised Silvano, the man from Anton's restaurant. Relief turned to rage as Kate drew level with him on the landing. He was about her height, and much smaller than he had seemed when he was looming above her.

'You scared me to death!' she said, waves of anger coursing through her.

Silvano's mouth curved into a smirk and she saw that he had enjoyed her fear. He pointed his cigarette to the trees above. Beneath dense foliage the red eye of a CCTV camera winked down at them.

'Everything here's under surveillance,' he said. 'You needn't have worried.'

He stood between her and the steps that led to the road. She could hear scooters wailing above and felt a strong urge to shove him out of the way and to run for it, but even though he was smaller than she had thought, she was no match for him physically.

'What the hell do you want?' she said.

'I was at the hotel this evening – in the bar. I wanted to speak to you there, but you were with your colleagues. When you left, I guessed the route you'd take.'

'So why not say something back there on the path? Why stalk me like this?'

'When I came off the phone you'd gone and it would have been worse if I'd chased you.'

Kate pushed past him. He grabbed her wrist but she twisted away, moving up the steps so she was now above him.

'I know what you're doing with the Falkon litigation,' he said.

As Kate peered down at him, Silvano shifted his stance. His face was now shadowed, eyes black, his mouth twisted in contempt for her.

'It's my business to know what's going on there, among the people who work for us.'

'Us?' Kate said.

'I work with Amir and his group of companies. I know you're planning to sabotage the litigation, to have the new evidence thrown out as fraudulent.'

Kate's immediate thought was that Anton had told him, but he couldn't have: Anton didn't know what she had done.

'Amir won't accept that outcome. His investment and his reputation would be ruined.'

There was a noise on the path below. Possibly people coming towards the steps, but then it faded out.

'If you go ahead you'll be exposed. I have proof you drafted that document. You'll never work as a lawyer again.'

'So you've come here to threaten me?'

Silvano smiled. 'I don't need to do that.'

'What then?'

'I'm offering an alternative: a generous settlement for the men. More money than if they'd won the litigation. You could negotiate a settlement and get the case withdrawn. It's in everyone's best interests.'

But surely not yours, Kate thought as she stared at him, puzzled. 'Why would Amir agree to this now? He's refused to settle all along.'

'We need your help. In addition to embezzling money, Rob's disappeared, leaving a lot of problems. We need someone at Meritus to help fix things before it's too late.'

'*Fix* what things?' She took another step up. Kate was now closer to the road than to Silvano.

'We need someone with access to the system. We need clarity on what Rob was doing before he disappeared.'

Kate shook her head. She knew Silvano and Amir were more powerful than Rob, Julia or Meritus, but more powerful also meant more dangerous.

'Why would I believe you about this settlement? At the restaurant you lied about Anton. He's not in Milan. Where is he?'

Silvano ground his cigarette into the wall. 'When you left him at the casino he returned to the tables and lost everything.'

'You were there?'

'I had someone watching him because we knew he was stealing. They all do, eventually. If you help us with this it will help him too.' Silvano then added with a sneer, 'You might be his last chance.'

There was a pause as a cavalcade of scooters shrieked above them.

'Why would I want to help Anton?' Kate said, drawing further away. She had now reached the road.

'There's a party tomorrow night at Casa di Stelle,' Silvano said. 'We can speak more then.'

Kate looked back to him. 'Casa di Stelle?'

'Tomorrow night, late. Come alone,' he said.

Kate had no intention of going to the party. Although she was worried her scheme to frame Rob and Julia had been sabotaged, she didn't believe Silvano about the settlement offer. She wondered how he had found out about her nocturnal activities in the office, and the next day at work she tried to find Marc.

293

He still hadn't returned her call from last week but as he had predicted, everyone in the IT department had been replaced with a batch of new consultants and none of them had any idea where he was. She could understand how he might want to put Meritus behind him, but it wasn't like him not to say goodbye or even call once he had left. Maybe she had been wrong about him too.

Kate returned home late on Friday night. She poured a glass of wine and sat on the sofa, looking up a delivery menu on her phone. The wine was delicious and distracted her mid-scroll. It was one of the bottles Anton had brought over. She topped up her glass and moved to the balcony thinking over their conversation the night they had sat there together for the first time. She recalled how much she had trusted him and told him everything about work, stupidly, as it turned out. She realised this was the first time she had been on the balcony since then and the chairs were still close together the way they had left them.

Kate gazed out at the lights of Monaco. An amphitheatre of apartment blocks studded the shoreline and rose up into the hills, empty residences looming over the dark bay. She heard the long drawn-out wail of a siren along the Corniche and the sound seemed to hit the exact pitch of her loneliness.

She glanced inside to the shelf and saw the miniature portrait Anton had painted, and she wondered how many people were sitting alone, like her this evening. How many others were ordering takeaway under the bright lights of their unused kitchens and then going to bed alone? She didn't have to be one of them, she thought as she drained the glass of wine. She didn't have to sit here wallowing in self-imposed isolation like the exiles on the hills. Kate stood and breathed in the warm night air and then went inside to get dressed.

The taxi dropped her off at the station and she walked towards the villa, its gates now wide open. The guards had replaced their army fatigues with tuxedos, and one of them escorted her up to the villa, the driveway flanked with fire pits.

The man had called ahead and Silvano was waiting in front of the house unrecognisable in a dark blue suit and a white shirt, his hair a smooth oily slick above eyes so dark-rimmed they looked like they had been blackened with kohl.

'You're just in time,' he said, handing her a glass of champagne then leading her up the steps into the house. They crossed a wide marble entrance hall into a lavishly furnished salon. The walls were elaborately panelled, draped in tapestries and silk, and rows of gilt-framed portraits kept watch over the gathering. On the far side of the room, glass doors opened onto a balcony with an unobstructed view of the sea.

There were about forty people in the salon, some lounging on sofas, others gathered around the gambling tables – poker, baccarat and roulette, each table with a pair of croupiers. In the corner, a pianist played jazz on a vast white Steinway. Everywhere she looked her eyes sought Anton, but he wasn't there.

Silvano guided Kate out to the balcony. The sea was calm, the sky so deeply blue it was almost violet, and a large moon had just risen over the water.

They walked down some steps and then past a swimming pool, shining like a jewel in the dark. The moonlit silhouettes of palm trees grazed the water and small groups of people surrounded the pool, drinking and talking in low voices.

Kate had expected something different from the party. Loud music, fountains of champagne. She thought she would feel out of place, uncomfortable in her clothes as usual. But this was altogether different. Quiet, sophisticated. A bit boring even.

As they walked past the pool Kate watched a woman slip into the shallow end, barely an expression on her face – no delight, no sign of whether the water was cold or warm. She thought Silvano would ask her to sit with him there beside the pool, but he just took her empty glass and placed it on one of the tables.

'Come this way,' he said, nodding towards the darkness where the path disappeared into a thicket of trees. They walked uphill to a clearing and once they had gained height, Kate saw the helipad and a small black chopper crouching like a gleaming mosquito.

The pilot handed Silvano and Kate a headset each and then leaped inside.

'We're going to the real party now,' Silvano said, helping her into the chopper.

There were four others already inside and the pilot spoke through the headsets.

'There's going to be a lot of noise, so keep your sets on and buckle up.'

Then, in a burst of floodlights, they were in the air, the helicopter lifting and juddering into the sky, the lights of the Côte d'Azur dancing beneath them as the chopper spun around and sped out over the dark sea.

Kate turned to Silvano with so many questions she couldn't ask now because it was so loud and the headset was on a single circuit with the other passengers, so she looked out of the window. On the sea were pinpricks of light – tiny constellations of yachts and fishing vessels spread across the void.

After about ten minutes flying, the helicopter descended towards a large, matt grey vessel. The ship they drew towards didn't resemble a yacht so much as a submarine that had just surfaced, radars and ballooning sonic equipment on the top. It was four or five storeys high, flood-lit and glowing against the black sea all around.

The chopper hovered over its mother ship as the pilot brought it down.

As they descended, Kate saw scores of people milling on the decks of the yacht.

The noise from the helicopter was deafening and as soon as they had alighted, stewards showed them into the control room and down some stairs to the main section of the yacht. When they reached the middle deck, the chopper took off again.

The scene on the yacht was much livelier than the house with clusters of people everywhere – some eating on tables inside, others talking excitedly, dancing, swimming in the on-board pool, all of them high on coke and champagne.

Silvano led her out to the foredeck. He wasted no time telling Kate what he required of her. Rob had been reorganising Amir's assets in anticipation of sanctions on Amir. Some of the assets had been transferred to Amir's wife Selena, and some to other family members and trusted associates. The work, however, had not been completed and many of the assets were still held by

Amir, although disguised through complicated structures. It was time-sensitive and they needed help finding out what Rob had done so they could protect the properties from being frozen once Amir was sanctioned.

'This has been coming for a while,' Kate said. 'Surely Rob has done everything necessary to shield the assets.'

'Frankly, we don't know exactly what he's done. Amir trusted Rob too much,' said Silvano, scowling. 'Rob's embezzled money and that's probably the least of it. We need access to the system at Meritus to see exactly what he's done with the assets.'

'Why not ask Julia? She'd have a much better handle on this than me.'

'She's tied to Rob financially as a partner of the firm. She can't be trusted. When he goes down she'll be caught in the fallout.'

Kate stared out over the sea. What he was asking her to do didn't make sense but she was cornered. 'So you just want information from the system?'

'Exactly. You just need to do some specialist detective work,' said Silvano, grinning as he lit a cigarette. 'It won't take long and it will be worth a lot. Whatever you need for your mother and sister.'

Kate turned away. She wasn't thinking about her mother and sister. She was thinking about what Anton had said about the drug-running he had done. 'What exactly do you and Amir do here in France?' she said eventually.

'We invest money. *Grow* it.'

'And where is this money from?'

'Different places.'

'I know about the drugs and the money laundering. I won't do any of that.'

'We don't call it *laundering*.'

'What is it then?'

Silvano waved his hand in the air. 'Investing. Buying things.'

'Buying what kind of things?'

'Most of what you see over there,' Silvano said, pointing towards the shoreline.'

'Like what?' Kate asked.

'Property. Country clubs, beach clubs, casinos. We run many of the hotels along the coast.' Silvano gestured towards the lights of Monaco. 'My family used to own land there, actually. Citrus groves. They were farmers until the government took the land where one of the beach clubs is now. The Monte-Carlo Bay, you were there last night.'

The crust of shoreline glowed beyond the sea, its epicentre where Silvano was pointing – the glittering jewel of Monaco.

'The work is well within your capability and it will only be for a very short time. Consider it,' he said before he walked away.

Kate breathed in the soft air, saw the sea glistening below and considered Silvano's proposal. In a perfect world, she would not work for criminals but the world was far from perfect and she had to be pragmatic. If she tracked down this information for Silvano, the litigation would be settled favourably for the men without any more risks, and she could leave Meritus with her reputation intact. In addition, Kate would be wealthy, her sister and mother catered for and she would be free financially, at least for a while.

Yes, Silvano was a criminal, but she worked for criminals already. At least Silvano didn't hide who he worked for, or what he did.

Nor did he fool himself he was changing the world, Kate thought as she leaned back on the railing and watched the party inside. The world was a tough place – it wasn't going to change. And anyway, these people didn't need to change the world. They had created their world right here.

Chapter Twenty-Eight

KATE STAYED ON DECK AFTER Silvano went in, listening to the waves slap against the yacht as she gazed over the dark stretch of water to the thin band of shore lights. The coastline was a flickering mirage, and despite the bulk of the five-storey colossus beneath her, she felt she was drifting far out at sea.

At some point during her reverie, Kate became aware of a presence at her side, an expensive waft of sandalwood and tobacco that snuffed out the fresh sea breeze.

'You don't get many nights like this,' the man said, lighting a cigarette. 'Nights when you can see so clearly the line of Cannes, Antibes, Nice, Monaco,' he added, pointing out the sequence of towns along the coast. As he spoke a constellation of fireworks burst into the sky above Nice.

Kate recognised the accent and turned to him. 'You're the photographer.'

'Amir,' he said, extending his hand.

Kate wanted to ask why he had deleted her photos but of course she knew.

'Privacy,' he said, a note of apology in his voice. 'More valuable than gold.'

Kate felt the rings on his hand as she took it, saw his expensive watch. 'The Côte d'Azur isn't normally associated with privacy,' she said quietly. 'People usually come here to show off.'

'It used to be very private,' said Amir, turning back to the view. 'There are a lot of people snooping around now though, unfortunately. Journalists and the like. Sticking their noses in where they have no business and then writing all kinds of nonsense, starting rumours. That day we met – I thought you were one of them.'

He pointed to the shore as more fireworks exploded.

'Why is it so clear tonight then? Atmospherics? The moon?' asked Kate.

'The clarity of distance,' said Amir, leaning on the rail. 'The distance between us and them.'

Kate looked for a trace of irony in his face as he exhaled smoke into the night, but there was none.

He raised an eyebrow as if daring her to mock him and then flicked his cigarette over the water. 'Come,' he said, offering his arm. 'Let me show you around.'

Kate went with him inside to the party and he introduced her to people she had seen online, in magazines and in the Monaco business pages as his *lawyer from London*. His guests looked her over politely, scattering breadcrumbs of small talk, their eyes drifting elsewhere once they assessed she was not in their league. Kate met Elanka, Amir's girlfriend, whom she had seen in Monaco when she was with Vanessa.

After more champagne, Kate relaxed a little and decided that while she was there she may as well experience life like they did.

She found that the more she stayed with Elanka, Amir and their entourage, the more she drank and the more interesting everyone became, at first, but as the night wore on she grew uneasy. There were a lot of young women on the yacht, most of them fawning over the men, laughing childishly at their stories and bad jokes. She had heard rumours about the hostesses hired by the dozen for parties such as this.

Kate refused several offers of cocaine, knowing it would just increase her anxiety and when Amir caught up with her later, he asked why she was so restrained.

'Nothing happens if you're cautious. By the time you've weighed up the pros and cons the opportunity has usually passed. You need to dive in,' he said.

He nodded to the shore. 'Over there, people are dying in front of their screens. It's one long retirement village from St Tropez all the way to the Italian border. You never know when you might join them.'

Kate thought back to where the evening had started. She had been one of those people alone on her sofa with her screen.

'You have the rest of your life to be cautious,' he said.

It was the cocaine talking, but it was also what she sometimes thought: she might be dead tomorrow, so she had better live now, before it was too late. It was a nice idea, but it had never suited her. The times she had lived recklessly, she had just done foolish things.

Kate watched Amir as he drew away. He was so self-assured, his movements smooth and languid as he smoked and laughed with his guests, bestowing a smile here, a friendly touch there, charming but never giving too much away. This laidback manner seemed natural but Kate knew it was a front. Like all successful criminals, there was a control freak beneath that charismatic facade. He hadn't made his money by being easy-going and reckless.

Then again, she hadn't achieved much by being cautious. She couldn't say that anything she had done had brought her any more clarity, any more happiness than recklessness might have. She never used to think like this, but surrounded by these people here tonight, she was overcome with self-doubt. She didn't think money meant so much either but in Monaco, where appearances mattered, it was paramount. If you didn't have money, people treated you differently: they dismissed you and pushed you around.

It was hard not to feel resentful.

Kate turned to Amir when he returned and asked him, almost as part of her own thoughts, 'Why do you do all this?'

He looked at her quizzically, his eyes narrowing behind a smoky exhalation.

'I mean besides the money,' she said, laughing at how ridiculous she sounded – as though she had missed the whole point of life. And in a way she had – all those days in the office, the nights alone in her apartment.

Amir gestured to the yacht as if to say: *Why do you think?*

Kate gazed at the decks of the floating palace and realised that despite working for the rich she had no real clue what motivated them.

'I do it to shape my world,' he said.

'*Your* world?'

Amir nodded. 'If I want to shape a bigger world I can do that. Money is power and it buys perspective.' He eyed her a moment as if reluctant to continue, but the cocaine had loosened his tongue. 'I see things that need to change and I have the means to influence that change. People listen to me.'

Kate wanted to ask what things he wanted to change. He had a fanatical look in his eye, his mouth stern, chin tilted above a perfect suit, a flash of white at the collar and sleeves like a billionaire preacher, his adoring flock luxuriously captive here, ready to pursue his ideas of change.

He smiled. 'All people want in their lives is a bit of hope – that their situation will improve, that they'll get a better job or win the lottery. But it never happens.' He sighed, as if he had experienced such disappointment too. 'It hurts to abandon hope, it leaves you feeling empty.'

He paused and Kate didn't know what to say.

'I understand that emptiness. I can help change it into something better.'

'With your hotels and your country clubs?' asked Kate sceptically.

'Why not? People can forget their lives for a while. That's all they really want – distraction.'

He had come to the end of his cigarette and a waiter appeared with an ashtray. Kate stared at him in silence. He was deluded but he believed what he said and was all the more dangerous for it. He would change the world while everyone else was distracted.

When he had stubbed out his cigarette he pointed to the shore. 'Enjoy the view. Not many nights are this calm and the coastline so clear this far out,' he said and then went inside.

Shortly before dawn, the helicopter returned to take Amir and Elanka back to Monaco.

'Amir says you should stay a little longer,' Elanka said. 'You can sleep on the yacht. There are bedrooms, you know.'

Kate didn't want to stay on the yacht, but she could see others heading up to the chopper and she knew there would be no room for her.

'I've asked one of the girls to lay out some things,' Elanka said. 'It will be fun. Silvano will take care of you. I wish I could stay too, but Amir needs to go back to London tomorrow.'

Kate didn't want to be taken care of by Silvano either, and she was about to object but realised there was no point.

As Elanka drew away, Kate asked if she knew anything about Anton.

'Who?' Elanka said.

Kate had to shout above the noise of the chopper.

Elanka pointed to her ears. 'I can't hear you,' she mouthed and then made a phone call gesture with her hand. *Call me.*

Kate grabbed Elanka, put her mouth to her ear. 'You must know him. He works with Silvano and the others,' she yelled.

Elanka stared at Kate a moment then opened her mouth but it was too late. Amir was at her side.

'It's too noisy. I can't hear you,' Elanka yelled as he ushered her away.

At dawn, more people left the party as the effects of the alcohol and the drugs wore off, the helicopter ferrying some back to Monaco, others leaving by boat or disappearing to rooms below deck. The first glow had appeared above the hills and the sea was a vivid blue, the breeze turning the water to ribbed glass. As the sun rose, the towns along the shore melted into the landscape and the mountains were streaked with gold where the sun touched the bare limestone ridges.

Silvano showed Kate to a cabin with a double bed, plush carpet and a white marble bathroom.

Kate slept all morning and woke after midday. Fresh clothes and a swimming costume had been laid out and so she dressed and went upstairs. She found Silvano and others from the party at a vast mahogany table flanked by waiters and on the rear deck, guests lounged by the pool sipping cocktails.

There was sea all around and no sign of land.

'Where are we?' she said to Silvano who was working his way through a huge plate of food.

'We thought we'd go for a cruise,' he said, barely looking at her, his mouth full of eggs and charcuterie.

'A cruise where?' Kate said, her eyes straining towards the horizon. The yacht seemed to be moving fast, a wide wash of foam in its wake.

'Corsica!' said Silvano and those around him cheered.

Kate turned to scan the vista behind the yacht. Beyond miles of sea there was a faint land haze.

She started to object, but then stopped. What would they do – make a U-turn just because it didn't suit her? It was Saturday, after all and there was nothing she had to be home for. She had no one waiting, not even a cat. She looked at the guests – unreadable behind their sunglasses. These people could throw her overboard and no one would miss her.

Silvano pulled out the chair beside him. 'Come. Sit down. Eat.'

They arrived in Corsica late on Saturday afternoon and spent the evening at a harbourside restaurant reserved just for them.

After dinner, a fleet of cars took them to a club in a nearby town. There were twelve guests on board and on Sunday they swam in a series of coves and cavorted on inflatables set up around the yacht. On board, a staff of ten attended to their every whim. The plan was for Kate and Silvano to fly back to Monaco from Calvi later that evening, while the others would spend a few days circumnavigating the island, enjoying the restaurants and clubs en route.

'There's something I need to tell you about what you'll be doing,' Silvano said in the car on the way to the airport.

Kate felt the hairs rise on her neck. 'What's that?'

'I wanted you to meet Amir first. That way you wouldn't let anything slip.'

'Let anything slip about what?' Kate said, alarmed.

'What I need you to do is slightly different than what I initially said.'

Silvano told Kate that things were about to get very difficult for Amir. He had been sanctioned in the US and they had heard he would finally be sanctioned in the UK and Europe next week. Although Amir was confident he could challenge the sanctions and keep most property in his or his family members' names, Silvano thought otherwise. It was too much of a risk for Amir's companies to keep any relationship with Amir, however well hidden. It wasn't advisable to have any legal association with Amir at all, he said.

Silvano told Kate that her job, officially, was to work for Amir. She needed to make it look like she was helping finish the work Rob had started, which was to make the ownership structures of his companies and assets more opaque with complicated offshore trusts so when the authorities came sniffing around, they couldn't prove Amir actually owned anything.

Kate's real job, however, was to assist in taking ownership from Amir outright. This was much more serious and involved transferring control of everything away from Amir and his family and into the names of people like Silvano, who were, in Silvano's view, much less likely to be sanctioned.

Silvano put up a pretence of making it sound as though he was acting in the best interests of Amir's companies, but what he really wanted was for Kate to help him stage a legal coup against Amir.

'But you said you just needed me to do a bit of detective work – to get some information. You didn't say anything about any transactions or moving property.'

'The plan has changed,' said Silvano, his eyes narrowing.

'What if he finds out what you're doing?' *What I'm doing*, she meant.

'He won't. Amir likes to think of himself as a big picture guy – throwing his weight around, deciding on strategy, discussing philanthropy and change. He knows the properties need to move around but the detail doesn't interest him.'

'Right,' said Kate, thinking this couldn't be right at all.

'In fact, he's a very small picture guy,' said Silvano bitterly. 'Amir trusted Rob and gave him wide authorities to act on his behalf, which was very stupid. Now Rob has disappeared, I need you to step in.'

'So what exactly do you need me to do?' Kate said, feeling as if he was asking her to not just step in, but to wade through a swamp that had just thickened further.

'First, I need you to locate everything on the Meritus system that relates to Amir.'

'Like what?' asked Kate helplessly.

'Details of all the companies that own his assets, how those companies are structured, full lists of directors and shareholders including identity documents. I need details of all trusts and beneficial owners. Get everything off the system and onto a memory stick. Once we have all that we can work out how to move it.'

Kate had no idea where any of this information was.

'We're working on getting someone into the IT department to help you. As soon as we can we'll get someone in. Your friend could have helped, but Rob dealt with him after his blackmail threat.'

'*Dealt with him?*'

'He had a bad cycling accident last weekend.'

'Oh my god! Marc? How do you know? Where is he?'

'He's in Brittany.'

Kate called Marc immediately. His mother answered his phone and confirmed a motorcyclist had forced Marc off the road in the hills above Roquebrune last Sunday. He was still recovering and would call her when he was better.

'I'll tell Julia that from now on, you are to take instructions solely from me,' Silvano said when the jet landed in Nice. 'I'll be your main contact. You'll have no other work except mine.'

When they parted at the airport, Kate wanted to call a stop to it all, to tell Silvano she couldn't possibly go ahead with this scheme. It was one thing to help him strip data from the system or even help hide Amir's assets from the authorities. It was an altogether different thing to get involved in some kind of mutiny within the group. But it was too late; Silvano had told her too much. He wouldn't let her walk away knowing he had such treachery planned against Amir. Kate was cornered on his side now and she had to go along with it all whether she liked it or not.

Chapter Twenty-Nine
Paris

IT HAD BEEN HARDER THAN Vanessa thought to disappear. She had taken the train to Avignon and spent a night in a hotel near the station where she passed herself off as an English tourist who spoke very little French. Her cover worked and the hotel staff mostly ignored her, but she remained cautious – staying in her suite and ordering room service. The next day she ventured out to explore the walled town, visiting the Palais des Papes and the famous medieval bridge. She had heard good things about Avignon and as far as she knew, she didn't know a soul there.

Vanessa found an apartment through an agency near the hotel and spoke to a man who would take cash if she paid a premium. The apartment was on the northern side of the Rhône, just beyond the town centre – a third floor studio in an uninspiring but inconspicuous block. It was neither on the tourist beat, nor in the suburbs and she took it for a week to begin with. On the very first day, however, her neighbour's cat made its way onto her balcony and got stuck. Vanessa tried to coax the animal back to the adjacent flat but it took refuge in a small cavity behind a drainpipe and refused to come out.

Vanessa had no choice but to knock next door. The neighbour, Gilles, was excessively grateful – the cat had belonged to his recently deceased wife who had used Vanessa's apartment as a painting studio. As Gilles left with the cat, Vanessa heard him mutter something about providence and afterwards, he took a very keen interest in her. Even though Vanessa varied her schedule, Gilles' outings coincided with hers and whenever they met in the lift or the lobby he asked increasingly probing questions about her life and how long she planned to be in Avignon. He was her neighbour so Vanessa answered politely enough, but she only gave vague details. This seemed to pique his interest further and two days after the incident with the cat he invited Vanessa to supper. Vanessa conceded – she really had no choice – and although Gilles was kind, Vanessa was reserved and distant, telling him she was newly divorced and penniless. She thought this would put him off but far from being discouraged, Gilles saw a green light and started leaving gifts at her door. At first it was just food he had made – a slice of terrine, or a jar of pasta sauce. Vanessa enjoyed the food and returned the empty containers graciously, thinking it was just her luck to meet a generous man who could cook when she was least able to take advantage of it. When he started leaving flowers, she knew she had to leave. Avignon just wasn't the kind of town to disappear in.

She thought the next logical place to try might be a remote village in the countryside, but that was even worse. The people in the town just west of Dijon were nosier than Gilles and Vanessa didn't even make it to a hotel without half the town knowing her business. A man from the café offered to help with her suitcase, and the woman behind the counter in the boulangerie asked Vanessa what she was doing there. When Vanessa said she was visiting for a couple of weeks, the woman introduced her to the person behind her in the queue who happened to run the tourist office. Both women and several other people in the shop then spent the next ten minutes giving Vanessa advice on the best places to see while she was there. Vanessa thanked them all and trudged back to the train station with her sandwich, realising that the smaller the town, the more obvious she would be.

Finally, just a week after she had left Monaco, Vanessa arrived in Paris. She needed to be among people who were more interested in themselves than others and she would only find that there. She paid two months advance rent on an apartment in the 11th arrondissement, which she knew was a busy stepping-stone for people on their way somewhere else. The apartment was modest – a simple studio in a modern block that smelled of bleach, and it was on the first floor so she could avoid meeting people in the lift. With her suitcase of cash, she could have afforded better, but she didn't know how long the money would need to last.

Vanessa had always thought of Paris as a place for beautiful people, but she now discovered it was an ideal place for plain people too. Vanessa's haircut was neat but ordinary and her second-hand clothes were really quite shabby, but she resisted the temptation to spruce up. In return, no one paid her the slightest bit of notice. Men gazed past her in cafés and women ignored her in the shops. After a lifetime of making the best of herself, it was a revelation not to have to try.

Every day, Vanessa woke thinking of David and he was her last thought at night. She made sure she wasn't outside on the streets after 4 p.m. because then she would see all the children returning from school. She avoided leaving the apartment altogether on Wednesday, because that wasn't a school day and children were everywhere.

Finally, Vanessa called Kate on one of the pre-paid phones. Kate had spoken to David twice, as agreed, and she passed on all his news. The school was providing pastoral support and despite the difficult circumstances, he seemed to be all right. Sports day was that weekend – on his birthday – and he had been chosen to run in the hurdle race. This was the highlight of the call.

Vanessa hung up and discarded the phone into a bin. She was relieved that David was doing well, but a heavy sadness gripped her heart. She wept as she realised she had never once attended David's sports day, even when she'd had the opportunity. She had always been too busy in the office. She tried to console herself with the thought that she had always managed to give him nice holidays – in the Caribbean or skiing, but then she remembered she often had to work then too and David usually spent his holidays in the kids' club.

As the days wore on, Vanessa's anger mounted, together with her unhappiness, and she felt as if she was suffocating under the weight. She had put her life into her work, had sacrificed everything, and for what? It was work's fault she was now in an ugly apartment in Paris, lonely and grey, nervous about social interactions and frightened of her own shadow.

Vanessa became obsessed with hurdles, finding out as much as she could about the race and having imaginary conversations with David about his strategy for winning it. She spent hours online at the library scanning the school's website and the sports day updates. It wasn't long before her daily walk involved a circuit of a nearby athletics field. As the sports day grew closer she could bear it no longer and called Joe to check whether the passport she had bought from him would pass through border security.

As soon as she hung up she went straight to the Gare du Nord and bought a ticket to London.

Chapter Thirty

Monaco

S HORTLY AFTER KATE ARRIVED AT work on Monday morning, Julia came into her office, shutting the door firmly behind her. The stony expression on her face made it clear the camaraderie from last week had vanished.

'Seems like you've made a good impression on the clients,' Julia said, picking up a random file from Kate's desk and flicking through in a distracted manner.

Kate kept her tone cool. 'How's that?'

Julia sat on the edge of Kate's desk. 'Silvano Bellaci just told me you spent the weekend with them in Corsica. I have to say, Kate, I'm impressed.'

Julia didn't look impressed. In fact, she looked furious. 'I've been working with Amir for ten years and I've never been on his yacht,' she said sourly.

Julia stared at Kate intently. 'To be honest I didn't think you had it in you.' She waved the file she was holding and then slapped it on the desk. 'Don't worry about this file. Give it to Lucie or one of the others. Silvano wants you working with him full-time trying to sort out this mess Rob's left us in.' There was a pause, then Julia added, her brow furrowed, 'He also said he wants Falkon Racing settled.'

The last statement was more of a question and Kate wasn't sure how to respond as Julia sat poised for more information. 'That's my understanding too,' Kate said eventually. 'I'm aiming to have it all agreed today.'

Kate and Julia discussed the matters Lucie would take over, and then Kate helped Julia find them in the cabinets. Just before she left the office, Julia glared at Kate above the stack of files and then appraised Kate's clothes. Kate hadn't had time to collect her good clothes from the dry cleaners and she had dressed quickly that morning in one of the staid old navy suits she had brought with her from London.

Julia was wearing a garish pink and yellow Missoni jumpsuit that matched her nails. 'It's just a thought, Kate. But you might want to make a little more effort with your appearance now you're going to be spending time with Silvano and the others.'

Julia saw the blood rush to Kate's cheeks. 'Don't get offended. It's just a piece of advice.'

Normally Kate would ignore such a comment, but she was tired, and stunned that Julia would say such a thing with all that was going on. 'Back off, Julia. Things aren't looking that good for you here at Meritus. Why don't you worry about your own *appearance* rather than harass me about mine?'

Silvano didn't visit the office, nor did he communicate in writing or even on the phone, so for the rest of the week Kate had to meet him wherever he happened to be. Mostly that was Le Grill restaurant on the rooftop of the Hôtel de Paris but sometimes it was his house in Cap-d'Ail, just west of Monaco. A couple of times Kate flew from the heliport at Fontvieille to Amir's yacht, which was stationed a few miles off the coast. Being at sea was strange when it was just Silvano there. The staff of ten were ever-present, of course, but that didn't make it any more lively. With the sea all around there was a desolate feel to the vessel, like a seaside hotel out of season, and whenever Kate was there, she sat with a view of the shore. She didn't think she would get stranded again, but she didn't want to take any chances.

Silvano had taken Kate through the structures of Amir's companies and assets as far as he knew it, and it was Kate's job to supplement that with more up-to-date information from the Meritus system. Amir had left Silvano with wide powers of attorney and other authorities, and Silvano was confident he could ensure ownership was transferred away from Amir once he knew exactly how the assets were held. Amir was now subject to sanctions in the UK and Europe, which meant he was legally powerless and stranded in London, and Silvano said it was urgent they transferred everything out of his control as soon as possible before anything was located and frozen or worse, seized.

Kate had searched the firm's database, but the only assets she could find of Amir's were a couple of apartments in London. These were acquired, as usual, through companies in the British Virgin Islands and controlled through trusts in Jersey. While most of the documents were kept offshore, Kate scanned all the emails and correspondence onto a separate file then uploaded it all onto a memory stick as Silvano had asked.

The Falkon Racing litigation was just a week away and Kate wrote a formal letter to the other side's lawyer saying that in an unanticipated new development, she now had instructions to settle the cases. She asked if he would agree to a further adjournment while they hammered out a deal. He called her immediately, pleased but confused, and enquired why the plans had changed. Kate said she couldn't discuss it over the phone, but asked him what he thought the men hoped to receive if they won the litigation. When he mentioned a figure, Kate told him to double it in his formal response to her settlement letter. She said she was sure her client would accept a higher sum to settle the claims swiftly.

Kate brought in one of the other lawyers to help finalise the settlement before Silvano changed his mind. As soon as she had finished the work for Silvano, Kate planned to leave Monaco and so she needed someone to take care of it when she was gone. The atmosphere at Meritus was increasingly chaotic and the office Rob used when he was there had been completely cleared out. No one had heard from him for over a week and even Julia didn't seem to know where he was. Kate heard a rumour he had been suspended from the firm pending an investigation into his conduct and that he was under some kind of house arrest in London.

Although Kate would no longer have the satisfaction of contributing to Rob and Julia's demise, she was glad the forged document was not required. The prospect of settling the cases amicably with the mechanics was the best possible outcome and it pleased her immensely, keeping her going during the strange time she worked for Silvano. Now she was no longer beholden to Rob and Julia, Kate could come and go from the office as she pleased. She realised she was being swept along, avoiding thinking about the kind of people she was now involved with, and the kind of businesses she was supporting. As soon as her mind drifted in that direction she shut the thought down and focused instead on her work. She would do this job for Silvano then quit. After several days she found she didn't even need to do that and whole hours would pass without her conscience being disturbed at all.

Kate continued to trawl the Meritus system to find out exactly what Rob had done with Amir's assets before he disappeared. When Julia was out, Kate searched her office and found paperwork relating to Casa di Stelle in the files beneath Julia's desk, together with a list of other properties in London and Europe. Kate photocopied what she could and scanned it into the database she had created. Structurally it was the same. The property had been acquired by a British Virgin Islands entity, but she was missing the crucial data that showed who owned this entity, and how Rob had changed this.

The missing information was the most crucial because the companies listed as owners on the public property registers were never the real owners – they were just fronts. Like a massive iceberg hidden under the water, the real owners and beneficiaries could change all the time by amending secret trust arrangements, while everything on the surface – the name of the company, its directors and shareholders, stayed the same. Kate's job was to find all this submerged data.

She knew from Marc there were many private databases on the system, but she didn't know how to find them. Since the firm had outsourced the IT department, the team came and went so it was impossible to build any kind of rapport with them. Nevertheless, Kate passed by the IT department each day and lingered on that floor in the hope of befriending one of them.

But they all sat glued to their screens, headsets clamped over their ears.

One afternoon, in the middle of the week after the trip to Corsica, Kate ran into Elanka as Kate was leaving the Hôtel de Paris. Kate had just had a meeting with Silvano on the rooftop and saw Elanka sitting alone in the bar restaurant.

Kate was curious as to how Elanka was coping now Amir was fully sanctioned, but Elanka was strangely cold and formal so Kate quickly changed the topic and asked about Anton again.

'I mentioned him on the yacht. I'm worried something awful has happened to him,' Kate said.

'I have no idea,' said Elanka, too quickly.

'He worked in that restaurant on the beach.'

'I don't go to the beach,' Elanka said irritably before turning back to her salad. 'You know Kate, these kind of guys they come and go.'

'What do you mean *come and go*?'

'They work for Amir for a while then one day' – Elanka clicked her fingers – 'they're gone.' Then almost as an afterthought, 'I don't like to think about it too much.'

'He worked for Amir at the casino.'

Elanka glanced at Kate. 'Probably.'

A strange look crossed Elanka's face, which seemed like worry, but then her features hardened. 'These guys are all the same, Kate. The ones who do this work. They're all desperate. Petty criminals. Conmen. Stay away from them.' She straightened her jacket. 'If you're so worried about him, why are you working with Silvano?'

'What do you mean?'

'Why are you helping him, Kate? What are you still doing here in Monaco when you could be anywhere else? You're just like the others, aren't you?'

'Like who?'

'Like Rob and the rest. You'll go along with anything for the money.'

Kate was too stunned by Elanka's comment to reply, she just muttered a goodbye then walked through the lobby and stood outside, facing the casino. At the end of Kate's meeting with Silvano he had confirmed he had transferred a hundred thousand euros into her bank account – the figure they had settled on for her work. She checked the account on her phone and saw the money was there. A powerful wave of gratification washed over her, bringing a sense of calm that overwhelmed any stirrings of guilt, and Kate felt herself detach from financial worries for the first time in her life as the world around her expanded. She was seeing things differently now, her consciousness unhindered by primitive worries about money. The casino was in front of her, the dazzling sports cars and the tourists. She was at the epicentre of Monaco now and no longer an outsider. Kate felt an uneasy sense that perhaps Elanka was right and that money was what she had been chasing all along.

Later, while she was sifting through copies she had made of the files she had found in Julia's office, Kate discovered that Rob had used a law firm in Jersey to help him with the restructuring of Casa di Stelle several years ago.

Kate went online to the firm's website and checked the list of associates against the initials on the file and then put in a call.

The initials belonged to a South African lawyer called Daniel and after introducing herself, Kate told him she was responding to a request from the authorities who needed ownership details of Casa di Stelle.

'We're currently prohibited from working on any Meritus matters,' Daniel said.

'I'm not asking you to work on them. I just need confirmation of the ownership structure,' she said.

There was silence down the line, but Kate pushed into it. 'I understand it's owned through the same kind of structure as the other properties.'

'That's right,' said Daniel after a while.

'So there are different companies for each of the properties, but it's essentially the same structure, with a Jersey trust arrangement beneath each one?'

'Yes,' said Daniel. 'Though that one's a bit different because there were changes made to the beneficiaries just over a month ago.'

'I can't see any of that on the system here.'

'We don't send any of those details to Meritus. All the documentation about the underlying trust structures is held here.'

'Yes, of course,' said Kate. 'So who are the current beneficial owners of Casa di Stelle?'

'Until recently it was Amir. But the beneficiaries are now Elanka and Lucia Aleksandras, who I understand is Elanka's mother.'

'Elanka and her mother,' Kate said, remembering what Vanessa had said over lunch at Marcello. 'Can you send me the transfer information?'

'I'm sorry, that information is protected.'

'Protected?'

'Only Rob had access to the database, and it's now locked. There's a block on anyone accessing these files while they invest-igate his activities. Not even I can access them properly. The best I can do is a one-off search against individual properties like I did for you just now.'

Kate thanked Daniel then hung up. There was nothing else on the Meritus system. Everything Rob had been working on had disappeared and the only records were at this firm in Jersey. Kate passed the information about Elanka's ownership of the villa to Silvano and told him if he wanted more information he would need to somehow hack into the Jersey database.

The next day, Kate was in her office as usual and there was a knock at the door.

She looked up and it was Anton.

Chapter Thirty-One

SEEING ANTON DRESSED IN A suit at her office door was surreal and Kate didn't know where to start.

'I'll explain everything later,' Anton said, coming around to her side of the desk. 'We need to be quick.'

Anton plugged a small device into the USB port of a laptop he had brought with him and then connected the laptop to Kate's office computer.

'Silvano wants me to try and access the Jersey database.'

Kate stared at him. '*Silvano?* Wait. I thought you had been stealing from him?'

'No,' said Anton, his eyes on her screen, hands darting over the keyboard of his laptop. 'From Amir.'

'And now you're helping Silvano in this coup against Amir. Are you crazy?'

Anton glanced up. 'I could ask you the same question.'

'What's that you just plugged in to the laptop?'

'It's a hacking device. I can access the Jersey database this way through the managing partner's login.'

'Napier's login?'

'Yes,' said Anton. 'He's the only one with access to Rob's files.'

When Anton brought up the database, Kate reeled at the amount of information flooding the screen.

'Go through the database and copy everything Silvano needs onto this memory stick,' Anton said, plugging in the stick.

'There's a massive amount of information here,' Kate said, sinking back into her chair as she stared at the screen. She took the mouse and scrolled through. 'It looks like the database for the entire Jersey firm. *Thousands* of documents. It'll take me hours to comb through this, let alone copy any of it.'

Anton glanced at his watch. 'You have one hour. I've had to override the restrictions so you can duplicate the files from here. But your activity will be monitored, and I can't override that.'

'Monitored by who?'

'Someone in the Jersey office. Access to this database is recorded there.' Anton tapped several more keys, then checked his watch. 'I've made it look like Napier is reviewing it now, but if it goes on too long they'll get suspicious.'

'There's so much here,' she said.

'Just go through and copy everything you recognise. There's an office down the corridor that's empty. I'll be in there if you need anything.'

When Anton left, Kate went through the material, cross-referencing it with a list she had been compiling of Amir's assets and companies. She saw that everything on the database was arranged logically. A reference number and a separate file was given to each of Amir's properties and assets, and everything was then placed into those files – emails, documents, payment instructions and transfers.

The database was, in fact, a gold mine: it contained historical information on scores of Amir's companies, properties and assets including everything Rob had done recently for Amir. Under the names of each asset were the company incorporation documents for the shell companies that owned the properties, passport scans of the directors and shareholders of those companies, share certificates, contracts and bank statements showing money flows at the time of purchase, and for all subsequent transactions and transfers. There were scans of the email chains with other lawyers, accountants and bankers. Most importantly, the files included details of the secretive trust deeds and powers of attorney, which were all held offshore and showed who actually owned and controlled everything.

Kate went into the details for Casa di Stelle. Everything was there, including the recent transfer of beneficial ownership from Amir to Elanka and her mother. She scanned through each of the other properties. Although ownership was well hidden, many of the properties were still held by Amir.

It took Kate the best part of the hour to find and then copy the material across and within moments of her finishing, Anton was at her door again.

After checking the USB stick, he made a copy of it, pocketed the copy then plugged the original into another laptop he had brought with him.

'I'm uploading the material to this URL, an encrypted site which connects to a secure drop box. Wait here until it's gone through.'

'Where are you going?'

'I'll find you afterwards. Elanka will call you soon.'

'*Elanka?*' said Kate, but Anton had gone.

'Has Anton set up the secure drop? Is it uploading?' said Elanka, seconds later when she called.

Elanka asked Kate to read out the URL address on the screen. 'What's this about?' Kate said. 'I thought this material was for Silvano.'

'You can't trust Silvano. Don't tell him anything about this if he calls. Silvano is worse than Amir.'

'*Worse than Amir?* But Anton is taking a copy to Silvano now.'

'No, he's not. And anyway, once the data has gone through to the secure drop it will be useless to Silvano. It will be too late.'

'Too late for what?' Kate said, staring helplessly at the laptop screen. The data was still uploading through the encrypted site. 'Tell me what this is about.'

'Do you really have no idea what they do?'

'Anton told me about the gambling and the drugs,' Kate said. 'Is that what this is about?'

'Don't be stupid,' said Elanka savagely. 'It's not just gambling and drugs! The helicopters. The helipad at Casa di Stelle. The yacht. You were there at the party – you saw all those girls. What do you think goes on there?'

Kate thought back to what Anton had told her, felt the same tightening in her stomach. '*A concierge service. Delivering things to yachts by helicopter,*' she said, recalling their conversation.

'If there aren't girls, there aren't gamblers. That's what they say.'

'That's what who says?' Kate said.

'Amir and Silvano. The helicopters transport the girls out to the yachts. They're supplied free to the biggest gamblers during the season.'

'There's a *season* for this?'

'It starts at Easter with the stag weekends. Then in May everyone comes down for the Grand Prix. Monaco has always been a major hub for this kind of thing – ever since they built the casino. People didn't ever really just come here to gamble, or at least not primarily. The Hôtel de Paris is practically a brothel and in the summer the whole world comes to the Côte d'Azur. The rich on their yachts, the tourists in the hotels and country clubs. They have money, they've waited all year and they want nightlife, entertainment, sex, distraction.'

'And the girls. Do they stay at the villa, at Casa di Stelle?' said Kate, recalling the girls on the beach the day she first saw the villa.

'There are a few apartments in Roquebrune, some in Monaco, a couple of hotels in the hills. They stay for a week or two, and move from yacht to yacht.'

Kate felt a wave of nausea, wondering if it was one of these places in the hills Anton had offered to show her that weekend which now felt so long ago.

'Amir oversees it. But Silvano runs it. He organises the girls' transport, their papers.'

'And you did this with him too?'

'Of course not. But I've seen it all for years,' Elanka said. 'And Silvano will just carry on and do exactly the same thing if he's not stopped. He wants Amir out of the picture so he can get on with it himself.'

'And how are you stopping him?'

'The data that's going through now shows how they traffic these girls and how much money they make from them and where it all goes. Once I have it I'll send it to my lawyers, to the police and the press. People need to know who's involved and how they hide it. This way I can prove it all.'

Chapter Thirty-Two
London

WHEN ALLEGRA WENT AWAY, LENSLEY'S evenings began in the kitchen with beers. If he looked up from his phone, he would notice the fading grey light slowly dissolve the diamond shadows on the marble surfaces into cold nothing. At around 8 p.m. he would consider his supper. Allegra usually left meals for him in the freezer – a range of inspired, one-tray items in recyclable packaging that had been purchased for their detoxifying effects. Lensley only ever thought of detoxifying when he saw these unappetising boxes and they only ever inspired him to reach for another beer. There was a calendar on the fridge with cheery messages, emojis and a schedule of what to eat when, but Lensley usually ignored it and ordered a takeaway.

Allegra was in Sri Lanka on a yoga retreat and this time there were no frozen dinners and no cheerful messages. Instead, Lensley met the delivery man at the door, set the bag on a tray with a bottle of wine and went downstairs to the media room. He intended to get drunk and lose himself in Netflix and sport. If there was a football game on he would watch it so he knew what to say to his boys when he spoke to them next.

He had just finished the spring rolls and had taken his first mouthful of chicken Pad Thai when he heard a faint scratching behind him. He turned the volume down, swivelled his chair around and listened. Beyond the kitchen, the glass door to the lower garden reflected his lonely image, silhouetted against the television's blue glow. He stood, his eyes straining against the dim light. As Lensley walked towards the door, something outside darted into his peripheral vision. It was too big to be a cat or a fox and its movements were clumsy and awkward, unlike the fluid gait of an animal.

Lensley was at the window, peering into the planted border when a murky shape revealed itself. It was dressed all in black and darker than the night. There was a balaclava stretched tight over its head and figure of eight eye sockets stared through the glass, mere inches from his own.

Lensley shrieked and leaped back, his glass of wine shattering on the stone tiles, and the figure screamed too.

'What the hell,' Lensley said, as the figure removed its headgear.

'It's me,' Vanessa whispered, finger to her lips as Lensley opened the door.

'Shhhh, be quiet. I need your help.'

When Vanessa called Joe about the passport, he told her it wouldn't fool the facial recognition cameras at the airports, but as long as she avoided those she should be all right. The best way to travel was by train, he said, and so she caught the Eurostar to London the next day. It was the first week in July and the station was packed. The queue stretched out of the holding area

all the way down the stairs onto the concourse and the attend-
ants' nerves were frazzled. Vanessa avoided detection as she
skipped over from the biometric queue and went through the
passport process manually.

'I'm not sure it was such a great idea to come here,' Lensley
said once he'd heard about Vanessa's flight through France. He
told her Rob had been suspended from work, his personal bank
accounts frozen and that he was now at home pending an
investigation into LuckyCoin and his dealings with Amir.

'The deal has completely imploded. It's been all over the
papers,' he said, handing Vanessa a glass of wine.

'I haven't seen a thing,' she said.

'It's been a disaster for Meritus. Rob's whole department has
been shut down and most of the clients have pulled work from
the firm. Napier has been trying to do some damage control,
but it's not going well. The firm will probably go under.'

'Oh my god,' Vanessa said, taking a seat at the dining table.
'What about you?'

'Nothing so far. For the time being their hands are full with
Rob. In any case, I pulled out of the deal after that evening at
his place. He was furious but I could see where it was headed.'

Vanessa raised her eyebrows as Lensley topped up her glass.
'*Teflon Len* Rob always called you. He meant it as an insult, but
you're smarter than all of us.'

'Let's see,' said Lensley grimly. 'It's not over yet.'

Lensley went into the media room and returned with the
takeaway food. He divided it between them and they ate together
as Lensley filled Vanessa in on the rest of what had happened.
He said Amir was in the UK now and had been sanctioned a
couple of days ago. Like Rob, his bank accounts had been frozen,

and he was under a travel ban, meaning that if he left the country he wouldn't be allowed to return. The authorities were trying to track his assets but apparently Rob had hidden them well. Julia and a couple of other Meritus lawyers had been suspended from the office too, their profiles taken off the website together with Rob's.

'I've seen Rob wriggle out of tighter corners but as the firm's Compliance Officer you're in deep trouble. You should have stayed in France. What on earth are you doing here?'

'That's not my priority now,' Vanessa said, as she grabbed his hand and led him upstairs. 'Let's discuss it later.'

She found the bedroom he shared with Allegra on the first floor.

'I don't think this a great idea, Vanessa,' Lensley said from the landing as she went into the bedroom and started removing her clothes. He had heard about Vanessa's exploits, but this was on another level.

'Don't be stupid. I'm not interested in you. I need to see David.'

'David?'

'My son, David,' said Vanessa, staring around the bedroom in her underwear. 'Where's Allegra's wardrobe?'

Lensley showed her the dressing room just beyond the en suite bathroom and Vanessa marched over. She flung open the walk-in wardrobes and began rifling through Allegra's clothes.

'Does she have anything above a size six?' Vanessa said, pulling out a gold sequinned cat suit. 'Or anything remotely normal.'

Lensley pointed to the balaclava, polo neck and jeans Vanessa had discarded on the floor. 'What about your assassin's outfit?'

Vanessa's voice was muffled by a long, flowing dress that hung over her face. 'That's my uniform until things blow over.'

'You might be waiting a long time.'

Vanessa tugged the dress over her bust. 'Just don't tell anyone I'm here.'

Vanessa spent a while grunting and yanking at zips, trying to get Allegra's clothes over her frame until finally she gave up and flung everything onto the bed. She stood at the wardrobe, hands on her hips.

'What does Allegra usually wear to the school sports day?'

'*The school sports day?*'

'Tomorrow. The Meetham school sports day. You and me. We're going together.'

Lensley stared at her, astonished. 'What the hell do you mean?'

'I'm going as Allegra.'

'You look nothing like Allegra.'

Vanessa glanced at her reflection in the full-length mirror. 'I know, but I'm guessing she doesn't go to many school events so who's going to know?'

'Christ knows. But surely someone will.'

Vanessa drew closer to the mirror and examined the skin on either side of her face. She looked tired and drawn. 'If anyone asks I'll tell them something dreadful happened at the dermatologist.'

'And the hairdresser,' said Lensley.

Vanessa glared at him and went back to the clothes. 'Come on, help me. I need to blend in.'

Lensley watched as Vanessa held up outfit after outfit, each more extravagant and outlandish than the last.

'Allegra's not really about blending in.'

'What about this?' Vanessa said, holding up a cream suede halterneck jumpsuit.

335

'That's her Barbarella outfit. She wears it with those silver boots.'

'I'll wear this navy jacket over the top and these flat sandals.'

'Allegra would never wear it like that.'

Vanessa held up a lemon mini dress with a midriff cut out. 'What did she wear last year, then?' she said in exasperation.

'She definitely wouldn't wear what she wore *last year*.'

'Well, what should *I* wear, then?'

Lensley walked over to the bank of wardrobes on the other side of the dressing room.

'What? She's got that side too?'

'And the room upstairs,' said Lensley, flicking through the racks.

He pulled out a lime green balloon dress made of silk chiffon. 'This one?'

'It's gorgeous,' Vanessa said, peering at the label. 'Alexander McQueen!'

'She bought it recently. Wore it to the races last week.'

'It's beautiful,' Vanessa said, running her fingers over the silk.

The dress was tight across the shoulders but loose everywhere else and fitted Vanessa perfectly.

'She likes to take inspiration from the colours around her,' said Lensley. 'If she goes to the snow she wears white fur. On the beach she likes a yellow bikini. A blue and white striped one on a yacht. But it's never about blending in. For Allegra it's all about standing out.'

'And a sports day with the grass all around, it's green.'

'She wore it with those shoes, this sombrero and of course the matching handbag. Allegra would never go anywhere without a matching bag,' Lensley said, gathering the items, all the same shade of green.

'Quite right,' said Vanessa in delight, taking the green accessories from him. 'The sombrero will cover my face. And the handbag is a bit big, but it's gorgeous.'

She leaned forward and pecked him on the cheek. 'Thank you, Lensley. It's all perfect.'

Chapter Thirty-Three

VANESSA WAS EXHAUSTED BY HER trip and once she had decided what to wear to the sports day, it was goodnight to Lensley and upstairs to the spare room to bed.

Sleep didn't come as easily as she had hoped. Now she was alone, Vanessa's thoughts turned to Rob and the deals they had done together, and Vanessa lay awake worrying about how many of them could be traced back to her. She tried to reassure herself they had always taken precautions – communicating privately over secure, encrypted networks and never through their work devices. In terms of the actual mechanics of the deals, the money they laundered always went through circuitous offshore routes with all the documentation kept offshore too. When she contacted local agents and service providers she always made sure instructions were given verbally or in code, and deleted afterwards. Most of it was deniable, or at least possible to explain away, except the seven million of Amir's money she had authorised to go through the Monaco trust account, of course. She had to hope Lensley was right and that the authorities were focused on Rob's role in other aspects of the LuckyCoin fiasco.

As night drifted towards the dead zone of 3 a.m., Vanessa fell into a restless sleep. With each stirring, she felt as though something was pressing hard upon her chest and gradually, her confidence began to erode until all that remained was a stark bedrock of fear. Of course there were things that could be traced back to her. Like everyone in London, Rob had pushed through some very aggressive deals. The whole City had interpreted the government's lacklustre enforcement as a green light to forge ahead in the spirit of free enterprise and if lawyers didn't cut corners they weren't in the race. As Compliance Officer, she had not only turned a blind eye to some dodgy things, she had positively authorised them, and that would all be laid bare when the files were audited properly. It was expensive to hide things and cumbersome too, and she had become very sloppy and cavalier.

She couldn't trust Rob not to implicate her either. He would do that in a heartbeat. He probably already had.

How reckless she had been! Vanessa's thoughts sifted back through the deals she had done, shuffling through the rules she had disregarded, her mind snagging on the omissions that would stand out as red flags to anyone reviewing the files with any diligence.

Throughout the night, Vanessa's mind swung between panic and dread, and she lay there frozen, staring into the void.

She hadn't been involved in the rest of the financing of LuckyCoin so that was something at least, she thought, as she fell back into a disturbed sleep.

Vanessa woke a couple of hours later feeling groggy and unrefreshed. She dressed and went downstairs where she made a pot of tea and sat watching Lensley's garden reveal itself to the rising sun.

'How do you know the investigation into Rob is limited to LuckyCoin?' she asked Lensley when he came down for breakfast.

'I don't. But that's where it started.'

'These investigations spread like wildfire,' Vanessa said, shaking her head.

'Sure,' said Lensley, 'but their focus is there.'

'For the time being.'

'Yes. For the time being.'

'And do you think Amir knows about it yet?'

Lensley handed her a coffee and turned back to the eggs and bacon he was preparing on the hob. 'It was in the papers. Someone leaked it to the press.'

'Sweet Jesus,' Vanessa said, then told Lensley how Elanka had conned Rob into transferring ownership of Casa di Stelle to her and her mother in return for helping Rob get his hands on Amir's Cyprus money for LuckyCoin.

'When was that?'

'Last month. At the time I thought it was strange that neither Amir nor Silvano were involved in moving that money. It was all very urgent and sudden one Friday evening and I had to authorise the transfer through the trust account.'

Lensley raised his eyebrows as he flipped the bacon. 'I thought there was something fishy when Rob said Amir had invested in LuckyCoin before we even had the investment documents ready.'

'Last night I couldn't sleep and I went back over all the deals we'd done together. That one sticks out, of course. I remember it was so urgent I had to go back into the office on the Saturday.'

Lensley brought over the food and as they ate, he told Vanessa he had seen Rob attack Elanka on the rooftop of the nightclub in London.

'I didn't know it was Rob until later but it still haunts me that moment. More than any of the other things I've seen Rob do.'

Vanessa put down her cutlery, appalled. 'What did he do to her?'

'It wasn't really what he did. It was what I did.'

'Good god, Lensley, what did *you* do?' Vanessa said, aghast.

'I did nothing. And then I turned and ran away.'

Vanessa grabbed hold of his arm. 'Thank god for that.'

Lensley shook his head. 'The point is I did nothing, just like I do at work.'

'You don't do *nothing* at UBank.'

'I don't do anything I'm proud of, Vanessa. I'm a coward.'

'You're not a coward! What were you supposed to do? You said you didn't know it was Rob until later. He could have had a knife or a gun.'

'He could have, but he didn't.'

Vanessa pointed her fork at him. 'But you didn't know that. Still don't.'

'I didn't bother to find out. I just did nothing. I turned a blind eye and hid from the truth.'

'We've all done that, Lensley.'

Lensley glared at her. 'We do it every day! We're all so servile to Rob, and for what?'

'For our jobs, remember?'

'So we can create these lives we hate. It's pathetic!'

'I wouldn't be too quick to hate all this,' said Vanessa, gesturing around at the beautiful kitchen.

Lensley collected the plates. 'I've always loathed this kitchen. It's like a morgue.'

'So what do we do about it now?' said Vanessa. 'Elanka took a huge risk transferring that money without telling Amir. How does she think she can get away with it?'

341

Lensley went over and poured more coffee. 'For the time being Amir is grounded here. From what I've heard Elanka's clever. She knows how to cover her tracks.'

'It's not enough to be clever with these people,' said Vanessa, thinking of the brazen way Elanka had continued to swan around Monaco after double-crossing Amir. 'Perhaps they just haven't worked it out yet. We still don't know what's happened to Rob.'

'He called me last night.'

'Rob called you? What did he want?'

'The usual. He wanted me to do something for him. I refused of course.' Lensley finished his coffee and walked to the window.

Vanessa thought she heard him sobbing. 'Lensley, what's wrong?'

It was then Lensley told her that Rob had been having an affair with Allegra.

'You were right when you suspected it that night at Rob's party. It had been going on for years. I hid from the truth of that too, but of course I knew. That's why Allegra's gone away. She said she needed a break from me, can you believe it?'

Vanessa went to stand by him, putting her hand on his back. She felt a huge amount of gratitude for Lensley. She was a fugitive and he owed her nothing, but he had been kind and hadn't hesitated to help her.

'I'm so sorry, Lensley. Rob's such a pig.'

'Both of them are as selfish as each other.'

'They deserve one another then,' she said quietly.

Lensley turned to Vanessa, the shadows under his eyes almost black. 'Allegra has finally got what she's always wanted – a rich and successful man.'

'Well, she's chosen the wrong one. Let's see how long she stands by him through all this.'

Lensley collapsed into an armchair and looked up at Vanessa, his eyes wet. 'Do you want to know the real reason Rob called me last night? He was trying to track her down. Apparently they have a secret lovers' account in Switzerland or somewhere and he needs her signature to access it.'

'Oh, Lensley.'

'You say I'm smart, but it's taken all this to make me realise how fucked my life is. I don't know what will happen to me but until then, I'm taking the boys to live in the country. This place is for sale.' Lensley threw his arms wide. 'This whole house, this whole fucking ugly kitchen, everything. It turns out none of it matters at all in the end.'

Half an hour later, Vanessa got dressed up as Allegra and the two of them drove out to Berkshire in Lensley's Audi. The instructions from the school were that parents should arrive before 11 a.m. and that after the sporting events, there would be an awards ceremony then a picnic beside the river.

They had fine-tuned the details of Vanessa's cover, agreeing that sticking as closely as possible to the truth was the most convincing way to lie. With her careful presentation and elaborate clothes, Vanessa hoped people would assume she was Allegra, and she would be introduced as Ally, but if enquiries went further, Ally would be a work colleague of Lensley's. Ally was there because she was looking at the school for her sister. Lensley had called his sons, telling them he was bringing a colleague and that Ally was also a friend of Mum's who would be taking plenty of photos to send to her in Sri Lanka.

Meetham was the kind of school whose parent body had little opportunity to mingle. Most parents lived abroad or were busy with work in London and so the requirement for parents to attend the school was minimal. The school was independently wealthy and as a charity it paid no tax. It had no need for any fundraising activities and so there was no well-meaning parents' group, nor any parents on the board of governors. Parental involvement in the school was actively discouraged by the head-master, and apart from the requirement to pay fees on time, the school behaved as though parents didn't really exist.

As a result, most of the parents who attended the sports day had never met each other and those whose paths had crossed couldn't remember let alone care who was there with whom. The same went for the teachers who came and went through a revolving door that moved with such velocity they could barely recall the boys' names let alone their parents'. For his part, Lensley had seen so little of his children and their friends that no one spoke to him, and Vanessa and Lensley sat in the stand and watched all the races undisturbed.

Finally, it was time for David's hurdle race – the last item on the agenda before the awards ceremony. Vanessa sat spellbound, her eyes glued to her binoculars and when David won the race, she leaped from her seat and let out an enormous whoop then excused herself and walked swiftly to the toilet.

It was all she could do to contain herself until she was in the cubicle where she sobbed for ten minutes.

Afterwards, Vanessa stood at the mirror, dabbing her red and swollen eyes, trying to correct her make-up while keeping the sombrero in place. At one point she glanced over to the woman at the next basin.

'Hello, Allegra,' the woman said.

'How wonderful to see you here,' Vanessa managed to say.

The woman must be the mother of one of Lensley's kids' friends, Vanessa thought. She couldn't possibly mistake her for Allegra at this close range. She must have seen her with Lensley.

Vanessa fanned her face and pointed to her eyes. 'I'm sorry, it's been such an emotional day. They grow up so fast, don't they?'

The woman stared at her blankly. 'I need you to walk ahead of me to the door.'

'I beg your pardon?'

'I don't want any fuss out there in the stand. I have a weapon and so does that man over there.'

Vanessa glanced over and saw a thug standing at the door. 'I think you have the wrong person,' she said. 'I'm not going anywhere with either of you.'

'We've been watching you since you arrived with your husband. There's someone out there guarding him now. If you don't come with me, Felix and Theodore will become our target.'

'Felix and Theodore?' Vanessa said, unsure for a second who they were, then recalled those were Lensley's kids' names.

Just then a young girl and her mother entered the toilet.

'Move,' said the woman quietly, jabbing something hard into the back of Vanessa's ribs.

Vanessa had no idea what was going on, but she knew it had something to do with Meritus and Amir. If she said the wrong thing she could expose Felix, Teddy or even David.

Vanessa walked from the toilets and out to the stand. She searched for Lensley and saw him talking to a man who was standing very close.

The woman took Vanessa by the arm and led her to the steps, the man close on her other side. The man smelled of stale cigarettes and cheap, airport aftershave. Vanessa could smell her own sharp scent too – one of tension and fear. When they got to the bottom of the steps they turned left towards the car park. Preparations were underway for the awards ceremony and the winners were assembled in rows on the grass with the headmaster circulating among the boys, taking some aside to congratulate them. Vanessa's eyes did what they had done all day – they peered into the faces of the boys searching for David, then, at the edge of the throng she saw him. He was alone and staring at something in his hands. She wanted to run over, fold him in her arms and never leave his side. But she didn't know what these people were capable of. Who knew what risks they presented to him, let alone her.

Just then, David looked up and stared straight at her, his face still flushed from his race. He should have been elated but he just looked forlorn and lonely. A second later, the headmaster came and put his hand on David's shoulder and his eyes broke contact. The headmaster led David over to the rest of the group and Vanessa tore her eyes from him as her captors led her away.

Chapter Thirty-Four

LIFE WAS STARTING TO TREAT Rob badly.

Things weren't meant to spiral out of control like this and for the first time ever, Rob was out of his depth with nowhere to turn.

He had woken up in his hotel room at the Chèvre d'Or in Èze twelve days ago, six hours after Vanessa had drugged him. Rob was still groggy and confused when he dragged himself from his dreamless stupor to the bathroom. He stood in the shower under a torrent of freezing water until his brain emerged from the fog. Naked and shivering, he crawled around looking for the cash he had brought with him until he realised Vanessa had taken it. Once he was dressed, he sat heavily on the bed and reviewed the situation. He was a sitting duck in the south of France if Amir knew what he had done, so he booked a ticket on the next plane to London and checked out of the hotel.

Vanessa had been right about Stephen, their colleague in the finance team. Napier, the managing partner, had seen Rob's demise coming and had asked Stephen to carry out an audit of the work Rob had been doing for sanctioned or soon-to-be sanctioned clients. Despite the precautions Rob and Vanessa had put in place to obscure their dealings, Stephen had discovered a rich seam of fraud, illegality and non-compliance stretching back many years. Rob had always been the firm's biggest biller, his main clients all from ex-Soviet states, so it really came as no surprise to the other partners. They knew Rob had been skirting the edges of the law but they had simply chosen to ignore it. Well, they couldn't ignore it now. Rob's gravy train had come screeching to a halt and had spewed its contents all over the firm.

Napier called an emergency meeting of the partnership and hatched a plan to cut Rob loose. This was no time for loyalty. The partnership's main concern was not to spook their other clients so Napier put out a statement, reassuring everyone they had ring-fenced Rob's deals and that the rest of Meritus was sound. The messaging was that Rob was a rogue player who by no means represented the values of the firm, and the rot he represented would be torn out immediately by the root.

Rob was not aware of any of this when his plane landed at Gatwick but when his security card didn't work at the office, he called his PA. Napier met him in reception and took him straight to a meeting room.

Napier was cold, but professional. He told Rob they had been monitoring him for several weeks and that a full internal invest-igation into his activities would take some time, owing to the complicated money flows Rob had devised. Napier suggested that if Rob cooperated with the firm to minimise the fall-out for Meritus, Napier wouldn't shop Rob to the authorities straight away. The deal was that Rob would be suspended from the office and confined to his home under twenty-four-hour surveillance pending the firm's investigation. Napier told Rob Meritus had brought in a forensic accountant who had found Rob's personal offshore accounts and that these had been frozen by the banks. As far as Rob could see he had no choice but to submit to the restrictions Napier had imposed.

Napier had a car waiting to take Rob home, and Rob sat in the back fuming. As they drove towards Highgate, Rob's mind cleared and he started casting around for people to blame.

Vanessa was the main culprit, of course. Rob was sure that despite what Napier had said, Vanessa had shopped him to Napier after she had drugged him in Èze then disappeared, leaving him to deal with this alone. Rob realised with growing outrage that he had been duped by not only one but two women. Where they were now was anyone's guess.

With the security guard next to him the atmosphere in the car was claustrophobic and Rob felt nauseous. He reached for the button to take down the window but it was locked. Realising he was fully cornered, Rob sat back and tried to think through his options. His first urge was to leave town somehow – he had a bit of cash squirrelled away in one of the safes in the house, but that wouldn't last long if he went on the run. And there was his safety to consider too. Although the security guards would make sure Rob didn't leave his home, their presence would ensure Amir's thugs didn't get to him either, and so Rob reluctantly conceded that Highgate was the safest place for him to be – at least for now.

For the first week of the investigation, Rob stayed home answering questions of the auditors whenever they called. Bit by bit they pieced together the transactions Rob had master-minded. Rob knew they were appalled, but he could tell they were a little impressed too and he got a kick out of it. The more Rob revealed about the ingenious ways he had hidden his clients' money and assets, the more arrogant he became and the more he divulged. He had really done some amazing work.

At the end of the second week of his Meritus house arrest, Rob began to feel restless. He didn't know how much time he had left, or whether the investigation would ultimately end in a jail term and he had no desire to live like a prisoner before he legally had to. He didn't have a lot of money in the safe, but it was enough to be able to enjoy a few good meals while he waited for his fate to be sealed.

Rob had been so cooperative with the auditors that he managed to persuade Napier to let him leave the house for lunch, provided he went with the driver and the security guard. They went to Bar Barolo, his favourite restaurant in the City, where he had discussed LuckyCoin with Vanessa and Lensley in happier times. Rob sat at a window table while the men waited in the car outside, watching him as he ate.

Bar Barolo was an old school place and the staff had never cared what Rob's business was as long as he paid his bills and Rob had always done more than that, tipping generously whenever he went there. He had never fully appreciated how much loyalty tipping generated among waiters, but he certainly appreciated it now.

'Would you like an aperitif, sir?' the waiter asked politely as he showed Rob to his table.

Rob ordered a dozen oysters and a bottle of champagne. The waiter brought over the champagne and made a fuss of it, rattling the ice bucket and peeling the foil off the cork with a practiced flourish. The bubbles hissed in the chilled crystal glass and Rob smiled as his life took on the illusion of normality.

'Celebrating?' the waiter asked, setting the cutlery down in front of him.

'Always,' said Rob, raising the heavily etched glass to his lips. The bubbles tickled his nose and the whole performance made him happy for the first time in weeks.

The oysters arrived on their bed of crushed ice and Rob leaned back to let the waiter settle the napkin on his lap. He glanced at the other diners then through the window to the view of the corporate tower blocks opposite. Rob took a sip of champagne and breathed a sigh as he relaxed into this, his favourite landscape.

Rob had always loved the City. The place made sense in a way no other place did. It was a world where a man could get by on his wits, by working hard and by working the system. The City had encouraged him to push the boundaries of human endeavour in the realm of corporate structuring in a way that made him feel creative. Whenever Rob came up with a new way to help the rich hide their money, he felt a rush of elation. He thought it was similar to the way those at the vanguard of the Industrial Revolution might have felt when they invented something like the steam engine, for example. They didn't know the full extent of its application, but they knew they were on to something.

The City had been a refuge, a place of safety, and Rob had fought for his job at Meritus. He had grown his practice from nothing by being smarter than the next guy and by doing the work no one else could stomach. The other partners at the firm had cheered him along, never asking questions as long as the money rolled in.

They had loved him once. What they were doing now was unfair.

Rob sat forward and breathed in the fresh iodine scent of the oysters, so rich and full of promise like a crinkly banknote. Rob loved the complex aromas embedded into the substrate of those old paper notes. When you slid them between your fingers and smelled the filmy grease on each roll and each note. The salty residue of countless unfair exchanges.

Rob singled out the largest oyster and plucked it from its bed of crushed ice. He squeezed lemon juice over its translucent flesh and watched its frilly edges ripple back on its pearly shell, like those silky knickers Allegra sometimes wore.

They had met three years ago at the UBank ball. Lensley was chatting to a colleague and Allegra had singled Rob out from all the other men in the room after dinner. She was wearing a beautiful dress – some kind of layered arrangement of shiny fabric in a kaleidoscope of silver and grey. Rob didn't want to stare – in fact he didn't know quite where to look – but at the same time he couldn't take his eyes off her.

In the beginning, they only met occasionally but it wasn't long before they saw each other every week.

Allegra reminded Rob of the endless possibilities of money. To him she embodied everything the City had to offer – money, excitement, power and other men's wives.

Rob looked over to the empty space beside him at the table as he remembered those early days with Allegra. He had set up an account in Switzerland in her name. It was something he did on a whim after a particularly debauched weekend with her in Paris while Lensley was in Dubai toiling away on one of Rob's deals. It was part of a fantasy he had about running off with her and he knew she would be impressed by the gesture. He couldn't recall exactly how much money he had put in the account. At the time it hadn't seemed like much but he had added to it over the years and there would be more than enough to escape with.

He remembered he hadn't been so lovestruck that he had lost his senses entirely. He knew she was as ruthless as him when it came to money, and although the account was in her name, it needed both their signatures to access.

He hadn't spoken to Allegra since he'd had the trouble at work. It was too humiliating, but now, with his other accounts frozen, he needed that money. He had tried calling her during the week on the secret phone he had given her but she didn't answer. He had tried calling Lensley too but that hadn't worked out well.

The oysters looked up at him like a silent jury waiting to see what he would do. He jabbed one with a fork and brought the quivering flesh to his lips. The briny juice ran down his chin while the oyster slid down his gullet. He took a sip of champagne and then wiped his mouth on the fine damask napkin.

Rob gazed around the crowded restaurant. If Napier had his way all of this would come to an end. It wasn't right. The whole thing was unfair.

He needed to find Allegra, she was his route out of this.

He took out his phone and dialled her number again. The phone rang this time, but there was no answer, so he sent a text.

I really need your help, darling.

To his surprise, the message was delivered. It looked like she had the phone on. He opened the tracking app he had paired with the phone before he had given it to her. She was somewhere near Windsor so he sent another message.

I need you to authorise a bank transfer asap. Is that OK?

He took another oyster and considered its pearly edges and its hard leaden shell – down the hatch it went – then he went back to his phone. Allegra had read both messages but she hadn't replied so he sent another.

Darling, please. This is important.

Rob finished his oysters and sat back. The waiter replenished his glass and removed the platter of empty shells.

As the waiter withdrew, a text arrived on Rob's phone from Allegra's number.

I'm here, darling.

Rob seized his phone and they had a text exchange. Allegra agreed to help him but he had to come out to Berkshire.

She sent him a map and he zoomed in on the address.

Rob called the waiter over and whispered something in his ear. The man nodded and walked briskly towards the back of the restaurant.

Rob followed.

He handed the waiter a roll of cash and then slipped out the back door.

The alley behind the restaurant led to a side street beside Farringdon Station where he caught a train to Reading. From Reading Rob took a taxi to the address Allegra had sent him.

Mill Wheel House was a beautiful red brick mansion on the banks of the Thames right next to a small parish church. The entrance to the house faced the river behind a couple of elegant willows whose fronds grazed the water.

As Rob passed a small muddy animal enclosure not far from a path that led to the front door he heard voices and the muffled scratch of a walkie-talkie tuning in.

That was the last thing he sensed before something hit him on the back of the knees. His legs buckled beneath him and then everything went black.

Chapter Thirty-Five

Berkshire

T HEY HAD GIVEN VANESSA SOME kind of sleeping drug, Temazapam or Ambien, Vanessa knew them all, but this was a lot stronger and she woke with her awareness lagging behind her physical sensations. Her head was heavy and there was a huge vacancy of memory. She was in her underwear but unhurt, apart from the ache behind her eyes, which she thought might ease if she just lay there a while.

The room was dim, but the light at the tiny window was intense for such a small aperture. It was full daylight outside, morning most likely and from the low bowed ceiling, Vanessa assumed she was being held in some kind of attic. Better than a damp basement, she thought, gazing around the dusty bare-boarded room, which held little more than the mattress she was sprawled upon. Someone had undressed her and Allegra's turf-green frock was hanging from a hook on the door like a deflated squid. If they meant to kill or violate her they would probably have already done so. A sense of relief forced its way through the brain fog and then petered out, feeble and unconvincing.

Fragmented recollections of the previous day appeared like random snapshots. She remembered seeing David alone on the grass as she emerged from the toilet wedged between her captors. He had looked over as if she had called to him and their eyes met briefly before the headmaster took him by the shoulder. Vanessa stared at the ceiling as her mind veered between two opposing but equally wretched thoughts: David had seen her and looked away, indifferent, or he hadn't recognised her at all. She hoped for her own sake it was the latter and she felt the bruise at the back of her ribs where the gun's nose had propelled her from the toilet, down the steps and into the waiting car. Vanessa shivered at the thought of what might have happened had David recognised her and come running.

She recalled the voices in the car, someone forcing her to drink from a paper cup, a bitter taste, her two captors plus a driver. The afternoon sun had taken on a surreal glare, light dancing around the car, individual colours refracting across the glass as the world tilted and she grew more confused. A mixture of Russian and some other language, the voices garbled and indistinct as the drugs took her out.

How long had she been lying here? She looked for her watch, but it had gone, together with Allegra's green handbag.

Vanessa went to the window. She was surprised to see the view was of a wide, fast-moving river beyond a broad sweep of garden. Large willows marked the edge of the lawn, their tendrils draping over the water and to the left there was a muddy field and a shed. Some rudimentary fencing surrounded the field but other than that, there were no physical obstacles between where she was now and the adjoining properties, one of which seemed to be a church. She was on the third, maybe fourth floor of what appeared to be a large red brick building. She tried to open the window but it was nailed shut. Vanessa didn't know what obstacles lay beyond the bedroom door, but if by some miracle she could get past whatever human menace was gathered there, escape might be possible.

Her predicament was mixed up with Amir and the things she had been running from, but specifically why she had been abducted she had no idea. Over the past two weeks she had played out many different and dangerous scenarios and how she might respond but now she had been caught, she couldn't think rationally. Her mind was too muddled; she was too frightened. This was why they trained people in situations where kidnapping was likely. The mind doesn't work when it's cornered.

There was a bathroom to the side with a small basin so she busied herself quietly and then splashed her face with water. She didn't want to make any noise that might summon her captors and bring a start to a day filled with dread.

As she headed back to the mattress there was a tap on the door, the politeness of which made her suddenly furious.

'Stay out!' Vanessa said, snatching Allegra's dress off the hook. She wriggled into it, pressing her weight against the door as a key ground the lock. There were no words from the other side, but she felt the man's power as he opened it easily, not struggling in the slightest against her weight.

He was a standard issue thug – shaved head, bony jaw, short and over-muscled. He was overdressed too, for the warm weather, in black trousers and a zipped up utility jacket. He didn't seem to be able to speak, just grunted and communicated in a series of facial gestures. The first one Vanessa interpreted to mean that she should consume the plate of eggs and the water he held out to her on a tray.

She wasn't hungry but took the bottle of water and checked the seal.

The man stepped back, placing the tray on the floor as she drank from the bottle.

When she finished, he indicated she was to follow him downstairs.

He was clearly undaunted by whatever fighting skills Vanessa might possess as he turned his back to her and walked ahead. Vanessa trailed a few steps behind wondering if she would be able to fell him with the benefit of height and gravity. At neither of the two landings did he even bother to check she was still there.

Any fantasies Vanessa had of escape dissolved at the sight of two more heavies at the far end of the hall, one of whom was her male abductor from David's sports day. These men seemed similarly unconcerned about her potential as a flight risk and just looked up briefly before going back to their phones.

The man she was following led her through a corridor on the ground floor of what turned out to be a manor house full of darkened rooms each one extravagantly decorated in clashing colours and styles. It wasn't eclectic taste so much as a total absence of taste. There were antique chairs around Perspex tables, Persian carpets beneath ugly modern sculptures and acres of animal print amid brightly coloured, tasselled cushions. Finally, at the end of the corridor, the man stepped outside into the garden.

A path cut across the lawn to a wooden gate that led to the field with the shed she had seen from the window. Another man stood guard outside the shed, and a couple of enormous spotted pigs lounged in the bog, their hairy bellies caked with mud.

The man at her side stopped at the gate. He gestured beyond the pigs to the shed where the other man stood.

Overwhelmed by the mud and the stench and thinking this shed was to be her new prison, Vanessa stood her ground.

'I'm not going in there,' she said. Apart from anything else, the prospect of sharing a small space with such enormous pigs terrified her.

The man next to her shoved her forwards.

'Go!' he yelled.

'Your boyfriend's in here,' said the man outside the shed.

Vanessa had no boyfriend so what did he mean? Her mind veered back to the various encounters she'd had before she left Monaco and she tried to fathom how any of those men could be in that stinking shed. Panic gripped her as she thought of David. Whatever they wanted from her they could easily get through him, so pretence at cooperation was necessary.

She made a plea to the man at the shed. 'What do you want? At least tell me that.'

The man beside her grabbed her in a full body lock that barely left her room to breathe and frogmarched her through the mud, opened the shed door and shoved her in.

Inside, the revolting stench of pig shit erased all other senses and Vanessa's eyes fought against the gloom. A small plastic skylight cut into the roof cast a sallow glow, covered as it was with dirt and leaves, and from the far corner of the hut came a scuffling sound. Vanessa backed away, assuming the mottled bulk on the floor was another of the pigs, disturbed by her arrival, but then miraculously it reared up on its hind legs and spoke to her from the shadows.

'What the *fuck* are you doing here?' it said.

It was then Vanessa made out the shape of Rob. He was naked and badly beaten, the bruises starkly livid on his vast white rump, which was stained with mud and pig shit. One eye was dark and swollen, the other just a slit.

The man guarding the shed opened the door. 'Now tell us – where's the money?' he said to Rob.

'I told you. All my accounts are frozen. But as soon as they're unfrozen—'

The man moved towards Vanessa while still addressing Rob. 'If you don't give us access to your accounts you and your girlfriend will both die horrible deaths in here and you'll be fed to the pigs.'

'Just tell them what they need to know, Rob,' said Vanessa, terrified but averting her eyes from Rob's naked bulk.

'I don't care,' said Rob. His voice was little more than a grunt and he looked savagely at Vanessa. 'This is all your fault. They think you're Allegra.' Then turning back to their captor, 'Feed her to the pigs for all I care.'

'Rob, please.'

'Fuck off!' said Rob viciously. 'You're on your own.'

Rob stumbled towards her but the man moved with lightning speed and whacked him on the jaw, sending him reeling back into the mud where he writhed and moaned. As much as Vanessa hated Rob, it was difficult to watch.

Rob pointed to Vanessa. 'She's not Allegra. She's Vanessa,' he said, slurring his words. 'They've frozen my accounts. I have no money and it's all her fault.'

'Please, Rob. We can get hold of Allegra if that's what they need. Let's get them to call Lensley.'

Rob pulled himself to standing. He was swaying badly. 'Her name's Vanessa. She's my colleague! She's responsible for this mess.'

Rob staggered towards Vanessa, and then fell. He pointed at her, his hand shaking. 'If it wasn't for her none of this would have happened.' His eyes were rolling back in his head now. 'If you want the money, ask her!'

Rob lay on the floor repeating himself, his words slurred and incomprehensible. Then he went quiet mid-sentence and Vanessa thought he must have passed out.

'Please, no more. He's badly hurt, can't you see?' said Vanessa to the man beside Rob.

With a terrible groan Rob raised himself to sitting. 'She's not Allegra, you fucking idiot! Bring my wine!'

The man kicked Rob again.

Rob lay there thumping his fist on the wall, his head rolling as his words slurred into nonsense, English mixed with Russian. 'Not her. Oysters! Wine! Vino!'

The man muttered something Vanessa didn't catch then, 'Stay here. Don't move.'

He stepped outside and Vanessa heard him speaking on his phone.

Rob gazed wildly towards the light from the open door. Vanessa could see he was bleeding from an injury to his head, his one seeing eye bloodshot and crazed.

'Oysters!' he yelled, his mouth frothing with sputum.

The other, more thuggish man entered the shed.

'He's unwell. You've beaten him senseless. Please take him to the house. Someone needs to clean him up and look at him. He needs a doctor,' said Vanessa.

Rob piped up from the floor, pointing a shaking finger at her. 'Don't waste your breath. That fuckwit doesn't speak English. Why aren't there any proper waiters here?'

The man clearly understood Rob's kind of English and kicked him back to the wall.

The man on the phone returned to the shed. 'You,' he said to Vanessa. 'Come with me.'

Rob reared up again, mumbling and swearing. 'She's the one with the money,' Rob screamed from the shed as they disappeared down the path. 'She knows where ALL the money is. She can get it. Take her and let me go.'

Vanessa could still hear Rob yelling when they entered the house. He was calling for oysters.

A bearded man was in the hall where the other two men had been sitting before. There were tea things arranged on the table in front of him.

'We haven't yet had the pleasure,' he said. 'I'm Amir.'

It wasn't a situation requiring a handshake but Vanessa complied.

'I just did what Rob asked in relation to your business affairs. It was my job. I thought you had authorised it all,' Vanessa said, smoothing the muddy green silk of Allegra's dress away from the chair as she sat down opposite Amir.

Annoyance crossed Amir's features as he poured the tea. 'I have a lot of financial obligations and these sanctions mean I have limited access to funds. Rob was supposed to have all that covered off, but he's let me down badly with this crypto fiasco. It's cash I need now.'

'You kidnapped the wrong person. I'm not Allegra. I don't have any cash.'

Amir stood and went over to a shelf near the door. 'I know Rob has put money into Allegra's name. Quite a lot of money he said. He boasted about it to me in Monaco last year, and we thought you were Allegra because you were with her husband. Then, when we found you—'

'*Found* me?'

'When we picked you up we went through your bag and found this phone.' Amir showed her the iPhone Rob had bought for Allegra which had been hidden in Allegra's matching green bag all this time.

'When we charged it and turned it on we saw Rob had been trying to contact her. He came to Berkshire thinking Allegra was here.'

'Why on earth would he do that?'

Amir scrolled through the phone. He read a couple of messages about needing Allegra's help to authorise a bank transfer.

'He came out here to try and get the money he'd stashed in her name.'

Amir handed the phone to Vanessa and she went through the messages, shaking her head, amazed that given all the trouble he was in, Rob's priority was still money.

She placed the phone on the table. 'You kidnapped the wrong person. So please, now, let me go.'

'I can't do that,' Amir said. 'Even if Rob's accounts in the UK are frozen there are offshore accounts and you must know where they are.'

'Really, I have no idea.'

'He indicated just now you knew where the money was.'

Vanessa let out a sob. 'He's desperate. He'll say anything. You should see the state of him.'

Amir spoke to the man at the door. 'Take her back upstairs.'

'Wait,' said Vanessa, her mind suddenly focused. 'I do know where Rob has money.' She looked from Amir to the other man. 'But it's in France, Not here.'

Amir nodded. 'Where then?'

'In Nice. There's money in a bank there.'

Amir snapped his fingers and called through to another room. A man came in with a laptop. 'You can make a transfer then. Show me.'

Vanessa shook her head. 'It's a dark bank. A stash house. Cash only. There's no account, nothing online.'

Amir nodded. 'Cash is good. OK. How much cash?'

Vanessa had no idea of the exact figure, as the money moved in and out according to schedules not even Rob understood, but she needed to make it sound good.

'There's at least five, maybe six million. Some of it's yours—'

'All of it's mine now,' Amir said. 'So how do we get hold of this cash in Nice?'

'*I* will get it but I have to go alone.'

He shook his head. 'Not alone.'

'Only Rob and I can access the bank. It uses bio-security – facial recognition and a DNA sample. And Rob is in no state to do anything with his face all beaten up like that.'

'I can't let you go by yourself.'

'I'll go with that guy there, then.' Vanessa pointed to the man at the doorway. 'And then release me once I've done it. After I hand over the money,' she said, her mind moving quickly.

Amir looked over to the man. 'Get two flights to Nice for tomorrow. Call Silvano for back up.' He then switched to Belarusian and Vanessa heard him say the name 'Elanka'.

'And get me some decent clothes,' said Vanessa.

Amir looked at Vanessa and then at the man. 'Guard her with your life and don't hesitate to kill her if she's lying.' Amir turned back to Vanessa. 'I do hope you're not lying.'

Chapter Thirty-Six

Nice

T HE OLD PORT OF NICE is sheltered from the tourist hordes by Castle Hill, which stands between the port and the Promenade des Anglais, and marks for the majority of visitors the town's eastern edge. Although the castle and its fortifications have long since been destroyed, the rocky peak that once defended the village of Nizza in the Middle Ages now shields Port Lympia from this modern invading force, and so there is still some charm left in the harbour and the quiet streets of the Old Port.

Even now, at the height of the tourist season, the port district was calm. It was mid-afternoon and, in keeping with the town's Italian roots, most shops were closed. The area's limited activity was centred on the restaurant terraces where diners sought refuge from the afternoon heat.

When Vanessa told Amir she had a fake French passport she thought he would abandon the plan to send her to Nice but instead, Amir assured her that Gatwick was the easiest point of departure for anyone with 'identification issues'. He made it clear he wanted the cash at any cost, and having her take the massive risk of crossing a border with a fake passport meant nothing to him. Vanessa warned Amir the document wouldn't fool the facial recognition cameras at British airports, but Amir was right – there had been none leaving Gatwick's South terminal, and nothing but a cursory glance at her passport when she arrived in Nice.

A black Mercedes was waiting at the airport for Vanessa and her travelling companion, Pavel, and once they had cleared the tangle of motorways on the outskirts of town, the car crawled east in the traffic along the Promenade des Anglais. As if to compensate for the smooth entry into France, the car slowed at every roundabout and stopped at every traffic light on the short stretch of sea-front tarmac. Through tinted windows, Vanessa watched the throng of brightly dressed tourists as they streamed beneath the palm trees towards the town's pebbly beach. Pavel sat in the front and exchanged a few words with the driver. He had barely spoken to her since they left the grey skies of Berkshire and even though she couldn't understand what he was saying to the driver, it was clear the sunshine hadn't improved his mood.

As they drew towards Castle Hill, Vanessa noticed both men checking the rear-view mirrors. When they turned left, Vanessa glanced behind to see they were now being followed by two black Mercedes vans. Amir had made it clear Vanessa was to transfer the cash Rob held at the stash house into suitcases. Five million would require at least ten suitcases, possibly more. There had been little discussion as to what would happen once she had transferred the cash, but she hoped not to be around for that.

Finally, the traffic eased and the black Mercedes convoy skirted around the northern edge of Castle Hill and pulled up outside the jewellery store next to the Hotel Lympia.

Pavel craned around. 'I thought you said it was a bank.'

'It is,' said Vanessa. 'It's the biggest cash bank on the coast.'

Pavel looked irritably at the hotel and then said something to the driver.

Vanessa opened the car door. 'I'm going in alone,' she said. 'Bring over two of the suitcases. There's an alley that runs behind the hotel. Get the vans to wait around there.'

Pavel leaped out of the car. 'I'm coming with you.'

Vanessa walked to the hotel. She glanced at Pavel who was at her side, and then pointed to the vans. 'I said bring over two suitcases. And wait for me in the alley with the next two.'

Pavel whistled to the guys in the vans. The grouping of thugs and the fleet of black Mercedes couldn't have been more conspicuous in the quiet side street as one of the men wheeled two large suitcases over the road.

Vanessa entered the code on the keypad beside the hotel door. When the lock disengaged she turned to Pavel. 'It's not that I don't want your company,' she said. 'But I'm the only one authorised to enter.'

'We're coming too,' Pavel said, and pushed against the doors.

'You won't get any further than the lobby.'

'We'll have to. Those are our orders.'

'Look, I know you think you can just bust your way in with your guns and your orders, but it doesn't work like that here.'

Both men ignored Vanessa and strode along the corridor to the desk. They looked around for an attendant then checked the breakfast room.

The men stood over her as she placed her index finger on the sensor. The screen on the wall lit up, scanned her face and then went black. The steel door to the left of the desk slid open to reveal the lift.

Vanessa turned to Pavel. 'The money's upstairs and there are three layers of security to get past. There are no people to threaten or kill, just these machines.'

She pointed to the lift. 'The lift only takes one person at a time and you need an image and a retina scan here, and another one to get out of the lift. Give me the bags and wait out the back like I said.'

Vanessa reached for the suitcases but Pavel pushed her aside and marched towards the lift. An alarm went off, the screen flashed and the lift door closed abruptly.

Pavel turned to her. 'What the—'

'I only get one more chance to enter the lift. If you mess it up again, my entry will be barred,' she said.

'My instructions are to stay with you.'

'Well, that's not possible.'

Pavel was blocking Vanessa's way to the lift. 'Those are my instructions.'

'Then we need to get your instructions changed. Call Amir, let me speak to him.'

Pavel pulled out his phone and spoke to Amir, then passed the phone to Vanessa.

'Your guys are wasting time and already attracting attention outside,' she said. 'It's a very inflexible process here. They need to do as I say.'

'He needs to stay with you,' said Amir.

'Well, he can't. He's not a client of the bank.'

'Why didn't you tell me this before?'

'Because I thought you'd know. Look, you have six guys here. Put two at the front and the other four at the rear. I'm not going anywhere.'

'Where's the money?'

'Upstairs. They won't let him up there.'

There was silence down the line.

'So who's there?'

'The people who own the place.'

'Call them. Get them to come down and authorise Pavel's entry.'

'I don't have their number.'

'You must have their number.'

'Rob deals with it all. I just deliver the cash. And now you've beaten Rob to within an inch of his life you won't get anything out of him.'

'Just get this done.'

'I'm trying. But your goons are stopping me. I want this over too.'

'So, what's the security protocol.'

'Facial recognition, retina and a DNA sample.'

'No ID?'

'No ID,' said Vanessa.

'OK. Then leave your passport and your phone and everything else – bag, driving licence, with Pavel.'

Vanessa handed the phone back to Pavel who spoke briefly to Amir. She gave her handbag to Pavel and took the empty suitcases.

'How long will you be?' Pavel asked.

'About half an hour. We have to go through a counting and sign-out process the first time. After that, it should only take about ten minutes each time.'

'I'll wait for you here,' he said, standing back against the wall. The other man stood guard at the front door.

Vanessa went through the facial scan at the desk again and then entered the lift. Pavel watched as she pressed the button for the third floor.

The lift closed and instead of going up, the lift took Vanessa down to the crypt where she went through the procedures to exit the lift and pass through the small antechamber to the bunker.

Franz met her at the door. He had seen and heard through CCTV the events that had taken place on the street and in the lobby so there was no need to explain anything. He was never one for small talk, anyway.

'Hello, Franz. I need help filling these suitcases and then I need access to the tunnels,' Vanessa said. 'The one that goes to the station.'

The secret network of tunnels and storage bunkers that ran beneath Castle Hill had existed for centuries and were originally linked to smuggling activities that ran along the coast. Those who kept their money with Franz knew about the tunnels of course; they were so numerous and ancient that there were rumours the tunnels were the burial place of the Knights Templar treasure.

The network fell into disrepair after the castle was destroyed in the eighteenth century, but the Germans had found the tunnels during their occupation in World War II and carried out extensive repairs. The Nazis had planned to build a submarine base at Nice and while the end of the war thwarted those plans, the improvements and additions to the tunnelling remained.

Franz was the grandson of the German officer who had been responsible for excavating and expanding the network. The French had kept Franz's grandfather on after the war as part of an amnesty because he was the only one who knew the tunnel layout, having overseen the engineering that had taken place.

Franz's grandfather had passed this information on to his son and then to Franz who saw the tunnels' underworld potential, this time as a smuggling and money-laundering hub.

Franz showed Vanessa to Rob's vault which looked untouched since she had seen it last.

'I'm going to take as much as I can in these suitcases now. I need you to transfer the rest of the money into one of the German or Swiss banks.'

Franz called over two of his assistants who started packing bricks of cash into the two suitcases.

Vanessa opened the safe and took the diamonds together with her old passport, laptop, SIM and driving licence, everything she had put there two weeks ago.

Franz took a copy of her old passport. 'At the moment we can move it to a bank in Austria or Dubai,' he said. 'But it will take some time.'

'I need it next week.'

Franz shook his head. 'To do it that quickly we'll need to charge double our usual commission.'

'Twenty per cent, not thirty,' Vanessa said, stuffing her papers into the front pocket of a suitcase.

Franz pointed to the bricks of money in Rob's vault. 'I can move it all in cash to Austria or Dubai on your instructions, but I can't release it to you personally unless—'

'Unless what?'

Franz clasped his hands together. 'Unless I take thirty per cent. We'll need to deal with those guys you've brought here. They won't be happy when you don't reappear.'

Vanessa didn't want to know how Franz proposed to deal with Pavel and the others, but that wasn't her problem now.

'OK then. Thirty per cent,' Vanessa said.

The men had finished packing the suitcases. One of them handed her a slip of paper, a receipt for half a million euros in each bag.

Vanessa tried the handles of the bags, testing to check she could wheel them in the tunnels all the way to the station.

'You'll need one of these,' Franz said, putting an LED headlamp around her forehead. 'And here's another should that one fail,' he said, tucking it into her pocket.

He pointed to the suitcases. 'Are you sure you can manage both of these? The tunnel that goes to the station is the oldest and the last stretch is uphill. It will be hard going.'

'I'll manage,' said Vanessa. She knew it wasn't part of their service to help clients transport cash beyond the bunker and so she didn't ask.

Franz led Vanessa to the back of the crypt and opened a small door. A cold draft wafted up smelling of mildew and sewers. The cavity ahead was lined in concrete and there were puddles in the middle where the concrete sagged. Vanessa shivered, realising they were below sea level. Franz took one of the suitcases and led Vanessa along the damp corridor to a vaulted door with a spindle wheel. They were both hunched over and there was barely enough room to drag the two suitcases.

'The only way to get this open from the other side is with explosives,' Franz said.

He took a while to unbolt the door, which opened to reveal a narrow tunnel clad in cobblestones and glistening in the torchlight.

'This is the main tunnel from the port so it's straighter than the others.'

The way ahead was dark and narrow and Franz's face shone ghoulishly in the torchlight as he described the route. 'This tunnel heads north. Follow it for ten minutes and you'll see a branching off to the left. Follow that for another fifteen minutes and you'll come to the underpass below the station.'

Vanessa shuddered.

'Are you sure about this?' he said. 'Once I shut this door, that's it. I won't open it again. If you get lost, you're on your own.'

Vanessa looked at her watch. It was 4 p.m. She glanced back to the bunker and then took the other suitcase from Franz. 'Understood.'

'Keep your head down and good luck,' he said and then slammed the door shut.

The grinding of the bolts and locks behind the closed door echoed along the tunnel as Vanessa forged ahead, dragging the two bags, her head down, the light from the headlamp bobbing crazily on the stone walls around her.

The tunnel was long and straight but on an incline and so it was arduous work to drag the two heavy suitcases. Rats scuttled over the stones up ahead and so she kept the torch moving from side to side to scare them off. At several intervals there were strange indents in the wall, places where the bricks had collapsed and tumbled out so she had to stop and haul each suitcase over the rubble. After five minutes she panicked, her heart thudding wildly and she stopped to catch her breath. What if she got lost down here? What if Franz had deliberately sent her off in the wrong direction? She couldn't see any intersection up ahead but she forced herself on and sure enough, she soon came to a narrower tunnel that branched off to the left.

It had been more than half an hour since she had left Pavel. He would be getting suspicious by now, raising the alarm with the other men and possibly also Amir. She didn't know how Franz would deal with them, but the stash house had been in business for years. They specialised in this kind of thing, exacting a premium from desperate people in impossible situations. She had heard about a gun fight that had broken out in the crypt a few years ago and both clients had been killed. That was why they only allowed people to enter one at a time.

Would Amir think to check the station? Perhaps they were already there, waiting for her. People like Amir didn't stay in business by not thinking ahead, and Vanessa quickened her pace, her shoulders burning with the weight of the bags, which snagged and pulled over the rickety stones. She battled hard to swallow down panic, telling herself that the further she walked, the further she was getting from Amir and his men, and the closer she was getting to freedom and, she even let herself dare hope, to David.

Soon there was a dim glow up ahead. As she drew closer, she saw that the tunnel came to an end at the foot of a steep, crumbling flight of stairs overgrown with weeds and smelling of urine and excrement. It took her a while to heave the suitcases up the stairs, the last few steps taking all her strength, her arms shaking with the strain.

She was euphoric when she saw the station. She had been worried she would attract attention in her dishevelled state, dragging two suitcases out of a tunnel in broad daylight, but it was summer and the station was heaving. No one even glanced at her.

She crossed the road and checked the timetable then bought a ticket for the next train heading west to Marseille.

It left in ten minutes, which was enough time to buy a new disposable phone from a shop opposite the station.

The train was crowded and Vanessa stayed near the doors with the bags.

On the train, Vanessa called David but his phone went straight to voicemail.

'I can't say much now, darling, but I'll explain everything when I can. I'll call you tonight.'

She then put in a call to Kate.

When the train stopped at Juan-les-Pins, Vanessa alighted. She found a hotel and took a room. Before heading upstairs she bought a change of clothes in a shop near the hotel and, after showering and dressing, she went straight to the marina with the bags.

Chapter Thirty-Seven
Roquebrune-Cap-Martin

AMIR HAD BEEN IN LONDON for nine days now and had been under sanctions for four. He had known that sanctions were coming, of course, and so he'd had plenty of time to decide where he wanted to live while they remained in force. A travel ban had been imposed throughout Europe meaning he was unable to move freely, and going back to Belarus was out of the question. Amir had fallen out with one of the President's sons in a business deal last year and it wasn't safe to return until relations had thawed. Everyone advised him that London was the most obvious place to live, at least initially. The sanctions regime in the UK was much more lenient than in France, and provided you had good lawyers, the harsher aspects of life under sanctions could be eased. It was still possible to use frozen funds to pay lawyers' fees, after all: the British would never make their lawyers go cold turkey from oligarch cash. Several of Amir's wealthy Russian friends were living a lifestyle in London that was more or less the same as it was before the sanctions came in. It was just ordinary people that sanctions affected.

Although he had a British passport, Amir was sceptical about the UK, but Elanka persuaded him saying that in London, Amir would be near Roman. If Amir stayed in the south of France, it might be years until he saw his son again if Selena was not minded to travel. Elanka promised she would join Amir in London at the end of July after she had visited her mother in Lithuania.

When he left France for the UK, Amir knew that Rob had embezzled three million of his funds for LuckyCoin, but he didn't know about the money Elanka had transferred to Rob earlier from Cyprus. To cover her tracks, Elanka told Amir she had used the Cyprus money to buy shares in a business that ran a gambling platform that had recently listed on the London Stock Exchange. Amir had been so busy organising his affairs in France that he didn't pay too much attention to the Cyprus companies, but he agreed that since they were going to be based in the UK, the more business they had there, the better.

Although Amir listened to Elanka's advice about his move to London, he kept other decisions to himself. Thanks to Rob, Amir's ownership of the country clubs, hotels, casinos and other businesses along the coast were well-hidden from the authorities behind offshore front companies and Amir agreed that while he was in the UK these could continue as normal under Silvano's management.

Elanka had always despised Silvano. He had treated her badly when she first came to Casa di Stelle as a hostess, as he did all the other girls. Silvano thought of the women as his property, calling them 'his girls', and even now he behaved as if Elanka was a member of staff. She didn't trust him and had warned Amir several times that he was trouble, but Amir had brushed her off, knowing there was a lot of bitterness between them. Now that Amir was out of sight, however, Elanka suspected that Silvano would muscle in and stage some kind of takeover, she just didn't expect it to happen so soon.

It was Silvano, not Amir, who discovered through Kate's investigations that Rob had transferred Casa di Stelle into Elanka's name. He visited her at the villa and said that as long as she allowed him full access to the villa, its helipad and the yacht for the night-time events, which incidentally he planned to ramp up over the summer, then he wouldn't divulge her secret to Amir, *for now*.

Going back to taking orders from Silvano and turning a blind eye to the sordid activities at the villa and on the yacht was not what Elanka had in mind. She had loathed Silvano for so long that she understood how his mind worked, but there wasn't an obvious way to deal with him, particularly now he knew what she had done with the villa. She needed to act fast – before he told Amir.

Rob was the only lawyer Amir had ever invited onto his yacht and so when Elanka met Kate at the party, her suspicions were aroused. When she asked about Kate later, Amir told her Rob had gone missing and that Kate was helping him fix the mess Rob had left behind. Amir said it had been Silvano's idea to bring in Kate, and to have her travel with him to Corsica, and so Elanka engaged a man to monitor Kate's movements. The man reported that Kate was spending a lot of time with Silvano at the Hôtel de Paris, at his villa in Cap-d'Ail and on the yacht, and Elanka guessed Silvano was using Kate to make some kind of move.

Elanka needed to get to the bottom of whatever Silvano was up to before she was caught in the fall-out. It was clear from the brief conversations Elanka had had with Kate that she was infatuated with Anton, so she knew that Anton was the key to finding out what Kate was doing with Silvano. Like all Amir's associates, Elanka knew Anton was easily bought. She also knew that Anton had just been caught in Milan with a suitcase of cash and was now back in France under Silvano's thumb.

'That English girl has been asking after you,' said Elanka when she saw Anton at the villa a week after the party on the yacht. Anton was in Amir's office working on some network issues they were having with the computer system.

'Which one?' Anton said, and although his eyes stopped moving over the computer screen, he didn't look up.

'That pretty lawyer. She seems to think you're in some kind of trouble.'

'Tell her to stay out of it.'

Elanka came around to stand beside him and scanned the screen. 'I didn't tell her you'd been caught in Milan with a suitcase of Amir's cash. It must have been Silvano spreading rumours about you that got her all worried. Cigarette?'

Elanka pointed outside, indicating they should continue their conversation there. She didn't put it past Amir or Silvano to have had the room bugged. Anton followed her to the balcony and they stood in the shade near the steps leading down to the gazebo.

Elanka lit their cigarettes. 'How long do you think Kate will last working for Silvano?'

Anton shrugged and said coolly, 'Is she working for him?'

'I assume so. She went to Corsica with him and they've been together ever since.'

Anton turned to face the beach. It was a beautiful cloudless day and there were people swimming and sunbathing right in front of the house.

Elanka stood beside him so they were both gazing down onto the beach. She waited a while then turned to face him. 'Silvano's up to something. He's been planning it ever since he knew Amir was facing sanctions. He needed someone at Meritus though, and that's why he sent you to seduce her.'

Anton laughed.

'Isn't that how you two work – you're the warm up act then Silvano's the main course?'

'No.'

'Yes it is – you've become his little gigolo. How easy was it to rope her in? Tell me, did you appeal to her ego or her sense of romance?'

'Leave her out of this.'

Elanka gestured around the estate. 'Leave her out? *You* brought her in and now she's running around for Silvano. Is that what you wanted for her? Another of Silvano's girls?'

Anton stepped away from the balustrade. Two guards were crossing the lawn with the dogs heading for the beach. One of them looked up and nodded to Elanka who waved back.

'Don't be a fool,' Elanka said, returning her attention to Anton. 'Silvano knows he can't trust you. You were *stealing* from them. You're only here now because he needs something from you. What is it?'

'Give up, Elanka. Go back home – to Lithuania.'

'Whatever Silvano's giving you, I'll double it.'

Anton stared at her and gestured around at the house, the grounds and the beach. 'You're playing a dangerous game – why would I want to be part of it? How on earth do you think you can keep this place?'

There was a deathly silence as the cicadas paused to change the tempo of their chorus and then resumed, even louder than before.

Silvano hadn't told Elanka how he knew she now owned the villa, but now she realised.

'Oh, I see now. Is that what Kate's doing for Silvano? *Spying?*'

Anton helped himself to another of her cigarettes.

'Of course she is,' said Elanka to herself, her eyes gleaming. 'And Silvano doesn't just want control of this place, does he? He wants all of it.'

'Wait here,' she said and then walked back into the house.

A little while later she returned to the balcony with an envelope of cash. 'I know he's not paying you anything after the stunt you pulled with the casino cash so take this and tell me exactly what they're doing.'

Anton glanced at the envelope and shook his head.

'I'll find out anyway, so you may as well tell me now,' said Elanka. 'Here.'

She pushed the cash towards Anton and finally, he took it. He told Elanka she had guessed correctly and that Kate was helping Silvano reconfigure ownership of Amir's companies so Silvano could take them over.

'There, that's their plan,' he said, flicking through the cash.

'And what's your role? Why are you here?'

'Kate can't find what Silvano needs on their office system. Rob's hidden it in a separate database and Silvano needs me to go in there and find it.'

Elanka went back into the study. She wanted whatever information Silvano was getting. She searched through her phone, wrote several web addresses on a card and gave it to Anton. One was the address of an anonymous platform routed to a secure drop box. 'When you find the material Silvano needs, download this browser and then send the data to this drop box from this URL. It's untraceable.'

'Are you out of your mind?'

'There'll be another fifty thousand when I have confirmation it's there. You can take the data onto Silvano afterwards. He'll never know what you've done.'

'A hundred,' said Anton.

Elanka thrust the card at him. 'A hundred then.'

'And half of it now.'

'Once it's been sent,' she said.

Anton finished his cigarette and ground the stub in the ashtray. 'Why are you messing around with all this? Why don't you just get out of here?'

'I could ask you the same thing.'

'I tried and got caught, but you could leave now. What's stopping you?'

Elanka sighed and pointed to the beach. The security guards were standing over a group of girls spread out on the pebbles. 'You've seen them – those girls here now. They're more desperate and younger than ever.'

As they watched the group on the beach, two of the girls broke away and started walking towards the restaurant but the security guards called them back. The girls refused and an argument ensued, the girls yelling and swearing at the men. The other girls huddled closer together on the beach and several of them began to cry.

'I told myself for years it wasn't my problem,' Elanka said, then turned away. 'But of course it is.'

Elanka's conversation with Anton took place on Friday morning. It was Sunday evening now and tomorrow, Elanka would fly to

Lithuania where she would wait for Amir and Silvano to be arrested before returning to France.

Elanka had been dealing with the UK authorities since they approached her several months ago, offering immunity if she helped them prove their suspicions that Amir was financing the supply of weapons to Russian forces in Ukraine. Through her lawyers, Elanka had supplied details of the Belarusian bank Amir controlled, passing on emails and other information she found in Amir's office and on his computer. The police had raided Amir's London properties over the weekend and he was due to be arrested at his house in Berkshire tomorrow.

Silvano would be harder to implicate and Elanka had no faith in the police along the coast. They had known about Silvano's involvement in illegal gambling and the trafficking of girls for some time, and they had never done anything about it. Once Amir was arrested in the UK and his network exposed, however, this would change, Elanka's lawyers assured her. The police would no longer be able to ignore Silvano's role in Amir's businesses and they would have to act.

Elanka wasn't sure she would be able to retain the villa in her name, but once Amir and Silvano were in jail, she would return to Roquebrune and commence the fight to keep it. Elanka's lawyers said that any legal battle the French authorities might launch to confiscate the property would take years – it could even drag out for decades – and in the meantime, she planned to live at the villa with her mother on the money she had amassed in Cyprus.

Elanka opened the doors to the balcony and scanned the front garden. By the time she returned in several months the new pool would be finished, and she smiled as she looked out over the lawn towards the beach. The digger had arrived on Friday and had already dug two wide trenches.

Elanka watched as one of the security guards crossed the lawn. She always made a point to meet the men who guarded the house but she hadn't met this one yet. When Amir left she had called the security company and arranged for a complete change of staff. She didn't want anyone at Casa di Stelle who would be loyal to Amir or to Silvano. On Friday she called the company again and requested an additional guard alongside the two they already had. The guard she saw now crossing the lawn must be the new one. She would make sure she introduced herself to him before she left tomorrow.

Elanka noticed how peaceful the villa was now that she was here by herself. The girls were still here, living in the village in the hills but soon they would be gone, thank god.

The sudden influx of younger, more hopeless girls was no coincidence. Amir's companies thrived in times of war, preying on desperate victims trafficked over porous borders. Lately the girls came overland from Ukraine through Poland, Slovakia and Hungary. Elanka had told Amir what she thought about it all a year ago but he had become irate and shouted at her. He told her what she had told Kate: if there weren't girls there weren't gamblers, and if there weren't gamblers then where would the money for her jewels and couture dresses come from?

She was angry too at first but then she realised he was right.

Sometime in the night Elanka woke and got up to check her bedroom door was locked. As she returned to bed she saw the full moon through the curtains. It was a beautiful, warm evening and she opened the balcony door and stepped outside. The light from the moon stretched over the water like a path to eternity, and she heard a couple laughing on the beach. That must have been the sound that woke her. She envied the couple their freedom as she watched them from the balcony and she wondered who they were – tourists perhaps, or a pair of lovers who had just met that night.

She was so absorbed in their lives that she barely felt the loss of her own.

Chapter Thirty-Eight

Antibes

T HE SILVER MOTORBOAT CUT OVER the sea from the jetty at Juan-les-Pins towards a rocky cove on the western tip of Cap d'Antibes. Vanessa sat at the rear of the boat and watched the town's beaches recede beyond the gleaming water as the coastline to her left rose into rugged limestone cliffs.

The boat skirted the yachts of Port Gallice and then arrowed across the water to the Batterie de Graillon. Rounding the cove, the driver cut the motor and entered the small bay, reversing the vessel up to the dock. Rolling against the swell, the boat's engine released a surge of bubbles around the hull creating a turquoise cushion on the deep blue harbour.

A deckhand moored the boat, opened a hatch on the stern and Vanessa disembarked onto a teak jetty that led to the Hotel du Cap-Eden-Roc.

The relentless sun beat down as two white-jacketed porters scurried for her luggage and a concierge held a sheltering parasol. Vanessa gave him her name and said she would accompany the porters to her room before heading to the bar for a drink.

When Vanessa came down to the restaurant overlooking the sea, all eyes turned towards her. Unlike the other guests, Vanessa was dressed plainly, but the people here were not inspecting her clothes for a change, nor were they assessing her handbag or jewellery. They had sensed something more subtle, something they couldn't at first see. It made them study her a little longer than usual, trying to work out what it was.

Vanessa strode through the restaurant her eyes shining with relief. She held herself casually but with an edge of detachment, confident that the victory she embodied transcended anything these people could buy.

She would wait for her friend in the champagne bar, Vanessa told the maître d', pausing at his little stand to observe the restaurant. From this vantage point, between kitchen and terrace, she heard snatches of conversation – a melange of languages and accents, the international murmur of the elite. You could always tell the pecking order of the world's gangsters by listening for the dominant language on the deck of the Eden-Roc Grill. Five years ago, it would have been Russian Vanessa heard if she had stood in this spot then, the hotel having been a favourite hangout for all manner of crooked businessmen from the former Soviet bloc who moored their yachts nearby. But things had swung dramatically since then – those caviar days were gone – and all around her now were stateside voices. The place had come full circle, order restored to the Americans who had returned to claim the summers their compatriots celebrated here long ago when summer resorts were unfashionable.

It was hard to believe that the Côte d'Azur had ever been unfashionable whatever the season, Vanessa thought as she walked up the spiral staircase to the rooftop champagne bar. She took a seat and gazed over the water to the islands off Cannes, and then further along the hazy shoreline to St Tropez whose lighthouse would, when night fell, cast a pinprick of green light. Vanessa watched a motorboat shear across the water, foam glistening in its wake. She saw the yachts in the bay, the coast-hugging apartments stretching on forever and she couldn't imagine its pulse subsiding.

Below her, swimmers bobbed in the warm saltwater pool, an eye-scorching spill of blue against the jagged white cliffs. The same voices she heard in the restaurant drifted up from the water – the holiday drawl of hedge fund bosses and real estate tycoons boasting of their latest ventures as they performed a languid breaststroke, comparing notes on the lucrative deals their lawyers had secured for them.

Surrounding the pool an amphitheatre of sun loungers were arranged according to status – the highest tipping guests and their buckets of champagne in the two front rows, the rest boiling behind in the cheaper seats. At the far end of the pool, on a raised plinth under the sheltering pines, was an exclusive zone reserved for the most loyal and fortunate guests. Those who had been coming to the Hotel du Cap for decades, each time staying more than a week. With rooms at two thousand euros a night, this area was for those with serious cash to burn.

The voices rising from the pool grew more indistinct as the breeze dipped and the crickets sang, their chorus reaching its high summer peak. They wouldn't stop until midnight when the temperature fell and the frogs took on the nocturnal shift, croaking through the night.

Vanessa was on her second Bellini when Kate appeared, pink-faced and breathless.

'Sorry I'm late. All this fuss meant the trains were cancelled through Nice. I had to get a taxi and it took *ages*.'

'What fuss?'

'I keep forgetting you don't have a smartphone,' Kate said, reaching for her phone. She scrolled through and held it out to Vanessa. 'There's been a shooting in Nice.'

'Where?' said Vanessa, but of course she knew.

Kate read from her phone. 'An armed burglary at a jewellery store in Port Lympia. Two men shot and four arrested.'

'Good god.'

'In broad daylight, can you believe it?'

'And they stopped the trains?'

Kate handed Vanessa the phone. 'They thought it was a terror attack at first, being so close to Bastille Day.'

'That's understandable, I guess,' said Vanessa, scanning through. 'The burglars had Kalashnikovs.'

There were no details as to who had been shot and she hoped Franz and his team were all right. They had dealt with this kind of thing before and they had been prepared this time, at least. Vanessa hoped she was not now on their blacklist.

Kate took her phone back. 'Sometimes though, those jewellery places are fronts for something else.'

'I guess so,' said Vanessa as the waiter brought Kate a glass of wine. 'What about you? We haven't spoken properly since Meritus imploded.'

Kate told Vanessa what had happened last week, how Kate had been tricked into helping Silvano compile information on Amir's assets, and how Elanka had seized it too.

Kate took a sip of wine. 'She's been dealing with the police in the UK for a while, informing on Amir and leaking stories to the press. Amir was arrested this morning on money laundering charges, which is just the tip of the iceberg. Thanks to Elanka they have material on the Russian arms profiteering, sex trafficking and details of all his properties. The offshore structures and the illicit money flows.'

Vanessa shivered despite the warm evening. 'Elanka's a brave woman. She could have just sat here and waited this out, like all the others.'

'Like us.'

'I hope she's a long way from here now somewhere safe.'

Kate agreed and they were quiet for a while.

Kate put her hand on Vanessa's arm. 'I'm sure you're worried for yourself too. Can you negotiate some kind of plea deal?'

Vanessa lit a cigarette. 'Maybe. I have a lawyer in London trying to negotiate something. I hope so. If not, it'll be Thailand or Argentina under a new identity and who knows when I'll see David again.' She bit her lip and glanced around the bar. The place was starting to fill up.

'Silvano will be arrested too, eventually. Maybe that's your way through this.'

'There's a lot I could tell them about Silvano,' Vanessa said grimly.

Kate cleared her throat and spoke softly. 'You knew what they did. Why did you go along with it all?' The question was low, barely there.

Vanessa looked away. 'I got sucked in. I made a terrible mistake years ago and it felt impossible to go back. Once I was in it was hard to get out and then it became a habit.' She paused and shook out her hair. 'You were working for Silvano too in the end, don't forget. You were on your way there.'

'I had no choice.'

'That's what I thought, too. It's easy to think you have no choice.'

Kate knew Vanessa was right. She was helping Silvano, however she tried to justify it. She would have probably helped Anton too, eventually.

'Speaking of bad choices, what happened to that grifter you were seeing?'

Kate took a sip of wine. 'He wasn't a grifter,' she said, but she knew she would never be sure.

The sun was setting over the hills above Golfe-Juan drenching the sea in golden light.

'Another drink?' asked Vanessa.

'Sure, why not?'

Vanessa smiled. 'Remember that night we couldn't get in anywhere around here? We kept getting turned away.'

'And now here we are, fitting in perfectly,' Kate said.

Vanessa pointed to the majestic Hotel du Cap just beyond the gardens behind the restaurant, its rose facade glowing in the setting sun. 'I've booked a room for the night.'

'You're kidding. A room *here*?'

Vanessa slid a key towards Kate. 'And one for you as well.'

The key was attached to a heavy silver ring in the shape of a lifebuoy.

Kate pushed the key away in disgust. 'You can't stay here. You're a fugitive. If this is another of your dodgy deals, I'm not touching it.'

'I can't vouch for the source of funds that paid for the rooms, if that's what you mean. But there's something I want to discuss with you.'

'What?'

'Now you're out of a job, I wanted to ask if you'd work with me.'

Kate almost choked on her wine. 'Work with *you*? Vanessa, you're practically in *jail*. Work with you doing *what*?'

'Law, of course.'

'What kind of *law*? Don't you know the kind of trouble you're in. You won't be able to practice law after this? And who would be our clients?' Kate said, imagining a range of hideous options.

'We would do legitimate work,' said Vanessa haughtily. 'Not everyone's a criminal down here.'

'No, not everyone,' admitted Kate.

Vanessa leaned forwards. 'Think about it. If I get through this.'

'Hmmm. That's a big *if*.'

'You can't always be so righteous,' Vanessa said softly.

'You can't always be so wicked, either.'

Kate settled back in her chair. 'If you get through this I'll be impressed. I'll be asking you to work with me.' Kate's phone beeped. 'The driver's here.'

'Where shall we go?' said Vanessa, smoothing her dress.

'Let's go back to that place in Monaco and demand an outside table. Afterwards, we'll go to Jimmy'z. I've always wanted to go back there.'

Vanessa looked at Kate's clothes. 'You're still not dressed for it.'

'I know,' said Kate. 'But this time it won't be a problem.'

The sun had set but true night was still hours away. The sky was violet, the sea cobalt, burnished gold above the hills, and Kate gazed in awe at its unearthly beauty.

A man sitting by himself at the bar caught her eye. He wore a blue, open necked shirt and as she took a sip of wine he raised his own glass, pointed to the stem.

She realised she was holding her glass by the bowl and sighed in annoyance. What was it with these pedantic guys?

She glared at him as she corrected herself and was about to look away but he grinned and so she looked closer. He had blonde hair, but she recognised the smile.

Vanessa stood. She had seen the exchange. 'I've got to make a call to David. He'll be just finishing supper. Let's talk about it all tomorrow.' She looked over at the man and then back to Kate, sliding the key ring towards her. 'You stay here and enjoy the view. We can go to Jimmy'z anytime.'

Requiem

ROB HAD SLIPPED OFF INTO an ocean of memory. Glassy eyed, struggling with consciousness.

The champagne, the ice bucket and the chilled glass.

'Celebrating?'

Rob gazed at the thug standing over him. He felt the last bolt of pain as numbness took over, warmth gushing from his nose, running over his lips. Rob remembered he liked oysters, the wet brine on his chin.

But not with Vanessa. Why was she here?

He would never eat oysters again in fancy restaurants with his face all messed up like this, but there were still places he could go. Little places on the coast. If he could just get up on to his feet.

A grind of pepper, a squeeze of juice.

He yelled for the waiter. He needed a pepper mill and a fork for these oysters. Rob tried to snap his fingers, but he couldn't find them. Why couldn't anyone hear him?

He could barely see now beneath his swollen lids, eyes watering as the man lay into him, kicking him all over. The pain had gone and his brain too, all grey and shrivelled. He no longer had a sense of smell, instead Rob imagined the faint whiff of seaweed and the things he loved, like the smell of money.

He reached for an oyster. If he had a fork he could ease the edge of his eye back from where it had caught a little on his skull.

He lay back, tried to bring his hand to his mouth.

'Swallow it in one,' he said, grinning and cupping his hand to collect the drool that slipped from his lip.

He saw Allegra in the luminous nacre hollow of an oyster shell.

A slug of champagne. An oyster down the hatch.

And he did it. He could still swallow. It went down without touching the sides. He did it again. More lemon juice this time, more champagne.

As his mind drifted further from his body, Rob saw around him a sea of money. Oceans of it. Chests and suitcases brimming with coins and gold bars. More than he would ever need.

The money fell from his hands as he tried to scoop it up and it slipped away.

The oysters and the juice dripping from his mouth. Sputum at his lips like sea foam.

Slippery plastic notes slithering through his fingers, hissing and receding the more he reached out to them.

In and out of delirium. Looking to see who was watching. There was no one here. No one had seen him. He had gotten away with it. He had no senses left, but it was all so perfect.

Tears fell from his eyes and slid down to join the briny, bloody juice on his chin.

He found his hands and cupped them over his ears. He was crying now but never happier than in that moment, gently nodding to a roaring of waves, the hiss of the cash all around him.

Acknowledgements

I would like to thank the following people for their help and support: my agent Peter Straus, Kelly Smith, Eleanor Stammeijer and Arzu Tahsin at Bonnier Books UK, Sophie Goodfellow and Helen Clifford at FMcM Associates. Thanks also to my wonderful friends in London, Monaco and elsewhere who listened to my ideas for the story, read extracts and provided generous insights, laughs and drinks: Emily Ruth Ford, Danielle Rowe, Alice Ives, Anna Funder, Sally Murray, Joseph Mundschau, Jeremie Alameda, Elizabeth Macneal, Helen Taylor, Dolf and Tracy Darnton, Euan Lawson, Simon O'Brien, Amanda Davis and the Roquebrune Dogs.

Thanks always to Tom, Louis and Dylan and to my parents, Annette and Leon Davis.

Don't miss out on Megan Davis's prize-winning debut thriller . . .

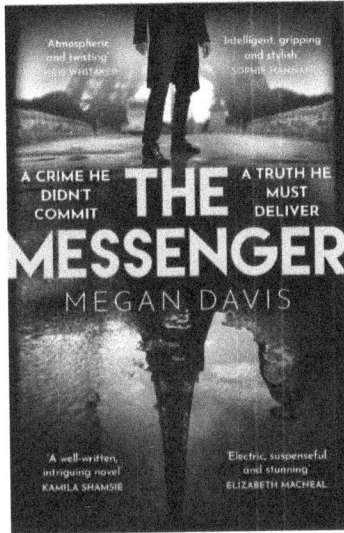

Wealthy and privileged, Alex has an easy path to success in the Parisian elite. But he and his domineering father have never seen eye to eye. Desperate to escape the increasingly suffocating atmosphere of their apartment, Alex seeks freedom on the streets of Paris where his new-found friend Sami teaches him how to survive. But everything has a price - and one night of rebellion changes their lives forever.

A simple plan to steal money takes a sinister turn when Alex's father is found dead. Despite protesting their innocence, both boys are imprisoned for murder. Seven years later Alex is released from prison with a single purpose: to discover who really killed his father. Yet as he searches for answers and atones for the sins of his past, Alex uncovers a disturbing truth with far-reaching consequences.

In the heart of Paris, against a backdrop of corruption, fake news and civil unrest, *The Messenger* is a mind-racing new thriller that follows one son's journey to find redemption and expose the truth.

AVAILABLE NOW

Prologue

Christmas Eve
Montparnasse Cemetery

A SHOUT FROM THE DARKNESS UP ahead.

Then a dog – some kind of muscled mongrel – nosed at my ankles, a low growl rolling in its throat.

A man jerked the leash bound double round his fist, flesh white and glistening, puckered by the links. He smacked the dog with a rolled-up newspaper, then laughed as it scuttled on, tail between its legs.

'Gotta show 'em who's boss,' the man said to me, as I stepped back against the railing that wrapped around the cemetery.

I glanced towards the corner – Sami was fifteen minutes late – enough time for the rain to soak through my clothes bringing with it second thoughts while dark, earthy smells crept over from the shadows behind me.

Up ahead there were yellow headlights and slanting rain, shiny umbrellas floating through the night. And when I turned back, Sami was there, hood up, his face shadowed under the street lamp.

'Start by just asking him for money,' I said. 'Tell him I owe you money.'

It was cold, and my breath hung in the air.

Sami smoked as we walked along the tall black rails with their gilded spikes, back towards the Boulevard Raspail.

'Tell him I'm in trouble. Get him to hand over his wallet. He always keeps a lot of cash. Cards and cash.' I was jabbering now, teeth chattering with the cold.

'Uh-huh. Cards and cash,' Sami repeated.

'In his wallet.'

'OK,' said Sami, checking the road before we ran across.

'I know the PIN codes – always the same ones. I told you.'

'Yeah.'

'If he thinks it's a one-off payment, he'll go along with it,' I said, grabbing Sami's arm. 'Make it clear it's a one-off thing.'

'It *is* a one-off thing,' Sami said quietly, drawing half a step ahead.

'He puts his wallet on a tray by the door,' I said, as a wave of nausea engulfed me, thinking of the warm apartment and Sami's cold intrusion.

Sami checked his phone and then scanned the street as though there was somewhere else he needed to be. He looked at me as if he'd only just heard.

'Yeah, yeah, you already told me.'

I tried to breathe, the air catching in my throat. 'There are gold cufflinks and stuff in his bedroom. On the chest of drawers in a little silver bowl.'

Sami grinned, and I felt like throwing up. He quickened his pace, and I ran to keep up, my stomach lurching like the sea. We hadn't talked things through, not properly, not beyond getting into the apartment and a few things Sami should take. As for what we'd do afterwards – we hadn't even thought about that.

We came to the church, crossed over and turned right into my street, the rain needling our faces, sharp and silvery under the street lamps. Our footsteps echoed along the narrow footpath between the buildings, dark and shuttered save for a faint glow on one of the upper floors.

'Just let me in and leave me here,' he said at the entrance to my building.

'It's raining. I'll wait in the lobby.'

'That's not what we agreed.'

'So what?' I said, suddenly not trusting him at all. 'It's better if I'm here. In case there's a change of plan.'

I pressed the numbers on the keypad, but the door didn't budge. A surge of relief coursed through me – they must have changed the code.

'Try again,' he said, his breath warm and rank on my cheek.

This time the door clicked open and we went inside, shaking off the rain. The radiators were cranked up and it was stifling. A Christmas tree stood in the corner, its red fairy lights dancing round the small, mirror-panelled lobby as if to some upbeat Christmas tune.

There was a note taped to the *gardienne's* door, her perfect cursive saying she was away for Christmas and New Year, and wishing everyone *Joyeuses fêtes*. Outside in the street, there was a shriek of laughter – someone singing a drunken song – but inside was quiet as a tomb.

I pressed the interphone and stood back. My father took a while to answer. I almost heard the squeak of the chair as he pushed back from his desk. In my mind I saw him take off his reading glasses, rub his eyes and smooth the thin grey hair from his forehead, his hand pausing for that last irritable scratch of the nape. I imagined the swig from the crystal glass before he stood, replacing it on the well-worn coaster with the faded sailing ship, lone ice cube swirling in the coppery liquid as he walked towards the door. I could smell the apartment – that sour, old man's reek, and the soft, leather-bound mustiness of the bookshelves.

Sami eased back his hood, checking his reflection in the mirrors all around. He cocked his face to either side, cheeks sucked in, and raked a hand through his hair. He puffed his chest and drew a finger across his lip, wiping clear a light sweat.

'Hello.' My father's voice crackled through the interphone. 'Yes? Who's there?'

A pause, as the interphone scratched.

'Speak.'

Finally, Sami stepped forward. 'It's Sami, Alex's friend.'

'Is Alex there? Alex, are you there?'

Sami glanced at me. 'He's on his way. He said I should wait for him upstairs.'

More static through the interphone, then the lock released. A rush of cold air blasted in from the back stairwell as Sami pushed the door open and then entered the lift at the foot of the stairs, his body strange and unfamiliar in the wrought-iron cage. He turned, and a halo of light cast shadows on his face as the lift jerked upwards. I had the urge to run upstairs, warn my father he was coming, to call the whole thing off. But I didn't move, and the door to the apartments closed softly in my face.

I stood there listening, counting off the floors as he glided upwards. I imagined the lift juddering to a halt with that familiar last jerk, Sami stepping out to the darkened landing, pressing the doorbell. I swear I almost heard the soft tread of my father's loafers on the parquet as he stepped forward and opened the door.

I turned and saw my image in the cold mercury glass of the mirrors that surrounded me. My face was damp with rain, flushed red, and the lights from the Christmas tree flashed crazily in time with my heartbeat. As I looked around, my reflections receded into the corners. The images mocked my movements, and in each of my eyes there was a tiny, flashing red blob of light.

A chill ran through the lobby and I wiped my hands on my jeans.

Minutes passed like hours and still Sami hadn't appeared. I walked to the door that led to the apartments, pressing my ear against the crack, against its cool brass edge. My tongue rasped on the roof of my mouth, humid breath over dry lips, blood throbbing in my ears.

Where was he? What if he'd screwed it up? What if the police were on their way?

I rattled the handle, pushed against the foggy glass. No sound from beyond the door, nothing. Then I pressed the buzzer to my home – three quick blasts – hurry up! I waited and pressed again, then again, longer now. Still no sound.

Then I heard it – someone coming down the stairs fast, taking them two, maybe three at a time, the pounding getting closer, louder. I stood back as Sami burst through the door, fear and adrenaline rising from him like steam. He held a white plastic bag, the handles twisted round his fist. There were dark shadows on the inside, the weight of the hammer warping the bag, pulling it sideways.

He fumbled with my father's wallet, shaking as he held it out.

'Take this,' he said, forcing the wallet into my hand.

I stared in horror at the blood on his hands, on the wallet, the dark smudges on his jeans.

'He was drunk. He went for me!' Sami said, wiping his face, my father's blood blooming across his cheek.

My head burned, the muscles in my neck like twisted ropes, skin flaming across my chest. I turned towards the door, catching it with my foot before it closed.

He grabbed my sweatshirt. 'Do not go up there! It's OK. He'll be all right. He was still speaking.'

'*Still speaking?* Jesus, Sami, what have you done?' I said, tears streaming down my face.

Sami's eyes were crazed, red and flashing, and they locked on mine. 'We've done this now. Come on.'

'Done *what?*'

He pulled at me. 'Come on. Don't be so gutless. We need to get out of here. Let's go.'

They say the human body replaces itself every seven years, but that some cells, like those in the lens of the eye, can last a lifetime. That's why, more than seven years on, images from the night my father died still haunt me. Most of the cells in my body have died and regenerated, yet these images recur. Each night the dream's different, but the feeling is the same, and it's like I'm seeing it again for the first time.

And in the back of my eyes there's always that tiny red flash of light.